A DIVIDED KINGDOM

THE FOUR-BORN BOOK 2

Joshua M Fitton

A Divided Kingdom

Book Cover Design and Interior Formatting by 100Covers.

ISBN: 978-0-000000-00-0 (paperback)

TABLE OF CONTENTS

Acknowledgements 1

Prologue 3

Guests and Goodbyes. 7

Lessons Learned 18

Deals In the Dark 35

Descent Descends 47

Ask No Questions Hear No Lies 61

The Night Brings Changes 68

Time To Play the Game 76

Favours and Fevers 87

Assassins 94

The Waters edge 104

In the Wake of Blood 110

Interrogations. 116

The Many Uses of Blood 126

Closer to the Truth 133

Challenges 144

Investigations 154

Anger and Understanding 176

Weddings and War. 186

The Arrival of Friends and Trouble 204

Words of the Faithful Actions of the suspicious . . 217
Blood and Water 224
White and Red 244
Answers and Truth 254
Words to the Dead 263
End of the Games 271
Rise as Men 282
Epilogue 287
About the author 291

ACKNOWLEDGEMENTS

First and foremost, I thank my family for all their support and encouragement. Thanks to my wife for giving me the time to do this. Thanks to my children for giving me fresh inspiration, my brothers for the memories, and for always keeping me grounded with insults. To all my friends who offer yet more inspiration. To all those who read and enjoyed the first book, especially those who found a way to get in touch and talk with me about it. Hearing from those who truly found joy in it is a fantastic experience. Thank you to all who supported me, from buying the book to interacting with me on social media. Hopefully, the next instalment matches expectations.

PROLOGUE

Vol, Prelim of Varliant, sat in the shade with two slave girls fanning him down vigorously. It was high summer, and the heat was oppressive. The city-state of Varliant was considered a wondrous place, and at first glance, there was little to deter such notions. However, dig a little deeper, and the reality quickly became apparent. The city and its people were on the verge of ruin.

Vol sipped wine as he lazed on the edge of consciousness, offering a barely noticeable nod whenever he wished one of the slaves to feed him. Being grotesquely overweight meant the movement was even harder to register. His thinning hair and wispy goatee did little to enhance his appearance. To look at Vol, anyone would think him perfectly relaxed. It wasn't so. He would not admit to such, but it was without doubt that much of the city's current state was due to his poor leadership. These were dangerous times. There were whispers of revolt.

He opened a single eye by a crack as the aide leaned in to get his attention.

"What is it, Salvadire? I am weary today."

"She is here, My Lord. The one that sent the message."

Vol acted as quickly as he could, given his bodily state. Clumsily sitting upright, he waved the slaves away. The room soon cleared except for Vol, his aide and the newly arrived guest. Vol quietly berated Salvadire for allowing the guest entry without giving him a warning. Salvadire gave an expression that said there was little he could do about it.

For long moments, there was a tense quiet. The only sound was Vol's laboured breathing. He sweated profusely and wished he could blame it on the absence of the slaves instead of the fear he now felt.

"Greetings," he offered. "Welcome to Varliant. It is the pleasure of the greatest city in the known world to host such a prestigious guest."

Silence. The figure before him was so small, wrapped head to toe in black rags, its face hidden in shadow, that it appeared almost childlike. Vol knew better. Stories had reached his ears. They'd reached many ears, spreading quickly throughout the known world. He would not have believed such things once upon a time, but the world was changing, and too many accounts had been heard to be ignored. The Fait were no longer the sole proprietors of magic. A significant shift in power was taking place, and Vol intended to move in the right direction.

Shuffling nervously on his seat, he began to wonder if he'd caused offence. Perhaps he should have stood. The silence stretched on. He looked to Salvadire, who could only shrug, appearing just as nervous as his master.

"It is not," came a voice like stones being ground to dust. It almost pained his ears to listen.

Vol's eyes darted back to the figure in black. He seemed shocked, as though a rock had just discovered the gift of the spoken word. Sweat trickled down his back, and he wondered why he had been foolish enough to allow this. It had simply been too tempting, promising so much. There had always been a part of him that didn't expect it to go any further, to never actually come face to face with this thing.

"Erm, apologies?" he said. "What is not?"

"This city," came the reply. Every word was hard to listen to. "This foul, stinking, feral city is far from the greatest in the world. You hold a barely maintained illusion of grandeur over a reality of destitution while you gorge yourself, pretending that your city is not crumbling to dust. Your vaults run empty. Your wells run dry. Your farms produce next to no crops. Your people starve, and you, great Vol." The words held more spite and contempt than he'd heard in a long time. "Prelim of Varliant will soon be dead at the hands of your own people."

Vol almost choked. His eyes grew wide with a mixture of shock and fear.

"I assure you, whatever rumours you have heard—"

"Enough!" The small figure stepped forward, throwing back the rag that covered its face. The stories he had heard were not as exaggerated as he'd hoped. They had not done the truth justice. An ancient face looked at him like a corpse had been dressed and sent for an audience.

The witch, known only as the Crone, stared at him with eyes that could turn blood cold. "I know the truth of things. Do not lie to me. But it could be. Oh, it could be!"

Vol drew deep breaths, trying hard to compose himself before his face scrunched in question.

"Could be?" he said. "What could be?"

"This city. It could be so much more. It could hold true power. The white walls could shine again. A beacon to all, surrounded in gold and splendour."

Oh, that sounded like music to Vol's ears. He could more than imagine it. He could hear it, smell it. He could see it right there in his mind as though he were a bird soaring above the streets, vibrant and beautiful. It invaded his mind and senses, touching and caressing his very soul. It felt glorious.

He heard a sudden snap, and the vision was gone. He looked again upon the Crone, almost embarrassed at falling into what felt like a dream. Despite the shining sun outside, his entire world now seemed all the dimmer. The vision had been so brilliant that the real world now lacked clarity.

Yes, it was obvious now. The stories were true. This creature before him had power. The Crone had taken a lowly man from the Sile clans and raised him above all others. Together, they had marched right into the castle at the Centre of the Cross, supposedly the most powerful nation in the known world. They had almost gained victory before the Sile champion fell. If she could do that with a savage from the Angosh plains, what could she do with a man such as Vol?

The rulers of the Cross, those self-righteous, pompous Fait, declared themselves the sole users of magic. The Crone was tearing away their façade. She was offering magic to the world. With such power, Vol could do such wonderful things.

"How?" he asked, falling from the chair down to his knees and scurrying forward, his hands clasped together and held out before him in pleading. The heat vanished as he got closer, and he felt a desperate chill but ignored it. "Please, I beg you. Tell me how? I will do anything. Anything!"

She held out a hand of pure white bone that seemed brilliant in its cleanliness when seen next to her rotted flesh, yet somehow, it was perhaps the most disturbing thing about her. The sharp bones of the fingers curled into a fist.

"It will take blood," said the Crone with a grin that forced Vol to stop dead. "With blood, we will change this world, but first, you will need gold."

"Gold," he muttered.

Vol grinned. He liked the sound of that. He liked it very much indeed.

GUESTS AND GOODBYES

At their furthest edge, the lower gardens of the castle grounds were more like a small forest. Four figures ran through wild bushes and trees before the land quickly began to change, becoming tamed and giving way to trimmed grass and meticulously kept flower beds. The for princes of the Fait were returning home from one of their secret excursions into the city beyond the castle walls.

Venturing beyond the walls without protection and supervision should not be possible, even for Aron, the eldest and a man in most people's eyes. After all, he was still a prince and heir to the throne of the kingdom of the Cross. Jacob was the youngest of the four but was already stretching out into the body of a man. No one considered the princes to be children. Not after what they'd already been through in their lives, not after the things they'd already done. They were not ordinary people. Not only did royal blood flow through their veins, but also the blood of the Fait. Blood that allowed their family and their family alone to use the Gift safely.

Despite being princes and Aron being the heir, the four spent as much time as possible out in the city beyond the castle grounds. They used the secret tunnel that ran beneath the wall surrounding their home. Over time, they had found that their lives beyond had become more desirable than their lives within. The four of them lived as different people with different names. They were not princes with Gifts or anything else special. All of them found freedom in this, a freedom they enjoyed.

They'd spent that morning visiting their friends. It was time to return home, or their mother would send search parties through the grounds again. She had no idea about the tunnel and the excursions. Their father, however, was a different matter. He knew about the tunnel and likely knew where they'd been. He had even used it himself when he was younger. An arrangement had been reached between a father and his sons, albeit under strict conditions. First, stick together. The boys had learned very quickly how dangerous the city could be. Also, they must never give away their true identities. The city was hazardous, let alone four princes. There were more rules, a lot more, but these were the ones that the boys considered most crucial. Also, an arrangement between a father and his sons did not translate to an arrangement between a king and princes. Their duty came first, so they must always return on time.

The gardens turned to the courtyard, and the four princes walked across it, nodding to those who stopped with dipped heads at their passing. They all paused momentarily, as they almost always did, at the massive stone in the courtyard. It seemed random. The stone, more a boulder the size of a small horse, lying in the otherwise pristine courtyard, looked entirely out of place, but the boys knew it for what it was. Once, the stone had been part of the castle itself. It had broken away when a man had crashed through the wall in a great battle. The stone should have broken the man, but the man had broken the stone, at least during their first meeting. The second meeting went the other way, but only just. It was what their father had used to crush the Crone's champion. Winning their battle and securing the safety of the Cross. The Crone, once considered an ally of the Fait, had been the deliverer of the Gift for generations. She was now their greatest enemy. The boys feared her more than anything.

"I still can't believe he lifted it," said Joshua. "It just doesn't make sense."

"I'll lift it one day," said Luke, twisting at the hips as though limbering up for an attempt. Luke, the Second-Born, was the most confident. Holding the Gift of Fortune could do that. Was it any wonder when the world seemed to fall so often at his feet? Aron found himself becoming increasingly annoyed at the differences between him and his nearest brother. Aron had bad dreams and a Gift he could little understand, never mind use. Meanwhile, Luke was becoming increasingly confident in his Gift, making him unbearable.

"It'll take more than Fortune to get this thing off the ground," said Aron as he reached out and touched the stone with reverence. Their father had decided that the stone would remain in the courtyard, right where it fell, as a reminder to all that the Cross was not invincible, that the walls were not insurmountable, that danger can always come, and the people of the Cross must be ready to face it. Aron, however, saw it as a reminder that his father was the strongest man in the known world. Not just in the power he held as the king of the Cross, but literally as the strongest man in the world. King Branthony had the Gift of Strength.

"Do you really think you could lift it one day?" asked Jacob.

"No," blurted Luke instantly. The word fell from his lips as though dragged out on the end of a string. "Hey! Don't do that?!" he protested.

"Sorry!" said Jacob, retreating a step. They'd discovered that Jacob's Gift was showing most often. Maybe it was simply because it had the most opportunity to be used. Jacob held the Gift of Truth and found controlling it a challenge. As the Gift seemed to make it almost impossible for anyone to lie to Jacob, people were becoming increasingly nervous around him.

"Don't use your Gift on us, Jacob," said Aron, removing his hand from the stone and continuing toward the castle.

"It just happens sometimes. I can't help it," Jacob said, walking away from the stone monument. "Just like you can't help your dreams."

Aron winced at the mention of his dreams. They were becoming more of a problem. He had the Gift of Foresight, which seemed to manifest mainly when he slept. At first, he couldn't remember the dreams, waking screaming most mornings but not knowing why. Then he could remember parts but wished he could not. Now he knew what made him scream, and even in his waking hours, the images threatened to force a fresh cry. Now, he was trying desperately to understand his dreams; there lay the real problem. They made no sense. One dream would conflict with another. They never seemed to be in any order. Some nights, he seemed to have ten different dreams, all moving from one to another in that strange way dreams do. However, one dream in particular kept coming back. This was the one dream he wished most to forget. This one he kept a secret. He kept hoping to find meaning in it all. He didn't. The Gift of Foresight should be known as the Gift of useless tiredness, or so he thought.

They made their way inside the castle and to their mother. The queen greeted them with hugs and kisses like she hadn't seen them in years.

She had been much more attentive to them since the Crone's attack, and despite it being some years ago, she had not let up.

"Where's Father?" asked Luke as he went to a table and started stuffing grapes into his mouth.

"He's in the council chamber."

"On a day of rest?" asked Aron. "They don't usually hold council meetings on days of rest." He would know. He'd been joining his father more in the meetings in preparation for the day when he would rule. Aron was, after all, the First-Born and would one day wear the crown. He didn't look forward to the day. He found the council meetings tedious at best and the council members annoying, most of them at least. There were some he liked more than others. His uncles, Michael and John, for example. Healing-Master Fredrick as well, though he was growing so old he would soon be stepping down.

"There was something that required his attention," said Debreace to her children. "It's not easy ruling a kingdom, you know. Your father works hard to maintain a strong and secure Cross."

"How strong and secure can it be with the Crone still out there?" Luke hadn't meant to speak the words so loudly, and he looked away as he felt his mother's eyes on him. They knew she didn't like to talk about the Crone. No one did, but Mother especially hated it. The fact that the Crone had come for her children and nearly succeeded made Debreace angry like nothing else. Ironically, only the boys came close to making her as angry as the Crone.

"What's the meeting about?" asked Aron.

"I'm not sure. Your Uncle Michael came for your father and said he was needed."

"Is Uncle Michael going to—" Aron never finished the sentence as the doors swung open, and Michael strode into the room with a smile. It would seem strange that he would walk through the door just as Aron spoke his name, but things like that seemed to happen often. Had Aron dreamt about this at some point? He strained his memory, trying to think if he'd seen this moment before, but nothing came to him. His thoughts washed away as his uncle grabbed him and started tussling with him. Aron was getting strong enough to push back a little. They both laughed as they separated.

"You're not the king yet, you know," said Michael with a smile. "So, tell me, nephews. What adventures have you been on today? Hiding from your mother again? You'll be the end of her, you know. She worries too much."

"Leave them be," said Michael's brother, John, as he strode past. "There is nothing wrong with boys having some fun. The God knows their father is hard enough on them."

"Where is Father?" asked Aron.

"He'll be here soon," said Michael. "His business won't take long. It didn't strictly need his attention, but I thought it was something he'd find interesting."

"What was it?" asked Jacob, hoping it was something exciting.

"Nothing that would interest you boys," answered John. "Just some envoys and businessmen from Varliant. Here to arrange some trade deals."

"And why would that need my husband's sudden attention?" asked Debreace.

"It wouldn't, usually," answered Michael as he sat and poured himself a glass of wine. "It's just the amount of business they're doing. They've been making some substantial deals."

"What's so special about that?" Joshua asked as he stared down at his chessboard. Joshua had the Gift of Guidance, which should advise him on any given situation, telling him what to do, how to achieve victory, and warning him of threats. He was gaining control over time, but it made living an everyday life all the more difficult. It was hard to concentrate when your mind was thinking of every variable for every situation.

"Well," said John as he swooped the glass of wine from Michael's hand just as he was about to take a sip. He gulped it down, saying, "The last we'd heard, Varliant was broke. No creditors would go near them, and they had little to bargain with. The whole city was damn near close to revolt. Now, their envoys turn up here trying to trade in everything from grain to steel. It just seemed a little odd. The Coin-Master will investigate them more carefully, but for some reason, your father likes to take note of these things, if only to pass the information on to your Uncle Christopher."

As uncles from their mother's side, Michael and John, along with their other brother, Grey, did not have the Gift. Uncle Christopher, however, had the blood of the Fait and the Gift of Knowledge. This made him one of the smartest men in the known world, and their father relied heavily on his advice.

"Varliant," said Debreace, a not-so-small hint of disgust playing over the word. "Slavers." She said nothing more, and her opinion was clear.

"Anyway," added John. "As I said, it's nothing that should bother you four. Aron may have some interest. It'll be his job soon enough, after all. But until that's the case, I'd pay it no mind. Why aren't you out having fun somewhere? All the times you're needed and can't be found, and now, on a day of rest when your time is your own, you're here with us."

"They've come to see their mother," said Debreace, smiling at them. "Because they know how much I love them." She stepped to Aron, who was closest and hugged him. Aron hugged her back appreciatively.

It sometimes seemed to Aron that he relied on his mother more than the others. Was it simply because he was the eldest? Because he'd spent more time with her? Or maybe it was because none of his brothers had so-called Gifts that made them wake up screaming at night. No one saw it, but Aron clenched his fists in frustration and fought the sudden anger rising at the thought of it all. That rising anger was becoming all too common.

"Well," said Michael. "Whatever the reason, they don't have to stay. Your father won't be back just yet, and even when he does arrive, I'm hoping to tempt him into a drink with us. John and I are leaving the Centre soon, so it's only fair we get a little time to enjoy ourselves first. So, if it's all right with your mother, you can go do whatever it is you boys do."

They all looked to their mother, who smiled, clearly enjoying the sight of the four of them standing together. "Off you go," she said, and they yelled their thanks, already heading through the door. Aron lingered a moment longer, pondering whether to stay. He chose against it and followed his brothers.

King Branthony walked the long corridors and felt a familiar sense of unease. There was always something on his mind, something troubling him. There was always something he just could not get right. He did the best he could in every aspect of his life. He tried to be a good king, yet there were still desperately poor people in his kingdom, bandits that raided and killed innocents and a never-ending list of other problems that he seemed unable to make a dent in.

He tried to be a good husband but was often dragged away by his other responsibilities, so his wife was left to raise their children alone. He tried to be a good father, yet his children seemed to think of him as mean and controlling for striving to instil in them the lessons he'd learned through his life.

Alas, it seemed to Branthony that he failed as often as he succeeded, but that didn't mean he intended to stop trying. Right now, he was determined to succeed in his quest to learn more about his family's history and the Gift.

For generations, the Crone brought the Gift to his family, taking a few drops of blood from each newborn child and giving the child milk through which they would gain their Gift. For generations, the Crone had been lying to his family; worse, she'd secretly erased their knowledge of the Gift and its history. She had used her magic, and who knew what other means to erase their records and knowledge, making them more dependent on her.

The relationship between the Fait and the Crone ended abruptly at the birth of Branthony's Fourth-Born son, Jacob. That was the day he'd finally realised that every time the Crone had delivered a Gift, she had also taken something in return. The blood. He'd always thought she used it to identify the Gift. He now knew that this small drop of royal blood gave the Crone her strength, magic and long-lasting life. What was worse, she had been taking the blood for hundreds of years. Who knew the true limits of her powers?

He had hoped to put an end to the Crone when she attacked the Centre. She had escaped with at least one of her Gifted Sile. A dark-skinned woman as deadly as she was beautiful. A woman named Cutter-of-Men.

Branthony reached a door and came to a stop. He took a deep breath and composed himself before knocking gently and entering. Inside, he saw a large bed and an open window, allowing the sun and fresh air to fill the room. A young woman sat at a small dressing table tucked into the corner. She smiled at him as he entered, moving to rise from her seat, but he held up a hand to stop her.

"Hello, Merleal. How are you today?"

"Much better, Your Majesty. Thank you for asking."

He took a seat on a chair across the room.

"Have your ailments subsided?"

"Somewhat," she assured him. "But they will never go completely. However, I can learn to control them with time, effort, and practice. For a while, at least. In the end, they will get the better of me, but then I must relinquish my position and pass the honour on to another who will take my place, as the Crone should have done centuries ago."

Branthony looked at Merleal, and although she said she was feeling better, he suspected she was lying, if only a little. He couldn't help but feel bad. This was, after all, his doing in a way. After parting ways with the Crone, Branthony had to secure the future of the Gift and his family. He'd made the desperate move of travelling through enemy lands to the Blood River. There, he had learned lessons that should never have been forgotten. Merleal had travelled back with him from the Blood River to the Centre. She had come to take the Crone's place as the one to deliver the Gift. She had done so with the birth of Branthony's first nephew, but it had come at a price.

"By giving the Gift and taking the blood, you've changed somehow?" He asked the question, although he must have asked something similar a hundred times. She nodded her head in response, always patient despite his repetitiveness. "The blood will give you new abilities. Gifts, you could say." Merleal continued to nod as he spoke. "But now you crave the blood?"

She giggled, and Branthony was taken aback for a moment. She was still so young, and until he'd met her, she had never left her village at the Blood River. How and why did she make him feel so small? He was a king, yet he felt inferior when in her company. Was it simply because she knew so much more about the Gift than he did? Was it because he felt guilt at dragging her away from her family and all she'd known to come and serve him in a faraway and unknown land? She had a son of her own whose childhood she was missing. Branthony knew the toll that could take. Either way, her giggling made him feel strangely put back.

"You make it sound like I'm some sort of blood-sucking monster."

"I'm sorry, I didn't—"

"It's all right," she reassured him. "And in a way, I suppose you are right. It's just a little more complicated. The blood will give me abilities, but they are tied to you and your family. It is the power my body will crave. The power that comes with the blood. I have taken it twice, though I have only delivered the one Gift."

Branthony's brother Christopher now had a daughter, Harriet, to go with his son, Oliver, whom the Crone had tried to capture on the day of his birth.

"My brother's second-born child did not receive a Gift. His bloodline will not take the throne."

"Exactly," confirmed Merleal. "His son had a Gift, though it will likely be weaker than his father's. His daughter could not carry the Gift, but her blood is still special in many ways. The Gift is limited. Only the direct line will carry it. However, if Harriet were ever to be the last of the Fait, her children would take up the Gift. The power cannot be denied. The world needs it."

It was Branthony's turn to nod along. He understood what she was saying but became lost if he thought about it too much.

"What is the cost?" he asked.

"The cost? The cost is that for all the power the blood gives me, it will never be enough. I will always crave more. Each time I take the blood, I will gain more from it but lose more. The cost," she continued, looking solemn. "Is that I will outlive all those I know and love. My people live long lives thanks to the river's power, but I will see them all turn to dust."

Branthony felt a fresh wave of guilt. Did he truly have the right to ask this of anyone? Did his family have any right to expect such a sacrifice?

"The Blood River," he said. "What part does it play? Why is it so important?"

"It is where it all began," she said, adjusting herself on her seat. "I know you pay little attention to the idea of the Divine or to the thought that the blood that flows through your veins is the blood of an—"

"Angel," he said, cutting her off. "Yes, I remember your father's story. A demon and an angel fell to earth in a great battle. The demon died, but the angel survived. His blood flowed into the river, and now the river is magical."

"In a sense," she answered, and again Branthony felt like a child receiving lessons from a patient teacher. "The river helps those who live from it, but it is pure only in that small place where the angel fell. To the people of my village, it gives longer life and vitality, but it does little else. But it does allow someone who has taken enough of the water to deliver the Gift. It enables my body to survive that which others would not and to pass on the power of the river through my milk.

"Only when paired with your family does the river have real power. The angel did not die. He was rescued by a woman and fell in love with her." She paused at Branthony's scowl. He had made it all too clear that he lacked great faith. Merleal could understand why. He had seen much death and strife in his life. It was an easy thing to doubt the Divine after seeing such things. The queen was much more religious; she believed the story wholeheartedly.

"He fell in love with a woman," she repeated, "and she bore his children. That is where your family line begins. That is why you have the Gift. That is why you rule. Not to hold yourself above all others but to guide them through the power and will of the God."

"If you say so," was all he could add.

"But I have told you all this many times. You know the story as well as I do."

He sighed. She was right. She had repeatedly told him the same story, answered the same questions and more, however often he'd asked. In truth, she'd been a gift in herself. She'd given him more answers than he'd hoped for, and his knowledge was greater than ever. He still wished he knew more about the individual Gifts and all they could mean or do, but he could not blame her for his shortcomings.

Yes, Merleal had been a great help to him, and the boys had enjoyed having her at the Centre but therein lay the reason for his questions. He'd decided to ask her one last time because her time at the Centre was ending. She had to return home to the Blood River. According to Merleal, the water would help her deal with the changes she was going through. Branthony had to admit she had lost much of the spark that made her such a delight. She'd seemed sick for months now, and it had gradually gotten worse.

"I'll be sad to leave," she said, as though plucking the thoughts from his mind. "This place, this city, this kingdom, has amazed me. I had heard tales of castles and forts, towns and cities, but never thought to see them for myself. Thank you, Your Majesty, and I will return in time. I very much look forward to the day."

"So do I," he said as they both stood from their seats. She went to give an almost awkward curtsey, but Branthony pulled her into a hug, and they embraced wholeheartedly. They both hoped that together they could re-forge the bond between their peoples and undo the damage the Crone had done.

LESSONS LEARNED

Jacob walked away from his lesson with mixed feelings. Practising using his Gift consisted predominantly of asking people questions. He had the Gift of Truth, but the truth was he could not control it. Not yet, at least. He asked questions to which people were supposed to lie. If they failed, it was because his Gift had prevented it and today had not been a good day regarding controlling his Gift. Almost everyone he'd asked a question had given him a false answer.

"I'm terrible," said Jacob to the maid, a large woman who waddled beside him as his escort. It would often be a guard's duty, not that an escort was needed. Jacob wasn't a child anymore, but today, he'd insisted the maid take the task. He secretly wanted more practice with his Gift.

"You're not terrible, Your Highness. Do not worry yourself. Your Gift will come with time."

Jacob appreciated the words.

"Are we going to see Mother now?" he asked.

"Not now, young prince. She is with your father. They are hosting a delegation from the city of Varliant. Some very wealthy gentlemen have come to trade."

Varliant? Wasn't that the place his uncles were talking about the other day? The people his father was interested in.

"What's so special about them?" he asked.

"Well, they appear very wealthy indeed," continued the maid. "The whole Centre is talking about them. They're making trades and deals with anyone and everyone. Many of the merchants are ecstatic. People are rubbing their hands together at the mere prospect of doing business with Varliant. It seems no one can lose. They're..."

Jacob allowed her to talk and slowed his step, waiting until they were near the corner. It was the perfect place. When the time was right, he hopped onto a large pot that held a small tree and used its branches to climb up onto the balustrade above. A manoeuvre he couldn't have completed not long ago, but he was growing quickly now. At this rate, he'd be taller than his brothers soon. He looked down at the maid just in time to see her realise he'd gone. She paused and looked around. "Oh no," she said, her voice full of dismay. "Not again."

He felt bad. It was the first time he'd successfully used his Gift all day. The maid seemed particularly susceptible to it. It wasn't the first time she'd blurted out information he wasn't supposed to be privy to. He liked her, so he felt doubly bad when he had to give her the slip, but what she'd told him had piqued his interest. Despite their best attempts, none of the maids, servants or guards were particularly good at keeping an eye on him or his brothers. No one knew the castle like them.

After losing the maid, he moved into one of the smaller halls, stood on a table to grab one of the long banners draped down the wall and pulled, noting that he'd soon weigh too much for this. He lifted himself into the wooden rafters and, from there, crawled through the spaces in the beams. He pushed on through dust and cobwebs, slowly but surely making his way to the great hall. He couldn't see anything as a fresh layer of plaster had only recently been skimmed onto the ceiling. A part of the repairs after the castle was damaged during the battle at the Centre. The repairs could have been completed long ago, but Father insisted on not taking any extra coin from other, far more deserving projects.

In the darkness, Jacob perched himself on the rafters. Though he couldn't see anything, he could hear perfectly. The voices of his mother and father were clear, along with some other accented voices—the delegates from Varliant.

Branthony sat upon the throne, his wife beside him. Together, they looked down the steps of the dais and listened patiently to the men from Varliant—four men, very carefully presented, wearing rich clothes and jewellery but nothing too brash or overbearing. The king's distaste for such things had become well-known. They talked elegantly and complimented their city and its vast wealth and power. Though they bordered on being overly boastful, they often declared their desire to share their power and wealth. Their words held nothing but the highest praise for the Prelim of Varliant, talking about all that was great about their city and its leader.

"He is the most gracious of men," said the delegation leader, a man named Salvadire. He was tall, with golden-tanned skin, dark hair slicked back, a perfectly shaped goatee sat below a hooked nose, and piercing green eyes. "It is because of Lord Vol's impeccable leadership that the city of Varliant flourishes."

"Yes," said Branthony, suddenly deciding to speak. For a second, the entire delegation, the lead most of all, looked surprised at the interruption, as though it were strange that the king had decided to use his voice inside his hall. "Lord Vol has indeed led your city on a most prodigious rise. It has been joyful to hear of your sudden economic upturn. I beg Prelim Vol's advice on such matters."

For the first time since this meeting began, Salvadire looked uncomfortable.

"Well, Your Majesty," he said, loosening his collar as though the temperature had just increased dramatically. "I am sure Lord Vol would be willing to share his vast knowledge. The first thing he did was disband the council of Varliant. For too long, their greed and selfishness led our city and its people down a path of destruction. It was their greed that threatened Varliant. Lord Vol has finally turned us from that path, and now our city and people flourish."

"It is quite amazing," said Debreace, her hand reaching to her side to take hold of her husband's. She smiled at him. A smile that said she was impressed by his tactful, if uncharacteristic, choice of words. When she turned back to the delegation, there was no hint of such an expression. Branthony listened as his wife continued. "The turn of Varliant's fortunes has been dramatic, to say the least. Not too long ago, we heard dire stories about your city. I hoped they were not true."

"Exaggerations, Your Majesty. I assure you. Yet, unfortunately, they stemmed from the truth. That is why Lord Vol's sole leadership was so desperately needed. This allowed him to instil his vision."

"And what exactly is his vision?"

"Progress, Your Majesty. His vision is the very reason we are here. Lord Vol envisions a world of trade and prosperity. A world of opportunity."

"Yes, you have been exploring many of these opportunities. I have it on good authority that you have made substantial agreements with merchants and traders from all four points of the Cross. Trading in everything from steel and wood to grain and gold. Even attempting to trade, what do you call them, Deliverers of serenity?" There was a not-so-subtle hint of distaste in Debreace's words

"They are a valued commodity in Varliant, Your Majesty. Highly trained to anticipate and meet your every need. They are skilled in many aspects of—"

"By another name, they are slaves," Branthony said, his tone icy cold. Once again, the delegation looked uncomfortable.

"In some places, they may be considered such," said another delegation member. "However, once here, it would be up to the one who purchased them to decide their stature."

"Purchased?" said the queen, and it was obvious they had chosen their words poorly. The four men stood still with almost blank expressions, suddenly unsure where to take the conversation. Branthony decided to alleviate them of the choice.

"You have made many deals during your time here. Shook many hands. Procured many products. Made many, many promises. All this in the name of a city that was not long since close to ruin."

When Salvadire opened his mouth to interrupt, Branthony turned cold eyes on him, and the delegate closed it again without a sound escaping.

"I sincerely hope these trades are successful. I will await such results."

"I can assure His Majesty that we have the capability to meet every deal made. The Arduous hard work of the people of Varliant has placed us in a powerful position. The Cross shall receive everything it has coming to it."

Branthony couldn't help but wonder if those words had been purposely chosen. He felt his blood rise a little, which was made worse by the break in protocol by interrupting him. He swallowed his anger, speaking in a lower tone. Not threatening, but not to be argued with.

"As I was saying, and this time, allow me to be clear. Your city and its leader have risen fast from the brink of disaster with no explanation that my advisors can give. I have my doubts about a city that deals in slaves, and I have doubts about a city so close to the edge of ruin suddenly becoming such a financial force. I cannot help but wonder where this newfound wealth has come from. You deserve a chance to prove yourselves, so I shall give you one. Prove that this rise in wealth is innocent. If you can make good on the deals you have already made, I shall reconsider our relationship. Until then, there will be no deal with the Crown. I thank you for your visit. That will be all."

The delegation's faces were surprisingly placid, and Salvadire's was particularly hard to read. The king and queen stood as the delegation offered slight bows and shuffled from the hall. The doors closed with a loud bang that echoed through the near-empty chamber.

"Well, that was interesting," Debreace said as she wrapped her arms around her husband's waist and rested her head on his chest. "Do you think that was wise? Many won't be happy that we spurned their offer. It could jeopardise all the other deals, and a lot of coin could be lost. People could blame us. Is that what we need right now, more trouble?"

"People are blinded by coin. Something is not right about all this. I need to know how they've risen so far so fast."

"I understand. Now come. The boys will be finished with their lessons soon. Let's—"

Branthony held a finger to his lips. Debreace looked at him like he was playing a game, but his expression told her otherwise. He looked upwards at the ceiling. She followed his gaze but saw nothing of interest.

"What is it?" she whispered.

A silent pause dragged out. Branthony's eyes narrowed, fixed on the ceiling. Debreace was about to ask him again what was wrong. That was when she heard the creak for herself. Her head spun to the ceiling, and together they stared. She felt her husband stiffen. His hands tightened into fists.

A loud crash sounded through the room. Debreace screamed and jumped back. Branthony held his ground as dust and debris fell upon him. In the end, they stood staring at a pair of legs hanging above them.

Branthony felt his blood boiling. Why? Why couldn't his sons do as they were told? Why did they constantly feel the need to climb into every nook and cranny? Why were they continually making nuisances of themselves? They weren't children anymore.

"How many times must I—"

"They were lying."

They couldn't see his upper body, just his legs. Still, as Jacob's voice called down, Branthony paused.

"When they said their wealth has come from the hard work of their people."

The king and queen looked at each other.

"You're sure?" called Debreace, who, despite her husband's anger, was trying to stifle a laugh at the fact that they were staring up at the ceiling and talking to a pair of legs.

"Oh yeah," called Jacob. "I could tell. I could feel it. They were definitely not telling the truth."

She looked back at her husband with raised eyebrows.

"So where did it come from?"

Whack!

Aron felt a pang of pain as the wooden sword clattered against his arm. The fight would likely be over if the swords were real, but they weren't, and Aron could be quite stubborn. With a scream of defiance, he attacked.

His opponent, Ollie, was taken by surprise. He'd thought the battle over after landing the heavy blow. He fell back as Aron's sword snapped across his chest. It was Ollie's turn to be angry. He didn't say anything; Ollie rarely did. He was deaf and seldom chose to speak, though he did at times.

The two of them stood in a stare-down with matching aggression. Ollie had grown in the last years and was starting to tower over Aron. Most of the boys his age now towered over him. Just one more thing to make him more defiant. Neither of them seemed of a mind to back down until the Weapons-Master came between them.

"Settle down," Austin commanded. He was relatively new to the position. His predecessor, Hogan, had died during the battle at the Centre. Hogan had fought and defeated one of the Crone's Gifted Sile. He'd won the battle, but it cost his life. Aron felt bad for Austin having to take Hogan's place. The new Weapons-Master didn't seem to believe he deserved the position, but as far as Aron could tell, he was doing an excellent job.

Austin pushed the boys apart. For all their aggression, they both quickly calmed. He was a large man, thick-chested and aggressive-looking. He had a bald head with narrow eyes that seemed to beg for a challenge.

"You two are peas in a pod, you know. Both have the same temperament. Both aggressive, but untamed aggression won't win you a fight. Most of the time, it will get you killed. You'll be good sparring partners for each other if you pay attention. Learn from each other. Now, go again."

Aron listened intently as Ollie watched the Weapons-Master talk. He'd become quite adept at reading lips. When instructed, they both raised their swords and began to duel. Austin watched on, careful to keep himself within Ollie's view, shouting as they practised.

"Swordsmen must trust themselves," he said as he paced. "You must trust your skills but also learn your enemy's. Pay attention to them. See their strengths and weaknesses. Learn what you can exploit. If you have allies, use their strengths to your advantage. You will fight side by side one day. Good. Good," he said as the boys sped up a little. "Yes, that's it. Learn to anticipate your opponent."

They sped up again, and the sound of their swords clashing rattled through the practice yard. Neither would yield. They kept going despite the sweat on their brows and the ache in their arms.

"Enough!" called Austin loudly, and they let their swords drop. "That's good practice. Well done. Like I said, you two were made for each other." Austin knelt over so that Ollie could see him clearly. "Who knows, you might make quite the swordsman. You could even be the head of his guard one day."

Ollie's eyes opened wide, and Aron knew his friend had understood every word.

"Wouldn't that be a tale," said Austin as he took the practice swords from them and placed them in a rack. "The peasant boy who saved a kingdom and became the king's Chosen-Sword. You'll go down in history, my boy. Now, off with you both. Aron, I'll be sure to tell your father about your progress."

The two offered a respectful head dip, then Aron gestured for Ollie to follow, and they set off from the practice yard. Aron walked backwards so his friend could watch his lips as he talked. "Imagine that. You, the head of my Chosen-Swords. The two of us. We could go wherever we wanted." Ollie smiled back at him, clearly impressed by the thought. "But aren't Chosen-Swords meant to be great warriors? You were barely hanging on then. I almost had you."

Ollie smirked sarcastically, then began to give chase with a raised fist. Aron laughed as he fled, and together, they crossed the training yard in moments before reaching the walls and heading back into the castle.

Aron couldn't express how grateful he was for Ollie's presence. His friend had a way of making him feel grounded, more normal. He appreciated that and knew how special it was for Ollie to be with him. Of course, Ollie had earned his place. He'd fled with the newborn baby of the Fait, keeping it out of the clutches of the Crone. Now, Ollie and his brother Joe had complete access to the castle grounds, receiving lessons with all their expenditures paid for by the Crown. Not to mention that the baby, Aron's cousin, had been named Oliver in honour of his saviour.

Ollie and Joe weren't always there. Unfortunately, they didn't take lessons on the Gift together, which Aron remembered was next. The two friends said their goodbyes and promised to meet up again later. Aron made his way into the castle and went to find his instructor.

Luke sat sternly in his seat, arms folded, shoulders hunched, and chin tucked into his chest. The very picture of a sulking child despite Luke now entering adulthood. There were only five years between the four brothers; the most significant gap was between Aron and Luke. He hated that. People were starting to treat Aron like a man, while Luke felt treated like a child. He could hear his father's voice telling him to stop acting like one. He only sulked more.

"This is stupid," he said, his face scrunched up in the most distasteful of frowns. The instructor looked back at him, shaking his head. He was a large, muscular man with long hair hanging in strands over dangerous eyes. He had a large nose and a stubbly chin and seemed entirely out of place as an instructor. He dressed in worn black leathers, nothing like the fresh tunics or emblazoned surcoats often seen around the castle grounds. No, he definitely did not seem like an instructor, especially with the name Hunter.

"It may seem so now, but I assure you, this will all make sense in time. Your father has left strict instructions that we both have to follow." Hunter spoke in a deep, raspy voice that seemed far too menacing for a room of learning. Luke's father had brought in several new faces to the castle in recent months. People whom Branthony trusted. People he'd worked with before. People he knew to be particularly good at what they did. Hunter, an instructor? No, it simply didn't fit. So, what was he really?

"But I don't want to," Luke replied petulantly. "I am a prince of the Cross. I can do what I want."

"Very well, My Prince. I'll let ***you*** tell your father if you don't mind?"

All in an instant, Luke looked a little less stubborn. He tried to deny it, but he was just as scared of his father as everyone else.

"Let's just get this over with." He leaned forward, resting his elbows on the table between them. Upon the table sat a deck of playing cards. The instructor picked up the deck and began to deal out a hand to each of them.

"The game is Fait's Gambit," began Hunter in a calm, patient voice, showing no adverse reaction to Luke's earlier attitude. "It's a popular game in the Cross, often played for high stakes. It is a game of skill. A player can play his cards in many different ways, whether aggressively or defensively. It's a game of odds and concentration. A skilful player pays attention to the cards placed and knows which ones have been used and which remain. Some would say these were the two main factors in a game of Fait's Gambit, but others would say they both place behind the third main factor, luck. Everything depends on the next card, and a game can be won or lost on the turn of each one."

They went through their decks and assembled their cards. Each player had three cards placed face down on the table with three more placed face up and three more in their hand, making nine in total.

"The idea is simple," said Hunter. "The first player to rid themselves of all their cards wins the game. Players take turns to place a card. If a player cannot equal or beat the most recently played card, they must pick up all the previously played ones. You can see why this would be detrimental to your chances of winning. Each card played must be of an equal or higher value than the previous one, but, like your family and the game's namesake, some cards are Gifted, meaning they have abilities."

Luke couldn't help the frown returning to his face. How was this supposed to help with his Gift?

"The lowest value card is the Peasant. However, this is a Gifted card; even the Peasant can hold great power. It can be played over almost any other card, even those of a higher value, and it will bring the game back down to its level, meaning the next player must once again beat or equal the Peasant, which should be an easy thing to do. However, the Peasant cannot beat one card, but we will come to that soon." Luke yawned, and Hunter bristled at the action. "You would do well to pay attention to the game's lessons, young prince. Even peasants can do remarkable things. Weren't your friends considered peasants? Now look at them. They saved the life of your cousin and perhaps the kingdom itself. Now, they live and learn alongside royalty. Is this not the very definition of the lesson the game is trying to teach?"

"What lesson is that?" Luke replied nonchalantly.

"That you should not underestimate people."

Luke took Hunter's sharp tone on board and sat up a little straighter.

"Shall we continue? The next card is the Servant, followed by the Farmer, followed by the Craftsman, and then the Merchant. Next, we come to the Mercenary, another Gifted card. When played, it draws its power from the previous card, meaning the next player must beat the previous card. The Mercenary can be played on any other, making it, in some ways, the most valuable card in the game, though the Mercenary's deadliness depends entirely on who surrounds him. It is the previous card's strength that the Mercenary relies on. Again, this can teach us a real-life lesson. Many wars are won and lost by the actions of mercenaries."

"You mean wars are won and lost depending on who has the most gold."

"Not at all, young prince. You should pay more attention to your history lessons. Remember the king of Golt who hired mercenaries when his people revolted? He hired the most expensive troupe he could find, but they were so expensive that they had not been hired in quite some time. This meant they had lost much of the abilities that made them able to charge such a fee in the first place. The result?" Luke could only shrug his shoulders. Hunter looked disappointed. "Well, Your Highness, let us just say that Golt no longer has a king." Luke shuffled uncomfortably at that.

"The next card is the Man-at-Arms, followed by the Knight. The knight is an incredibly special card in the game."

"It has the power to change the tide of battle," blurted Luke. The instructor let the interruption go and even gestured for him to continue. "When played, the Knight switches the tide. Then, for one turn only, the next player must play a less valuable card."

"Correct. It's an invaluable weapon when played at the right moment. Played wrong, and it simply gives your opponent a chance to rid himself of yet more lower-value cards. Played right, and it can stifle the most powerful cards in the game."

Luke nodded. He'd heard how well the Knight could be deployed, and this time, the real-life lesson the game taught was not lost on him.

"What's next?" asked the instructor, encouraging Luke's participation.

"The Lord," he answered. "This is also a Gifted card. Some players consider it the most powerful card in the deck. The Lords control the land. They can burn the deck."

"Precisely," nodded Hunter. "A move also known as the Lords revolt. Yes. The Lord is mighty, sitting only beneath the royal family. When played, he will burn all the cards already used in that game, meaning they are out and cannot be picked up. There is a downside to this: it protects all players from the possibility of picking up should they not be able to make a move, but there are bonuses as well. Whoever instigates a Lords Revolt will then take another turn. The timing of this card can be critical."

"Come on already." Luke couldn't hold his frustration any longer. "Can't we just play?"

Hunter breathed down his frustration. "Your father asked me here because he needed people he could trust. After the lords came to the Centre demanding answers, it became clear how precarious his position is. The game, Prince Luke, listen to the game. The Lord's Revolt can burn any card beneath it, even a higher-value card. You know what will happen in the coming months. This lesson could be invaluable."

Luke understood all too well.

"Next, we move on to the royal family. The highest value cards in the game. The Prince, the Queen and the King."

"Yes, yes. That's it, so let's play."

"Your Highness," frustration was starting to creep into his voice. "You know full well there is one more card. Only one thing is more powerful than the members of the royal family: the Fait. The powers of the family combined. This is the highest-value card in the deck. The Peasant cannot bring it down. The Lord cannot burn it. The only way to pass the Fait is to play the Mercenary, who then draws an equal strength from the card, or play another Fait. There are, of course, four cards of each kind."

"Yes. I understand. I know the cards and how many of them there are. I know their Gifts. So, let's play, and you can try to teach me whatever lesson you're trying to teach."

"It was your Uncle Christopher's idea for us to play together. You know this, yes?"

"Yes, so?"

"You do know that your uncle is a knowledgeable man?"

Luke looked confused at the sudden turn in the conversation.

"He has requested that we play Faits Gambit together. You have the Gift of Fortune. He hopes that playing a game such as this may help your Gift bloom, and you may learn to control it. But also, the game itself can teach us lessons. Not just the obvious ones surrounding the cards. Lessons you can take out into the world and use throughout your life."

"Such as?" asked Luke mockingly.

"Such as patience!" he spat. "Now, shall we continue?" Once again, Luke could only scowl in response, though he looked a little scared. "There are some more rules to the game, of course; if four of the same cards are played on top of one another, either in one turn or more, they will mimic the power of the Lords Revolt, thus burning the deck and allowing the player who burned to go again. Four of any kind, even with a Mercenary between them, will have the same effect, and cards of the same value can be played at once. A player can swap any of the first three cards in their hand for the upturned cards on the table. I would suggest placing any Gifted or high-value cards down on the table if you were fortunate enough to get some when the cards were dealt."

Hunter looked at Luke as Luke looked at the cards in his hand. He had a Peasant, a Knight and a Lord. All three were Gifted. On the table sat one Merchant and two Man-at-Arms. He swapped all three cards in his hand for those on the table. The instructor swapped only one card. Luke watched him pick a Farmer from the table and replace it with a Prince.

"As I dealt, you go first."

"You watched me swap my cards. I know you looked at what I had on the table, so you know what I have in my hand."

"Of course."

"Just checking you're paying attention," he said, then played his first card.

"Each player picks a card from the deck after each move until the deck is depleted," said Hunter as the game started to move. "If players cannot go, they pick up the discarded cards. A player does not have to pick from the deck if he has more than three cards in his hand. Once the deck is depleted and a player uses the cards in their hand, they may pick up their three upturned cards from the table. Once these are used, the player may turn over his downward-facing cards one at a time. The player will not know what is on those cards until he moves."

The game was moving at speed now, with both players placing cards and then picking up from the deck, which was already almost half depleted. So far, neither player had been unable to make a move, and the discarded cards were piling up. If a player had to pick up now, it would be devastating to his chances of winning.

As the game progressed, Luke began to feel confident. The cards were falling his way, and as the deck ran out, the Gifted cards on the table would help. He looked from his cards at Hunter, who was smiling. The last card Luke played was a King. It would be tough to beat, yet the instructor's smile grew as he placed down a Fait card. He sat back, confident.

"You've been paying attention to the cards played?" asked Luke.

"Certainly."

"Then you know all four Mercenaries have been played?"

"I do."

"Then you know how hard it is to beat a Fait?"

"I do," Hunter said again.

"Then I hope you can do it." Luke placed his card triumphantly. It was his turn to sit back with a smile. He'd played another Fait. He picked the last card from the deck, not bothering to look at it; with no cards left in the deck, he only had to use the ones in his hand before moving on to his table cards.

The instructor looked dismayed. The pile of discarded cards was a large portion of the complete deck. He did not look impressed at the prospect of picking them all up. It was the last thing Luke expected when the instructor smiled once again. He positively beamed as he placed down a third Fait card.

Luke sat suddenly forward, slamming his palms against the table. What were the chances? He felt defeated. He knew only one card left could prevent him from picking up. He had a Man-at-Arms and a Queen to play. They were good cards, but not good enough. Wait, he had another card. He'd picked the last one from the deck. He knew there was still one Fait card. Had the instructor been lucky enough to pull a third from the deck before it ran out? Or was it one of the six down-facing cards on the table? Luke had to hope.

"You could have played both your Fait's at once," said Luke sulkily.

"Strategy, young prince. I knew you could likely beat one Fait, leaving me without a defence, but two? Not so easy."

Before turning his card, Luke focused, picturing the Fait card, the one thing he needed.

He turned the card.

What good Fortune.

The last Fait stared up at him.

Luke slammed the card down. Not only did he not have to pick up, but he'd made four in a row of the same card, burning the deck. He was relieved when he pushed all the discarded cards to the side, knowing they were now out of the game. As Luke had burned the deck, he got to go again. He played his Man-at-Arms. Hunter matched the card. Luke played his Queen next, then picked up his three upturned cards from the table and finally looked at his opponent.

"Well," said the instructor. "What were the chances of that?"

"Slim."

"Indeed. There was only one possible card to save you, and you found it in your moment of need. Was this simply good luck? Or Fortune?"

"Who can tell?" said Luke. It was one of the drawbacks of his Gift. Such a thing was not impossible, just unlikely. Was the card always there and destined to be picked up, or had Luke's Gift had an effect?

The game was now tipped in Luke's favour, but he still had his blind cards to play. He had a Peasant, a Knight and a Lord in his hand. The same three cards he'd started the game with.

"Shall we finish?" he asked with a smirk.

"Yes, let's," said Hunter, matching Luke's expression.

Joshua and Joe, or Joseph as most of the adults around the castle preferred, stared with open mouths at Healing-Master Fredrick. The old man had his back to them as he pointed to various parts of a diagram depicting a dissected human body. He explained in some detail what the different organs were and their functions. He rambled on, barely stopping for breath and without turning around, completely unaware of the expression on his students' faces. Fredrick was the Healing-Master, but he was also ancient. More Master in name now than anything else, thus why he was teaching. This would not usually be the responsibility of a Castle-Master.

Finally, when Fredrick turned around and noted his two students, he paused and chuckled.

"I'm sorry. I may have gotten a little carried away with myself there." The two of them simply nodded. "Well, I do believe we may have overrun our time together. You may tell your next instructor it is my fault, although I am sure Hunter will have some angry words. That is, if he's done with your brother yet. Run along now."

After a simple, silent nod, the boys shuffled awkwardly from the room. They walked several corridors before either could bring themselves to speak. Finally, it was Joe who broke the silence.

"Did you know what the intestines did?"

"I didn't even know we had intestines."

"Me neither." They both tried to shake the so-called lesson from their minds. "So, what's next? Oh, it's a lesson on the Gift. Should I meet you later?"

"Why don't you come with me? I'm sure Hunter won't mind." He wasn't sure at all but pressed on. "You could just sit and wait in the corner. We're late, so it should be a short lesson."

"Why not? Worth a try at least."

They reached a door. Joshua knocked, and a voice called for him to enter. He opened the door, about to apologise for being late. Instead, he looked on in shocked silence, surprised at what met them.

A huge model filled most of the room, a giant landscape of hills and fields, rivers, forests, and forts, all carved from wood and meticulously painted. Joshua reached out a hand, reverently stroking the beautiful craftsmanship.

"Quite something, isn't it?" said Hunter.

"Yes," he replied, mesmerised. "Erm, Sir," he added, remembering where he was.

"Come, you may have guessed, we will not play chess today."

Joshua started to walk around the room, surveying the model from all angles. It was marvellous, like a vast map. Just as a question came to his mind, a voice spoke it aloud.

"Is this the Cross?" asked Joe.

Joshua suddenly remembered his friend.

"Erm, is it all right if Joe joins us? We do our other lessons together."

"Of course," said Hunter. "Your father suspected we may have company at some point. He encouraged it, in fact. Maybe Joseph will be as good for you as Ollie is for Prince Aron. In answer to your question, yes, this is the Cross. A portion of it, at least, however, the model can be changed. Well done on your observation. Many do not see it." Joe looked incredibly pleased with himself.

Upon closer inspection, they saw that the model's base split into different sections that could be added or removed. Almost everything else on the surface was an extra piece placed upon the board. Forests were small groups of wooden trees put together. The rivers were tendrils of blue cloth. The forts and castles were generic grey cubes. Their placement on the map told the boys which castles they represented. One was different, though, standing out from the rest.

"The Centre," said Joshua, examining a beautiful replica of the city. "What's it all for?" he asked.

"From today, we will use this board to play out what many refer to as 'war games.' It's much like chess in ways. We will play out a strategic war against one another. We each have forces at our command. Infantry, cavalry, archers. We have forts to protect, rivers to cross, terrain to consider, all things a real commander must think of."

"This will help my Gift?"

"I believe so. As far as we know, Guidance is a Gift that allows you to navigate complex situations instinctively. Your Gift guides you so that you, in turn, can guide others."

"Can I help?" asked Joe.

"I hope so. Question him and demand explanations. If you have doubts, express them. Joshua's Gift may tell him to do something, but it could lead to trouble if he doesn't understand why. We are all learning here. I was selected as your instructor because of my tactical skills, but I have never faced people with Gifts. Playing Fait's Gambit with your brother Luke has been most educational."

"Did Luke beat you?" Joshua asked. Hunter simply smiled back at him.

"My lessons with Luke are between me and him, for the moment."

That sounded a little ominous to Joshua's ear.

"I don't really know how to use my Gift. It's just a voice in my head," he said apologetically.

"Like I said, we are all here to learn. So," said Hunter with what could only be described as a slightly menacing grin, "it's time to play the game."

DEALS IN THE DARK

The Centre was a vast city with people from all levels of society living on both extremes of the spectrum of wealth. From the castle's grandeur to the depravity of the lower town and the old market. Sir Bolevord Bront was the Scroll-Master and, as such, spent most of his time in the castle in what was undoubtedly the higher end of society. He did not, in any way, enjoy debasing himself by traversing the squalor of areas such as he found himself now. Bolevard held himself above the average citizen of this city. He considered himself far above his current course of action, but the time had come to do what he must.

He entered the dimly lit tavern and saw several tables spread over a dirty, straw-littered floor. The patrons of the tavern were much as expected, filthy ingrates who would never contribute anything good to the world. Bolevard counted ten faces spread across four tables. Three looked up at him as he entered. They'd see little in the gloom and dim candlelight, especially as Bolevard wore his hood up.

With a gesture to the barkeep signifying his desire for a drink he had no intention of drinking, Bolevard took a seat with his back to the wall where he could keep an eye on the other occupants. Before he had become the Scroll-Master, he had been a knight of the Cross. He'd been proud of that once upon a time. Not anymore. He hadn't felt pride in anything for a long time. How could he be proud of being a knight of the Cross when the Fait ruled the Cross? Bolevard knew what so few others did. He knew the true source of the Fait's power. The witch!

People had seen the witch. She had attacked the Centre in broad daylight. Bolevard had thought that would be enough, but no. People were desperate to cling to the status quo. Still deluding themselves that the Fait were special.

He sat in the gloom, staring at his murky reflection in the dirtied glass panels of the window. He became lost in his eyes, staring himself out as though waiting for the reflection to back down. *Coward*, he thought as he looked away. The image caused almost as much revulsion as the witch. He was glad for a distraction as the door opened, and a figure entered. A man scanned the room, his eyes eventually settling on Bolevard. He approached and took the seat opposite.

"Sir Bolevard," he said in a thickly accented voice. Bolevard shushed him aggressively.

"Don't speak my name," he whispered, cautiously glancing back over his shoulder.

The man dipped his head in apology. "My name is Karim. Salvadire sends his regards." He kept his voice low.

"So," said Bolevard, sitting back on his chair a little and pretending to sip his drink. "The meeting with the king went well?"

"Exactly as planned."

"The Crown has signed trade deals with Varliant?"

"No. There will be no deal. The king has stated he does not trust Varliant and has no intention of trading with us."

Bolevard was surprised. That didn't sound like the meeting went well.

"I thought you said—"

"I said the meeting went exactly as planned."

"You wanted the king to say no to a trade deal?"

Karim smirked as he took out a pipe and lit it. The smoke drifted in the air, with Karim's grin lurking behind it. Bolevard waved the smoke away, annoyed by its sight and smell.

"How did you know the king wouldn't just say yes?"

"We didn't," Karim grinned annoyingly. "But we are well aware of the king's cautiousness. He acted as expected."

"Lord Vol has sent his most trusted envoys to the city, my companions and I, led by Salvadire, but we are not the only men from Varliant to come to the Cross. In each of the four points, our envoys have been visiting the lords and merchants of the land and making great promises and fantastic deals worth more gold than you can imagine. Now, the king has offered a blank 'no' in response to our offers. Many of those who have already said yes will feel aggrieved by the king's decision, especially when, as a result of it, Varliant pulls itself from these previously agreed deals."

Bolevard listened and watched the man through the thickening smoke, and everything fell into place. He was impressed. These filthy foreigners had concocted quite a plan.

"So, the lords, merchants and anyone else who will be out of pocket will blame it all on the king."

"Precisely," said Karim, his smile growing after another long drag on the pipe. "We are allies because you want to see the king fall. This is one step in many that will bring about such a thing."

"Not just the king," Bolevard quickly interjected, though he was still sure to keep his voice to a minimum. "The entire Fait. They must **all** go. They are in line with the... With the..."

He strained himself, his face growing red as though he were suddenly choking. His eyes began to water, and it seemed he might collapse until Karim's hand landed on top of his own with a firm grip.

"Relax, my friend. Relax. Do not try to fight their devil's magic. We know who the Fait are in league with. It is the very reason we have come. The world must be rid of their evil."

Bolevard drew a deep breath. It took a few moments to calm himself, and, in his mind, he said another thousand curses for the Fait, but most of all for Princess Susan, who'd laid this affliction upon him. Hers was the Gift of Obedience, and she'd used it on Bolevard many years ago. He could not talk about the things he knew. He did, however, take reassurance that at least some others thought as he did.

"So," he said after a moment to compose himself. "What do you want from me?"

"Simple," answered Karim. "When Lady Celia told us of your distaste toward the Fait, we knew we could be allies. We want you to use your influence at court to stir the tension between the lords and the king."

"And what does Celia get out of this?"

"She is an ambitious woman. If the Fait are to fall, she seeks to replace them."

That sounded exactly like Celia. Pure greed. It was not something he agreed with, but when Celia offered this alliance, he accepted anyway. Greed, whilst deplorable, was understandable. Working with creatures such as the witch was not. Anything or anyone was better than the Fait. Even Celia. He would be happy enough to see her on the throne.

"And then what?"

"Patience, my friend. Salvadire will send word in time. For now, sow discord. The time for our next move will arrive soon enough. The Fait's time is ending. We will see to that together."

In the end, to Bolevard at least, that was all that mattered.

Karim walked through the door and looked at his companions. Their current holdings were not luxurious, but he still felt out of place in the ragged cloak he had worn to meet with their agent inside the king's court. Whilst not a man of extreme power or influence, the Scroll-Master was proving useful.

"How did it go?" Salvadire asked whilst sipping wine and enjoying a pipe. A woman of pleasure hired from the establishment in which they spent their time sat behind him, rubbing oils into his bare torso. She was not as skilled as the Deliverers of serenity, but her touch was pleasant.

"Excellent," he replied, taking a seat across the table. "The fool has no idea what is really happening. His hatred for the Crone and the Fait is all that guides him. If only he knew that by working for us, he works for her."

"Can he do as we need?"

"He certainly believes so, but there was something else. Something that disturbed me."

Salvadire sat straighter in his seat, shrugging off the girl, who looked aggrieved as she moved away. "Go on," he urged.

"Bolevard, he tried to talk about the Crone, to say her name. He couldn't do it. He tried so hard, but the words would not come."

Salvadire scrunched his brow. "We knew to expect this. He has been infected by the Fait. The king's sister used her Gift on him. He cannot talk of the Crone."

"Yes, it was not unexpected. It is just that." He removed his pipe from his inside pocket and began to pack it with tobacco. "He tried. He tried so hard I thought he would kill himself with the effort."

"What is your point?"

Karim put a spill into a candle, then placed it to his pipe and a fresh cloud of smoke began to fill the room. The smell was bitter against the sweet incense that burned elsewhere.

"The magic of the Fait is strong, my friend. I saw a man almost die from trying to speak a word." He shook his head as he took a long drag. "We are meddling with great powers here. Powers we do not understand. I fear where this path may lead us."

Salvadire leaned forward and stared intently into Karim's eyes.

"They received their powers from her; now she works with us. The plan is coming together perfectly." Salvadire sat back and ushered the girl to return but pointed her toward Karim. "Do not fear, my friend. All is going according to plan. Now, freshen up. Enjoy a woman. Let *me* worry about the Fait."

Celia opened the door to her chambers and peered out into an empty corridor. She paused there momentarily, listening for telltale sounds of anyone nearby. When there was nothing to hear, she gently closed the door and locked it before heading to the small desk in the corner of her room.

As a representative of a Point-Warden, Celia lived on the castle grounds. Her father, the Warden of the Eastern-Point, expected her to carry out his wishes here at the Centre and represent their Point in all things. She did this job to the utmost of her ability, which was a damned sight better than most. In the years she had been here, she had made quite the reputation for herself. Celia was the only woman ever to represent a Point-Warden. She was also the sole heir to the Five Fingers, which made her one of the most powerful people, let alone women, in the entire kingdom. Yet Celia wanted more. Much more.

She reached into her desk, pulled out the small glass vial, and surveyed its contents. The red liquid seemed so inconspicuous. It was blood, but not just any blood. The blood of the Fait. Who would think it could do so much? The truth was she didn't actually know what it could do. What were the limits of such a thing? The mere act of obtaining it would be enough to see her in chains. Celia's heart began to pound as she removed the stopper from the vial.

She had done many questionable things in her life, but few caused her to question herself. Some decisions, some exceedingly rare ones, still haunted her to this day. Decisions that made her heart and gut twist whenever she thought of them. She had been pregnant once. What she had done then was a decision she often worried over. The decision she was making right now was another that troubled her. There was no doubt that this was an act of treason, and if she were ever discovered, her head would be forfeit. No amount of power would protect her, not even the power of her father. He may well be the first to call for the axe. He had never been Celia's biggest fan. What was between her legs had always been an unscalable barrier between them, and nothing mattered more to Lord Carter Trone than his reputation.

After the battle at the Centre, she had aligned herself with the enemy of the Fait. Celia had accepted an offer from the Crone. She would spy and work towards the Crone's goals in exchange for power. Celia would be there to claim what was left behind when the Fait fell. A dangerous ploy. She would have to play both sides, but Celia was nothing if not confident in herself.

With the utmost care, she poured a single drop onto the desk before her. She stared at it intently, waiting. Nothing happened. Had she poured enough? She reached for a nearby cloak and wrapped it around her shoulders, the air feeling colder. Thoughts of pouring another drop came to her, and she lifted the vial again.

"Do not waste it!"

The icy, gravelly voice made Celia jump in her seat. She turned and looked about the room but saw nothing new besides the cloud of her breath as it drifted against the frigid air. She wrapped the cloak tighter as the cold grew despite the warmth of the summer night. This was a relatively new experience, and she had to admit it still made her skin crawl. Though she could not see the Crone, the sound of her voice was enough to send shivers rampaging down Celia's spine.

"What you hold in your hand is the most precious substance in this world. That is the blood of the Fait. A single drop is worth more than all the gold in the land."

Celia looked out into the room, unsure where to direct her gaze. "Many would disagree," she argued.

"Many are fools!" The Crone's voice snapped. "That blood can make gold, so what value could gold have compared to such a thing? You see the truth. Some believe that gold will buy power, but true power cannot be bought."

The blood can make gold? she thought but said nothing more.

"Those with the most power are born to it," she replied.

"No," came a whisper. "Not anymore. I can create power. You must obtain more blood as soon as possible. Only with the blood can we continue to communicate."

"It's not exactly the easiest thing to come by."

"You are resourceful."

Celia felt a wave of confidence and already knew she would somehow find a way.

"That I am, but you talk of power. Of giving and creating such, but to do so, you need the blood of the Fait. So, who truly holds the power? You or them?"

A low chuckle sounded through the room, and Celia would swear the temperature grew colder still. Who knew a sound could be so disturbing?

"The blood is but one part of the equation. The Blood River is another. I am an exception to the rules."

'How? How does it work, and what makes you so special?"

"It is the blood of an angel. It lives within the Fait. Such power does not simply die. Living and feeding from the Blood River grants the ability to awaken the Gift. The Gift resides within the blood but needs extra strength to awaken. The angel bled into the river; its power resides there. The men at the river gain health and long life, but women, the women gain so much more. Only a woman could carry such responsibility. The Gift is awoken by giving the Fait that extra power through the milk. I fed from the river for years and have other powers beyond that. I am forever linked to the Fait."

"Is that what makes you the exception? Because you took so much of the blood and fed from the river for so long?"

"That is what they would believe, what those fools at the river believe. They are wrong, but enough with your questions. I have a question for you. Do you believe in my power?"

Celia spent a moment in thought before she replied.

"I believe… I believe I have climbed as high as possible in the current state of play. Yet, I wish to climb higher. So, the only available option is to change the state of play. The Fait are at the top of the ladder; if I wish to surpass them, they must be removed. You are my best chance of doing such a thing."

The chuckle sounded again. This time, even more dreadful.

"I knew I was right to choose you. I knew you had the vision to see how the world changes. We shall both rise in power, but first, we must move carefully. Until the Fait are brought to their knees, they are dangerous. I sought to control the world around them, thus shaping it to fit my needs. Now, I will shape the world ***through*** them. For too long, I have feared the powers beyond this world. I thought to act just enough to fulfil my desires without earning the ire of the beings of creation. I now know I failed. The God himself moves against me."

Celia was shocked. Were the Crone's words true, or was she delusional?

"If the God moves against you, does that not make you fearful?"

"On the contrary. It emboldens me. It proves I have been too soft on this world. It proves how much more I could do. The God or any other power cannot interfere directly with this world. I can. That is why they fear me. That is why they try to eliminate me. He grants stronger Gifts to his little pawns, but I grow stronger with every move he makes against me. The Fait are the only obstacle."

"Their problems are growing by the day," said Celia as she began to feel more relaxed. Acceptance of one's decisions can often bring about fresh resolve and clarity. "The battle at the Centre has opened the eyes of the world. What you did here, what you showed people, you have created a whirlwind. The people now know that magic does not solely belong to the Fait."

"Without me, anyone who uses magic will die. The river may offer some respite for those who have taken sufficiently from it. Besides that, and the Fait themselves, I am the only option. Even that takes great sacrifice."

"Yes, but people don't know that. Many of the lords of the Cross now believe that the Fait have been lying for generations to keep their power. The Fait rule through the Gift. Now, others believe that they could have a Gift and that maybe they should rule. The king is no fool; he already knows that much of his authority is now called into question. The power and honour of his family are in doubt. It has been a long time since the Fait have faced such wide scepticism."

The Crone growled. Somehow, the sound conveyed that everything was as expected.

"My plan with our friends from the east is moving forward. You must continue to grow discord amongst the lords of the Cross. They will play their part, and little Branthony's problems will only grow worse. I will show him the error of his ways. He will pay a heavy price for thinking himself above me."

Celia could understand that all too well. She could not abide anyone looking down on her. She begrudged admitting how many traits she and the Crone shared.

"There are more tasks I must ask of you."

The Crone's voice made it clear that these were not requests.

"The king's new little plaything will soon return home to the Blood River. You must have one of your people with her. I must know what is happening there."

"If the girl Merleal and these stupid river people are such a threat to you, then why not simply be rid of them? I have seen what you can do. You can move places. You did it here at the Centre. Brought yourself and your Sile here. Why not simply go to the river and have done with it?"

"She is ***not*** a threat to me!" The Crone snapped. "Their time will come soon enough, though some things are not so easily achieved. What I did at the Centre took great power. Getting out of there after the attack and taking Cutter-of-Men with me was no simple trick. Besides, the river is protected. For now, we need eyes and ears there. See what the king has planned."

"That's easy. He plans to establish a presence there, and for the people of the river to have a presence here at the Centre in time. He is determined to build new, stronger alliances with the Sile and the people of the Blood River."

"He will need to fortify the river if he hopes to protect it. Find what he puts in place there and report to me. I cannot see what happens there. It is a place I cannot breach without great sacrifice. When the time finally comes, I must have every chance at victory."

"I shall see to it." She already had the perfect candidate. The boy, Res, would be taking a trip. "What else?" she asked.

"Hmmm," a low chuckle rang in the air, and somehow it was the most disturbing sound of all. "You have grown close to the First-Born."

Celia felt that familiar shiver run down her spine. How did the Crone know so much? "I wouldn't exactly call us close, but I believe he trusts me. I've worked hard to gain that confidence from Prince Aron and his mother."

"Yes, you have done well. Continue to garner the boys' trust. I must know of his dreams. Tell me what he sees."

Prince Aron's dreams were well-known throughout the castle. At least, his state when he woke from them. How many times had he returned to the waking world screaming in terror?

"He barely remembers his dreams. They're as confusing as they are terrifying."

"The boy was born too early. He was not ready. He may never truly gain control of his Gift, but he can still be dangerous."

"I understand," said Celia. She already felt that rare tug at her conscience. Aron was becoming a fine man, albeit one with a temper. Even Celia felt sympathy for him when she heard the terror in his voice when he spoke of his dreams. However, she would do what she must.

"Good,' said the Crone. "Be prepared. Things will move swiftly."

The room grew instantly warmer, and Celia knew the conversation was over. She moved to her window and looked out onto the night, pushing down the knot within her stomach.

Vol sat sweating. The damned heat was relentless at this time of year. He almost welcomed the rare meetings when he would speak to the Crone. Her presence, even when ethereal, always brought bring a chill. Alas, this was not one of those meetings. Time in her physical presence was rare indeed. Overall, Vol was immensely grateful for that. Everything about her was overbearing and wore him down. The very sight of her was hard to stomach.

She did, however, converse with him slightly more often. They had spoken recently, and Vol had listened. It was not hard to see that the Crone thought of him as an asset, a tool to be used. He understood this. It shamed him to admit it, but everything she said about him was true. When they had first met, his city was on the brink of collapse. He had nothing to resolve the situation, and without her, he would perhaps already be dead.

How quickly the tides of fate could change. Now, Varliant was on an unparalleled rise, and Vol was considered a hero to many. The Crone had used her considerable skills to create the ramp on which he rode upward.

He wished now to repay her. He also wanted to prove his value, to show her that her selection of him had not been wrong. He had questioned her often about the Fait. Despite her words that they were nothing without her, Vol knew of their powers. Even if they didn't have the Gift at their disposal, they were still the ruling family of the Cross, whose might was not to be underestimated. She planned to divide the people of the Cross and have the kingdom pull itself apart, but there were still problems to be solved. Vol would prove his worth. He was desperate to. He knew he was far from essential in all this.

He entered the room where his meeting would take place, pulling at his silk trousers as they sagged. When did that start happening? Was he losing weight? Yes, definitely. Quite a bit. Perhaps the stress of his new activities was causing such?

"Your services come highly recommended," he said. "Has my man explained the task to you?"

A figure stepped from the darkness and pulled a hood down, revealing a face covered in dirt and grime. Once upon a time, Vol would only have seen a peasant, someone far below him, not worth the time of day. Now he realised this was a clever disguise. Assassins liked to blend in. This assassin did an excellent job. He barely seemed to deserve a second look.

"You wish to take the life of a Fait," said the assassin. "This is no easy task. All in the known world fear them. The price for an attempt will be high."

"The cost is no object, but I do not want to pay for an *attempt*. Can you succeed?"

"It can be done," the man said confidently. "No one has a better chance than us."

The assassin was correct. He represented the Nerium. An order of assassins whose name derived from a poisonous plant, the Nerium Oleander. They were known and operated throughout most of the known world, and their reputation alone was frightening.

"And you know your target?"

"I was told one of the Fait. I would assume it to be the king. His Gift is well known, and the Heir is still young."

"No!" said Vol, regretting the sharpness of his tone as the man turned upraised eyebrows on him. "No," he repeated in a much calmer voice. "The king's Gift is useful only in battle. We do not intend to be in open war with the Cross. Not yet, at least. No, your target is the youngest, Prince Jacob."

Vol knew the Crone had apprehensions of the young prince. His Gift of Truth offered the most danger to her plans. The cracks in the relationship between the Crone and the Fait finally broke open on the day of Jacob's birth. The moment she'd learned his Gift, she knew that sooner or later, it would mean the end of their time together. She chose not to wait and made her intentions clear that day when she turned on the king.

Vol would prove himself to her and have the little brat eliminated.

"The youngest prince is the target, but you must take precautions. No one can be questioned."

"We understand the task," came the simple reply.

"Good. Then I await word of your success."

The Crone would surely be grateful, and there would be one less Fait to worry about. Now, time to rest. His work would soon resume. Raising Varliant back on high was not cheap. It felt like creating the wealth needed to accomplish the task was killing him almost as quickly as leaving the city in ruin would have.

DESCENT DESCENDS

The boys stood in a line as their mother inspected them; even Aron, despite his age, did not escape scrutiny today. Each dressed in their finest tunics embroiled with the royal emblem of the Cross, stitched in golden thread, they most certainly looked like princes today.

"They will begin arriving soon," said Debreace as she checked over them again, fussing over every slight imperfection.

"Yes, Mother,' said Luke, who tried to pull away as she attempted to tame an unruly lock of hair. "We've done this before, remember? All the lords of the Cross came when Father disappeared."

"This is ***nothing*** like last time, and that was not 'all' the lords of the Cross." She looked them in the eye with that stern expression that told them now was the time to pay attention. "Listen to me," she urged as she pulled her children closer. "These people are coming here to question your father, to question ***us***. Many believe we have lied about the Gift. What the Crone did." They all saw the flicker of emotion at the mention of that name. "What she did when she gave that Sile warrior a Gift has sent the world down a new path. The Sile reached all the way into the Centre, and now the world sees weakness where before there was only strength.

"It is up to ***us*** to show them we are strong. A strong Fait means a strong Cross. Do you understand?"

"The lords think they can come here and question us? They need to be put in their place," said Luke aggressively.

"No, Luke. They are the lords and ladies of the land. They have every right to be upset, and our job as leaders and rulers is to answer their questions. We owe our position to them in many ways. They each hold their own power in their lands. That power answers to us only as long as we are worthy."

"It's like Fait's Gambit," he said thoughtfully. "The lords could burn it all if they turned against us."

"That's right, " she said. "So, we must ensure they are satisfied and stay on side. If any of your Gifts tell you anything, this is the time to use them." She hugged them all tightly. "Come, your father is waiting."

The massive doors opened, and the boys stepped out into momentarily blinding sunlight. The roars of the crowd immediately hit them, and when their eyes adjusted, they all gazed upon the packed-out streets of the Centre. Everywhere they looked, people filled every corner and peered from every window. Thousands had even climbed upon rooftops to watch the passing procession.

The boys stood at the top of the giant stone steps that led to the main entrance of the castle, an entrance that was rarely used, but todays were no ordinary guests. They looked to their father as he turned and ushered them forward, then stepped out with their mother so the people could get a better view of the entire family together. The noise rose as the people saw them. It was not lost on the boys how they were viewed by many.

There had never been four children born to one generation of the Fait. Some believed their births meant a golden age was imminent. Others, including their father, believed a great threat was coming and that it would take all their Gifts to defeat it. The boys sided with their father. They already had a name for the threat.

Aron stepped to his father's side, who placed an arm around his shoulders.

"Take it all in, Son. It's days like these when being a king truly means something."

Aron tried to appreciate it all: the grandeur, the spectacle, the adulation. The people looked to the Fait, and he truly believed they were some of the few rulers in the known world who tried to put the people first. He'd noticed a change in how people looked at him recently, now seeing the man and the future king instead of the boy and childish prince.

"When will they start to enter?" asked Joshua.

"Soon, but this could take some time. Look." Branthony pointed out into the distance, and the boys followed with their eyes. They could see the procession making its way through the streets. Horses and carts, knights in full armour, lords and ladies dressed in all their splendour. Trumpets blew aloud as flags and banners waved proudly announcing the arrival of the lords of the Cross. It trailed most of the way through the city.

"Mother was right. It's not like last time," said Jacob, referring to when the lords last descended upon the Centre. They'd come in secret to confront the queen regarding the king's disappearance. The boys didn't even see the lords arrive; they were too busy playing in the city somewhere with Joe and Ollie, but Jacob was right, this was vastly different.

"Last time they came with their hosts," said Luke. "Rushing to demand answers, knowing Father wasn't here. They all thought they could get away with murder in his absence. Talking to Mother like she was beneath them!"

"That didn't go too well for them, though, did it," said Aron, remembering how his mother had commanded the respect a queen deserves.

"This time they're making a show of it. All pomp and pretence now they know Father is here." Luke had that familiar snarl on his face.

"It won't stay like this," said Joshua. "Things could turn ugly. It all depends on how many of them support us and how many think it may be time for a change. They think our family has lied to them for years. They think the very thing that has given us power is a lie. The Crone has tricked them all."

"Well," said Jacob, now pointing forward. "Here's one at least that we know will support us."

The first banner entered the castle grounds. The boys recognised their father's friend, Lord Richard Dawsel of Rodley, who approached them with his wife Donna by his side and their three children, two boys and a girl. They climbed the steps as a family, and when they were close, they took a knee. When they stood, the king and queen embraced them.

Joshua watched and felt a strange yet familiar feeling running through him.

"What's wrong?" asked Luke, sensing his brother's agitation.

"It's my Gift," he said, feeling almost strange confiding in Luke, who, of all his brothers, Joshua had always had the most challenging relationship with.

"What about it?" Luke pushed.

"It's explaining things to me."

"What does that mean?" asked Luke, keeping his eyes forward and a smile on his face.

"Lord Richard arriving first isn't an accident. Father needs friends and allies. It wouldn't look good if the first lord to enter the gates was rebellious. Having Richard arrive first and bow so deeply sends out a good message. He's a powerful lord, and showing support for Father may already have dissuaded some of the others from going the other way. They'll all be taking note of who does what."

Luke lost the pretence of being interested in the greetings and turned to his brother with wide eyes.

"Your Gift told you all that?"

"Erm, kind of."

"I prefer Fortune," he said bluntly, looking back at the crowd. "That was just boring."

Joshua merely sighed.

They watched on for what felt like an age as the procession slowly made its way through the gates. The boys paid close attention to how each lord and lady greeted their parents. Some were warm and embracing, like Lord Richard. Others, such as Lord Dwayne of the First Fort, seemed slightly more subdued, choosing to bow but not so deeply. Others were downright frosty. The slightest of bows to adhere to protocol, then straight back to their feet. Even these, however, were met with warm welcomes from the king and queen.

"They're trying to charm and win them over," said Joshua.

"We don't want the lords burning the game, do we?" Luke replied with narrowed eyes.

Time dragged as the procession continued. The boys filled their time by looking out at the city and finding areas they knew and had visited in their alternate lives. Now and then, Father would look over and smile knowingly.

They paid close attention as the banners of the Black Fort came through the gates. Lord Basel was a powerful man who openly spoke out against the Fait when their father travelled south during the Sile invasion. Basel's short and sharp bow was followed by a little more than a dip of the head before he moved on, his eyes drifting over to the boys. They all felt ice in the glare.

If the Black Fort was one of the powerhouses of the Western-Point, then the same could be said of its opposite. The Red House was one of the most powerful lands in the Eastern-Point. Lord Victor Hive was well-known; his influence would go a long way in swaying others. No one knew which way he was currently leaning. His bow and greeting gave little away. It was deep and long enough to show respect, but nothing more. He nodded to the boys, and his eyes drifted to Lady Celia, standing not far away. As the representative of the Eastern-Point Warden, Lord Hive had a duty to serve Celia. It was well known that he had vied for the position of Point-Warden against her father. He spoke quietly into her ear before moving off. She did not look pleased with whatever he'd said.

The procession was ending, and the boys felt their legs aching. "How much longer?" asked Jacob.

"I think that's it," said Aron as there were no more banners to come through the gates despite the long tail of the procession.

The king and queen turned and were about to head inside when their eyes returned to the gate. The boys turned with them as trumpets rang out again. New banners that had for some reason remained hidden were suddenly thrust into the air. The boys looked on expectantly at the surprise announcement.

"Is that?" asked Jacob

The banners blew in the wind as the trumpets rang out, and the crowd, who had begun to lose interest, was suddenly reignited. The royal emblem of the Cross was suddenly displayed proudly, and the boys ran forward to stand beside their parents again.

"Aunt Susan," said Luke.

Even their father, it seemed, was surprised by the arrival. Susan appeared at the gates wearing a long flowing cloak and climbed the stairs to stand before her brother. She looked over and smiled at her nephews.

Branthony embraced her, but the boys could not help but see and feel tension between them. Everyone knew the relationship between the king and his sister was not warm, but the boys had no idea why. It was not something their father had ever spoken about.

"Susan, it's good to see you," said Branthony.

"It is good to see you, all of you." She looked at Debreace and then back at the boys again.

"I wasn't expecting you," said Branthony.

"I know," she replied. "And you won't be expecting what I've come to say."

Michael slowed his horse a little, allowing those trailing to catch up. The group would soon reach the destination where they would split. Michael and his brother John would return north to the Centre. Merleal and many others would be continuing on through the Angosh plains, the home of the Sile.

The group they'd come to meet was not far in the distance and drawing closer. Michael waited for Merleal to pull her horse up alongside him, wanting the chance to speak with her before they parted ways.

"Your riding has improved," he said, and it was an understatement. "When I first met you and we travelled north together, you struggled. Now you sit a horse as well as anyone."

She smiled warmly. Merleal was one of those people who had a gift for making everyone around them feel a little better. She had a calming presence, and Michael enjoyed being around it.

"Spending days on the run from pursuing Sile will make anyone improve."

Michael laughed. It now seemed so long ago that they had made the same journey together in the opposite direction. "Funny, I had somehow almost forgotten about that. So much has happened since then."

"It has been eventful," she said with a smile that made him feel even more at ease.

"Merleal, before we part, I wanted to thank you, and I wanted to apologise. We didn't know what we'd find when we came south to the Blood River. If my brother-in-law had known what would be asked of you."

"He would not have asked, and the Crone would still be the one to deliver the Gift. Now, after generations, that cycle is broken. The Fait have a new deliverer, and the link between them and my people has been reforged. We shall all be better for the renewed bond. This is as the God planned."

He nodded back at her. Michael, Branthony, and the others had realised that Merleal's faith in the God and the stories of the origin of the Fait was unshakable.

Michael looked forward again at the waiting party, who were drawing closer.

"Well, I wanted to thank you. I look forward to the day we meet again."

"Thank you, Michael. Let's hope it is not too long."

He nodded, knocking his heel into his horse and pulled away toward an approaching man from the waiting party. The two came alongside one another with warm smiles, embracing each other with firm grips.

"Christopher."

"Michael. It's good to see you."

Prince Christopher, Warden of the Southern-Point, brother of the king and holder of the Gift of Knowledge, was genuinely happy to see his old friend.

"And you," replied Michael, and he meant it.

"How is she?"

"She seems to be in good health, but it's hard to tell with her. She is certainly different. Ever since she took the blood and delivered the Gift, she's seemed strange. Somehow, almost…" he searched for a word. "Ethereal."

Christopher nodded appreciatively at the word choice. "She has changed herself, but there is danger in such things. She is now more like ***her***." They both knew who he meant.

"And our escort?" asked Michael, peering over Christopher's shoulder to the rest of the waiting party.

"Eager to be underway, but I must admit to enjoying their company."

"Can they be trusted? This is a huge gamble. Showing the Sile the Blood River. We have only just reclaimed a bond to it. Now we are asking one of our greatest enemies to help guard it?"

"The river is on the southern plains. We cannot hope to protect the village without the help of the Sile. Besides, after what the Crone did, they know she is their greater enemy. She turned one of them into her champion and, by doing so, ripped the clans of the Sile apart. Many Sile believe they would not have escaped her champion's grip without my brother."

"They'd be right," Michael affirmed. "But just to be sure, we're sending someone with them who can hold his own."

"Who?"

"Sir Walter."

Christopher winced.

"Well, that will be entertaining if nothing else. Where is Sir Walter?"

"Bringing up the rear. He doesn't like stragglers."

"He is a firm man, to be sure. I can see the sense in sending him, but I think the Sile will hold up to their end of the bargain. No Sile is more appreciative than our escort. I hope to join them at the river in time, but I am needed elsewhere for now. Come, we best not keep Morbius waiting."

Merleal trotted along and watched Michael and Christopher embrace, giving them a moment to converse. She was startled as a young man rode up beside her.

"Excuse me, My Lady. Is there anything I can get for you?"

"No," she said with a smile. "Thank you, and I am no lady. I've spent most of my life at the Blood River, we live mostly in tents and from the land, much closer to the ways of the Sile than the life of a lady."

He nodded at her before looking off into the distance across the plains. "I can't wait to see it."

"You're coming with us?"

"Yes, I'm part of the retinue heading to the village."

"You look young for a man-at-arms."

"I'm nearly a grown man," he said, puffing his chest out exaggeratedly. "And I can use a sword pretty well, but..." his chest deflated again. "I'm no man-at-arms. I'm part of the team sent to study your people. I'm a disciple in the library at the Centre."

Merleal looked back at the lengthy line of riders and carts that followed. Servants, diplomats, scholars, disciples, holy men, historians, squires and more. All coming to learn from her people. All that, before she even counted the fighting men. All led by one of the tallest, loudest, sternest men she'd ever met, Sir Walter.

She would be escorted the rest of the way by Morbius Duvec, a man known by most as the Lord of the Sile. Once considered the greatest enemy of the Cross, he united the clans of the Sile in a war against the kingdom. He lost power when the Crone's champion usurped him. He regained power when he helped Branthony return to the Centre and defeat the champion.

Morbius and Sir Walter did not know each other. Not yet, at least. They were quite opposite in terms of personality. Walter was known throughout the Cross as a man who brooked no argument to his authority. A man renowned for being stiff and unbending. Morbius was a man with natural charisma who loved to push buttons. Merleal felt a pang of guilt for the disruption she would soon bring to her home.

"What is your name?" she asked.

"My friends call me Res."

"Well, I should very well like to be your friend, Res."

"I'd like that too." He said the words as he started to drift further back. Merleal turned and smiled at him as she moved away.

"I hope we speak again soon, Res." When she looked forward again, she met the eyes of the waiting men.

"Hello, Morbius, Shimmer." She looked past Morbius to the grizzled figure of Shimmer-of-the-Night, Morbius's right-hand man. He nodded to her with a grunt.

"Merleal," said Morbius in a far more polite manner as he dipped his head to her. "It is good to see you again. You look well."

"Thank you. You look much better than the last time we came into each other's company."

He smiled, but it was not an expression of happiness. She could tell he was reflecting on the circumstances of that meeting. Morbius and his men had captured Merleal and her party, including Branthony. Capturing the king of the Cross should have been a great victory for the Lord of the Sile, but Morbius had fallen far from such a position at the time. He'd worn rags, his face hidden behind a long beard. He'd looked and felt desperate. In his desperation, he had aligned with Branthony, and together they had defeated the Crone's champion.

Merleal was not lying when she said he looked better now. The beard was gone, and his long hair was tied back. He wore a loose shirt, more in the style of the Cross than Sile, but it did not look out of place. Morbius was a man born to lead. The only man Merleal could compare him to was Branthony. She was happy to see him restored to his former glory.

"I want to thank you for agreeing to escort me. I know you are a busy man."

"It will be my pleasure; besides, I dare not refuse the great king. How is he up there? Still fearing a knife in the back from one of his own lords?"

He said the words with a smirk, enjoying the fact that Branthony was having difficulty. The Sile and the Cross had been enemies for years, and though they now shared a not-so-easy peace, it still seemed the Sile found some humour in the Cross' misfortunes.

"He's very good, thank you," answered Michael.

"Remind me again why he doesn't just smash their faces in and beat them into submission like any good Sile would? After all, it would be easy for him with his Gift."

"You would know," said John, bristling a little at the insulting tone as he came up alongside them. "He smashed you around once or twice, didn't he?"

Morbius's smirk fell from his face. He was not used to insults, which were often met with violence in Sile lands.

Merleal felt the tension and urged her horse between them.

"I thank you for your company, Sir John, and all who honoured me with an escort, but the journey is still long. Morbius, shall we be on our way? We have much to discuss. First among them is how we can stop the men of the Cross and the Sile from tearing each other apart."

She glanced back down the line. The introduction to Sir Walter could wait as long as possible, as far as she was concerned.

"Stop pushing," whispered Aron over his shoulder into the dull light.

Once again, the boys found themselves in the hidden passages spread throughout the castle, and this was a particularly tight one. Aron was growing too big for many of their old routes through the rafters or beneath floorboards. He could still fit down the narrow stone corridor, but it was getting difficult, especially when his three younger brothers were all vying for position to see and hear better.

Luke pushed his way forward and put his eye to the spy hole. Looking out into the room. "I see them," he said, referring to two figures.

"Well, be quiet and we might hear what they're saying," ordered Aron.

The boys squirmed and twisted around each other until they all had at least a narrow view of the room beyond the wall. Their father and Aunt Susan had gone inside shortly after her dramatic arrival. The two of them now shared the room together.

"That was quite the entrance," said Branthony. "Why not send word? Why not tell me you were coming? Were you trying to embarrass me?"

"I'm sorry, Bran. I meant no disrespect." Branthony must have looked unconvinced because she pressed her sincerity. "I swear it, Bran. I haven't come to make trouble for you. I knew you would need support and that many see my absence from the Centre as a sign of my discontent with you."

"Isn't it?" asked Branthony, and all the boys thought they heard a familiar hint of anger in their father's voice. They couldn't see much, but they all noticed their aunt bristle at the sudden tone. She took a deep breath, composing herself.

"In ways," she admitted. "I know I have not always acted as I should. I know that my staying away and," she swallowed a gulp and took a breath, the words were hard to speak. "And refusing to use my Gift has made things difficult for you. But my problem is not with you or our family. I certainly have no problem with the Fait ruling the Cross. Most of those who do, do so out of ambition and greed. The Fait are meant to rule."

"We rule through the Gift." Despite his sisters' efforts, his tone seemed no lighter than before.

"Must you jump straight to it, Brother? I am trying to be civil. I'm trying to tell you I came here, hoping my actions may redeem me a little in your eyes."

This time, Branthony took a composing breath, and the boys could see the effort it took.

"I'm sorry," he said, and the boys looked at each other in shock. Apologising really didn't sound like their father. "You never needed redeeming in my eyes, Susan. I know why you do the things you do, and I understand."

"The Fait rule through the Gift," said Susan, her tone still calm. "When used properly, they are what make the family good rulers. You are a good king, my brother. Nothing that has happened between us has changed that. Our father died young. You say the Crone killed him, and I believe you. It only means that you've had a harder job being king. You took the throne young and didn't have time to learn the many lessons he had to teach. None of us did. I am proud of you, Brother. I know we have our difficulties but never doubt that I am proud to be your sister."

Through the small gaps, the boys could see that their father was taken aback. It was a strange sight.

"Do you think things would have been different if he'd lived longer?" Branthony's voice was soft and reminiscent. To the boys, it didn't seem like listening to their father at all.

"Perhaps," said Susan with a sad smile. "I needed more teaching, Bran. I needed more than you or Christopher could give. That's not your fault, but I didn't have it, and when I did what I did, it changed everything for me. I said my problem has never been with you, and I meant it. My problem is with my Gift. The very name brings a *sour* taste to my mouth. The Gift makes good rulers when it is used properly. When used otherwise, well, look at all the damage I caused. How many lives were lost? How much blood was spilt because of my so-called Gift? It certainly wasn't a Gift to me. More a curse."

Aron bristled in the small confines of the secret passage. His aunt's words resonated. He'd said that to himself many times and had no idea anyone else felt like he did. All the others always seemed so happy with their Gifts, growing ever stronger and more confident in them, while Aron only grew more fearful of his.

"We've been through all this before, Bran. As I said, I have not come here to argue. I have, in fact, come to ask you a favour of sorts."

The boys watched their father take a breath and hold it as though expecting what Susan was about to ask of him to be something he did *not* want to do. Susan seemed to think the same and faltered. They watched her brace herself, determined to say what she had come to say.

"I have not travelled here alone. I have brought a friend. If truth be told, he is more than a friend. I have come here, Bran, to ask your permission to marry."

All four boys had seen their father wear many expressions, and they'd surprised him many times, but they had never come close to this. The shock on his face almost caused them to laugh aloud and give away their position. They grabbed each other and forced composure on one another.

Silence stretched out, and Branthony was lost for words.

"Well," said Susan, swallowing her nerves. "Aren't you going to say something?"

"I… I can't believe this."

"Branthony," said Susan, sounding panicked. "I know I have not always been the best sister and have disappointed you, but I—"

She didn't finish her words as Branthony crossed the room and embraced her. Tears were suddenly flowing from her eyes, and she hugged her brother like she had not done in a great many years. The boys watched it all in hiding, unable to take their eyes from the scene.

When they finally separated from their embrace, Branthony looked Susan in the eye. "I am so happy for you, my sister. Who is it?"

"His name is Robert. He comes from a small family in the Shield lands. I know it may not be a favourable marriage, but I—"

"You have my permission, Susan. It doesn't matter who it is. After everything that happened, I am happy you have found love again."

Susan sobbed. "Thank you. Thank you, Branthony."

They seemed caught in the moment for a long time, and Branthony had to pull himself away.

"Well, for all the trouble these next few weeks will bring, I am glad it brought us something good. We will talk more later. For now, I have to get back out there. Perhaps at some point, I could lighten the mood by telling the lords we may have a royal wedding while they are at the Centre."

Susan smiled, they hugged one last time, and Branthony left.

"Come on," whispered Aron. "Let's get out of here." He tried to twist in the tight confines but couldn't quite turn. He felt something hard dig into his back. "Watch out."

"You're standing on my foot!" protested Luke.

"Move back," said Joshua. "One at a time or we'll—"

It was too late. Someone lost their footing, and the next thing, all four boys were tumbling. There wasn't even room to fall to the floor in the small confines, so they crashed into the wall and all four froze as a loud bang was clearly audible.

"Show yourself!"

Susan's voice rang into their ears, but it was unlike anything they had ever heard. All thought disappeared. All they could feel was the desperate need to obey.

ASK NO QUESTIONS HEAR NO LIES

Bolevard turned to the door as it opened. The occupants of the crammed room looked to the king and queen as they entered. There had been an unexpected delay. The king had taken time to speak with his sister. Princess Susan's return was unexpected, and the room filled with chatter and gossip.

Bolevard had found himself retching into a nearby flower bed when he'd caught sight of Susan. *I am not only a coward but also a coward who cannot control himself.*

As the royals entered, the games began immediately. Some clamoured forward for attention, while others hung visibly back in defiance. These two groups did not interest Bolevard; their minds were almost certainly made up. He watched the others, the ones who seemed uncertain, the ones whose decision could still be swayed, and they were numerous.

Bolevard sipped at his wine and stuck to the outskirts of the large hall, watching the proceedings with a careful eye whilst being sure not to draw any notice. He couldn't help but feel disdain at those who so desperately sought the attention of the royals. *Pathetic!* He could not keep the snarl from his face and hid it behind another sip of his drink. *The fools have no idea what they're doing. The Fait lie to them, betray them, control them, and the dogs lap it up with open mouths, begging for morsels.*

Bolevard approached his first target casually, offered a respectful bow, and began his act.

"Lord Gether," he said with a smile. He could tell instantly that Andross Gether didn't recognise him, but such a thing was expected. "I am Sir Bolevard of House Bront. I am also the Scroll-Master. We met once, many years ago during the Western Rebellions."

He waited patiently for a moment and hid his insult at still not being recognised even after announcing his name. Andross Gether, at least, had the good sense and manners to pretend his memory had jogged.

"Yes, of course. Sir Bolevard. How are you? Scroll-Master, you say? Well, you're certainly doing well for yourself."

Yes, I thought the title might be what you noticed.

"Yes," he replied with nothing but pleasantness. "I have my uses, apparently." They chuckled at the joke, and Bolevard took another sip to hide his anger. "I wanted to say how sorry I was to hear of your lost contracts with Varliant. I had just begun writing up the details for the Coin-Master's inspection when I got word. It seemed quite the prosperous deal."

He hadn't started writing anything, of course, but he could see the effect his words had. Bolevard knew Lord Gether, more than most, was desperate for that deal to go through. Andross was pained at the loss of it, as he should be. It was outrageously generous. Now it was ripped to shreds, and Andross obviously held some animosity, just as Salvadire had hoped. The Varliant plan was working.

"Yes." Andross struggled to downplay his disgruntlement. "It was upsetting to hear that the king had chosen not to deal with Varliant. Especially as it now seems they have less interest in dealing with the rest of us."

"Perhaps, but I know some very interested parties are still looking at Varliant despite the Crown's refusal to deal with them."

The words immediately angered and flustered the Lord of Bolgar, who visibly clenched his teeth. "Is that so?"

"I've said too much.' Bolevard feigned embarrassment. "I didn't mean to rub salt in your wound. I only meant to—"

"Your intentions matter little, Scroll-Master. Only the truth of your words." Andross looked across the crowded room toward the king, who was making his way around the occupants, shaking hands and rubbing shoulders. "Tell me, why did the king refuse to deal with Varliant? A foolish decision given all that they have been doing recently?"

"I am uncertain. I am sure His Majesty had his reasons."

"He just doesn't deem it fit to share them with the rest of us," said Andross. This time, it was he who took a slow sip of his drink, hiding his anger behind it.

"The king does seem to have a habit of withholding information."

"Yes, and until recently, the Fait had never allowed an enemy inside the Centre. Until recently, the Fait were the only people in the world with magic. Perhaps their judgment and power are not what they used to be. Perhaps there's a reason they are keeping secrets."

"Perhaps?" responded Bolevard. "And let us not forget, there was an enormous amount of wealth going to the lords and merchants with those deals. With wealth comes power. Power that does not belong to the Fait."

Without waiting for a response, Bolevard turned and left, giving himself a mental tick on the list inside his mind. That was one for him. Now, who's next?

The boys stared at their aunt as she, in turn, stared back at them. There was a void between them that they'd never felt before. It filled their minds, cold and black. Luke was the first to come around. He shook his head and felt the void begin to withdraw. Clarity and warmth returned to the world. Slowly but surely, his brothers joined him.

"I'm sorry," said Susan.

Though they had not spent much time with her, they had always felt love for and from their aunt. They could see she meant the apology, though in their daze, none of them quite knew what had happened. It seemed they'd spent the last few minutes in a dream. They'd woken with a fuzzy memory of that dream, but it grew more distant with each passing moment.

"I shouldn't have done that. I didn't know who was listening. I thought… I lost control, I apologise."

"You used your Gift on us," said Joshua, reality now solidifying. He shuddered at the memory of the void where nothing mattered but obeying the command.

"I did," she confirmed. "Something I try never to do. Unfortunately, there are occasions when it is necessary. Other times, it is used by mistake. I placed a lot of strength into that command, so its effects were potent."

"Aunt Susan," said Aron, stepping closer. "What you said before, to Father, about your Gift. About it being a curse. What did you mean?"

Susan gave him a soft smile, which she turned on the others. Suddenly, in an instant, she was their aunt again. The cold influence of her Gift was all but forgotten. She moved to a chair and sat down, gesturing for them to make themselves more comfortable.

"It's so easy to forget how young you all are, even you, Aron. Children of the Fait, you may be, but that only adds to your problems. It is hard to understand your place in the world, especially when you have a Gift that is supposed to be for some specific reason. Gifts that often do as much harm as they do good. How is anyone meant to deal with such a thing, let alone someone so young?

"Has your father ever told you how much trouble he used to get in when he couldn't control his Gift?" The boys all shook their heads. "I bet he didn't. Well, the Gift of Strength can be a menace, let me tell you. The number of broken chairs and doors, and the God knows what else. How many men got sent to the healers because your father couldn't control his Strength?"

Once again, this did not sound like the father the boys knew. Their perception of him had changed so much over the last few years, and Aron was especially beginning to see the man behind the titles of father and king.

"What happened?" Jacob asked. "With you and your Gift, between you and Father?"

An immense wave of sadness washed over Susan. No, it ***crashed*** down upon her like a torrent, threatening to wash her away. All four boys felt a sudden desire to go to her, hug her, anything to dim that sadness, but she pushed it aside with a great effort. They could each see the resemblance to their father at that moment, the resilience, and the determination.

"I can feel your Gift, Jacob. It compels me to answer."

"I'm sorry," he replied. "I didn't mean to use it."

"No need to apologise. As I just said, I know how difficult it can be to control the Gift. There is also no need to use it. I will tell my tale in the hope that it teaches a lesson."

She took a deep breath.

"It was a long time ago. It's why I choose not to use my Gift and why I call it a curse." Her eyes locked with Aron's at this last part. "When I was young, I fell in love with a man called Jonathan of House Moore. You may not know that family name. They are no longer a powerful family, but that comes later.

"Back then, the Sile were always making incursions past the southern border, and men from the Cross would go down to the Edge, the furthest part of the Southern-Point, to join the fighting. Small fights and skirmishes. This was before Morbius Duvec had come to power and united the clans. Nothing like what we'd see in later years. The men of the Cross thought it was a way to test themselves. Some thought it would make men of them, others just liked fighting. Your father was a young prince whose Gift seemed designed for war, but he had never had an actual fight. He wanted a challenge. He wanted to go south to the Edge, and if the prince and heir were going, then others wanted to join him.

"Jonathan wanted to go. He thought he could begin to make a name for himself. I didn't want him to. We argued. I was angry and, in my anger, I said something that would change the course of all our lives. Something I will regret until the end of my days. I said…" She paused and swallowed a hard lump down her throat. The steely determination showed through once more. "Go and die then, I said. That was when my curse came down upon me."

The boys listened in silence, anticipating the next part of the story.

"He marched out onto the balcony. I thought he was going to get some air. To step away from the argument. I waited for him to come back in and apologise." The tears ran freely down her cheeks and dropped to the floor as the boys listened on, mesmerised. "In the end, when he did not return, I stormed out to the balcony ready to renew the argument with more fire than before, but Jonathan wasn't there."

A moment of silence stretched out as the boys waited for an explanation.

"He'd done what I commanded. I said go and die, so he marched out to the balcony and jumped off."

Jacob recoiled, and the others looked on in frozen shock.

"Your Gift made him do it?" Luke asked, and Susan nodded.

"I had accidentally used it. My Gift didn't usually work like that. I had to be more specific and more controlled, but I suppose, in my anger, I let it pour into my words. Jonathan had walked straight outside and killed himself out of ***Obedience***." Disdain filled the last word.

"What… What happened next?" asked Aron.

"Well, Jonathan's father did not take the news of his son's death well. Understandably so. He raised his armies and waged rebellion against the Crown. He convinced many that the Fait were dangerous and that we could not control our Gifts. If we could kill his son by accident, what could we do if we really wanted to hurt someone? I think most of them were simply scared by such a powerful Gift. The ability to command someone to do *anything* you say. This was too much power even for a Fait to hold.

"Your Uncle Christopher believes the Gifts have gradually grown stronger over the last generations. More Gifts. Rarer, more powerful. Mine is both, almost as much as yours, Aron."

It was his turn to swallow his fear. So much of his life seemed parallel to Susan's.

"Your father finally got a war, only it wasn't the one he'd wanted. After that, he never yearned for war again, though it seems a constant these days. Be careful what you wish for."

"House Moore used to control Bolgar," said Joshua. "Lord Victor Moore was a tactical genius. I've studied him in my lessons."

"You're talking about the Western Rebellions," said Luke, putting the pieces together.

"I am. So, you understand? My Gift, my curse, caused the death of the man I loved and then led to civil war. Your father and grandfather led the forces of the Crown and those loyal against the rebels. Your father wasn't the same man when he returned."

The boys tried to take it all in, and once again, their view of their father had changed and evolved. Was this the reason he often seemed so cold? Was the weight of those memories still heavy on his heart?

"I always just thought everyone else simply mastered their Gift," said Aron. "I thought it just came naturally to everyone." He looked at his brothers, and they realised he included them in his analogy.

"It takes much practice to master a Gift," said Susan. "Even your Uncle Christopher had to learn to use the Gift of Knowledge. He struggled for years to contain the things he learned, and then it seemed his head would explode with all the knowledge he'd acquired.

"My advice to you all would be to practise constantly. Whenever you think you're being pushed too far, or you feel bored and aggrieved at your lessons, remember my story. Master your Gifts, or they will master you."

THE NIGHT BRINGS CHANGES

Celia left the party behind. Music and chatter drifted away as she walked the torchlit corridor. It was a shame to go. The lords and ladies had become quite inebriated, and such events were great opportunities to gather information. Loose lips were rife when the wine flowed, and she always found it amusing to listen to people insult one another behind each other's backs. Alas, she had a prior engagement to attend. Besides, many of the young lords had begun to feel brave enough to make advances toward her and she was in no mood for such things. Perhaps she might have indulged one if it were a different time of the month. Nothing gets a favour in the pocket like a night in the sheets: men, such simple creatures.

She didn't head toward her room or the library or any other place she would typically be seen visiting but instead headed outside toward the barracks. A short stone bridge passed between the main castle building and one of the outer towers. Often, people would stand on it to enjoy the view, but Celia knew it would be deserted this late at night. She felt the refreshingly cool air wash over her as she headed outside and stopped on the bridge, looking out. The view was quite spectacular. The castle grounds and the Centre beyond stretched out before her. The distant lights and sounds of the city played their nightly chorus.

She waited until she heard three knocks from the roof above, then knocked four times in response and waited in silence again. Finally, a soft voice spoke into the night.

"How can I help, My Lady?"

The youthful, female voice was light as the wind and almost drifted away before Celia could hear it. Celia looked up at the ceiling, knowing the girl was likely propped on the tiles above, entirely out of sight. Of all the spies in Celia's employment, the girl was by far the best and most valuable. She had such a gift for being almost invisible that Celia would practically think her a Fait.

"What do you have for me?"

"It has been an eventful evening, My Lady. The lords do so love to talk."

"Don't they just," Celia whispered to the night air with a smile. "Which way would you say opinion sways?"

She had to wait momentarily for a response, but this impressed her. It showed the girl considered her answer rather than blurting out any old thing in an attempt to impress.

"Hard to tell," came the soft voice. "There is much anger. Some are angry about the attack on the Centre, others at the king's refusal to make deals with Varliant, but I do not think it is enough for most to side against the king. There will always be those who fear and trust the Fait."

Celia understood that in many ways. The things they could do were beyond the understanding of normal men, and most fear what they do not understand, but Celia also knew the Fait as a family, not just as the rulers of the Cross. They would never use their Gifts against their people out of malice or hatred, but she would not say such a thing aloud. She would instead secretly speak the opposite. Fear of the Fait may hold some at bay, but enough fear would eventually make many take up arms. There was only so far that they would allow themselves to be pushed. It was fear of Susan's Gift led to the last war.

"So, you think most would still side with the king?"

"Yes, though Master Bolevard has begun to sow discord. He had a great effect on several lords this evening."

It wasn't the answer Celia was hoping for. She needed people to side against the king. She needed him distracted. At least that's what the Crone ordered. Still, she couldn't help but smile at the mention of Bolevard. "He's a wily old dog, isn't he, but extremely hateful and vengeful. He will be dangerous if he ever discovers how much of a pawn he is in this game. ***Never*** reveal yourself to him. Am I clear?" She put force behind her words and wanted the message to get through.

"Of course, My Lady."

"Good. Is there anything else?"

"Lord Basel is most vocal against the king. He waits for the audience and plans to question the king regarding the Crone, but he fears it may not be enough."

"No," said Celia with a smirk. "No, it may not, but I may have another card to play there. I can offer Lord Basel something extra to fan the flames. You've done well. We shall speak again soon."

"I await your signal, My Lady."

Celia heard the faintest of creaks and knew her little spy was gone. She spent another few moments enjoying the beautiful view. No one would see the turmoil on her face. She was thinking again about those decisions in her life. Those few that she still questioned. Those that still haunted her.

It was late into the night before Aron was ready to sleep. Aunt Susan's story had stuck with him and so had her advice. Master your Gifts, or they will master you. Aron knew his Gift had been winning the battle of supremacy between them.

He'd spent so long trying to remember his dreams, but now he wanted to forget and avoid them, anything but face them. It only seemed to make them stronger. The ***one*** vision that came clear, the one he always remembered, was the one he most wished to forget. The vision of his own death. Of his brothers dying. He'd seen this particular one many times, though never identical; it always ended the same way.

My Gift is showing me this for a reason. I must be able to change it. Surely that is why I see it, to stop it from happening.

He thought about all that he'd learned in his lessons on the Gift, the meditation techniques he'd practised. He'd placed parchment and a quill to the side of his bed and was ready to write anything he remembered. He would try again. He had to.

Lying on his bed, he began taking slow and steady breaths, in and out, his chest rising and falling. The only sound was his own breathing, in and out, in and out. He'd done this many times, usually to no avail, yet rarely was he so determined.

Breathing became harder, and he gulped in air faster. There was noise around him. Commotion. Chaos. Fires burned. He could feel the heat and choked on the billowing smoke. He heard screams and shouts coming from all around. Where was he? He thought he recognised the place. Somewhere in the Centre? What street was it? Why was he here?

Aron screamed. He didn't know why. He wasn't hurt, but he screamed. The sound held such anguish, such pain. He touched his face and felt a beard wet with tears. An arm wrapped itself about his shoulders and pulled at him. He heard a strange, yet familiar voice speak to him in odd-sounding words.

"Come, My King."

King?

Aron turned to look at the speaker, but instead, he looked at a man bent over maps. The commotion was gone, the smoke replaced with cool, fresh air, but the atmosphere felt hollow. Aron had seen this room and the man before. He seen this very moment before, back on his first ever practise with the Gift, under the tutelage of Uncle Christopher.

"Joshua," he said, remembering the past vision. Joshua was dressed in a fine tunic and hunched over a table. Why did he look so old? Not in his age, though he was older, but in his demeanour. He seemed a broken man. He pointed at the map, and Aron looked. It showed a map of the Cross, and Joshua's finger was pressed just above the Northern-Point, at the White Mountains.

"There it is, Brother. That is where our path leads us."

Aron didn't understand. He looked back at his brother to ask what was happening, but Joshua now looked different. He was younger and dressed in a full suit of splendid shining armour, and the weight of whatever troubled him was gone. Aron could see his distorted reflection looking back at him. His face no longer had a beard, but it was still older.

"What's wrong, Aron?"

Aron turned to the voice and saw Jacob smiling back at him. They were both on horseback. He looked about and saw all his brothers riding alongside, each dressed in armour, all prepped for war. They were not alone. The four of them were at the head of a vast host marching to battle. Jacob went to place his Helm on his head.

"Relax, Brother. We've seen all this before, remember?"

As Jacob pushed his Helm down, he disappeared. Aron spun on his horse. Everyone was gone. Where were his brothers? Where was the host? It felt as though he were suddenly falling. He was surrounded by brilliant white, as though he'd fallen into a serene cloud. A stain of deep red suddenly spoiled the perfection. It splashed across the scene and marred it, making it grotesque. He felt the warm red liquid, sticky to the touch—blood.

Aron scrambled away, desperate to distance himself from the deep red. He found himself on his knees again. He could hear his breath once more, short and sharp. Hard to draw in. His chest was tight and painful. He glanced up, just as a sword came crashing down.

Aron startled awake.

He looked to the window but saw only the dead of night. How long had he been there? It felt like seconds as well as hours. He pushed the thought aside and started to recall what he'd seen, quickly taking up the parchment and quill, scribbling down words.

King.

White Mountains.

War.

White.

Red.

Can't breathe.

He read them back to himself aloud, and though the list sounded gibberish, each word brought a distinct image. A piece of memory of things yet to come. At least the visions had been different. He hadn't seen the end this time. He remembered that dream enough. So why these new things?

"What does it mean?" he asked himself, not for the first time.

Celia had waited in a quiet side room for Lord Basel to return to his room. The night drew late, but Basel had just decided he'd had enough for the evening. It was expected. He was the lead voice for those opposing the Fait. He'd need to be around as much as possible if he wished to convince others to side with him.

Despite the tension surrounding the visiting lords, the royals still knew how to throw a good party. They plied their guests with wine and food, played music and did all they could to distract from the fact that they could be on the edge of revolt. Lord Basel had joined in the festivities and had unsteady feet by the time he left. Celia was all too happy to finally see him leave. She needed to speak with him, but doing so in a room full of watching eyes and listening ears was far from optimal. She could hear the old man's irritation as she knocked on his door.

"You!" is all he said as he stared at her with drunken eyes once he'd opened the door. At least he still had the wits to stand aside and let her in. He likely remembered the last time she came to his door like this, and a beneficial arrangement was made.

Celia entered the room and glanced about.

"We are alone," he confirmed, discerning her thoughts.

"Good. Have you enjoyed yourself?" she asked, feigning pleasantries.

"You do not care a shred about my enjoyment, so why not just come out with it? I am tired and wish to sleep."

"Oh, but I do care." An overly sad expression appeared on her face. "I care a great deal. I want you to have an enjoyable time, especially tomorrow. With that in mind, I have something for you."

She always enjoyed how easy Lord Basel was to read. He couldn't hide his thoughts and emotions if he tried. His hungry eyes bulged at the thought of something juicy. He would not make a good Fait's Gambit player.

"Go on."

"You wish to sway opinion against the king. Well, what if I told you that two years ago, his Northern-Point warden sent a body to the Centre all the way from the White Mountains."

"What relevance is that?"

"Because the Warden believed Valfargs had killed the man. Only the king was too busy preparing for his excursion south. The same excursion that led to his absence when the Sile attacked. The journey he took to ensure his family's power, while placing the Cross in danger."

Lord Basel shook his head. As well he should. Valfargs were the ancient enemy of the Cross. It was said that years ago, the Fait brought the feuding points together under their rule and waged war against the invading Valfargs, forcing them back to the White Mountains and beyond. They had not been seen for hundreds of years. Yet, Celia had seen the body that came from the north. It had wounds from a creature with six digits, a characteristic known only in Valfargs.

"I knew it. Reckless and foolish. Well, I am sure this will upset many. So, tell me, woman." Celia had to hide her rage at being addressed in such a way. "What do you hope to gain out of this? Even if opinion sways against the king, this is not a democracy. He will still be king. The only way that changes is if the lords rebel against the Crown. Is that what you want? Is it war you crave, knowing that the women stay safe behind walls?"

"Only as long as they're on the winning side, remember. If not, then perhaps it is the women who suffer the worst fate. Dying on a sword is the common demise of men in war, whilst the women must be content to be raped and beaten until they are worthless, and death seems a welcome friend." He only sneered at her with those beady eyes. "Besides, isn't war what you want? A chance to prove that Lord Basel is more than just the fool who let the Sile walk right past him."

"The only reason those Sile walked past me Is because they were using magic! The very thing the Fait insisted no one else could do. I don't ***want*** war," he growled, barely able to contain himself. "I want justice, and I want truth. I want a safe and secure Cross. I want a king that I can trust. The Fait have sat upon their pedestal for far too long, untouchable because of their Gifts, but now we know the truth. The Gift is ***not*** theirs alone. They have ***lied*** to us. You saw it with your own eyes. What is to stop our enemies from using this power again? What is to stop someone else from having a Gift? The Fait have shown they can no longer protect us. What is to stop someone else from sitting atop the throne? Someone who would do a better job. Someone who would not abandon the kingdom to fulfil their own selfish needs. If it takes war to secure our future, so be it."

She had to be careful; his anger was boiling over. Perhaps she'd pushed him too far; alcohol had a way of shortening tempers. She wouldn't admit it, but he'd surprised her. The ferocity with which he spoke. Passion, and conviction were not attributes she would generally associate with the Lord of the Black Fort.

"And that someone could be you?" she asked, wondering how far his ambition went.

"Perhaps," he said with a grin, seeming to calm a little. "Though I have never pictured myself on the throne, if truth be told. This leads me back to wondering what you want. Where does your father stand on this debate?"

"My father!" She couldn't keep the venom from the word but quickly regained her composure. "Lord Hive brought word from my father. He wants what you want. A safe and secure Cross, but he is always looking for opportunity."

"And he sees himself atop the throne, is that it? Is that why you're doing this? You think to use others to do your dirty work and overthrow the Fait, and then the grand Lord Carter Trone can step in and take the throne for himself."

"Calm yourself, Lord Basel. You are getting far too ahead of yourself. Rest assured, I have ***no*** desire to see my father be king."

"Oh, I understand." His overconfident grin was agitating, to say the least.

"As I said, you are getting far too ahead of yourself with all this talk of rebellion and insurrection. Remember the last rebellion? The king commands vast and powerful forces. We must be sure that as few of those forces as possible would answer his call if it came. Use the information I have given you. See who else we can turn against the Fait." *And yes, do my dirty work for me, you simpleton. Only you have no idea how dirty the work really is. I may remember you when I am queen and keep you around as my pet.*

TIME TO PLAY THE GAME

Rain, Joshua thought with frustration.

He shifted his gaze from the scroll to the giant wooden game board that dominated the room. The scroll outlined the day's fictional conditions, including weather, wind direction, and ground conditions. For every five minutes of game time, additional information from the scroll would be revealed to correspond with an hour in real life.

If this game were real, I'd be soaking wet right now and in a bad mood, and with bad moods come bad decisions. I suppose the game can't simulate everything. Still, it gets pretty close. Think, Joshua, think! How can I win? Calm yourself. Let your Gift speak to you. Let it guide you.

He hadn't told his brothers, but he was becoming increasingly skilled at using his Gift. The war games were the perfect training method, and his Gift facilitated the learning process.

Not that I can share this with my brothers. It wouldn't help them at all. Aron gets upset, and Luke would see it as another reason to dislike me. They think I'm too confident. Aron would call me a cocky little git, and Luke, well, I won't dwell on what he'd call me.

"Concentrate!"

Joshua's thoughts snapped back to the present as he looked at his instructor. Hunter wore a fierce expression, as if preparing for real battle. Joshua had also noticed that he was easily distracted. Having a voice in his head that wasn't quite his own meant there was always someone to talk to, though that voice was becoming louder.

"Sorry." Joshua kept his face neutral, even as his heart raced. They had been studying and playing this round for hours. He knew his forces were at a disadvantage regarding ground conditions, but he had the advantage in cavalry and the element of surprise. The sand timer and scroll indicated it was early morning in the game, and Hunter's forces were unprepared.

Joshua manoeuvred his pieces from behind the wooden hill they had been using for cover and initiated his attack.

"It's dark," said Hunter, "and wet. Your attacking power will be diminished." The shake of his head only fuelled Joshua's determination.

"I know," he replied. "Attacking at night decreased my attacking power by three points, and the wet ground reduces it by one more. However, I still believe in my strategy. Your forces aren't ready, so your defensive points are reduced. You pushed them hard yesterday, so they haven't had ample time to rest, so your points are even lower."

He heard a growl of disapproval from Hunter.

"If you know the game, you understand you're attacking a fortified position, which adds to my defensive points. That's why I marched, to reach a safe position."

Joshua moved his pieces closer to the enemy camp and glanced at Joe, who spun the hourglass to resume time. Another hour had passed in the game, and the scroll now indicated that the sun was rising. Visibility had improved, and Joshua's reduction in attacking power decreased by one point.

"Oh, look," he said, unsuccessfully trying to suppress his confidence. He could almost see Aron and Luke's irritation in his mind's eye. "The rain has stopped. That means one more point for my attack." He and Joe exchanged smiles, and Hunter noticed.

"You're not taking this seriously! If this were real, those little wooden figures you're moving around would be real soldiers. Lives would be at stake. Would you be smirking at your friend, knowing you were sending men to their deaths?"

Joshua felt his smile fade, heavy with the weight of reality. His resolve to win only intensified. The voice in his head grew louder as his emotions threatened to overwhelm him. He turned his attention back to the game and pushed his pieces further forward.

The fortunate change in weather was a boon, but he didn't solely rely on luck. Hunter began positioning his pieces defensively, having left scouts in the field, allowing him to move his forces even though Joshua's were still far away.

Joshua walked around the table, viewing the board from different angles while Hunter followed suit. They circled each other, and Joshua leaned forward as far as he could.

"Looking at it won't change anything," Hunter said aggressively. "You've committed your forces, and you could have attacked faster. Maybe even caught my scout. You're holding back. I can see it."

Joe turned the timer again, adding another point to Joshua's attacking power. However, the delay also strengthened Hunter's defence.

"I push one-fifth of my infantry forward and move my cavalry into position." Joshua leaned against the board again, pausing for a moment.

Joe stepped toward the board and adjusted some of the wooden pieces representing soldiers, moving them into striking distance.

"Into range of my archers. Are you even trying?"

"I commit my second wave," Joshua declared as he leaned over the table again.

Joe leaned forward onto the board and knocked over several of Joshua's eliminated pieces. He also pushed forward more of Joshua's infantry pieces.

Joshua's forces reached the fort, and the battle truly began. He remained at the table's far side, and as he called his moves, Joe pushed the corresponding pieces. Joshua's forces were advancing but taking heavy losses, and it was becoming evident that he wouldn't push through and take the enemy position. Hunter growled and grumbled with each move, growing increasingly frustrated, but his eyes didn't leave the battle.

"You don't have the attacking power to breach the fort. This is over. End it before you lose every man you have!"

Joshua remained silent, staring at the board. The sand in the timer fell, and each second meant more losses.

"Joshua!" urged Hunter.

"Josh," mirrored Joe, his face paling as though he were watching a real-life massacre.

"Fine," Joshua succumbed. "I retreat. Pull them back."

Joe began to reposition the pieces. Hunter, it seemed, was ready to teach a lesson.

"You waited too long. Hesitation when in command costs the lives of your troops," he stated with a shake of his head and evident disappointment. He moved his remaining pieces out from the fort and pushed them onto the field to give chase.

"I commit my cavalry," Joshua said, and Joe moved his pieces for him. However, this time, Joshua came around to stand beside Hunter, but he wasn't alone. He leaned over and pulled some pieces from a wooded area of the board. Trees made of wood and cloth had hidden them from view— cavalry pieces.

"What?" asked Hunter. "Where did they come from? You can't just place pieces on the board."

"I didn't. They broke away from my forces days ago. They've been in those woods since I circled them. I've been pushing them forward with each move. You weren't looking in the right place."

It now seemed obvious why Joshua had moved to stand at the opposite end of the board and had Joe make his moves for him. Hunter began furiously counting the pieces on the board to be sure no others had been added. He smacked his hands on the table as he realised the numbers were correct. The timer spun again, and the scroll opened further. The sun was now shining on the battlefield, and Joshua's attack points had almost returned to full. What's more, he now had forces attacking from two directions, and Hunter had already pulled his men out from the defensive perimeter, losing his defensive bonus.

The game didn't last much longer. Hunter spat and raged about the newly revealed cavalry, but it was a fair move, and he soon had to admit defeat. He stared at the giant board, and Joshua thought he was about to flip the whole thing on its head. It was unexpected when he saw a large smile through the long hair that hung over Hunter's face.

"Well played. Well played indeed. I commend you, My Prince. I really do. You as well, Joseph. I can see you played your part in this. You tricked me, and sometimes tricks work on a real battlefield, but what you did there was a foolish gamble. On another day, I could have simply counted your pieces and realised some were missing, or I could have seen your pieces hidden in the trees or seen you move them. If I'd had scouts out that way, you'd have been obliged to give up your secret. The game doesn't account for everything. You must incorporate the differences into your strategy. Another player could have caught you out."

"But I wasn't playing anyone else. I was playing *you*. You had the advantage and the ground, and you asked me to devise a strategy to beat you. You were expecting my Gift to devise a special plan to outmanoeuvre your pieces, but it didn't. The game is the game, and the rules are set. My Gift didn't tell me anything new about the game; it told me about you."

Hunter was staring at him intently now, taking in every word.

"I could see you ignore the wider board. You focus on your areas of play. You hadn't sent scouts to your flanks, only toward my main force. I knew you'd push hard tore act the fort and not pay attention to the wider game. I knew you would get frustrated, seeing arrogance and lack of cunning with my attack and in the end, in anger, you would pull your pieces out from cover, thinking the game over. You were so sure I wasn't trying that you stopped trying. You're right, another player probably would have seen it, but my Gift didn't guide me in how to play the game or someone else, it guided me in how to beat you."

"Ha!" bellowed Joe before clapping a hand to his mouth. He removed it, and though he looked sheepish, he also looked mightily impressed, and Joshua couldn't keep the grin from his face.

"Interesting," said Hunter with his own smirk. "Very interesting. Then it appears we're ready to move on to the next stage of our training. I thought we might get to this, so I've had a little surprise waiting outside. Luke!"

Joshua and Joe looked on, stunned, as the door opened and Joshua's brother entered. Luke looked at the giant board with its hills, rivers and fields and then at Joshua with a menacing grin.

"So then," said Hunter. "Your Gift has helped you beat me, but I wonder how it will fare against your brother?"

Joshua had been enjoying the game, but now he wasn't sure he wanted to play it anymore.

"It's all a game," Debreace whispered into Branthony's ear. "Remember who you are." He braced himself as the massive double doors to the grand hall opened. "These people will push and pull at you and try to bend you to their will, but you must be strong. Remember, we are the Fait."

Her words reinforced his will. Together they entered the hall. Everyone stood. Good, at least the outright insurrection hadn't started just yet. The king and queen walked down the centre aisle, and as one sat upon their thrones. One more deep breath. One more quick cast of the eyes to judge those who stared back. Despite his wife's words, Branthony knew deep down that this meeting could change everything. He knew many of his people had lost faith, and he was fighting to prevent war and rebellion. If it went terribly wrong, there might not even be a war. If enough lords turned against him, there would be nothing he could do. What if he'd already lost before it even began?

As though sensing his sudden doubts, Debreace squeezed his hand. It was time.

"You have come here," he said before a pause, his voice loud and clear, ringing through the hall in booming tones that spoke of authority. It was a voice of cold steel. Many in attendance had heard it before, but not so many had suffered it directed at them. "You have come here to question my right to be king. I will brook no such question. I ***am*** the king. However, I am not a foolish king, nor a king who does not listen to his subjects. As lords of the Cross, you are all entitled to speak your grievances. So," he spread his arms out to the hall. "Who will be the first man to speak?"

There was a long, drawn-out silence, and the occupants of the room stared at each other, wondering who was going to be the first. It was a dangerous part to play, no matter which side the person spoke for. The quiet drew on, faint mumbles rising, but no one raised a clear voice. Finally, someone seized the moment, but it was no man.

Princess Susan stood from her chair. She had chosen to sit at one of the tables near the front, though she could have chosen to sit upon the dais as part of the royal family. Some had already wondered if this was a sign of her allegiance.

"Well, if none of the brave lords will speak, then I will."

Branthony almost winced. Insulting the lords with her first words was not a brilliant move; however, he noticed some of them bristle, as though hearing her words, taking note of them, and realising their truth.

"I will start by making my position very clear." Susan's tone was sharp, her eyes even more so as she stared at the room's occupants. "I am of the Fait and stand firmly with my family. Anyone who believed otherwise has been wildly mistaken."

Branthony scanned the room and could already see some of his sceptics begin to wilt. Perhaps they had thought to use Susan. With her on their side, they would have a significant advantage. He caught her eye and nodded his appreciation.

"Let me also say this," she added, again turning and facing the room. "My brother is the king of the Cross. The fact that he has allowed you all to come here to voice your concerns and worries should show that he is a ***good*** king. How many of you would take your subjects into your home and listen to them tell you why you should no longer be their lord? What would you do if the people of your lands decided to question you in such a way? Threatening you with revolt."

"It is an event that has happened many times throughout history, Your Highness."

"That is true, Lord Lister. As your family well know. However, you are still Lord of the Dawn. Tell me, who did you turn to for help when your lands were ravaged and burned? Oh yes, the Crown. The Fait."

"We cannot allow open insurrection," he tried to argue.

"Perhaps you are right? Then maybe I should use my Gift on everyone in this room and end this farce right now?"

Gasps filled the room along with the sound of chairs pushing back as though some were about to jump to their feet and run or attack. Branthony again caught his sister's eye, warning her she may be pushing too far.

"You can all relax," Susan said, hands out in a calming gesture, though she would admit to some amusement at the fear on some faces. "I would never do that. Besides, my brother would never allow it. That is because he is a good king. A ***just*** king, but let that be a reminder to all of the power the Fait hold. We are not simply the royal family. We are the holders of the Gift, and our power is vast. It has made the Cross the most powerful kingdom in the known world, and it will keep it that way."

She spared the room one more glance and then sat. Branthony felt his pride swelling. It had been a long time since Susan had even shown her face in such a public manner, and yet somehow, she had found the courage and determination to face down the realm's lords, even cowering a few of them.

He waited again to see who would be next.

There was a slight cough as a figure stood from a table toward the centre of the room. Branthony recognised John McNulty, the Lord of the Sword, a region on the Northern Point. Branthony had hoped to count on his support, but he could tell almost instantly that Lord John was not with him. He could not deny he felt a great stab of pain. Losing a large House in the north would be devastating. Lord John seemed hesitant to speak, and when he did, he kept his eyes low. Branthony knew then that this had not been an easy decision.

"Your Majesties, Your Highness." John looked at Susan and addressed her as he continued. "Your words have many truths to them. I want to thank the Crown for allowing us to speak our minds here. The Sword has always been a faithful and loyal servant. We have always trusted the Centre and the Fait, but the problem lies therein. You say the Fait have the Gift. You have always said that ***only*** the Fait have the Gift. It's the very foundation on which your dynasty was built. Yet now we know you have lied. Whether knowingly or not, I cannot say. But we now know for ***certain*** that others can use the Gift. If we had known this before, perhaps we could have been better prepared. It appears this was not a surprise to you as it was to us. All I know is that I trusted the Fait, and the Fait lied, and their lies led to many deaths. I can no longer say in all honesty that I still trust them."

Lord John sat, and it looked as though speaking those words had sapped the strength right from his bones.

Branthony stood. "Thank you, Lord John, for saying what you felt was right." John McNulty offered a weak and almost embarrassed nod back. It was out of character for the usually charismatic lord. "Firstly, allow me to clarify. Only the Fait can use the Gift. Magic, as some would call it, is fatal to all others. It will eventually kill anyone who uses it. The Sile that attacked and had any hint of a Gift were decaying from the inside out. They were pawns in a greater game they did not understand."

"Pawns of hers!"

The angered voice shot through the room like an arrow, and Branthony would almost say it had the same impact. Heads turned with vigour to see who had spoken in such a way. Who had spoken with such anger and hatred. The pain of the arrow grew as it was again someone Branthony had believed he could count on for support. Lord Patrick Hughes of the Crossed Hills, Lord of South Crave Castle, stared back at him with none of the timidness or indecisiveness of John McNulty.

"Those Sile attacked my lands, and when my men scoured those lands, they found nothing. The enemy slipped right past us. The Sile came straight to the Centre, something only possible through some kind of sorcery. But they were not alone. That creature was with them. It cannot be denied. She! It! Batted men aside like flies. How many men fell at its hand? The creature used magic openly and in many ways. Not simply one kind, as each of the Fait and even the Sile seemed to do. It is said you knew of her. I can't help but think you're lying again."

The emotions flowed from Lord Hughes like water from a spilt cup. Branthony now understood how deep the wounds of that day had cut. Part of him had believed that the lords were only threatening revolt to further their own ends. A way of garnering more power for themselves. He knew Lord Hughes and Lord McNulty to be men of honour. Now he understood how deeply hurt and betrayed some were by what had happened.

"Lord Hughes. Patrick. We have known each other for a long time, you and I. I know you are a good man and a good lord. I know the deaths of those men have weighed heavily on your heart, as they have mine. I am sorry, my friend, for any way I have let you down.

"That creature of which you speak is called the Crone. She came to the Centre to hunt my newborn Nephew. For a long time, she delivered the Gift to the newborn children of the Fait. An exchange. One that has allowed her to gain the powers she has. She is no longer the deliverer; without us, she too will soon die." He left out the part about her taking the blood. Suppose that story got out, who knew where it could lead and what some may do. Branthony greatly feared such things.

Another figure stood, and Branthony felt the knife twisting in his gut. This one he had expected, yet Lord Basel's timing was impeccable, as always. The room waited patiently for him to speak, his opposition to the Crown well known.

"Your Majesty," he said with a respectful head dip. "The real question here is not if others can use magic or have a Gift. That question has

already been answered. They ***can*** and they ***do***." The man was a wonder with words. Before Branthony even had a chance to retort, Basel had somehow closed that part of the conversation with him as a definitive winner.

"The real questions are these. This creature, this Crone as you call her. Where is she now? Our enemies know the Fait are weak. The Centre was attacked and breached. Lowly Sile ran through these very halls and killed at will. Our enemies see opportunity. Everyone in this room had better believe they are planning their moves against us." He clenched his fist and showed it to the room. "It is only a matter of time. They are coming, whoever they may be. They are coming."

Branthony stood again. He would meet his fiercest opposition on his feet.

"I don't know where she is." Grumbles ran through the room. "And you are correct, Lord Basel. The threat has not gone away; on this we agree completely. We need a strong, united Cross to face this threat. So, remember this. My children and their Gifts prevented the Crone from achieving her goal. It was my Gift that saw off her Champion. We have kept our Gifts to ourselves for far too long; no more. I have four children. Four! An event never seen before in the Fait. It is our custom to keep the names of our Gifts within the council until such a time as they can be controlled and used properly, but I want you to know the names of these Gifts: Foresight, Fortune, Guidance and Truth. My children carry these Gifts, and their power is immense. If an enemy wishes to try itself against the Cross, then let them. Let them smash themselves on our walls. Let them be crushed beneath the hooves of our horses. Let them run into the steel of our blades and the wood of our shields. We are the Cross. We are the Fait, and our Gifts will see us to victory against ***any*** enemy?"

Branthony spoke the words with passion, and many in the room showed their appreciation. It was a show of strength and defiance, a rallying call. It took a moment for the noise to die, and despite the support of much of the room for Branthony, Lord Basel remained standing.

"It is nice to hear you talk as though the kingdom comes first, but of course, we know that not to be true. You put yourself first. You put your family first. You did it when you chose to abandon us whilst you travelled south. You've done it other times as well."

Branthony narrowed his eyes. Where was Basel going with this?

"You say we must be ready to face any enemy. Does that include the enemy you choose to ignore? I have it on good authority." Basel was turning now and speaking to all corners of the hall before he pointed an accusing finger. "That you, King Branthony, had warning over two years ago of Valfargs on the move." The room erupted in commotion. "You chose to ignore those threats so that you could disappear on your selfish quest to ensure the Fait kept their grip on this kingdom." People were on their feet. Arguments burst out across the room. Tensions suddenly skyrocketed with the mention of Valfargs. "You lied and hid the truth about the Gift!" Lord Basel's voice still somehow carried clearly. "You lied and hid the truth about where you were going! You lied and hid the truth about ***Valfargs***! What else are you lying about?!"

The commotion took over. Branthony felt himself deflate. Only his wife, standing at his side, held him firm. All hopes of a quick resolution were firmly swatted away. This would be a long night.

FAVOURS AND FEVERS

Celia watched Prince Aron as he walked out onto the training yard with all the energy and vigour of a young man. She felt quite the opposite. You would never know to look at her, but she was exhausted. The audience with the king had dragged on into the obscenely late hours. The sun was already sliding into view before she found her chambers, but there was no time for sleep.

"Tell me," she whispered seductively as she placed her hand on the thigh of the man beside her. Well, man may have been pushing it a little. He was barely older than Prince Aron, but he was a fine figure for such a young one. Albert Smithe Jr was the Son of Lord Albert Smithe of the Gate. As the son of a lord, he had the honour of training with the prince today. "Does Prince Aron have any skill with a sword?"

"Well," said Albert, simultaneously trying to show some bluster despite the obvious fluster he was hiding. "He's nowhere near as good as me. He's too small."

She glanced back at the prince. It was becoming clear that he would not grow into a man of great height. Most of the others his age were beginning to tower over him.

"So," she said, rubbing at the inner thigh of Albert, who began to grin uncontrollably. The little git dared to put his hand on her thigh. She allowed it for the moment. "I want you to beat him today."

"Easy," he butted in.

"Listen." She turned her massaging into a tight grip, and he suddenly froze. "I want you to show me how good you are. I want to see how a real man fights. I want you to make him bleed." She spoke the words in lustful tones whilst grabbing and squeezing at his bicep with her other hand.

"Bleed!" Albert blurted. "He's the future king. The blades aren't even sharp. "

"Nothing much," she said, soothing once again, massaging of the inner thigh recommenced. "Just a little cut. It doesn't matter where. Nothing serious. Just show me you can do it. Show me how big and strong you are. How fearless. Even a king cannot stand against you."

He looked nervous, understandably so, but after a little more rubbing, he nodded his agreement.

"Good. I shall be watching." She offered him her most seductive smile, biting her lower lip to add effect as he swaggered away from her, rounding the corner and striding onto the training field.

She waited a moment before following him and sitting in the spectator's stands. There was a small crowd of ladies whose husbands were most likely still in bed after a late night. They all nodded to her, and some immediately tried to start a conversation. She indulged them, of course, but kept her eyes on the field.

Aron walked onto the field, tightening the straps on his armour. As heir to the throne, some might assume he had splendid armour, but his father insisted he train like all the others, and that meant no favours. The plates were old and dented, the leather straps worn. Still, Aron enjoyed putting them on. He joined the circle of students as they listened to Weapons-Master Austin's instructions for the day.

Aron spared a glance at the boys around him. He was the shortest in the circle and pursed his lips in frustration. He noticed Albert Smithe grinning at him as though he were some stupid little thing. Aron could already feel a tingle of anger in his belly. What was the smug git looking at? Usually, the other boys were hesitant about duelling with Aron. No one wanted to offend the future king despite instructions to treat him the same as any other. Otherwise, he would never learn. That's why Aron liked to train with Ollie, who didn't hold back. Maybe it was just his imagination. Right then, Albert shook his head whilst pointing at himself. A sign saying that Aron shouldn't want anything to do with him. So, definitely not his imagination.

Aron could barely believe it. Fine. If this pretender thought he was scared of him, he'd have another thing coming. Even if he was a foot taller, he was no bigger than Ollie.

"Right," announced Austin, but Aron had missed whatever instructions he'd given. "Pair up and begin."

Aron heard that. He stepped straight to Albert. "I'll take you."

Albert only smiled in response and began to roll his shoulders. Damn, he was big, and Aron had seen him train before, and he was quickly proving himself as one of the most able, especially with a sword, which was not Aron's best weapon. He was more of a blunt force kind of fighter, preferring a hammer or axe, but apparently, such things were not as princely.

"Prince Aron, you team with someone else."

The order from Austin only made Aron more determined. He couldn't have others doubting him, and if the instructor didn't believe in him, none of the others would. If he were to be king, he had to prove himself.

"Sir, I'd like to stay where I am."

Austin paused in his step and took a long, assessing look at him. "So be it," he said.

"Don't worry. I'll go easy on you," Albert said as he took a training sword from the rack. Aron followed suit.

Oh, this bugger is gonna get it! Aron heard the voice of his alter ego, James. The voice not of a prince but of a young man from the streets of the Centre, who did not take attitude from others.

"Positions," called Austin, and the boys made themselves ready. "Have at it."

Aron charged forward, and Albert was caught entirely off guard. Aron swung as fast as he could with all his strength and clattered his opponent on the shoulder, just beneath the pauldron. Albert cried out in pain and fell to a knee. Aron knew it was unbecoming, but he couldn't help taking his moment to gloat. He stood over his opponent.

"I guess you were just going easy, right?" He pointed at himself and shook his head.

He stepped away and could almost imagine Luke's smile when he told him this story. Still, before, Albert had looked cocky; now he looked mad. That anger only grew as Austin came over and clipped him around the head for being caught so easily.

"Go again, and take it seriously," Austin chided. "Starting positions. Have at it."

This time, it was Albert who launched, but Aron was ready. He parried the first three blows, as hard as they were, before returning one of his own that was easily defended. They separated and began circling.

"Good," commended Austin. "Good. Charging in can work sometimes, but it's risky. Assess your opponent. Find weakness. Find a moment."

Albert's form seemed near perfect. Every time Aron feigned, Albert was there. He swung and was blocked, barely managing to deflect the return off his shield, but he was off balance, and the next shot took his feet right from underneath him. He hit the ground hard but sprang straight back up. Albert was glaring at him with a cocky grin.

"Again," Aron declared with a glance at Austin, who nodded. Aron would even go so far as to say he saw a wry smile through the instructor's goatee. Austin liked a bit of spirit in his pupils.

Starting positions once again, and they were off. This time, Albert came at him with a completely different stance. Aron struggled against the taller man, now using height to his advantage. It took a moment, but Aron found himself on his back again. He sprang up once more and began marching to the weapons rack.

"Enough of this," he declared, more to himself than anyone else, as he threw his sword and shield down and picked up two axes. He enjoyed the nervous look on Albert's face, who was now looking to Austin for some word of reprimand, but none came. The Weapons-Master simply shrugged. He wanted to see this.

"All right. We can both play games," said Aron, taking his stance. The call came, and they launched forward. Albert's shield saved him once, twice, but failed the third time as Aron drove the blunt steel into his opponent's abdomen and knocked the wind from him.

Aron felt the adrenaline rush and held the axes out at his sides. Was this how Father felt on the battlefield? If so, then Aron liked it.

"One more time," said Austin, and they obeyed.

Albert was good and quickly adjusted his style to match Aron's. What's more, he seemed more determined than ever. His attack was relentless. Aron deflected what he could, but when the shield came at him, it couldn't be avoided. He felt his chin knocked into the air before the point of the sword stabbed into his ribs. Of course, it didn't pierce him, but by the God, it hurt. Aron went down and saw drops of blood splatter on the floor. Albert showboated to the other boys, who had all stopped their duels and watched on intently. He even looked at the stands where the ladies watched and paraded for them.

"One more," cried Aron, breathing deep as he stood, trying to shake off the pain. Albert looked on in shock.

"That's enough," said Austin.

"One more!" Aron insisted, and though he could see a flash of anger on his instructor's face, there was a nod of acceptance. It was the first time he'd ever given a command to a Castle-Master.

"But I have already drawn blood," Albert pleaded.

"Does drawing blood mean victory on the battlefield?" Austin roared back. "Go again."

Albert accepted the order and took his position, but something had changed. Aron could see the hesitation on his opponent's face. The bigger man was starting to have doubts. He hadn't expected such defiance. Was that a little regret Aron could see? They went at it once more. It was the longest duel of them all. Parry after parry, dodge after dodge. Both fighters moved around each other, earning nods of acknowledgement from tutor and fellow students alike. Sweat began to drip from both.

Aron felt the sword jab his back, and it should have been the duel, but he pressed on regardless. His axe whacked against Albert's wrist, who cried out in pain, but also refused to quit. The pair of them pummelled one another with blows, but neither withdrew.

It felt like a harsh twist of fate when Aron slipped and felt a sword clatter across his ribs. He stumbled forward and fell to a knee, struggling desperately for breath. Realisation dawned on him immediately. He'd seen this before. In his dream. The notes that he'd written. Can't breathe. *Wait*, he thought. *That means.*

He glanced up just in time to see the sword come smashing down at him. The world went black.

Celia ran along the grass, her dress hoisted high. She shoved the crowd aside and found Austin cradling Aron, who seemed unconscious but was shaking vigorously. She spared a quick, scathing glance at Albert Smithe, who had turned as white as a sheet. He should be scared, the oaf. She wanted a little blood; the small cut under the chin was enough. Why had they carried on? The last thing she'd wanted was for Albert to knock the boy's head off.

Aron's eyes suddenly opened. "Jacob!" he cried. "Jacob's in trouble!"

There was a moment of shock when no one knew what to do. What he was talking about was anyone's guess.

"Relax, lad," said Austin. "You've had a blow to the head, but that was one hell of a fight. You should be proud."

Celia couldn't help but scoff internally. What a stupid comment. Why did men find pride in fighting? The boy just nearly got himself killed because he couldn't admit defeat, and now, he seemed downright feverish.

"No," said Aron, trying to get to his feet but failing. He shook his head as though it would somehow bring his thoughts back into line. "I saw him, he was hurt."

"Jacob isn't here," said Austin, lifting Aron to his feet but keeping a firm grip on him.

"You're not listening. It's my Gift. I saw him. He may not be in trouble now, but he will be. They're coming for him."

"Who?" asked Celia. Austin only just noticed her presence and was surprised to see her there. "Who is coming for him?"

"I don't know, but I saw him bleeding. He was hurt. Please, you must listen."

Celia looked at Austin. "The king went out into the city an hour ago," he said. "The youngest was with him."

Celia hesitated for a moment.

"I'll take Prince Aron to the infirmary. Austin, find the King and Prince Jacob. Tell them they are in danger. You," she pointed at some random boy. "Get word to the queen she is to report to the infirmary."

Austin nodded and moved without hesitation. The boy was a little slower to act, but once Austin moved, so did he. One thing Celia found she could admire about certain men, especially soldiers, was their remarkable ability to take orders.

"Come, My Prince." Celia took him by the shoulders and ushered him away on shaky feet. "The rest of you are dismissed. Keep this to yourselves, or I will find each and every blabbermouth and deal with you myself." None doubted her words.

As she walked off the field with Aron in tow, she began to dab at his wounds, sparing one last scowl back at young Albert. Aron had a small gash on his chin and a large cut on the back of his head. He winced in pain and didn't notice as she held a vile under his chin, catching the drops of blood that fell. By the time they got to the castle, her arm and dress were covered, but she had collected more than enough.

ASSASSINS

Jacob sat beside his father in the carriage as it wheeled its way through the bumpy streets of the Centre. Although his father knew about his son's little forays into the city, they didn't discuss them. Perhaps he thought some things were better left unsaid. Joshua would call it plausible deniability in case Mother ever found out. Jacob had no idea what that meant. He just knew he enjoyed watching out from the side of the carriage at the passing streets, trying to recognise them. He recalled the different adventures he and his brothers had been on with Ollie and Joe. All the games they'd played with all the other children of the city. The evenings they'd dared to stay out longer than they should to see the night full of vibrant life with music, laughter and so much more than they ever saw inside the castle walls. He also glimpsed the old market and remembered running for his life from the men trying to abduct him. The same day that they first met their friends.

The conversation inside got a little more interesting as Branthony talked with Hunter. They sat across from one another, heads swaying with the movement of the carriage, discussing the meeting with the lords the previous night.

"So, how do you think it went?" asked Hunter.

"It was exhausting. For every argument, there was a counter. The lords argued as much as listened. I lost one to the opposition for every new lord I seemed to convince. Round and round in endless circles, but there's more to it. The realm has lost trust in the Fait. Lost confidence. Worse, some seem determined to push this trouble to its maximum. There is so much anger. Something seems wrong. Half the night was spent talking about the damn trade deals with Varliant, as though they were the most important thing going on lately. But enough of that. I talked long enough last night. Tell me, how did the training go with Joshua and Luke? Are they getting along?"

Jacob was suddenly intrigued by the conversation and turned away from the outside world to look at Hunter, eagerly awaiting the response. Jacob had been wondering who was winning the game. It was the first time any of the boys had been pitted directly against each other. Well, the first time that revolved around using their Gifts.

"The game is still in play. We didn't have time to finish. I don't know if we ever will."

"How so?" asked Branthony, glancing at Jacob with a grin, noting his son's interest.

"Well, their Gifts are obviously working extremely well. It's mesmerising, Your Majesty. It's like watching the jesters with their tricks, but only so much more impressive. Every turn of the timer releases a new benefit to Luke. Every downpour of rain, every gust of wind, every dry day seems to fall in his favour. I would think he was cheating if I didn't know better. It's as though the game wants him to win. It's supposed to be random, but it seems set to him. I wrote the conditions. I know what's coming. Yet even when I expect it to go against Luke, he seemingly randomly changes strategy, so the new condition benefits him. I don't believe he's aware of it most of the time."

"Fortune favours him," said Jacob, grinning.

"Indeed, it does," answered Hunter, scratching at his stubble. "But Joshua's Gift is also strong and much the opposite. Despite Luke gaining almost all the advantages Joshua continues to gain victories, if not questionable ones. I learned the hard way that Joshua's Gift does not necessarily tell him how to play the game, but the person playing it. He plays to Luke's ego and anger, lures him in with traps his brother is all too eager to spring. Joshua knows Luke is relying on the terms of the game falling in his favour rather than properly strategising. His Gift knows Luke will have the better terms and adjusts accordingly."

"You said his Gift is the opposite of Luke's?" said Branthony.

Hunter nodded. "Joshua is acutely aware of his Gift. Sometimes he stops and listens to a voice within himself explaining what to do and why."

"So, Joshua's Gift is winning?" asked Jacob.

"Not at all. I cannot say who is winning. Any new reveal on the game timer could spell the end for Joshua, or perhaps he will find a way to guide himself to victory. It is only…"

"What?" asked Branthony, sensing his friend's hesitation.

"It's nothing, Your Majesty. I'll wait till the end of the game before I comment."

"No fair," blurted Jacob. "What were you going to say? Tell us."

Hunter stared Jacob in the eye for a moment. "Joshua can be callous with the lives of his men."

"Jacob!" shouted Branthony, and his youngest son shrank into the chair.

"I'm sorry, old friend. Joshua and Luke aren't the only ones using their Gifts well these days."

Hunter seemed to shake himself back to reality and understood what had happened. "It's quite all right, Your Majesty. I've been wondering about the Fourth-Born. He's starting to change and become a man. I see he is becoming just as powerful as his brothers. That was quite… unique."

"Yes," said Branthony, and Jacob felt his father's eyes burrowing into him. "It will be quite handy when used properly, and ***if*** he can learn to control it."

"I'm sorry, Father."

"No need. You are young. These things will happen. All the Fait have struggled with their Gifts, including myself, but you ***must*** learn control."

"I understand, but please, Hunter, what did you mean? Why is Joshua callous with lives? It's only a game, right?"

Hunter looked to his king for permission to continue. Branthony nodded.

"It is a game, My Prince, but it is supposed to simulate reality. We are training them to command real armies. I said that some of Joshua's victories are questionable. If it were real, those would be real men. I have tried to express this to Joshua, but I believe his Gift shows him the best way to victory, despite the cost. He is quick to expend lives. Quick to send men to die if his Gift tells him it will gain victory."

"Victory at any cost," said Branthony, but Jacob could tell he was troubled. He heard the truth in his father's words.

"But it is still a game," said Jacob. "If it were real, he might choose differently, be guided down a different path. He knows the difference between playing a game and real life. His Gift may know the difference."

"Perhaps," mused Hunter. "But there may be no way to tell until real lives are at stake, and of course, the next question is whether he's right or not. Some would say that victory is all that matters when it comes to war."

The conversation was suddenly interrupted as the carriage came to a shuddering halt, sending Jacob and his father jolting forwards.

"What's happening?" shouted Branthony.

"A blockage in the road, Your Majesty," came the voice of one of the guards.

"I'll take a look," said Hunter, and climbed out. Jacob and his father sat silently for a moment before Hunter returned to the door. "A cart has lost its wheel in a ditch, spilt its load over the road. They're trying to pull it out but struggling. We could hurry it along, perhaps?" Branthony understood what Hunter was asking and stepped out. "Wait here," commanded Hunter as Jacob made to follow.

Jacob looked back outside and saw the mounted guards surrounding the area, holding people back. He watched eagerly as his father ushered back the horses and men with rope, before he bent toward the cart. He pulled it from the rut with a great heave and held it aloft as men began trying to reattach the wheel. It still seemed strange for Jacob to see his father using his Gift. It was a rare sight indeed. Not often would people find a king doing such menial jobs, but it wasn't often that a king could lift an entire cart on his own. Finally, Branthony placed the cart back on the ground, but there was still the spilt load to deal with. Wooden logs blocked the path, and it was not beneath the king to put his back to the task. Witnesses watched with awe as he picked up the largest log under his arm as though it weighed no more than a child. A lift that would have otherwise taken several men.

Even with his father's Gift, it would take time to clear the road. Jacob opened the door and stepped out onto the street. It was a dull, wet morning when the whole world seemed tinted with grey. Small drops of rain began changing the colour of his tunic. The light tipper-tapper of each drop somehow made itself heard. He looked up at one of the guards astride a horse, who let out a long sigh as the rain ran down his armour, his horse snorting loudly.

Jacob looked around at the scene. Several men were helping his father. A few others stood around caring for the horses. Jacob looked at the damaged cart. What had caused it to run into the ditch? He felt an odd sensation running through his body. Familiar and yet still so strange. Something was not right. Something about the situation did not run true.

He glanced at a small man standing at the side, his face dirty, his hands trembling as his eyes darted from side to side. He looked terrified. Why?

"You there," said Jacob, who was finding that being princely wasn't the challenge it used to be. The man looked at him with wide eyes, but rather than respond, he turned and walked away. Jacob pursued. "Hey, you there. Sir. Sir, I am talking to you."

The man nearly walked straight into a rump of one of the nearby horses, which startled it a little, and the armed guard astride turned angrily at the man.

"You!" said Jacob. "Tell me, how did the cart run off the road?"

There was a long moment of quiet when the man stared back at Jacob, trembling. The shaking grew worse until it seemed the man was in terrible pain, and Jacob felt his panic grow. He hadn't meant to upset the man, who looked like he would break down in tears at any moment. The tendons on his neck strained, veins bulged as his face grew purple. Finally, he blurted out words at speed.

"It didn't run off the road, we set it there knowing you were coming so we could lay a trap!"

If there had been quiet before, it now seemed all sound had gone from the world. A pure, undistilled silence took hold. Jacob stared at the man. Did he say what Jacob thought he said? Jacob drew a deep breath.

"FATHER!"

Branthony held one log on his right shoulder, another beneath his left arm. He turned at the sound of his son's voice. Everyone around them seemed to freeze for an agonising second, eyes darting to each other in an odd moment of tension that didn't seem to make sense. The gentle tapping of the rain could be heard alongside the breaths of men and the snorting of a horse.

Then all erupted in ferocity.

Branthony suddenly felt something tighten around him. The ropes from the fallen load. He'd been distracted, hadn't noticed the men loosely surrounding him. He dropped the log from his shoulder, but it fell onto the ropes and helped tighten their grip. The reality of the situation dawned as the air filled with screams and the sound of drawn steel.

The guards reacted like the trained men they were and drew close to their king, forming a protective perimeter, but it was hard to tell what was happening. Branthony yanked at the ropes held by man, horse and log. He felt the ropes give, but the scene was crowding in, only made worse as man and beast alike were pulled inward. He couldn't see what was happening. There was no room to move.

He heard the twang of bows, and two mounted guards dropped.

"You dare!" Branthony bellowed at the sight of his men falling.

Whoever these people were, they certainly did dare. One leapt off the now mended wagon onto the back of a horse and frantically stabbed at the guard. Over and over again, he plunged his knife into the guard's neck until they fell from the horse.

The clotting only grew as the riderless horses began to panic. The smell of blood was now clear in the air. Grunts of men fighting for their lives came from all directions. The royal guards were forced back. The enemy was everywhere, swarming like locusts. Branthony could not stop his mouth from hanging open as he saw his attackers.

Not armoured men or soldiers. Normal men and women fighting with whatever they could get their hands on. Some held rusted knives or blunted kitchen instruments. In the absence of any real weapon others held rocks. What was happening? What had driven them to such extreme madness?

Another of the guards went down, the enemy falling over him like rabid dogs as they scrambled forward to their next target. The other guards had formed a tight perimeter, despite the numbers against them, and they began to show their training. The enemy started to fall, man after man cut down, but still, they kept coming. A horse went down, crushing both guards and attackers.

Branthony waited for an attack to come his way. A blade, an arrow, something. It didn't come. Then the truth dawned on him. The guards had surrounded him, coming quickly to their king's aid, but Branthony now realised he was not the target.

"My son. Get to my son!"

Jacob fell to the floor as the ragged man suddenly leapt at him, brandishing a blade. He felt the bite of the weapon on his forearm, a hot burning sting followed by warm blood. He held up his arms to ward off a second attack, but none came. Jacob dared to open his eyes and saw the dirt-covered face staring down at him with wide, frantic eyes. The face suddenly contorted, eyes losing focus, then disappeared altogether. Hunter took his place, a bloodied sword in his hand.

"Up, My Prince. Up!"

Jacob held out his good arm, and Hunter pulled him up and along as he searched for a means of escape. They both watched as men and women of the city poured forward, attacking the guards. Some came toward them, determined to get to Jacob. Hunter turned his weapon on them, and it was apparent that he was far more than a simple instructor.

Jacob felt himself dragged along as Hunter cut down anyone who got close. The crowd and fighting were thickening. Hunter turned, pulling them to the side. Again, the route was blocked. He disposed of the attackers with frightening speed and precision, but more were coming. They moved in the other direction, but there was no way out, and suddenly, they were retreating back the way they came.

"The carriage," said Hunter. "Get in it, under it. Anything!"

"What about you? What about Father?"

"No time, go!"

He shoved Jacob towards the carriage and turned just in time to defend himself. Jacob watched as Hunter turned to fight, but they were on him. A hand grasped his wrist, his sword now held aloft. Hunter thudded his head forward, fighting tooth and nail. He scratched, bit, and raged, but in the end, he disappeared beneath the horde.

Jacob scrambled away and crawled on hands and knees beneath the carriage, which soon began to creak and rock from side to side as the fighting surrounded it.

Jacob waited, expecting someone to lean down and drag him from cover at any moment. He fought down his terror and dared to reach out a hand to grab a discarded blade. He'd trained with Austin. He could defend himself, or so he hoped.

Then he heard her, the Crone's raspy voice in his head.

"I can sense your blood, Fourth-Born," she groaned. "They're going to kill you. They're going to rip you open and pull your insides out. You will die today because your father and your family thought you were better than me." Jacob tried to shut it out but couldn't. She tormented him from within his mind. He could hear her amusement, her joy. "Tremble, little prince. Tremble at how easily they turn on you. Did you think they loved you? That they cared. See how easily they are swayed. Where is the power of the Fait now?"

She laughed, and Jacob held in his fear.

Branthony flung a dead horse aside and lifted the guard trapped beneath it. The man was injured but would survive. Branthony handed him off to another guard, took the first guard's sword in the process, and then turned to the battle.

Chaos, utter chaos. His men were trying to push forward. Cutting down those in their path, but there were so many. The royal guard had consisted of twenty-five men. How many attackers were there? A hundred? More? Despite their numbers, they fell in droves to the practised, skilled, fully armoured and in some cases mounted royal guards. It didn't seem to matter, they simply kept on coming. The only thing holding them back was their own numbers, too tightly packed to move with any speed.

One of the guards was overwhelmed, the attackers scrambling over his body like hyenas come to feast on a corpse of fresh meat. Only half the guards remained, and Branthony could not see Hunter. Worse, he could not see Jacob.

With desperate panic, he surged forward.

There was no path, nowhere to go, nothing but the congestion of battle and writhing bodies. Branthony threw men aside, tossed them like dolls. He kicked and punched and caused devastation, yet it was no use. The space he created was filled as quickly as it emptied. In all his years and battles, he had never felt panic like this.

"Jacob!" he screamed as he searched. "Jacob!"

He could hear nothing over the fighting. More of his guards fell, and those that remained began drawing into one another, trying desperately to hold a protective perimeter.

How? Branthony asked himself. How can it end like this? Not Sile or the Crone, but his own people. In the streets of his own city.

The enemy's forward motion seemed to slow. Many of those who had been pushing against him suddenly turned away. They turned toward a new threat, but Branthony could not see it. All he could see was a hundred or more figures. The people of the Centre suddenly turned into would-be king killers.

No, wait, not all of them. He could see it now. His attackers were people of the city, but so were his defenders. More had come. More and more still came, and these had the ambition of saving a king, not killing one. The battle began to turn. Those attackers whose intentions were clear were dragged down. Realising their chance had been and gone, others began to try to meld back into the crowd. Branthony's guards, now unburdened, stepped forward swinging their swords.

"No," ordered Branthony. "Kill no more. I won't see our rescuers mistakenly cut down. I want prisoners! Take them!"

The guards rushed forward, and finally, Branthony found himself with space. He turned and surveyed the area, eyes darting across the carnage. There was no sign of Jacob.

He saw Hunter. The man was down on the ground, beaten bloody, his face a mess of cuts and already swollen into a grotesque mockery of his usual face, but he breathed. With a trembling hand, he pointed at the royal carriage.

Branthony ran towards the carriage. He braced himself and sent his foot forward, crashing into its wooden side. It lifted from the ground and spun down the cobbled street, smashing into pieces with each new rotation. Jacob looked up at him, his eyes wide but his expression firm.

Branthony lifted his son from the ground.

He turned back to the fighting just in time to see fifty or more mounted guards suddenly surrounding the area, Austin at their head, bellowing orders. How had they arrived so quickly? Despite their speedy arrival, the battle was already over. Bodies littered the floor. Only five of Branthony's guards remained standing, but those members of the city's population who had decided to stand with their king had managed to end the short-lived uprising.

Such carnage. So much death in such a short amount of time. Branthony could barely believe his eyes. The street itself ran red. The people of the city had slaughtered his men. Then the people of the city had saved his men. They had come so close to claiming his son. For all his Strength, there had been nothing he could do. Nothing.

THE WATERS EDGE

Merleal embraced her father. They hugged tightly, both squeezing hard. When they finally separated, his hands remained on her shoulders, and they took in the sight of one another, smiling.

"Father," she uttered lovingly. "It is good to see you." She felt such relief at being home. It wasn't just seeing her father, friends and soon her son. There was something inside of her that was beginning to feel wrong that now felt right. Merleal knew that not returning to the Blood River was what had turned the Crone down the path of degradation. She knew she needed the river's blessed waters to heal what was poisoning her. She could not help but wonder why the Crone had stopped using the healing powers of the river.

"You succeeded," said her father, Graf. "I can sense the difference in you. You are much changed from the young woman who left here just a few years ago."

Her smile remained, but she could feel the weakness behind it. "I was gone too long, Father. I should have returned sooner, but it was hard. The Fait. They have strayed far from the path. The Crone's deceptions run far deeper than we had feared."

"You did what you must," he said, pulling her back for another hug. "You have renewed the bond between us and the Fait, and you have removed ***her*** as the deliverer of the Gift. Now we can set them on the path again."

They separated once more, and this time Merleal turned and pointed at the vast array of people behind her. All waited patiently, though some were more used to doing so than others.

"Father, allow me to introduce Morbius Duvec, Lord of the Sile."

Morbius stepped forward and dipped his head respectfully. "All these years," he said. "This place has been here on the edge of the plains. King

Branthony asked me about it years ago. I thought it was a mistake. Some trick, maybe. I wondered what significance a village on the plains could hold for one such as he."

He looked off behind Graf at the sprawling array of tents and huts that made up the small village at the edge of the Blood River. Almost everyone seemed to have come out to see the new arrivals. Still, that population was smaller than most clans.

"You knew we were here," said Graf, bowing his head. "You did not know our significance. The king of the Cross must trust you greatly to tell you of us and our importance to him. A great act of confidence considering the history of your two peoples."

Morbius nodded. "I must admit to finding great respect for Branthony of the Fait. He is an extraordinary man. I want you to know you can trust me, too. I have sworn to Branthony that the Sile will protect this place and that his secret shall remain with a select few. I owe him a great debt. Let it not be said that Morbius Duvec does not pay his debts."

Graf smiled and offered a hand, which Morbius took gratefully. "Then be welcome here, all of you."

Morbius moved on, and a very different man was next to step up for introductions. He wore a surcoat displaying the Cross. As tall as any man Graf had ever seen, with a stiff back and rigid shoulders. His jaw was covered in a short, neat, greying beard, yet held to the sky even as the man bowed his head.

He was much the opposite of Morbius, a man born to lead and very much at ease with his position. It came naturally. This man, Walter, was a man obsessed with his position and determined to prove himself worthy of it. Everything, every word, every action was a carefully thought-out process.

"Good day to you. I am Sir Walter. I have been placed in charge of the men of the Cross by His Majesty King Branthony. We are here to learn from you and protect you should danger arise, from any enemy."

Graf nodded, glancing at Merleal, whose face told him all he needed to know. Not all the men of the Cross shared their king's trust for the Sile. Being here, so deep into what had been enemy territory for so long, must have them all on edge.

"It is a pleasure to meet you, Sir Walter. Please, allow your men to rest and make themselves at home here. We have food being prepared. Drink from the river. Refresh yourselves. You are to stay for some time. Let us be friends in this holy place."

Walter nodded again. "I thank you, and I hope that can be so."

He moved off and began barking loud, precise commands at his men as Morbius commanded his own in a much more flippant way, with a casual word or a thumb pointed over a shoulder. Yes, very much the opposite of one another. Graf stood beside his daughter with an arm around her.

"There are many more introductions to make," she said. "These can be complicated people. Sile and the men of the Cross both. It will not be easy to keep hostilities from rising."

"No," agreed Graf. "But I have a feeling Branthony knew this. I believe he has chosen to use this as a little experiment."

"Yes," agreed Merleal. "But experiments often go wrong. Before we get to them, where is my son?"

The following days passed in constant commotion as Sile and Cross made their respective camps next to the village. Both sets had decided to keep themselves distanced from each other and rarely mixed. Merleal and Graf tried to integrate all three groups, but the task was challenging. Neither Cross nor Sile had much problem talking and interacting with the people of the river, but the resentment was apparent when it came to each other.

Merleal knew she had a great task before her but was not worried. She felt better than she had in a long time. She had seen her son, now so much bigger and changed in many ways compared to the little boy she had left behind. She felt the sadness at their separation and the enormity of all that lay on her shoulders as the new deliverer. Yet even this did not dampen her spirits. Being home, drinking from the river had refreshed her.

She walked the river's edge, taking a rare moment for herself. It was a pleasant surprise when she spotted the young man, Res. She startled him a little as she sat down beside him.

"Lady Merleal," he said, making to stand, but she stayed him with a hand as she made herself comfortable. She was no lady but had now long since given up on trying to correct people. The men of the Cross were determined to address her in such a way.

"Good morning, Res. How are you?"

He smiled at her, and for such a simple question, he took a long time to answer. She understood why.

"I'm… good," he finally replied. "I'm **really** good. I feel fantastic these last few days."

She smiled back at his enthusiasm. "It is the river nourishing you."

He looked out across the river, then back to her. "I heard the story that your people tell. That an angel fell and bled into the water. You believe in such things?"

"I do," she answered assuredly.

"Then you believe in the God?"

"Of course."

"Then…" he hesitated. "Then you believe the God is all knowing, and that he has some grand plan for everyone. Everything is just part of a plan. We're just acting it out."

"No," she answered, with no hint of jest. "The God is the Creator. He watches us. He loves us, but He does not control us. His biggest gift to us is our free will. He has given each person the chance to make their own way in life. Why would he create life just to control it? He has designs, but it is up to us how our lives are lived. That's the point. We can't blame anyone else for our actions."

Res shook his head. "I don't know."

"This world was and is the envy of beings we can barely comprehend. They fought for it. Angels fought to protect it whilst demons wanted it for themselves."

"And you think the Fait are what is left of these angels. That they have the blood of the Divine within their veins?"

"Something like that," she said with a smile. "It is their role to protect the world. They are instruments of the God to preserve that which He created. Their Gifts are given to make the world a better place."

"Then what is the Crone's part in all this. I saw her, you know, at the battle at the Centre. I watched as she tore a hole in the castle wall and strode into the courtyard like a creature from a story to scare children. I saw her blow herself up like a great bag of air, then scream. I watched men around her fall to the floor, writhing in pain. I saw her tossing men aside with a wave of her arm. I saw her champion heal from everything that was thrown at him."

"Not everything," Merleal countered, and Res nodded in acceptance of her point. It was easy to see his fear at the memory, but Merleal also saw some of what she feared most when men saw such power: wonder, amazement, and perhaps a hint of desire.

"The Crone is a lost soul who no longer knows her place. She stopped coming here and drinking the water. She stopped accepting the Holy River's healing. No one knows why. She has become corrupted and now seeks control and power above all else. But her time is coming to an end. She is no longer the deliverer of the Gift, and with the renewed relationship between my people and the Fait, we shall teach them all what she forced them to forget."

"How can you defeat such a thing?"

"Together. With the Fait, all their Gifts and the guidance of the God Himself, we will see in a new age. One without the Crone who has meddled and controlled this world for far too long."

"Can I tell you something?"

"Of course."

"My mother died giving birth to me."

"I'm sorry to hear that," she said genuinely.

"The woman who raised me told me I was a miracle. That I shouldn't have made it, but I did. I've always wondered if that was a part of the God's plan or in defiance of it. Thank you, Lady Merleal. I've found your words very comforting."

"I am glad to help," she said as she stood. "Let's hope I can have a similar effect on the leaders of the Cross and Sile. I feel they may be a little harder to calm than you."

"You are the perfect person for the task. Now, I have some letters to write."

"Letters?"

"I am to send reports back to the Centre to inform them of our status here."

"I didn't know that was your role here."

"Yes, I mentioned I am a disciple of Scroll-Master Bolevard. My skill in reading and writing is the reason I'm here. Not something I ever expected, but we all have roles in life we weren't expecting."

"Yes," she said with a smile. "We certainly do."

IN THE WAKE OF BLOOD

Aron lay on a bed in the infirmary, one of the healers beside him gently wiping his face and cleaning the dried blood that stained it. He tried to shake her off, telling her he was fine. Training accidents happened, and besides, he'd proven a point. If any of the others thought that they could try him, now they knew they would get a damn good fight. Even if he lost, he would sure as hell go down fighting.

Once the healer left, he tentatively touched a finger to the cut on his head and winced at the sting. It still bled, but not so much now.

"Does it hurt?" asked a gravelly voice inside his mind. Aron knew instantly who it was. The Crone had spoken to him this way before. He looked around and knew he was the only one who could hear the voice. "This is nothing compared to what will come. I will make you suffer! All that blood going to waste. Soon it will be mine!" He tried to ignore her. "Your brother is dead." He couldn't contain his gasp. "They'll all be dead soon, but not you. You, I will keep as my pet."

Aron clenched his eyes shut, trying to force her out. He grabbed a fresh cloth and pressed it against his wound.

"Be careful, My Prince."

Aron opened his eyes as the voice came from beside him. It belonged to Lady Celia. He thought it was strange she'd been at the training field. It seemed stranger still that she'd stayed here with him, but he was thankful for the company. Lady Celia had never made him feel like a child, never talked down to him. Now that he was older and becoming a man, the divide between them went almost unnoticed, but there was always something unshakeably not quite right with her. He would swear she was always a little nervous around him.

"What was that fool playing at?" she exclaimed. "I'll make sure he learns from his mistake."

"What?" Aron protested. "That was the best sparring match I've ever had. I can't wait to go again. All the others are too scared to push hard, too scared of offending me. I think Albert was finally smart enough to realise how to truly gain my favour."

"Right," Celia replied, though she sounded unsure. "May I ask you a question?" she said, shrugging it off.

"Of course," he replied, concentrating on her and shutting out the Crone's voice. It seemed to work. The voice in his head had fallen silent.

"Out there on the field, when you were unconscious, what did you see?"

Aron looked off into nothing and sighed. "I saw my brother rushed into the infirmary in my father's arms, covered in blood." He noticed Celia's flicker of emotion. Was she squeamish with blood? She certainly didn't seem so when she'd helped him inside. "Father was yelling about assassins. There was a lot of commotion. But you'll see for yourself soon enough."

"What do you..." She paused mid-sentence and perhaps should have guessed what would happen, but hearing about the Heir's Gift and seeing it in action were two vastly different things. The doors burst open, and the king rushed in carrying his youngest son, blood dripping to the floor. The boy was drip white. For a moment, Aron thought him dead, but Jacob pushed himself from his father's grip, determined to stand. Aron was proud of him in that moment.

The next hour was a blur as the healers treated Jacob and the others who returned with him. Many were injured, some grievously. Meanwhile, the queen arrived in a whirlwind of emotions, barely dressed and unable to contain herself. She hugged Aron and squeezed him so tight he thought his eyes would pop. He couldn't help but pay attention to Celia. She was looking at them. That same sadness he saw in her so often was there and yet amplified. Was it something to do with the embrace between mother and child?

The queen seemed torn between caring for her children, berating others that any of this should be allowed to happen, and asking questions that, as of yet, had no answers. Most of her questions revolved around why the people of the Centre would suddenly turn against them in such a swift and violent manner and how no one had a clue it was coming.

Mother had dragged Joshua and Luke along with her, and, for the moment at least, needed her children in direct line of sight, fearful that they were still at risk even here in the safety of the castle. After all that had happened, who could say they weren't?

Father gave orders to Austin, who left to command the forces heading back into the city to reestablish some order. From what Aron could gather, the whole thing had been quick yet extremely violent, but word had spread, and disorder with it.

It was some time before he had a quiet moment again. The infirmary was beginning to quieten down after the chaos of not one but two royal injuries and the fact that there had been some kind of uprising from the people of the city. Jacob slept. Father had stormed off in a rage, and Mother seemed unable to decide between staying with them or following him. Ultimately, she chose the latter but told Aron she would be back soon.

Through it all, Celia remained. "You've gotten much better at using your Gift," she said, retaking a seat beside him.

"Not really. I don't remember most dreams, just images or sounds, nothing that makes sense. Then there's the one dream I can remember. The one dream I wish I couldn't."

"Is there nothing you can do?"

"I've tried to practise, to get better. I tried to write things down to help me remember, but it's still not enough."

"Perhaps you just need some help." Her hand fell comfortingly onto his arm, and her smile seemed warm. The sadness was still there, but she seemed genuinely willing to help.

"I have a list."

"A list?" she enquired curiously.

"Yes. It goes King. White Mountains. War. White. Red. Can't breathe." He tried to tell her what he remembered of each part of his dream. He told her how he saw himself and his brothers as older men leading a host to war. He told her he now realised that "can't breathe" was the moment he got struck. That he realised just seconds before it happened.

"What good is seeing the future if you don't realise until it's the present? My brothers are getting better with their Gifts, but not me. It never gets easier."

Celia stared at him. She had no good answers. How could she?

"Perhaps in time you will learn to control your Gift more, and if you have seen yourself and your brothers as older men, you are seeing things far in the future. By the time these events come to pass, you may understand them more. Maybe you can even change them?"

He offered a weak smile and nodded. He supposed she was right.

"Thank you."

"Think nothing of it. What's more, I want you to know you can talk to me anytime. Why don't we make this a regular thing? Tell me more about your dreams, and we will try to figure them out together. As for your brothers, why don't you keep this between us? Perhaps we can help you catch up. Maybe even surpass them. You are the future king, after all. Maybe it's like the practise yard, you just need someone to push you."

Aron nodded his agreement. It sounded like a good plan to him.

Debreace listened as Branthony told her a tale of assassins and death of the streets of the Centre. He knew she was angry. Angry that someone had come for their son, angry that Branthony had all but walked into their trap, angry that despite all their power and authority, someone had once again come so close to claiming the lives of one of their children.

"You need to stop thinking this is a battlefield like you're used to," Debreace chided. She didn't shout and rage. She didn't speak down to him; this wasn't a wife disciplining her husband like a naughty child. This was a wife giving advice. A wife trying to help. She was angry. She was as angry as a storm at sea but didn't take it out on him. He was grateful for that. "The Crone is not like any other enemy. One thing she does not have is honour. She will use any dirty trick she can. You are used to pitching armies against one another, to fighting with sword and shield. This is a different kind of warfare, and we are falling behind."

"You're right," he agreed, placing his hands on her shoulders. His grip was firm but not tight. "You're right."

Debreace sighed. "Why Jacob?" she asked.

"I don't know, but I will find out."

"You took prisoners?"

"Yes."

"You're going to question them?"

"Yes, and I am taking the boys."

"What? Why?" Her disagreement with his plan was apparent, but he was determined. He had that steel in his voice that confirmed his mind was made up.

"We are all in this together. Our Gifts are chosen for a reason, and we need to start using them. ***All*** of them. The boys are in danger. It is up to us to fight back. Jacob's Gift could be our greatest asset in a war like this, a war of trickery and deceit. It is no coincidence that he received the Gift of Truth. No coincidence the Crone finally turned on us when she learned his Gift and why she fears him now. He can find the answers we need."

"Can't you take Susan? She can make them do anything."

"Even if Susan would do it, which I won't force her to, her Gift compels people to act. She could tell the prisoners to answer but would not know if they spoke the truth."

"She could command them to tell the truth."

"Her Gift doesn't work like that. She may get some answers, but I need Jacob for this. They tried to take his life, Debreace. It is only right that he gets to ask them why."

It was obvious she wasn't convinced. "Haven't they been through enough?" she asked.

Branthony sighed and took a moment to calm himself. Emotions and tensions were high. He had to be careful not to let them get the better of him.

"They've been through a lot," he acknowledged, looking his wife in the eye. Despite everything, she held herself together, and he appreciated the monumental effort it took. "But this is just the beginning. They will face threats throughout their entire lives. They were born with targets on their backs. I know this is not easy, but the sooner we teach them to face these threats, the better. Today should prove that point.

"Jacob knew something was wrong out there. They may have had us if he hadn't confronted one of the attackers. He was using his Gift, and it saved his life."

Debreace listened, and though it was not easy, she nodded her agreement. "One condition," she said. "You get the bastards that tried to hurt my family."

INTERROGATIONS

The boys stood with their father in an area of the castle they had rarely visited. Though they had been here before out of curiosity, it was not somewhere they would choose to be. They explored for fun and excitement, but there was little of either to be found in the castle dungeon. It felt strange to be there with their father at his request.

They could each tell that something had changed. The attack on Jacob the day before had pushed their father to a decision. Each of the boys felt a little older in that moment. All the times their father talked of responsibility, they knew that he was finally putting some of it on their shoulders. It felt unmistakable that, for the first time, he was treating them all as adults.

Branthony nodded at the guard, who turned the key to the massive iron gate and swung it open. They made their way down the dimly lit corridor, and it reminded the boys of the time they'd snuck into the crypts years ago. On both sides of the corridor were more gates, each leading down another bleak, stone passage with more gates to either side, leading into small cells. Who was held down here and what they had done were questions for another time, but each of them felt a shiver creep down their spines at the dread emanating from that place.

They made their way to the end of the corridor to one of the last gates, where two more guards stood waiting along with Hunter, who spotted the boys and quickly put his hands behind his back. Not quick enough that they didn't see the cuts and bruises on his knuckles. Compared to those on his face, they were trivial things.

"Your Majesty. Your Highnesses,' he said with a dipped head.

"You look exhausted," said Branthony. "Have you slept?"

"What do you think?"

"Me neither, how's the head?"

"Sore," said Hunter, yet he still managed a wry smile.

"I wanted to thank you," said Jacob. "You saved my life. I should never have gotten out of the carriage."

"Nonsense, My Prince. You are on the path to becoming a man. Telling you to sit and wait like a child was foolish of me. I should have taken you with me. Perhaps we could have avoided the whole situation. Either way, you forced them into early movement. You may have saved us all."

"Not all," said Jacob, forlorn.

"Have you learned anything?" asked Branthony, his voice low, almost a growl. They could feel the anger emanating from and felt relieved that it was not directed at them this time, though they could tell this was a different type of anger. One that they somehow knew was far more dangerous.

"Nothing much. They're stubborn, but I have not… pushed too hard as requested. We detained over thirty people, many of whom were injured. Some have not survived the night. Many claim they were fighting for us, not against. Perhaps Prince Jacob could clear this up later. For now, I have three men to question. This whole situation is difficult. Something is not making sense."

"How?" asked Branthony.

"Most of the attackers seem to be part of a mob. Determined to cause havoc and destruction, to make a point. Why suddenly so aggrieved that they would go to such lengths? Someone has been stirring them into a frenzy."

"You said 'most' of the attackers," prompted Joshua, who'd picked up on the word choice.

"Yes, there are others, including the three inside, who had another objective. I believe they were firmly set on getting to Jacob. An attack hidden within an attack. It was these that set the trap."

"Have you any idea what caused them to act out?" Joshua asked, his Gift searching for pieces to help solve this puzzle.

"There seems to be a sudden hatred for the Fait amongst the poorest citizens. Perhaps this is nothing new, but their willingness to commit violence certainly is. They speak of greed on your part. There is much talk of gold."

"Gold?" asked Branthony.

"Exactly. Many of those questioned speak of seeing enormous quantities of gold. Hordes of it, kept by the Fait from the people, so they say."

Branthony couldn't hide his confusion. "Where did they claim to see this gold?"

"Hidden somewhere in the city. There was talk of a ship in the docks. I'm looking into it. Either way, gold is the main word coming from their lips. They all seem to agree."

"They think we keep giant chests of gold coins randomly stashed around the city?" asked Luke.

"Oh no. That's the other strange thing. Not coins. Random objects of solid gold. A cup. A plate. A child's toy horse. Even a full-size wheel for a cart. All solid gold. All seen by many. All of it supposedly belonging to the Fait in blatant mockery of those who have nothing. Much of it was promised as payment for anyone who killed Prince Jacob."

"Who wants or has a wheel of solid gold?" asked Aron.

"Exactly. I think they are fools who have taken fool's gold for payment."

Branthony merely nodded.

"We are missing something here. Well then, I guess it is our turn."

Hunter opened the gate into a cell. There, chained to the wall, were three men, all of whom looked to have had a terrible night. Blood spattered the floor as well as their faces, and the boys glanced at each other, wondering if this was not pushing too hard, then what pushing more would look like. They could imagine. Perhaps such treatment was deserved for would-be child killers.

Hunter waited at the gate as their father stepped forward. All three men looked on in terror at the king before them, the silence only broken by their sniffles and sobs. The boys waited, half expecting their father to attack. He didn't. Instead, he turned to his sons.

"Your Gifts, do they tell you anything?"

None of them answered at first, and it was hard to tell. None had mastered their Gifts and using them under pressure was still a problem.

"This isn't a lesson, nor a test. There is no right or wrong here. This is us, a family, working together. If you feel anything at all, then say it without fear. Jacob, it is time for you to ask some questions."

The youngest brother stepped forward, rubbing at the bandages on his arm.

"What should I ask?"

He looked to his father for an answer, but Joshua prompted the first question.

"Ask them if they were there to kill you."

Jacob looked each of the men in the eye, and behind him, his brothers felt pride watching him stand so firm. He repeated Joshua's question to all three men. Though they fought against it, each of them nodded a yes through shuddering sobs.

"Why?" asked Jacob. "Who hired you?" The question was directed at the man chained to his left. The man stared back at him but didn't speak. "Who hired you?" he asked again, but still no answer was forthcoming.

"You will answer him," said Branthony. "Or you will be made to answer him." The boys shuffled nervously. They were not fools. They knew how interrogations worked, but they had never witnessed one before. Besides, most interrogations didn't have someone with the Gift of Truth.

"You won't need to do anything, Father. He will answer." Jacob stepped closer, looked the man in the eye, and asked for the third time, "Who hired you?"

The man took a deep gulp, trying to resist. He held his breath, desperately trying to prevent the words from escaping. Finally, he could hold it no more, and the words came tumbling out in a mumbled cacophony.

"I don't know. I was just part of the group. I just knew the job was to get to you." He gasped for breath like a man finally breaching water and finding air.

Jacob took deep, calming breaths. Despite only being eleven, he seemed even further beyond his years in this moment. He felt it, too. Jacob knew this was a turning point in his life. He would not be the same person after this.

"What was your plan?" he asked. It wasn't an instructed question, but Branthony let his son work.

"Cause a block in the street and attack the king as a distraction whilst someone goes for you. It wa'meant to look like a botched job. Make the king think he was the target when really you were."

Jacob looked to his father, who nodded for him to continue.

"Why was I the intended target?"

The man struggled again, trying to hold back, but eventually the words spilled from him. "I don't know. We didn't ask. They offered so much. We knew not all of us would make it out, but that only meant more for those who did. I'd be rich and I could take care o'my family. I've a daughter. We're living on the streets whilst you lord over us in the castle. That's all that mattered to me. It's the truth, I swear it."

"I believe you," said Jacob sympathetically. He turned his gaze to the centre man and repeated his earlier question. "Who hired you?"

"I don't know," came the same whimpering answer between huge gulping sobs.

"Why did you take the job? Was it just for coin?"

"My mother is sick. She needs'elp, we need money. The gold was there waiting for us. I couldn't believe it when I saw it. Gleaming like it wa fresh. I knew it wa stupid, but I had to try. Why should you'ave so much when the rest'o us have nothing?"

"All this out of desperation?" said Luke. It was not something he had comprehended before. He began to feel even more appreciative of his life and privileges. All the times he'd joked or jested at those less fortunate without considering the pure, deep desperation of their situation.

Jacob stepped over to the last prisoner. "Who hired you?" he asked yet again. The prisoner stared at him, eyes bulging, jaw clenched. "Don't make me ask again," Jacob pleaded.

"I don't know," came a trembling, sickly voice.

Jacob looked to his father. "He is lying," he stated confidently.

Branthony stood beside his son, kneeling to look the prisoner in the eye. "My son can hear your lies," he said, his voice oddly soft. "It is part of his Gift. He can also ***make*** you tell the truth. Do not fight it. It will gain you nothing."

The prisoner's eyes flicked between the king and the youngest prince. There was terror in those eyes, but also determination.

Jacob inched closer still. This time, he narrowed his eyes and concentrated. He spoke the words again, but slowly and precisely.

"Who. Hired. You?"

The prisoner stared at him with his jaw clenched shut. If he looked sickly before, then the effect doubled instantly. He trembled in his chains, eyes bulging further. It seemed he would pop with the effort. He was far more determined than his fellow prisoners, shaking visibly, chains rattling as he convulsed in agony. Inevitably, he broke and finally shouted a name."

"Gabor!" The word spilt from his lips. "A man named Gabor." The prisoner whimpered and sobbed, a long line of blood and drool falling from his lips to the floor.

"Tell me more of this Gabor," said Branthony.

"He lives near the old market."

The boys remembered the place well.

"What else?"

"He sells the Silent milk. That's how I know him. I went to get some. I owe him. I owe him big. Wouldn't sell but told us he'd heard of a job. Showed us the gold. I couldn't believe it. I'd never even seen gold before. Not like that. So shiny and new. He said if we could get a crew together and get the job done, there was more where that came from. Everyone was mesmerised. No one ever dreamed of 'aving so much. It was easy to find people willing to take the offer."

Branthony turned to Hunter.

"I'll send Austin immediately."

'Go with him," he commanded. "I want this man alive. He will not be the head of the snake, but he may lead us to it."

Hunter turned and left.

Branthony placed a hand on Jacob's shoulder and ushered him back before taking his son's place before the three men.

"We have your names. With those, I can do the rest. I will find your daughter and make sure she is taken care of. I will find your mother and have my Healing-Master look at her. If she can be helped, she will be." He turned to the last man. "There is nothing I can do for your addiction but rest easy that it shall not haunt you much longer. I am sorry your lives have led you to such desperate acts. I truly am. It is my failure as king that has allowed such things. But you attempted to take the life of a child, ***my*** child and your lives will be forfeit." The men whimpered, yet two of them at least held eye contact with Branthony and nodded their acceptance.

Aron looked to his father with surprise. The judgment wasn't what he'd expected. He knew the men would die for what they had done, but the compassion shown to them even after they had tried to kill one of his brothers, well, that was something Aron didn't know if he would have been able to give. Branthony saw his First-Born and understood.

"This is my judgment," he said with finality. "These men are pawns in a bigger game, manipulated by desperation. They will die before the dawn for their crimes. I shall seek out the ones who hired them. It is those who will suffer more. A king must be just, but a king is not without fault or blame." Aron nodded his understanding.

"What of the one that hired them?" said Joshua. "If these men are the pawns, then they were hired by the knights. There are other, more powerful pieces on the board. What about the queen? The most powerful piece. The one pulling the strings. We all know it, Father. We all know who is really responsible."

Branthony's face contorted into stubborn rage.

"Her end will come. ***We*** will see to that. Come. We are done here."

Merleal had her head in her hands and felt the pounding behind her eyes that she had hoped would lessen with her return home. Though the source of her feeling unwell was completely different, the effects were no less dramatic. She looked at her father and felt sympathy and regret. It seemed to fall on his shoulders to be the intermediary and peacemaker between the two warring factions she had brought to his home.

The Blood River had always been a peaceful, tranquil place. Now, it was filled with men who hated each other and were determined to argue on every possible point, leaning little in the way of compromise.

Morbius Duvec was a man who had earned his position as Lord of the Sile through years of pain and struggle. He was not accustomed to having his authority challenged, especially in what would be considered by most to be Sile lands. Usually, such a challenge would be met with one thing: violence. As bad as Morbius' anger was, it was matched by that of his men. The Sile were made up of every variation of man Merleal could imagine. They screamed and tensed as their blood boiled with each new insult to them and their leader.

The men of the Cross were equal in their refusal to back down. Sir Walter was a man who, much the same as Morbius, had earned the respect of the men under his command. More important to Walter himself, he had earned his king's respect. That was why he had been chosen to lead this expedition and was charged with protecting the village. It was a task the man obviously took extremely seriously.

Merleal jumped a little as Morbius slammed his hands on the wooden table separating the two groups. It seemed a flimsy shield between them, destined to be pounced over at any moment. Behind Morbius stood his closest allies and advisors. The prominent, round-bellied but powerful figure of Shimmer-of-the-Night glaring at the opposition. They were all dressed in leather and small furs. Mostly bare torsos displaying tattoos and scars that all Sile wore with honour.

The opposite side of the table was the dwelling place of the Men of the Cross. At their head was Sir Walter, the tallest man in the tent. His hair had long since turned grey, and his youngest years were behind him, yet he still maintained an intimidating figure. The Sile loved to fight, and it was not hard to see that Walter was a man who knew how to. He'd received many challenges from the Sile. He merely sneered at such things.

"We are not savages,' he was quick to say. This only invoked more anger and further challenges. The Sile, far from savages, had very different ways. They often ended disagreements quickly and efficiently through violence, allowing those involved to move on. With no challenge met and no resolution found, the same arguments continued.

In quite the opposite fashion of the Sile, the men of the Cross all wore surcoats over gambeson despite the heat. Walter was sweating as he leaned over the table. His height allowed his head to stretch over the length to meet the latest argument from Morbius.

"We must dig trenches and build fortifications!" argued Walter. There is an abundance of trees nearby. Sacrificing some to build defences is a cost worth paying."

Morbius shook his head. This was an argument he'd heard before.

"You men of the Cross with your holes and little houses. You have no idea of the delicate balance here on the plains. This is not the Cross where forests cover half the land. The trees are needed. This village has existed here for years, and now you wish to dig holes around it! The only hole you should dig is your own grave!"

The men behind Sir Walter pushed forward, hands drifting close to the hilts of swords that weren't there. Graf had ordered no weapons in the village. It may be one of the wisest decisions he'd ever made.

"Those little houses and holes, as you call them, kept your scavenging, murderous kind at bay for generations," spat back Walter. It was now the turn of Morbius' men to surge forward and shout their anger and insults.

"Ah, but even your great stone fortress was taken by Sile, or did you forget?" countered Morbius.

The other side rallied again as the insult was volleyed back at them.

"Which is exactly my point. An enemy took Fallow Hold with powers we could not defeat. We do not know our enemy here. We must be prepared for anything. You should know this better than most."

No insult, and no quick response from Morbius. In truth, he had to accept the point as he knew full well those Sile who took Fallow Hold were the ones who had worked against him and accepted the Crones' hideous alliance.

"I will send my men scouting far and wide. I can also call for reinforcements. I could have another clan here soon. Bolster our numbers and our defence."

"And also outnumber us, placing us at your mercy!" argued one of the men behind Walter.

"You are in Sile lands now, you are already at our mercy!" shouted one of Morbius' men. One of those stood behind their leader, all too willing to take up the fight in their leader's name.

Merleal blocked out their voices as the same argument continued. The problem was that they both made good points, and she agreed with them in ways. She was sure they were only arguing for the sake of it, or out of some foolish sense of pride. All she wanted to do was go and be with her son and father and make up for lost time. Also, she could not escape a feeling of dread that was building within. It was hard to explain. Perhaps those who'd delivered the Gift before would be able to do it better. She felt a connection to the Fait now. Sometimes it seemed she felt them individually and could discern which one the feeling connected to. Other times, it was more like she felt them as a whole. She would not mind. It was nice to feel connected even though they were so far away. A connection to the Fait was exactly what her people had sought for a long time. However, the problem arose with the way the connection felt. She had a growing sense of apprehension. Something was coming for them. *That's obvious*, she thought to herself. *The Crone is coming for them.* Only it wasn't that simple. She could tell that the danger was growing all around them. Something had happened, of that much, she was sure. Her thoughts cut off as her father's voice finally interrupted the arguing.

"Please, please!" Graf called, holding arms in the air in a calming gesture.

Merleal wondered if he believed they had made a mistake in re-aligning themselves with the Fait. Was this what he had imagined upon her return? Was this what he expected when they finally removed the Crone as the deliverer of the Gift and regained their place by the side of the Fait? Is this what he thought it would be like to be reunited with the closest thing to the God that exists in this world? Surely not.

"I thank you all," said Graf, and both leaders looked surprised. "Despite your... differences of opinion, I can see you both have the best interests of this village and its people at heart. You are both correct in your assessments."

He looked at Walter. "You may cut down some of the nearby trees." Walter grinned and glanced at Morbius as though he had won a victory. "But Morbius is correct. The balance between man and nature is much more fragile here on the plains. Even here near the river, where the power of the blood flows, if you cut down too many, they may never be replaced."

Merleal felt so grateful for her father and listened as he somehow began to reach an agreement between the two sides. She never knew he had such skill as a diplomat. Even after all she had witnessed over the last years, this, she thought, could well be the most miraculous thing of all.

Outside the tent was the boy Res, sitting inconspicuously amongst the many piles of clutter brought south from the Cross. No one noticed as he listened to the planning for the defences. He wrote down what he heard. The birds would fly north soon with an update. One of them would carry his words to Lady Celia.

THE MANY USES OF BLOOD

Once again, Celia waited until the dead of night to accomplish her task. The corridor cleared and the door locked, she removed the vial of blood she had obtained from Prince Aron. As before, she placed a single drop onto the table and within moments she felt the temperature plummet, though this time, she was prepared with a shawl spread over her shoulders.

"You achieved your task?" came the raspy voice of the Crone, cutting through the air like a jagged blade through bone. It jarred Celia's nerves to hear it.

"It is done. I have an ample supply."

"Yes, I could feel it when he bled. I could taste it. I was going to keep my presence hidden from him on this occasion, but it was too tempting. I do so love to torment them. Their pathetic whimpers are sweet music to my ears."

Celia could hear the joy in the Crone's voice.

"You know when they bleed?"

"It calls to me. The blood ***wants*** me to have it. To put it to use like those fools never could."

"What uses would there be?" she asked the empty room, eager to learn more. The Crone, whatever she may be, knew of things Celia could barely imagine. Knowledge is power, so Celia craved it.

"Remove one more drop and swallow it."

Celia looked around the room, wishing she had somewhere to direct her disgust.

"I will not!"

"Do it," commanded the Crone, and Celia felt her anger rise at being spoken to in such a manner. Wasn't the entire point of working with the Crone to rise above all others so no one could talk down to her? It seemed all she had achieved so far was gaining one more person, if the Crone could be called such a thing, who thought of her as theirs to command.

With reluctance, she placed a drop of blood on her tongue and swallowed it with audible disgust.

"Good," said the Crone, but now her voice was different, more solid somehow. Celia turned and leapt back in her seat, scrambling from it to the corner of the room. Quickly, she pulled a dagger that she always kept with her. Her dress lifted and revealed her underclothes in a desperate motion to gain distance.

She was there, in the room, the Crone. Her crumpled, hunched form was standing in the corner, smiling malevolently. Those cracked black lips and gums stretched into that odious grin, releasing a low growling chuckle as dark saliva dripped from her mouth. Her hand of bone pointed at Celia as she laughed.

"Did I startle you?" she asked, mockingly.

Celia took a few moments to regain her composure and calm her breathing. Finally, she adjusted her dress and asked. "What are you doing here? If anyone were to see you!"

"No one will see me." Every word sounded strained, yet the Crone herself seemed to take delight in speaking them. "No one ***can*** see me. Only you. Only for a short while."

"The blood," Celia replied, now understanding. Slowly, whilst still feeling unsure on her feet, Celia moved back across the room and retook her seat. She kept the dagger in her hand for now. "How does it work?"

"I have told you. The blood is power."

"If I took more, what would happen?"

"You would die. You were not meant for such things. Even if you had taken from the river, you would not survive. Only a deliverer takes the blood, and then upon feeding the new child, they release that power. It affects them still, but they live. Never take more than a drop."

"What more can it do? Why can I see you?"

"The blood calls to me. I am linked to it. But by ingesting it, a small amount of its power briefly resides within you. I can connect to that power."

Celia suspected the Crone was lying about the blood's limitations and wondered what other abilities it could instil. Surely, communing with the Crone was not the only power held within. She stared at the liquid in awe.

"I have spoken Prince Aron regarding his dreams," she said distractedly.

"Tell me. What does he see?"

Forgoing the questionable protection of the dagger, Celia poured herself some wine and drank it down. It did the trick. She regained some of her composure and cursed herself for showing such weakness to the Crone. This creature thrived on such things, and Celia did not wish to give her a morsel.

"The prince is troubled by his Gift. He foresaw the accident in which he was injured but did not know it until the moment it occurred."

"Ah," the Crone groaned, raising her hand of brilliant white bone and curling the fingers inward to form a fist. "But there is more, isn't there?"

"The prince has started logging his dreams, trying to make sense of them. He remembers little, but he retains certain images or thoughts. He has made a list." Another sip of wine followed by another glance at the misshapen thing in the corner. "The list reads as follows. King. White Mountains. War. White. Red. Can't breathe. The last was when he was injured, so it has already come to pass."

Celia paid close attention as she relayed the list, and only once noticed a reaction. The Crone flinched, ever so slightly, at one of the announcements. "What is in the White Mountains?" she dared to ask.

The Crone snarled at her. Mad at being caught out, perhaps? The anger went as quickly as it came. "Only death," she replied.

"Does this have anything to do with Valfargs? Are they truly moving again?"

"Do not concern yourself with what lies in the mountains. Nothing there is as important as that which is here."

Celia decided not to show that she had noticed a reaction this time but was certain the Crone lied. The mountains were of immense importance.

"You have done well. You must grow your bond with Prince Aron. He was born too early. Mastery of his Gift may never be achieved. Such a thing may hinder him for the rest of his life. There are few physical signs of his early birth, but his struggle to use his Gift is a consequence."

"But if he ever does master his Gift?" Celia asked.

"Then he could be very dangerous indeed. Gain his trust. Discover what he dreams and keep me informed. Do you understand?"

Celia took another sip of wine and refilled her cup. The effects were starting to spread, and she felt far more comfortable in herself, especially after reading the Crone so well. Despite her disfigurements and overpowering presence, Celia could get a read on her. That gave her some confidence.

"I understand," she said, adjusting herself in her seat. "I understand that I am taking great risks to do what you ask, and so far, I have seen no reward. I am in the same position and have the same power as I did before I met you. So why continue to take such risks?"

"Careful now, Celia. I admire your ambition, but do not overextend yourself. My plan is coming together, and your desire is minuscule to what I have in mind."

"I desire to be queen of the Cross."

"I know your desire better than you. The Cross is but one small place in the world. I plan to have it all!"

Celia stared at her. It was a concept she could hardly fathom, yet one she found desperately tantalising. It was like a hand had reached into her soul, plucking at a part she did not know existed and drawing it forth.

"The whole world?" she whispered.

"The whole world," the Crone repeated in her low, drawn-out growl. "All that you know was created by beings of power beyond comprehension, and this world is the prize they seek. They cannot touch this world directly, but ***I*** can, and I will claim it for myself and spit in their faces by doing so."

Celia could not pretend she knew what the Crone was talking about, but she did understand part of it. The part where they ruled the world. That was the only part she needed to grasp.

"If you have this power, why not use it?" she asked. "Why not kill the Fait and take control?"

"I have told you!" The response was a hiss of words. "It is not so simple. I need the blood of the Fait. We are linked. Intertwined. We are part of the same essence in a way."

"So, they will remain in power?"

"Once again, you fail to see the bigger picture. In the end, they will answer to you."

"But I will answer to you?"

"Would that be so bad? When the entire world bows at your feet?"

Celia frowned. It was hard to decide whether it sounded bad or not.

"The Fait are nothing but cattle. Their only purpose is to feed me."

"You still have to beat them. Your attempt at killing Prince Jacob didn't go well."

The Crone snarled, showing her black teeth as a fresh line of saliva fell to the floor. "His death would have been favourable, but the attack had more than one objective. I have known for some time now that this battle was coming. Ever since Branthony's birth."

"The King?"

"His Gift is rarer than they know. Most Gifts have a more mental applicability where his is physical. This was a departure from the norm. Then came Christopher. Then a third-born. Very rare indeed. When Princess Susan was born, and I felt her Gift, I knew the time was growing closer. The time that I would have to make my move and sever the link with the Fait. I maintained the illusion until I tasted the blood of the Fourth-Born. I knew it would be Branthony's last child, and with the complete list of Gifts, I knew what I was up against. I also knew the little one could cause me trouble. Perhaps even more than the others."

"How?"

The Crone growled again. "Even I am not immune to their Gifts. If he asked the right questions, I would give him the right answers. Truth," she spoke the word with utter revulsion. "It is a dangerous thing. Be sure you are never questioned by him. If the day should come when you find yourself on the receiving end of his questions, you would do better to take your own life before spilling your secrets, and they do it for you in a far more painful manner. Avoid him as much as possible. As his strength in the Gift grows, so does the danger of being in his presence. He will not even need to ask questions to sense your lies." Celia's eyes grew wider, and the Crone merely laughed.

"Do not worry. Even the Fourth-Born's Gift can be manipulated. Plans are in place."

"Why didn't you just kill them at birth, at least the youngest if you knew the time had come?"

"I tried, but the king was too close, and I was dazed after taking the blood. Not in full control. Look what a single drop has done for you. I took a great deal more from the Fourth-Born. Their time will come. All of them."

"You may have even more trouble. Now that Susan is back."

"What?"

Celia knew it was petty, but she took delight in surprising the haggard old thing. When it came to the creature lurking in her room, she would take any small victory she could, be it petty or not.

"Didn't you know?" she asked mockingly. "Princess Susan made her grand return and has sided with her brother."

The Crone's growled response was feral and terrible. Celia quickly wondered if the small victory was worth the cost.

"I thought I had dealt with that one years ago."

"What do you mean?" Celia asked.

"Her little man friend who jumped off the balcony. You should have seen his terrified little face when he walked outside and found me there. The terror! It was delightful. One small push was all it took. It cost me more energy to travel there and escape again than it did to kill the man."

"You pushed him? All these years, Susan has been haunted by his death, and it was you?"

The growl and disdain came again. "You pity her? You have done worse, have you not?"

Celia felt a familiar knot in her stomach and wondered, not for the first time, if the Crone knew ***all*** her secrets. Could she know that Celia had once been pregnant?

"His death led to war. Thousands died."

The amusement and terrible smile now took its chance to return. "His death led to a rupture in the family. A divide between them and a war that would break the young Branthony's spirit. It took years for him to end that war, and it prolonged the birth of his children. I was hoping he might die, then the line would pass to Christopher. Then, if he could be dealt with, the line would pass to poor little broken Susan. She would have been easier to control. One of them must always be left alive. A broken one is all the same to me, preferable in fact. I told you, even back then I sensed the end. I made my move to force that end further away."

"You're afraid of them," Celia mused, expecting wrath in response. This time, the Crone remained unexpectedly calm.

"You would be a fool not to fear them. They are dangerous beyond words. They are the only part of this world with a direct connection to that which lies beyond, but I fight against higher powers than the Fait. I have not survived all these years by being foolish. The Fait come and go, yet I remain. Remember that."

Celia considered the Crone's words. They were true. No matter the powers and Gifts that the Fait have, the Crone has always been there. Manipulating them, controlling and twisting the world to meet her needs. Despite everything easy to hate about the Crone, Celia admired this. She had orchestrated wars, controlled kings and queens like puppets, and no one had ever known.

"What would you have me do?"

"Give the blood to my men from Varliant, I will get it from them. They will not remain in the city for much longer. I will need it soon for what is to come. Also, I need word from the Blood River."

"I expect it any day. I will inform you immediately."

"If that's the case, we'll talk again soon. Until then, I leave you with a gift. Sleep now and see all that you desire."

Celia blinked, and the Crone was gone. She suddenly felt tired beyond words and nearly fell upon her bed. Her eyes closed, and she fell into a deep sleep. There she dreamed. She saw herself atop a golden throne. Queen, not only of the Cross but of all the known world. It was clearer and more pristine than any dream she had ever had before. She could touch, taste, smell and feel everything. It was mesmerising. Hypnotising. It was perhaps the greatest disappointment she had ever felt when she woke the next morning, which was saying something powerful. All her doubts and insecurities about her alliance with Crone had washed away. All she could think of was the dream and her desires.

CLOSER TO THE TRUTH

The boys waited anxiously alongside their father as Hunter entered the room. The last few days had been an odd mix of chaotic moments between prolonged periods of tense calm. Hunter had been out in the city with a few chosen men, living up to his name by hunting down those responsible for the attack on Jacob.

Now and then, sometimes hours apart, sometimes more than a day, he would return to the castle with a new prisoner or witness to question. Jacob used his Gift efficiently, and most could not withstand it for long before spilling their secrets.

Between these interrogations, there were still the different lords and ladies of the Cross to deal with, but Branthony had decided to turn this into an opportunity to display the power of the Fait. He had allowed a few to witness the questioning and the Gifts at work. Many of those chosen to watch had voiced opposition to the Crown.

"Let them see what we can do," Branthony had told the boys. "We've kept our Gifts hidden and shrouded in secrecy so much that the people have begun to doubt them. Let us remind them that we are the Fait."

So, the boys had. All tried hard to use their Gifts. Even Aron had begun having a little more success. After he'd run through them with Lady Celia, several of his dreams had become a little clearer. Though he was careful not to tell her everything, he'd kept to her advice and not told his brothers about the time he was spending with her. He had to admit it had been working. One of his dreams had shown him directing Hunter to a house in the city. With Celia's help, they discovered the house and took Hunter there, where he found one of the men he'd been looking for.

The thing that Aron couldn't figure out was that he didn't know the house, but his dream had shown him directing Hunter there. If he hadn't had the dream, would it have happened anyway? Had he simply made things move faster, or did his Gift have a way of using itself to make the future happen? Just thinking about it brought on an excruciating headache.

"So?" said Branthony to Hunter. "What do we have?"

"Well," said Hunter. "As you know, our first port of call was the man named Gabor. A seller of the Silent Milk, amongst other things. He was the one who had made the offer to the men who attempted the assassination."

"But we questioned him," said Joshua. "He didn't know anything. Just another middleman."

"Yes, but he led us to another source."

"Which led to another which led to another," butted in Luke impatiently. "We know. We've been questioning them for days now."

"So we have," accepted Hunter, though Luke noticed the stare from his father that warned against further rude interruptions. "One person led to another; the only unifying thread was objects of solid gold. We even managed to locate some of them. A boot, a knife, a child's rattle. All solid gold, just like the stories said. All this has finally led us to something of interest, but also something that may prove difficult." Hunter's eyes flicked to the boys.

"They've gotten us this far, my friend. I won't exclude them now."

Hunter nodded and continued.

"There were a lot of mentions of the docks. Reports of shipments coming in every few weeks. Small, but heavy."

"Gold," said Branthony.

"Yes. I started checking the manifests. The ships were from all over the known world. Someone had gone to great lengths to hide the link between them. Many had at least one port in common. Those who hadn't been to that port had at least docked with ships that had. It was a complicated mess, and many ships didn't keep proper records. None of the evidence I solid. In the end, this is just a guess. We could be wrong, My King."

"Where?" asked Branthony.

"Varliant," came the unconfident answer.

The boys looked at each other and their father. Aron asked the question that everyone was thinking.

"Why? Why would Varliant try to kill Jacob?"

Hunter had no good answer.

"We have no real proof that they did," said Hunter.

"Revenge for spurning their trade deals?" said Luke.

"Let's think through this," mused Joshua. "They come here and make huge deals with every merchant and lord they can get close to."

"But then Father refuses to deal with them," replied Luke.

"Many lords weren't happy about that," added Jacob.

"No," said Aron. "Which only makes things worse as Father is trying to gain their favour."

"So, Varliant wanted to turn the lords against Father," said Joshua.

"They've been stirring the pot," rumbled Branthony. His voice had that coldness to it, and the boys could tell he believed that Varliant was responsible for the attack. "I think we should ask them some questions."

"It will not look good if we go at them with force. Not without proof," said Hunter.

"Didn't you hear me? I said, we ask them. The delegation is still in the city, is it not? Perhaps I have been rethinking my position on those trade deals. Let's give them a visit and see what they have to say. Only I have a feeling they may not be keen to talk."

"I'll prepare the guard," said Hunter.

"The boys will be joining us, and if the Varliants were responsible, they may be dangerous. Fetch Austin, Michael and John, we need our best men. We will get to the bottom of this, one way or the other."

Celia found Bolevard sneaking out of the kitchens. He was the Scroll-Master, and just as the library was his domain, the kitchen was Agatha's. Neither Bolevard nor Celia would openly cross her, especially on her own territory. Rumours had spread that Agatha had killed several Sile during the battle at the Centre, and her fearsome reputation had only grown. Celia would say with quite some honesty that Agatha was one of the scariest women she'd ever met. Crossing her would be knocking on Death's Door.

"Where have you been?" Celia asked accusingly. Bolevard did not like the tone. He drew himself up to his full height and looked down at her with a snarl of distaste.

"What business is that of yours?"

Celia cursed at the volume of Bolevard and looked around to see if anyone was watching. Damn the man, he could be infuriating at times.

"I only meant that I have been looking for you. I thought to find you in your library, but you weren't there."

"Even I must eat."

"Of course." She took his arm, to which she could tell he was slightly offended and began walking down the stone corridor, appearing as old acquaintances taking a friendly stroll. "I have something for you." She handed him a small package. He went to inspect it, but Celia gently pushed it from view. "Not now. It is for our mutual friends." She looked him dead in the eye as they walked. She could see the wash of emotions run over him.

"You expect me to deliver it?"

"Oh, come now, Bolevard. Do you expect me to take it myself? Won't that look completely normal? This is a complicated game we play. Who knows who is on whose side? I can't trust this with just anyone," she said with a slight grin. "I need you to get this to them. They will know what to do. I cannot move about the city like you. I cannot protect myself like you should someone think to harm me. Our friends have been very complimentary of you, Bolevard."

"What good has it done? Their little plan hasn't accomplished much. Were they hoping the kingdom would implode simply because of a few broken trade deals?"

"Their plan is not yet at an end, but this will help them."

"Why should I do your dirty work for you again?"

She was just about to answer when they both stopped in their tracks. They were heading from the kitchen to the main castle when they saw several armed guards crossing the courtyard heading toward the stables. It wouldn't be a sight out of the ordinary if they weren't led by the king alongside Hunter and Austin. Not to mention the king's brothers-in-law. A conspicuous crowd.

"What is happening?" whispered Bolevard.

Celia's interest had piqued, but it surged at the sight of all four princes striding out to follow their father. It was obvious from their added bulk that all of them were wearing gambeson. She saw mail and some light armour over surcoats that all displayed the sign of the Cross. They carried small swords and daggers at their hips. Celia watched in shock as they walked with purpose, and she could see their father in each of them. They looked older, sharper, and more regal than ever before. Everyone seemed to stop and take notice. Celia knew then that none of them could be called children any longer. Aron looked every inch the grown man, but even the youngest looked far beyond a child. In fact, Jacob seemed to have grown most of all.

She knew that of all the princes, Jacob had been using his Gift the most lately. Perhaps such things take the youth out of a person. Maintaining one's childish innocence must be hard when you can see all the world's lies. Celia had risked getting close to him and watched one of the interrogations. She now understood the Crone's warning. If he turned to her right now and asked her the right question, she would spill her secrets like wine from a fallen cup. She shuddered at the thought.

"Prince Aron," she called, and he paused to look at her.

"Go on," he said to his brothers. "I'll catch up in a moment."

The other three looked a little annoyed but did as requested. Aron approached Celia, who had moved away from Bolevard. The prince had a speed to his step, obviously not wanting to fall too far behind.

"What is happening?" she asked.

"We're heading out to find the delegation from Varliant. We've got some questions for them."

She could hear the tone of his voice and knew he believed it may be far more than questions.

"But why?" she asked, though she already had suspicions.

"It's just some questions. Father wants to know more about these trade deals they're offering." He glanced back over his shoulder, and his brothers had disappeared. "I've got to go," he insisted apologetically. "We can talk later." He ran off to catch up with his brothers. Celia turned to Bolevard.

"Have you ever heard of the king changing his mind like that?" Bolevard shook his head. "You've got to get to them first. Give them the package from me and warn them! The king is coming for them. He must know something."

"Why would I take such a risk?"

"Are you such a fool that you do not understand?" She had to fight the urge to slap the man. "If Prince Jacob questions them, they will tell him the truth. Whose names do you think they'll give up?"

The colour drained from his skin.

"I know where they are," he said. "I can get to them first."

"Go then, and if you don't reach them first, I suggest you take your own life before the king does it for you in a far more painful manner."

Celia hated the fact that she was repeating the Crone's warning, but it made sense. Bolevard was gone in a breath, and she hoped he had the speed and wits to complete his task. Meanwhile, she had things of her own to do. She felt her heart pounding as she left the courtyard.

Sweat poured from Bolevard's brow as he headed out into the Centre through one of the smaller gates on the western side of the castle grounds. The night was young, and the streets still busy, so he knew he'd be faster on foot. Besides, he knew exactly where he was going, and it was not likely to be the first place the king and his devil spawn would think of. They would go to the wealthier areas where Salvadire and his friends had paid for expensive accommodation that they rarely used. That side of the city was not to the taste of the men from Varliant. Other areas were far more discreet.

Still, Bolevard did not dawdle. He ran through the dense, complex maze of the Centre. Homes packed side-to-side, back-to-back, and above and below one another. He ran through some hanging clothes left out to dry and found some britches tangled around his neck. He threw them off, spitting out his disgust.

By the time he reached the pleasure house where the men from Varliant secretly spent most of their time, he could barely breathe. He crashed through the door and almost caused a panic as patrons and workers leapt to their feet, believing it to be a raid. He turned his face away from them and approached one of the women he knew to have some authority.

"Where are they?"

"Don't know who you're talkin'bout," she snarled.

"Unless you want the king himself and fifty city guards crashing through these doors, you'll tell me where they are!"

That got her attention, and she pointed to a back room. Bolevard entered to see the men from Varliant sitting as usual, surrounded by women and puffing their pipes. The room was thick with incense and smoke.

"Librarian. What is all this commotion?"

"Salvadire! The king! He is coming for you. You are discovered. I think he has traced the attempt on his son's life back to you."

Salvadire looked a little surprised, but by no means in a state of fear or panic.

"I must say this has come much quicker than expected. I suppose we have the young one to thank for most of the work."

"Which is precisely why I helped you to get to him. I told you exactly where and when, and still you failed. Now look at the mess we are in. If the prince can question you, you will all spill your secrets."

"I have no doubt." Salvadire was not taking the situation as seriously as Bolevard would have expected.

"Then you need to leave. If they question you, it will lead to me." His eyes bulged, and he grasped Salvadire by the scruff of the neck. The other men from Varliant did not take kindly to that and reached for blades. Bolevard suddenly realised he was surrounded.

"Calm," urged Salvadire to his men. "Calm, my friends." The others slowly lowered their hands and eased away. Salvadire looked back at Bolevard and gently removed his hands. "My dear Librarian. We have prepared for this eventuality. We have always known it would come. We will make our escape. It has all been planned. You have been a good ally to us, and rest assured, our plan is still in motion. We will see the Fait fall."

Salvadire smoothed his clothes and then his oiled beard and hair. The arrogant smirk never left his face. That used to be Bolevard. He used to be the one who was always so sure of himself, so confident. Things had changed. He hadn't felt that way since the battle at the Centre. How could he? How could he feel confident knowing that he had failed when he was needed most, when he had his chance for vengeance, an opportunity to kill the Crone? He ran away like a coward to cry and piss himself.

"You must go," is all he could think to say as he shrank a little. He missed his old self. "Oh, and this is for you. From a mutual friend." Damn, in his panic, he'd forgotten to inspect it. "What is it?" he asked.

Salvadire took the package and smirked. "Better you do not know. For your protection, my friend. The less everyone knows, the better. That way, the little devil cannot gain all our secrets, eh?"

Bolevard knew that technically it made sense. He also knew the man from Varliant was talking out of his arse, and Salvadire sensed Bolevard's distrust.

"I can see your mind is not eased, my friend."

"You don't know who you are messing with. I don't know what has given you your confidence, but it is overreaching. Whatever you think you know of the Fait, they are far more dangerous than you know. Everything involving them is more complex than you can imagine."

For the first time, the solid wall of self-assuredness showed a crack. Salvadire made a small step toward Bolevard and spoke in a quieter, more serious voice.

"Plans are in place, my friend. ***Trust*** me. Things will not be easy for you over the coming months. We know this, but you have been a good friend to Varliant, and we will not forget. Know this. Whatever happens today, do not fear. Do not panic. Let it play out. It is all part of the plan. The king will spout lies about us, desperate to convince the people of the Cross that we are the deceivers. You know the Fait and how they manipulate. Do not be fooled. The Fait will fall, my friend. Believe in this if nothing else."

Bolevard was unconvinced. Salvadire stepped closer still, grabbing him by the shoulder and holding him close in an embrace as he whispered into his ear.

"Listen to me now. Do not be questioned by the boy, but if anyone from Varliant is questioned, you must be there when it happens." Bolevard went to pull away, his face contorted. What was this madman talking about? Salvadire only increased his grip and pulled him closer again. "Listen to me," he whispered, but his voice had a force to it. Bolevard listened to the instructions with surprise. He couldn't believe what he was hearing. Oh, things were starting to make sense. These foreigners were clever. Finally, Salvadire released his grip and stepped back with a smile etched on his face once more. "You will hear from us soon," he said loudly. "The Cross will hear a lot from Varliant, rest assured of that. We will take care of everything."

With those last words, their discussion was over, and Bolevard was slightly relieved not only by Salvadire's whispered words but also by the fact that he and his men began to pack some belongings and make ready their escape hastily. He watched without a move as they mercilessly slit the throats of the women in the room who knew too much.

Bolevard found himself trudging back to the castle grounds in a much more relaxed fashion than that in which he left. He even felt... what was that? Could it be confidence?

Across the city, it seemed to take an age after the first men had entered before their father finally called them in. The boys stepped into the lavish rooms and spread out. There seemed to be nothing unusual to see, not even several men from Varliant, as expected. Guards filled the rooms, some posted at the doors and windows, while others searched through the few belongings left. Other than that, the rooms were empty.

"The proprietor says most of them barely stayed here," said Hunter.

"I've got men searching nearby establishments," added Austin.

"Then you're probably checking in the wrong places," said Michael.

"Where would you check?" asked Austin, with a touch of irritation in his voice.

"Easy," answered John for his brother. "Pleasure houses and anywhere that has good wine and ale."

"Why do I get the feeling we're not going to find anyone anywhere?" said Joshua.

Branthony turned to the Third-Born. "You think they're already gone?"

"It would make sense, wouldn't it? If they were involved in a failed assassination attempt?"

"But it would also raise suspicions about them. They didn't know we'd found a link leading back to them. Running away would only look bad," said Aron.

"Perhaps they knew they'd been found out."

"A traitor?" said Hunter, distaste flowing through the word.

No one had time to speculate further. All eyes suddenly turned as a guard called out. Raised voices came from just outside. Hunter and Austin both ran out towards the commotion. The boys found themselves pushed back behind their uncles and father.

A moment later, the guards returned with a man tightly squeezed between them. One of the men from Varliant. He looked shocked and more than a little angered at his current predicament.

"What is the meaning of this?" he demanded.

"The meaning?" Branthony's presence suddenly made the man realise that his level of importance was not as high as he had believed.

"King Branthony," he said, surprise more than a little evident. "To what do we owe the pleasure of Your Majesty's visit?"

"We, you say. I see only you. Where is the rest of the delegation?"

The man swallowed, his eyes casting around the room as though searching for someone to save him. No such saviour would come. "They are…" He searched for words. "Out on business. Meeting with the merchants of your glorious city."

Branthony's jaw clenched as he drew a deep breath through his nose. "Jacob," he said, and his youngest son stepped forward.

"Where are your friends?" asked Jacob.

"They spend their free time at the pleasure house near the financial district."

The words spilt quickly, the man cupped his hands to his mouth, shocked that the answer fell from him in such a way.

Branthony nodded to Austin, who quickly shared a glance at Michael and John before pointing at several of the guards and ordering them to follow him. They stormed from the room with intent.

"What is your name?" asked Branthony to the pale Varliant man.

"Meroth," he answered, though it was a natural reply this time.

"Well, Meroth. Would you be so kind as to accompany me back to the castle?"

CHALLENGES

Sir Walter stepped from his tent into the daylight and straight into commotion. The backs of men were all he could see, all looking inward at some spectacle. He growled to himself. *What now?*

He stomped forward and began pushing men aside, forcing his way through the crowd, shoving men left and right.

"Out of the way," he called. "Out of the damned way!"

Finally, he made it to the centre of the circle formed by the crowd, and there he found an open space occupied by two men. One was a Sile, heaving heavy breaths. His dark skin gleamed with sweat, and a layer of dirt and sand was spread over his bare torso, covering many scars and tattoos. The man had a smile on his lips as he spat blood.

One of Walter's men was on the opposite end of the space, though it was hard to tell the difference. He, too, wore only his boots and britches. His top was bare, and though it had none of the tattoos or ritual scarring, it held its signs of previous battles and was equally covered with dirt. This man, also, seemed to grin as he held his hands forward and curled his fingers back in a 'bring it on' motion. The Sile obliged.

The two men came together in a storm of fists.

Walter stormed the centre of the circle and came between the two men. He kicked the Sile, sending him tumbling then grabbed his man by the shoulders and threw him like a rag doll. Both seemed aggrieved at the interruption.

"What in the name of the God do you think you are doing!" Walter bellowed.

"He is answering a challenge," came the voice of Morbius Duvec as he, too, entered the centre space with a swaggering walk.

"You allow this stupidity?"

Walter was enraged. How was he supposed to keep the peace and maintain some order and discipline when the leader of his so-called allies seemed determined to undermine such things?

"Of course I allow it. It is the Sile way. In fact, I am glad to see one of your men finally stepping up and accepting. I was beginning to think you all cowards."

"Cowards!" Walter almost choked with indignation. "There is nothing cowardly about maintaining order. We save our strength for the enemy. These two have beaten seven bells out of each other. What good will they be if our enemy comes today? We will have two fewer men to fight off whatever comes at us."

Morbius didn't have an immediate reaction. He considered the words, though in the end all he offered was a shrug of the shoulders.

"Is that all you have to say?" asked Walter, his voice now a low, menacing growl.

"You men of the Cross may be used to saying what you want with no repercussions, but when someone runs their mouth in Sile lands, they must be prepared to back up their words. Your man and mine had plenty to say, so they must settle the dispute. This is the way. After the challenge, they shake hands and move on, and nothing more will be said."

"If someone runs their mouth in a tavern, then they may have to answer to someone. Does this look like a damned tavern to anyone? We are supposed to be an organised, fighting unit."

"You're right," said Morbius, stepping closer. "We are far from a tavern. We are far from the Cross. These are our lands and our ways. The challenge has already begun."

Morbius now stood only an inch from Walter, who was by far the taller man. Still, when Morbius lowered his voice, Walter had to lower his head to hear, though he was weary of an attack and tensed at the ready.

"The challenge has already begun," Morbius repeated in a whisper. "It must be settled. If not, it will only lead to further arguments and hatred. Let it end, Sir Walter, and I promise I will hold my men from further challenges but stop this now and they will hold no respect for you or your men. It's not just the challenge itself. It's about where we are. We must show that your men understand this is not the Cross."

Walter growled. He did not like this at all. It went against all his training. Discipline and control were the lessons he learnt, but as he glanced at the faces of both Sile and Cross men alike, he could tell they all wanted to see this through.

"This once ***only***!" he said through gritted teeth. "And if either of them is seriously injured, it is on you."

Morbius nodded. As he stepped away, he raised his voice again for all to hear.

"The challenge was made and answered. It will be seen through to its end. Fighters, resume!"

The announcement was met with rapturous cheers. Walter's old friend, Austin, may have agreed with such things, but it was not the way Walter commanded. He strode to the circle's edge, purposefully taking position next to Merleal.

"You have been watching this foolery?"

"It may seem like such to you, but to the Sile, this is how they settle their differences. It may be good to try to put an end to this."

"What if it isn't an end? What if this is simply the beginning of a new challenge every day? Challenges that my men now believe they are able, or even ***expected*** to accept?"

"That is not how the challenges work. There is an order to them. They must be accepted not only by the two involved directly but by a majority of those there to witness. The same challenge or accusation cannot be made again once answered."

"And what accusations were made for this particular challenge?"

She smiled softly at him. "That the men of the Cross dare not fight because they don't know how."

Walter merely growled again and watched as the two men came together. The fight lasted several minutes, with both men giving and receiving heavy blows. He growled further as the man of the Cross went down and failed to rise. The cheers of the Sile riled him as they congratulated their fighter. However, he found himself with some be-grudging praise as the Sile lifted the man of the Cross from the ground and wrapped arms around his shoulders in a show of gratitude for a battle well fought. Within moments, the fight was being retold by witnesses, each giving their view of it. Walter found his eyes locked with Morbius' from across the crowd. The Lord of the Sile held out his hands. 'You see,' his motions said. Walter offered the faintest nod of his head before heading back to his tent.

"They were already gone when we arrived?" Hunter told the king and the princes when he arrived at the castle. "Though it seems they made a quick escape. As if they were suddenly warned of our coming."

The boys looked at each other, wondering ***if*** the secret had gotten out then how. Any number of people could have seen them preparing while they were still at the castle, but the thought that they may have a traitor in their midst was disturbing.

"Did they have someone watching their residence?" asked Branthony.

"Perhaps. We cannot say, but there's more," said Hunter. "We found several bodies. Only recently killed."

"They must have known something," said Joshua. "Killed to keep a secret."

"Yes," agreed Hunter. "The identity of whoever tipped them off."

"More crimes to add to the list. It is time," said Branthony. "Bring him in."

Hunter left momentarily, then returned, followed by two guards who had Meroth between them. Austin followed with a hand on the hilt of his sword. Also with them was Susan, who nodded to her brother and nephews but spoke no words. She moved toward the back of the room as though she were merely a spectator, though the boys now knew full well the extent of her powers. Then, to the surprise of the boys, flanked by her brothers, Michael and John, came their mother.

Debreace entered the room, and her children recognised the look on her face. She approached them and held out her arms. The four gathered close, and she spoke to them in hushed tones.

"My boys," she said with that gentle, comforting smile. "Look at you all. So grown up. I want you to know I am enormously proud of you all, but our job is not yet done. Do what you must. If this man is in any way responsible for the attempt on the life of one of my children, then I want to hear it come from his mouth."

They all nodded their acknowledgement. The queen moved to the side of the room without another word and took a seat. Her eyes were fixed on Meroth, once again, the boys knew not all of the steel and determination within them came from their father.

Meroth was placed on a seat with a guard on each side. Austin and Hunter remained close. Branthony stood directly before the man, who looked on in nervous silence. His eyes darted from the king to each of the boys.

Branthony looked to his Fourth-Born, who stepped forward, knowing he was being called upon once again. Jacob stood before the suspect and drew a breath, ready to ask his first question.

All eyes suddenly shot to the side as the doors again flew open. None of the room's occupants expected the Scroll-Master, his arms filled with scrolls and pots of ink with quills.

"Bolevard," said Branthony impatiently. "I did not summon you."

"I am aware, Your Majesty. However, I believed I may be of some assistance. If this man is indeed involved in the attempt on your son's life and is also a direct representative of a foreign nation, then perhaps it is best if this interrogation were recorded. I will take a transcript of what is said here today, and if indeed he is involved, we shall have a signed confession. I have prepared the necessary documentation."

Branthony considered Bolevard's words for a moment, then nodded. The Scroll-Master took a seat close to Meroth. "I best be sure to hear everything so as not to make a mistake," he said, preparing his equipment. It seemed to take an age as he fumbled with his scrolls and quills.

"Today, Scroll-Master," ordered the king.

"Of course, Your Majesty. Apologies. You may begin."

Branthony looked back at the prisoner.

"Meroth, we went to the pleasure house. The rest of your party was nowhere to be seen. In fact, they cannot be found anywhere within the city, though if they are still here, they will be found soon enough."

"I assure Your Majesty, they are here somewhere. What is this about? Why would they have cause to leave?"

Branthony had first intended to make these questions more subtle, not wishing to accuse directly if there was a chance a mistake had been made. The men from Varliant disappearing was almost proof enough, but not quite. The discovery of murdered bodies changed things.

"I believe they may have been tipped off that they are suspected of being involved in an attempt on my son's life."

The king's words and demeanour were far from the anger that the others knew he was feeling. Meroth opened his mouth to speak, but Branthony silenced him with a mere glare, and the man from Varliant was wise enough to take the hint. "They have fled, which could be a sign of their guilt. We may know soon enough."

"Your Majesty, I assure—"

"Stop. You will not give your answers to me. You will give them to my son. The son whose life assassins tried to take. Jacob."

Jacob was ready. He drew a deep breath. Using his Gift on demand no longer seemed to be a problem. Now for the question. Now for the truth.

"Was Varliant involved in the assassination attempt?"

"Absolutely not!" declared Meroth with certainty. Jacob didn't even use his Gift o compel him. The words came willingly. The answer completely changed the atmosphere of the room. Apart from the guards, each of the occupants looked at the others. It was not the response they had all expected.

"Who was responsible for the attempt?"

Meroth scoffed with outrage. "As far as I am aware, it was ***your*** people, not mine, that attempted to kill you."

Jacob was lost. This was the opposite of how he'd expected this to go.

"How is Varliant funding its recent rise? How is it that they suddenly have more gold than ever before? How do they plan on upholding all the deals they have made with the lords and merchants of the Cross?"

The question came from Branthony, who stepped in for his shaken son, but Meroth answered freely anyway.

"Prelim Vol is a magnificent leader. With his wisdom, he has guided Varliant from the ashes to become the power it is today. We have been nothing but honest in our dealings with the Cross and have made generous offers to any who wished to thrive through trade with our glorious city."

Branthony looked to his youngest son.

"He's telling the truth," Jacob said. "Everything he said is truthful."

"Of course I am telling the truth." Meroth seemed genuinely shocked, as though the mere prospect of lying was utterly alien to him. "We came here with nothing but good intentions, and despite our greatest efforts, you have spurned us. Now, even worse, you have accused us of a monstrous crime. My people will not take this insult lightly."

Branthony stared daggers into the man, unappreciative of his threatening tone, but there was an obvious shred of doubt. Had all this been a mistake?

The room again fell silent, and the Fait were undeniably off balance.

"If all this is true, then why have the rest of your friends run away?" asked Jacob.

"Perhaps they got wind of the lies laid against them and thought to flee before they found themselves in the position I am now in," argued Meroth with more than a bit of indignation. "Perhaps someone is setting us up. Those murdered could have exonerated my people, not condemned them."

"Funny that you were left here alone?" came Joshua's voice, and eyes turned toward him.

Instead of adding to his point, Joshua took a few steps away and turned his back on the group. Branthony and the other boys moved toward him and spoke in hushed voices so as not to be overheard.

"What are you thinking?" asked Aron.

"Is he immune to Jacob's Gift?" asked Luke "You're sure he's telling the truth, right?" Jacob nodded.

"Or at least he's telling ***his*** truth," Joshua said. "He believes everything he's saying. As far as he is concerned, he speaks no lies."

"What the hell does that mean?" asked Luke, confused.

Joshua shook his head and seemed to be in pain. He winced and closed his eyes. "My Gift is trying to talk to me, but it's too much. It's giving me a headache."

"I know the feeling," said Aron.

"Calm yourself, Son," said Branthony as he placed a comforting hand on Joshua's shoulder. "Do not try to force it. Let it come naturally.

He took a moment to compose himself. "If he thinks he's telling the truth, he's been lied to himself. It's no coincidence he was left here alone when the rest of his party escaped. He's been planted. They've fed him lies so that he can pass them forward when Jacob questions him."

"But that would mean they've planned against the Gift," said Luke. "How can they know so much?"

"Because they are not working alone," said Branthony, and all his sons looked to him, understanding his meaning. It all made sense.

Joshua grimaced against the pain of a headache again. "If the Crone knows how to work against the Gifts, she could be working against them now. Every move we make could be playing into her hands. How can we know what strategy to take? I can't…it's too much."

"Joshua," came Debreace's soft, calming voice. The boys turned to their mother. "Come here." He did so, and she hugged him. As they embraced, she whispered in his ear. "I may not have a Gift, but I know my children. You're straining yourself. Your Gift is trying to form a strategy, a plan. That's what Guidance does. But there are too many variables right now. There's no way we can plan properly, Gift or not. Don't push yourself. Relax. This is not the time to form a plan. That time will come."

She released him, and he smiled at her. Sometimes, even though they were all meant to be so special, their mother seemed to make the most sense and know what to do. "You're right," he said. "Thank you, Mother."

"He said not to trust you," Meroth's voice cut through their meeting.

"Who?" asked Branthony.

"Salvadire. Before coming to your country, Salvadire expressed his misgivings about our journey. He said the men of the Cross could not be trusted, but Lord Vol insisted we give you the benefit of the doubt. Is this what Salvadire suspected? Is this how the people of the Cross treat others? Is this how goodwill and the offer of friendship are met? You are so fond of asking questions, but can you answer any of mine? Here is one more. If you are so certain of the accusations you have laid against my people, then where is your proof? I have yet to see any form of evidence that anyone from Varliant was in any way involved in the attempt on your son's life."

There was another moment of silence, and Meroth let his gaze fall on everyone in the room. Somehow, it suddenly seemed as though he were the one in charge.

"I will find you your proof," insisted Branthony. "Then we will talk again."

"Am I to be kept here against my will? Is this yet more of the hospitality of the Fait? Another showing of the great power of the Cross, to hold one man accused of a crime he did not commit, with not a shred of evidence. When even your son has declared my words truthful."

Those words stung them all.

"You are to be detained within the castle for the time being whilst we investigate," said Branthony. "You will have every comfort that can be offered."

"You will find no evidence against my people because we are not guilty of the crimes of which we are accused," Meroth pleaded.

"We will see," said Branthony, walking from the room. He knew that if Meroth was right, he, Branthony, had just made a terrible mistake that could have even worse consequences.

When all had left the room, leaving Meroth behind with guards, Branthony turned to them all. "We need to keep this quiet for the moment, but what we really need is evidence. We ***need*** it!"

"If we need proof, then the answer is simple," said Joshua, who was getting over the headache, though he still seemed a little unwell. "The gold," he announced as though it were obvious. "They left in a hurry. They cannot have taken the gold. Someone somewhere can tie that gold directly to Varliant. We follow the gold. We find our proof."

By the time Aron climbed into bed, the night was late. Pulling his covers over himself, he lay in the bed, the candles casting a gentle light. He stared at one of the small flames as it flickered, keeping the darkness at bay. His eyes began to close as he drifted into the dream world.

When he opened them once again his vision was impaired. Rain poured from the heavens in huge drops. His hair stuck to his head as he tried to blink away the water that flowed into his eyes. He thought of his mother's stories of the storm that accompanied his birth.

He looked around. Where was he? The lights and sounds of the city were around him, but all was dulled and misshapen by the rain. He was in the middle of a cobbled road. Buildings stood to either side, but he didn't recognise them. He tried to hold a hand against the rain, but it did little.

"Hello!" he called, but no one answered. "Hello! Anyone!"

He walked against the rain as it drove into him. Warm lights were coming from a nearby tavern. The noise from inside began to spill out as he got closer. The sound of men cheering and whooping, whilst others booed and shouted in anger. Aron heard glass smashing, and a moment later, the door to the tavern flew open. Men began to fall out into the street and the pouring rain in a mass brawl. Fists flew and feet stomped. Blood began to join the deluge that ran down the cobbles. Through the chaos, Aron saw Luke emerge from the door. He ducked and dived through the madness, deftly avoiding any contact heading his way. Aron called out after his younger brother, but if Luke could hear him, he paid him no mind. Once Luke had put a little distance between himself and the brawl, he turned and ran from the chaos. Aron tried to follow but suddenly found himself back in his bed.

He panted and felt his body and bed sheets, expecting them to be soaked with rain. He was warm and dry.

"What does it mean?" he asked himself. Perhaps just as important was when? When would it come to pass? He grabbed his quill and began to write.

INVESTIGATIONS

"Why was I in a tavern?" asked Luke the next morning as Aron relayed his dream to his brothers. It was obvious that Luke found the prospect exciting. Aron held vivid memories after writing them down. The only problem was that despite remembering the dream quite well, he still had no idea what it meant. Why had he seen that particular moment?

"I don't know," Aron replied. "Maybe it was just to get out of the rain."

"So why were you out on the street?"

Aron could only shake his head again. "I don't know, but the dream must be trying to tell me something."

"Do you remember anything else?" asked Joshua. "How old did he look? What was he wearing? Is this something that's coming sooner or later?"

"Soon, I think. I can't remember what Luke wore, but he didn't exactly look like a prince."

"Well, none of us look like princes at the moment," said Jacob as he pulled on his top. They stood in the torchlight, underground. A rope was before them that they'd need to climb to exit the secret tunnel beneath the castle wall. They left their tunics, leggings and fine boots, replacing them with clothes that would blend in with the city's people.

"Well, it doesn't help us now, does it?" said Luke as he approached the rope and began pulling himself up. He reached the top, unclasped the trap door and pushed it open before disappearing, forgetting his duty to lean back in and help the others up.

Aron helped his other younger brothers up before making his own climb. Once the trap door was shut again, the boys went through the gardens and soon emerged into the city beyond.

"So where now?" asked Jacob.

"I don't care," replied Luke, "I'm just glad to get out of the castle for a while. It feels like an age since we've managed to get away fro there. All the lords and ladies prancing about like they own the place. Acting like they're the ones in charge of us. It's been chaos even without assassins and interrogations. I need a break from it all."

"We're here to do a job," Aron reminded him.

"Yeah, but it's still better than being in there."

"It's about time you lot showed up," said Joe. The boys smiled as he and Ollie approached. They all embraced one another. Strangely, they still saw each other often, but they had most of their interactions now on the other side of the castle walls. Something about being out in the city together made them all feel free.

"So, what's the plan?" asked Joe.

"Simple, really," said Joshua. "The one lead we have is the gold. Someone somewhere must have dealt with the men from Varliant directly. We need to find a link. So, the first thing we need to do is find someone who's got some of it. Hunter said they were paying in random gold items. Things like that must stand out. We ask around, see if anyone's been spotted with anything of the sort."

"What if folk don't wanna talk," said Joe, only to find himself gently nudged by Ollie, who used both hands flattened out to indicate Jacob. "Oh yeah, silly me. But this could get dangerous. We start asking after gold and following its trail. Folks'll think we want it for ourselves. Besides, Chris here starts asking questions that people can't lie to, and someone will cotton on quickly."

"Joe's right," said Aron, looking to Jacob, whose alias was Chris. "We need to be careful."

"So where do we start?" asked Jacob.

"Easy," answered Joe. "We ask the best source of information in the entire city."

"Who's that then?" enquired Joshua.

"We go to the minstrel."

Ollie tapped Aron, then waved his arm in a wide arc, a follow-me gesture, and they did without question.

The minstrel was young. He sat tuning his lute, twisting the nobs at the end of the wooden neck whilst plucking the strings till they gave out just the right note. According to Ollie and Joe, the minstrel knew everything there was to know about happenings within the city. He played in all the taverns and on every street. Everyone knew him. He was part of and overheard many conversations. If anyone knew anything, it would be him.

The boys had to wait until he finished a song on a street corner, then wait longer as he collected the coins thrown his way. He was talented. They'd supposedly had the finest minstrels in the kingdom come to play at court, yet all four princes thought this performance was as good as any they'd seen before.

Finally, as the crowd dissipated, they took their chance to approach.

"You're the minstrel?" asked Aron.

The minstrel looked around sarcastically. "Really," he said, eyes and mouth opened wide. "Is that me? Oh well, I'm glad someone cleared that up. There I was thinking that perhaps I was the king."

"Very funny," said Luke, annoyed by the attitude. Of all the boys, he was still the one who had the hardest time remembering that out here, they were normal. People had no reason to show them any extra courtesy.

"Relax, my friend. I only jest. Yes, I am the minstrel. One of many, I'm afraid. My friends call me Mini for short. Helps define me from the others I find."

"Mini the minstrel," said Luke with a grin.

"Easy to remember, whilst my performance is hard to forget."

"Isn't that the same thing?" asked Joshua.

"Not at all, my friend. Not at all. One is easy to recall when required, the other is hard to get out of your mind. Replaying itself over and over. Now, what can I do for you, fine young sirs?"

"We're looking for gold," said Joe bluntly.

'Aren't we all," replied Mini with an extravagant wave of the hand.

"Not just any gold. Gold that's been formed into random objects. Not coins, other stuff. Everyday stuff you'd never expect to see in solid gold."

That got Mini's attention. He glanced around a little nervously, then stepped closer and whispered.

"I'll warn you now, this is a dangerous path you're treading. Did you not hear about the damned mess a week back? What a disaster. The streets ran red with blood because of this gold. The king himself was fighting out on the cobbles. Insanity, I tell you."

"We know all about it," Jacob said, repressing the memories.

"Then you know how many are already dead because of this gold. Not much good being the richest man in the graveyard."

"We don't want the gold, we want to know where it came from," said Aron.

"Haven't you heard the rumours? It belongs to the Fait. They keep it all to themselves and forge it into these things to mock the rest of us with their vast wealth."

"Do you believe that?" asked Jacob, opening his Gift a little to listen for the truth.

"I grew up in Silden. It was one of the city's worst areas not too long ago. The Fait commissioned the building of new homes and an orphanage. All at the expense of the Crown. My family had a home thanks to them. So no, I don't believe the same people that would do that would also hoard enough wealth to build the whole damned city again."

"Have you seen any of it?" asked Joe.

Mini sighed and looked saddened in the process. "Unfortunately, yes. Though nothing too grand. There was a dice and some playing cards. Perfect, shiny little things they were. The engravings on the cards were as detailed as if the finest artist had painted them. A friend of mine came into possession of them, and now that friend is dead. So again, I warn of the dangers of pursuing this course."

"Can you point us toward someone? Anyone who may know more about where it came from."

"Check down near Ingles Way. It's a rough part of town, usually only home to orphans and urchins, that's where I saw the items. I'll tell you now, some of the lads down there won't hesitate to stick a blade in you for coppers, never mind gold. They were already falling out over it. I left them to it."

"Thank you," said Joshua.

"Ah, think nothing of it. However, I am not hard to find if you should happen across any of this gold and wish to repay my kindness. Perhaps then I could buy myself a new lute worthy of the song I am composing. The story of the Four-Born. It shall be my masterpiece. On second thought, ***some*** gold isn't worth the trouble it brings."

On any other day or time, they would have stayed to ask questions about this so-called masterpiece, but Mini was already packing his belongings, and the boys had more pressing issues. "Remember," he called as they were leaving, and all the showmanship had faded. He looked at them with stern, serious eyes. "Whatever this gold is, it's cursed. I've lost friends to it. Families are torn apart. I meant what I said. Some gold is not worth the trouble. You can't spend it in the afterlife."

They nodded yet were undeterred.

Morbius walked through the village with his usual effortless swagger, laughing and joking with his men. He had a relaxed way with them, but all knew he could turn in an instant if the situation called for it. His easy-going nature had fooled many who thought they could push him. They soon discovered otherwise. Shimmer was close by as always. He was a man whom no one would mistakenly believe was easygoing.

As they approached the edge of the village that joined with the camp of the Cross, Morbius noticed a large number of his men grouped together, laughing. They all looked over into the camp.

"What are they doing?" asked Morbius.

"They come to watch the Cross men train," answered Shimmer. "They always train at this time of day."

Morbius squinted as he looked up at the blazing sun. "It's boiling," he exclaimed. He pushed through the crowd of his men to investigate and saw that Shimmer was right. In organised ranks stood the men of the Cross, running training drills! They wore full mail over gambeson, and some had armour on top of that. At their head stood Sir Walter, roaring commands.

"He's going to train them to death," said Morbius. Right on cue, one of the men fell to the dirt, exhausted. The Sile laughed as he was carted away toward the river for a drink.

Morbius strode over the makeshift line that signalled the edge of the camp. That easy-going nature had now gone.

"What in the sands do you think you're doing?" he growled to Walter. He kept his voice low so as not to be heard. Mindful not to undermine the man before his men, yet his voice clearly showed his anger.

"It is called training," said Walter, matter-of-factly. He kept his eyes on his men and called another order. They responded with perfectly timed swings of their blades. Morbius saw the synchronicity of their movements from the corner of his eye and had to hide how taken aback he was.

"It's midday, the sun is at its hottest."

"The enemy may come at any time. We must be prepared to fight in all conditions."

"What if the enemy comes in an hour. Your men won't be fit for a damned thing."

Walter paused and finally looked at him. "Then we will rely on the Sile, after all, they have barely lifted a finger since we arrived. They should be plenty rested."

"Is this for our benefit? I assure you that any point you are trying to prove is missed."

"This has nothing to do with you or your men. This is to do with my men and the people of this village. I want them ready. I want the people to see that we are ready to protect them should the need arise, that we have not simply come here to enjoy the weather and their hospitality."

"All they see is fools cooking themselves. They see a man so determined to impress that he works his men to death."

Walter grunted and turned his attention back to the training.

"Fine, do as you will. Don't blame me when your men revolt. You dare to tell me the challenge was foolish."

He turned and walked back to his waiting Sile.

"Leave them to it," cried one of his men. "Gives us something to watch." They all laughed except Morbius. He was about to walk away from them all, his good mood abruptly ended when he heard Walter bellow.

"Last exercise.'

Some short, sharp commands followed this. Morbius turned back to watch as they executed a marvellous manoeuvre. The men in the heavier armour stepped to the front, chopping down in unison as the others stepped back before thrusting forward between the first line. They all skirted backwards, lifting their shields into a tight interlocking formation.

They shouted a great 'Harum,' sound as spears propelled through gaps in powerful thrusts before being pulled back. The spears came three more times, the unified call of the men accompanying each thrust, followed by downward sword swings from the front men. It was done with such precision and timing that it seemed like a dance.

Morbius watched it all with wide eyes before Walter called an end, and his men gratefully dropped their weapons and removed their armour, heading straight to the nearest water source. The other Sile, Morbius noticed, had suddenly stopped laughing. One or two, he thought, looked rather sheepish, or was it impressed? Morbius locked eyes with Walter. What was that look? Was it...gratitude?

Ingles Way was undoubtedly one of those areas of the city where you wouldn't want to be caught at night. The boys asked around, leaving Joe and Ollie to do most of the work. Although the four of them had become reasonably well-known amongst the youngsters who called the streets of the Centre home, Ollie and Joe were still far more familiar faces. The kids talked to them openly and easily, which saved Jacob from having to use his Gift. The more they could find without it, the better. Ollie nodded, watching intently so he could read lips. It was much easier with people on the other side of the castle wall. They spoke clearly, out here in the city everyone talked in slang or dialect or with a thicker accent. He could still read them but had to concentrate a little more.

It didn't take long to get a lead. Someone had been making too much noise lately, and word had gotten out. A boy named Marcus. Their questions led them to an old, abandoned building near the river. Once used to store goods coming fresh off the boats that sailed down the river, it was now more of a charred shell after a fire. The boys remembered Father talking about a massive fire in the city not too long ago. He was redistributing funds to help rebuild, and it was obvious why such a thing was needed. But one man's loss is another man's gain, and the city's youngsters had turned the remains into their newest playground.

"You, Marcus? " Joe asked the ginger-haired boy surrounded by a small group of girls as though he were a handsome prince, and they would be his suitors.

"Maybe, who wants to know?"

"My name is Joseph."

"My name is Joseph," the boy mimicked in a joking impression of a posh voice, causing his little group of admirers to giggle. For a second, Joe looked embarrassed. Like his brother, spending time in the castle was starting to rub off on him. "The name's Joe," he said, his accent and tone much different. "And I wanna talk to you."

"Oh yeah, so do allot'o people."

"You the one who claims to have gold?"

"Nah," he said with a shake of his head. "You've got me mixed up with someone else. So be off with ya."

Jacob leaned towards Joe's ear and whispered. "He's lying."

Joe nodded, though he could have guessed as much. "Listen. We don't want your gold. We've just got some questions?"

The boy rubbed his teeth together as he seemed to consider them. His eyes glanced at the girls around him, who all awaited his response. When he looked back at the six boys staring at him, one of them in the form of Ollie, who was exceptionally tall for a boy his age, and the other in the shape of Aron, who was older and had a scowl that was becoming particularly threatening, the boy considered his options limited.

"Gi'me a second, will you ladies?" The group of girls around him, none of whom looked any older than Jacob, giggled and smiled as he walked away from them. He ushered the group further away and spoke in a hushed voice. "Look, I don't know what you've heard, but the gold I had was a tiny amount. A lot to me, yeah, but I may have…erm… exaggerated the size of it to others, if you get my drift." He offered a nod of his head towards the girls.

"What are we talking about here?" asked Jacob. "A boot, a baby's rattle," he said, recalling some of the items Hunter had mentioned. The boy scowled.

"What, no! It was some dice. Just small golden dice. Weighed no more than a few coins. There were some gold cards as well, but I never got my hands on them. I sold the dice days ago and spent the money quick. I may've exaggerated the size of the gold to some, and I may've been, let's say, a little frivolous with the money afterwards." He said the words whilst rubbing the back of his head with one hand, clearly a little embarrassed. "May've tried to impress a few people," he said with a red-faced, awkward smile.

"Where did you get it?" asked Joshua. "How did the dice come into your possession?"

"Would ya listen to'im," said Marcus with a smile and a sideways nod. "Lad thinks he's come straight out the castle."

It was Joshua's turn to look embarrassed. "Where'd you get it?" he asked again, returning to his practised accent.

Marcus considered his answer for a moment. "See, the thing is, the money I got for it is gone. So, if you kind fellas could perhaps pay for such information, then maybe it'd jog my memory."

"You cheeky—" Luke stepped forward, fist raised, but Aron held him back.

"Relax, ***Dave***," said Aron, reverting to their chosen fake names. A moment later, he held a few coppers in his hand. The boys had learnt not to go out without a little something on them, but they'd also learnt from one of their first times out in the city that gold can attract the wrong type of attention. It made their current investigation a little ironic. Marcus scowled at the amount yet took it anyway.

"Well, ya see, I kinda stole it, but not from anyone who needed it," he hastily added.

"Who doesn't need gold?" asked Joshua.

"That's easy. A dead man." The boys looked at each other, remembering Mini's story. "Well, he was supposed to be dead," said Marcus. "No one'd seen him in weeks, and when I saw him, he was in a right old state. Been stabbed. Bleeding like a stuck pig."

"So, he's alive, the one you stole from?" said Joe. "Who is it? We need a name?"

"Erm, first, I consider it payment, not theft, for dragging him to the stitchers, but technically, yeah. A fella named Hursty. He was a common sight round'ere and down near Old Hill before he disappeared. I'd assumed he hadn't made it but wrd is he's back. I ain't seen him myself. Kinda been avoiding him, for obvious reasons, but apparently, he's returned to the city, been spotted at some of his old hangouts. He's a demon for card games, ya see. Loves to play, and pretty damned good too. Especially as he's only the same age as me, it's the only reason they let him in most o'the time. Plays for money and, well, he may need some on account of his gold going missing."

"So," said Aron. "We head there and find this Hursty."

By the time they reached Old Hill, the afternoon was drawing on. The boys knew they were taking risks by staying out of the castle grounds this long. Even worse, they were a distance away from home.

"So, what do we do now?" Joe asked as they walked the streets, which were starting to clear as people made their way home for the evening. The sky had clouded, and it now looked certain to rain at any moment.

The entire group looked around, hoping something would jump out. It was one of those rare, fortuitous moments when fate intervened.

"That's the spot," said Aron.

They all stopped and looked as Aron pointed at a tavern. A worn wooden sign swung and creaked on its hinges in the wind. It read 'The Tapping Foot.'

"That's the place I saw in my dream. That's gotta be where we've got to go."

"So, what now?" asked Joshua.

"Easy," said Luke, strutting across the cobbles as though he owned the very ground beneath his feet. He walked straight to the door, pushed it open and headed in. The others looked at each other in shock before quickly following.

Inside, the light was dimmed, and a stink of sweat and worse was in the air. The place was busy. Men and women filled chairs and stools around a large room, someone was shouting off about "the damned Fait keeping all the money for em'selves." It seemed the false rumours had spread beyond those who'd attacked Jacob.

A large man with a dirty apron and a rag tossed over his shoulder approached the boys.

"Hey, what are you lot doin in'ere? This ain't no place for kids. You two are no problem," he said, looking at Aron and Ollie. "But the rest o'yous can Bugger off."

"Piss off," spat Luke, and the others would swear their jaws hit the floor. They looked at him as though he'd gone crazy. Joshua choked down a cough and looked at his brother with a mix of disgust and adulation.

"What did you say you cheeky little—"

"You see that guy there?" Luke pointed off behind the man, who turned to see the source of Luke's attention. "That's my da, and he said we better come'ere and wait for him. He said we ain't to leave until he says so."

The man turned back to them, and they could all see the doubt in his eyes.

"You're Mergo's kids?"

"Yeah, that's right. Mergo's kids."

"All of you?"

"Yeah. What of it?"

"Bloody hell, your mum must be knackered," he said with a hint of suspicion. "So, how is your mum?"

Luke paused for the slightest second before putting his hands out to his side and lifting his shoulders. "Drunk," he said with confidence.

The man stared at him before bellowing with laughter.

"Well, I suppose she'd have to be to put up with Mergo for a husband. Never mind six kids?" Another loud laugh escaped the man, and the boys nervously joined in. "Well, Mergo's here for the game. He's a good player, your old man." He drew in breath through his teeth, considering his options. "Right, you lot stay out of the way, all right. I don't wanna hear a sound from you, and don't be distracting your da, you'ear! And don't be tryin to elp'im."

He ushered them into a corner and began collecting mugs.

"How did you do that?" asked Joe, more than a little impressed.

"I just pointed at someone and hoped for the best," answered Luke with a cocky smile.

"You don't even have to think about using your Gift, do you?" said Aron with raw jealousy. "It all just comes easy for you."

"He doesn't even know he's using it," added Joshua.

"Hey," said Luke with a shrug of the shoulders. "Don't get mad. What can I say, I'm just talented."

Ollie suddenly pointed into the room, and the attention of those sitting around it focused on a table in the centre. Several people started to take seats around it, and each handed over a small pouch to the man that Luke had so deftly tricked.

"This must be the 'game' he was talking about. It's a card game," said Luke, looking on hungrily.

Ollie began another round of pointing whilst tapping enthusiastically on his brother's shoulder.

"Look," said Joe. "The player on the left. He's barely older than us. That could be our guy."

The boys watched as the spectators started handing over their money, placing bets on who would come out on top. Finally, a large deck of cards was brought out and the dealer took centre stage, speaking loudly so the whole tavern could hear.

"Right people. The game is Fait's Gambit." Luke drew a gasp, grabbing his brothers in excitement. "Each game will go down to the last two players, the one that doesn't get rid of all his cards, well, someone may have to be kind enough to buy'em a drink after, eh?"

The crowd laughed and jeered as the players stared each other out with different demeanours.

"The last game will be a one-on-one and the winner..." the dealer paused for dramatic effect. "Will take it all!" The crowd erupted again. "So, ladies and gentlemen, you can bet on each round, and you can also bet on the overall winner. Odds are on the board." He pointed to a large chalkboard with different names and odds scrawled on it. "But get your bets in quick because the game is about to start."

Joshua pointed out that one of the names on the board read 'H.'

"Oh, this is gonna be good," Luke announced with a smile. "Get comfortable, boys."

The cards were dealt. Three cards to each player face down, three face up, and three in their hands. The players changed any cards in their hands for the face-up cards on the table, and then the game began. It was played at a furious pace. One player after another threw down cards, the play moving in a circle around the table. It didn't take long before the players moved on to their table cards. The first player to get rid of all his cards was the youngest. The one the boys were watching. He laughed loudly as he placed his last card down, then sat back in his chair, hands clasped behind his head. He ordered a drink, and the barman obliged despite the boy looking no older than Joshua. The boy gulped it down with practised efficiency.

The game went down to the last two. The only woman at the table, named Sarah according to the blackboard, gracefully pushed her dark hair back before throwing down a king. The man couldn't beat it. He stood from his chair as though about to protest or more, but the crowd and those working at the tavern quickly forced him to think otherwise.

Once the crowd had quietened, the woman retook her seat, and the dealer collected the cards and began to shuffle.

The barman came wandering around again, collecting mugs, some of which the boys noticed were still half full, but he swept them away anyway. When disgruntled customers began to look for their drinks in the chaos and were unsure where they'd gone, they started waving for a fresh one. When the barman came over with a fresh round in his hands, carrying several at once in a perfected motion, Luke dared to shout out to him.

"Hey," he called, and the barman looked their way. "The young player, on the left. What's his name?"

"Him, that's our phoenix. Risen from the ashes to claim his throne. Already caused quite a few upsets, so your dad better be careful." He pointed at the blackboard. "Name on the boards 'H.'" he said.

"H for Hursty," said Joshua. "Risen from the ashes. That's gotta be our man."

The next few games were played, and the players began to fall. Half the bar cheered each time someone advanced to the next round, while the other half booed. The situation worsened with each round, and the barman had to fight hard to keep everyone calm.

All too soon for Luke, the tournament reached its conclusion. The next game would be the last. Mergo went through first, and the boys found themselves cheering along with him to keep their cover and because without him in the game, they'd have to leave without getting the chance to speak to Hursty.

Sarah and 'H' were the only ones left. It was a close game, but Hursty, as the boys became more certain of his real name, claimed the victory. Sarah stood with a smile and gave a gracious bow to the room, where everyone cheered.

"Well then," said Hursty loudly. "Shall we get this over with?"

The final game moved fast. Many had left the tavern after losing their bets. Those left crowded in close, even the boys had dared to leave their designated corner. The tension was palpable. Men gripped at small betting slips, as though their whole lives were on the line. If some had placed bets at the beginning of the tournament, they could be set to win a substantial amount. Not that the barman seemed concerned. He grinned ear to ear in the corner, counting the winnings of the house so far.

"The game is almost up," said Aron. "Once it's finished, we need to get to Hursty and ask him some questions."

"Looking at the game, Mergo should have this," said Joshua.

Hursty glanced around the room as though weighing up the spectators. "What do you think?" he asked the room. "He's only got one card left. Can I stop him?"

There was a mixture of support and discouragement. Hursty turned to his opponent and looked Mergo dead in the eye. "You got a good card there?" he asked as though he was discussing something as mundane as the weather. Mergo only grinned in response, ready to play his card and finish the game.

Hursty played his card.

Mergo slammed his down on top of it. A Fait. The highest card in the game.

Half the crowd erupted into cheers and applause, hugging and congratulating each other in a drunken stupor, while the other half wilted and dipped their heads in disappointment.

"Wait," said Hursty, he had a lopsided grin that seemed ever-present. "I think you'd better check that last card again, my friend." The room fell quiet again, and Mergo looked on with sudden horror. Slowly, he reached his hand toward the table, grabbed the Fait card he'd played and lifted it. There, staring up into the room for all to see, was a Knight. A Gifted card. It meant the next card played had to be of the same or lesser value. A Fait card could not be played on top of it.

"That means you pick up, my friend."

That spelt the end for Mergo. It was all over soon after that. The cheers and groans in the room completely swapped as victory was pulled from the grasp of one side and handed to the other.

Mergo stared on with murder in his eyes.

"Be calm, Mergo," ordered the barman, and his associates began to crowd around, ready for any trouble.

Mergo stared at them all, then back to Hursty and with one final scowl, shouted, "To hell with you. I'm going home!"

He stormed from the tavern to a round of laughter aimed at the sore loser.

"Wait here," said Luke, and he ran after him, screaming, "Da." The others looked to each other, Ollie putting his hands up by his sides in a 'what's he doing?' gesture. None of them had an answer. They waited nervously, knowing they only had a few short minutes before they were told to leave. Then Luke ran back inside, wet from the heavy rain that had started falling.

"Where'd you go?" asked Aron.

"Just stood outside for a minute. Gotta keep up the charade."

"For what?"

"I can beat him," said Luke with confidence. He approached the table where Hursty was still celebrating and counting his vast winnings. "My da, erm… Mergo. He sent me in here?"

"He hasn't got his son to come beg for his money back, has he? I've seen some pathetic moves, but this one's new," Hursty laughed, or coughed, it was hard to tell, but those around laughed with him. It was one of those delightfully infectious laughs that encouraged others to join in.

"No," said Luke, drawing up a seat and sitting opposite him. "He sent me in to play a game with you."

"Really?" answered Hursty, sitting forward and putting his elbows on the table. Luke merely stared back. "Well, you've got to have something to bet if you're gonna play."

"How about this?" Luke placed a dagger on the table, beautifully ornate with solid, sharp steel. It had a small scabbard with a horn hilt and a small jewel. Hursty wasn't the only one suddenly paying attention, though he was the one who Luke pushed it to for inspection. After scrutinising it, he slid it back across the table.

Aron leaned down and whispered in his brother's ear. "Where'd that come from?"

"I never leave the castle without it. Not since that time that we got chased through the old market."

"How much do I have to wager?" asked Hursty loudly, cutting in on their conversation.

"How about everything you've won tonight?"

"Ha," he baulked. "It's a nice knife, but it ain't that nice."

"All right, how about this? You only bet what you won from Merg... My da. But if I win. You answer some questions."

Hursty tilted his head at Luke, distrustful. For a moment, the boys thought he wouldn't go for it, but his greed got the better of him. "All right!" he shouted, laughing again. "We have one last game for you all." A new round of bets started, and the barman was all too happy to take more of people's money, though the boys noticed that nearly everyone wanted to bet on Hursty. When the odds were written on the board Luke was a far outsider.

The dealer shuffled the cards and was about to start when a massive crack of thunder shook the building. "Bloody hell," someone muttered, and now people began to notice the heavy rain as it pounded the cobbles outside.

"Oh no," declared Aron, suddenly realising how late it was and how overdue they were. He turned to Joshua and Jacob. "You two, get back home," he ordered.

"But we want—"

"No arguing. We're in too deep to walk away now, but you two need to get back. Run as fast as you can. At least all four of us won't be knocking on Death's Door."

"We'll go with them," said Joe as he signalled to Ollie that they were leaving. Ollie looked none too happy about it.

"It's pouring down," declared Jacob with misery.

"Tough luck," declared Aron, pushing one younger brother after another. "And Joshua." He took a deep breath, not quite believing he was about to say the words. "You may have to send someone for us."

"What?! " Declaring that they had been out of the castle grounds, revealing their secret, and likely ending their excursions did not sound like a good idea, not to mention the thought of their father's wrath.

"I've got a bad feeling about this," declared Aron. "My vision, the fight."

"Then put an end to it. Grab Luke and let's go."

"How many times have I got to tell you? We have to fight our battles. We can't leave. The game already started. Besides, we still need answers."

"Not ***all*** battles have to be fought."

Aron thought of his vision. They had to mean something. He had to see this through.

"We're staying," he declared with finality.

"I'll do what I can," Joshua sighed.

"Good, now go."

Aron pushed his brothers out into the rain, Ollie and Joe joining them, and they quickly disappeared into the deluge. He turned back to the inside; the game was underway, and both players were moving swiftly. The pickup pile had grown rapidly.

Aron moved to his brother's side but did not interfere. He kept glancing around the room. If his vision was right, this whole tavern would erupt into a fight at any moment.

The game moved into its latter stages, and the tension grew. Both players had made their opponent pick up several times, and it was apparent they were both good. Hursty played the more tactical game, yet the cards fell Luke's way.

Luke moved on to his last three down turned cards. One by one, they revealed themselves to be the perfect cards needed to beat his opponents' moves. Hursty watched with dismay as Luke beat him every time, despite placing high and powerful cards

Hursty moved to his down-facing cards; he needed something good. Luke was on his last card but had yet to see it. Hursty's hand drifted toward his left card.

"You sure?" said Luke. His stomach was doing flips. A feeling gripped him. He had memories of Boxy, the Stable-Master. Luke had once accidentally used his Gift on Boxy, which felt the same. Fortune could only go so far. His Gift was telling him the card Hursty was about to pick would be very bad for Luke's chances of winning. He pushed his thought at the feeling, urging his Gift outward. Could he influence others? Make them do things that would benefit him? That's what seemed to have happened with Boxy.

Hursty's hand suddenly moved to the centre card. He turned it.

A Peasant. A good card at almost any other time in the game. It was Gifted and could allow a player to make a move. It also meant the game reverted to the lowest value card. Luke couldn't lose. He turned his card. Man-at-Arms. Not that it mattered. The game was done.

The crowd fell silent and almost seemed puzzled by the result, looking at the cards as though they didn't make sense. Hursty looked on with a furrowed brow and an open mouth. He turned his left-hand card, which he would have chosen if not for Luke's influence. A queen. It would have made Luke pick up.

Aron stood at the ready, expecting the outpouring of violence. It didn't come. The crowd seemed to drift away, some to collect their winnings, others to get another drink and drown their sorrows, and others to head off into the storm to go home. The whole thing seemed like a lacklustre event, an anti-climax. Hursty sat at the table, staring at the played cards, wondering what had happened.

"You can keep your winnings," said Luke in a low voice and finally Hursty looked up.

"What? Why?"

"Answer me some questions, and you can keep your money."

"What questions?"

"You had a golden dice. Where'd you get it?"

Hursty's face scrunched up again. It was hard to tell what had confused him more, the game's result or Luke's question.

"How'd you know about that? What's it to you?"

"Doesn't matter. You can either pay up or answer the question."

"Did they send you? Is that why you're here?"

"Did who send us?" said Aron, confused.

Despite the great offer, Hursty seemed to think about it for a moment, as though suspecting some trap. Ultimately, his desire for coin and Aron and Luke's confusion seemed to win him over. He drew his coins off the table and stashed them away.

"I won it. In a game."

"Who from?"

Hursty released a breath, and it was evident he was still unsure of answering. Luke held out a hand for his winnings, and Hursty recoiled as though it were poisonous.

"All right, all right. There was a group hosting games down by the docks. They had more gold than anyone knew what to do with, and they weren't afraid to gamble it. So, I thought I'd go down and relieve them of some."

"Who were they?" asked Luke, suddenly wishing his little brother were here to verify the truth of Hursty's words.

Hursty paused again. It was easy to see he was nervous. More than nervous. Downright scared was more like it.

"How do I know you're not in with them?"

"We don't know who 'they' are. That's what we're trying to find out if you'd spit it out already." Luke slapped two hands on the table, his impatience pushing through.

"Well, they didn't exactly want it to be known. They were here on some official business or something. No one knew who they were playing until they got to the table."

"Who was it?" the boys said in unison.

Hursty leaned over the table, his head only inches from theirs. "The Varliants," he whispered, eyes darting as though expecting to see one of them standing over his shoulder.

Luke's face lit up. "I knew it," he declared.

"You," said Aron. "Come with us. We need to—"

The barman blocked out his voice as he shouted, "Mergo! You've taught your son well. He's only gone and won you your money back."

Aron and Luke looked to the door in horror as Mergo stumbled back in, drenched from the rain.

"Son?" he asked. "What son? I ain't got a son? I'm only back coz the old lady locked me out again for losing all our money."

The barman looked at Luke, still sitting at the table but now looking altogether less confident.

One of the crowd pushed forward, a large man, beard dripping with spilt drink, as he held up a fist. "Is this some kind of hustle? You tell everyone the little rascal is Mergo's boy, so everyone bets against him when really, you've brought in some pro! I want my money back!"

"It's not like that!" declared the barman, grabbing a bat from below the bar and holding it up as a threat. "And no refunds!" he declared. It wasn't enough, and just like that, chaos ensued.

Something smashed, and bodies suddenly pushed together in a mass brawl of fists and feet. Chairs and mugs were soon added along with shouts, grunts and insults. Luke looked to Aron, who pointed to the door, but a pile of brawling men separated them. Some decided this fight wasn't for them and moved to the sides to watch with shouts of support and amusement whilst staying safely away from any trouble. Others tried to do the same and suddenly found themselves dragged into the violence. Others made for the exit. Aron pushed along with them. He called for his brother but suddenly lost sight of him.

Luke ducked low as the fighting surrounded him. He felt like a mouse in a house of cats as the bigger men brawled, some reaching for him as he seemingly became the source of their anger. Luke felt calm despite the threat of injury, the urgency and the downright danger of being squarely in the middle of a mass brawl. He made to follow Aron outside. Ducking, diving, twisting, and pulling, he found his way to the door. As he stepped out into the rain, the madness followed him. He decided to move low just as a chair came crashing through the murky window, leaving glass and wood on the cobbled floor.

A fist came toward him, but at that exact moment, he slipped on a wet cobble, the fist flying past his head harmlessly.

Someone had decided that fists weren't enough and produced a knife, slashing wildly at anyone who came close. He stepped in Luke's direction, but just as the young prince seemed to be in danger, two other men, tussling together, crashed into the knifeman's back.

A boot came swinging upward as someone kicked out, but a moment before it connected, Luke tumbled backwards, tripping over a now-unconscious figure on the floor. He did a backwards roll and came back to his feet. A knock on the back sent him stumbling forward as a man charged the position, where he had stood just a split second before. Luke couldn't help the laugh that escaped him.

He turned and forced his way through the fighting. Any time a threat seemed to come near him, some small yet all so significant action would take place, pushing him from danger. Luke knew his Gift was working hard to keep him from harm. He had never seen Fortune work in such a way. His whole body seemed to tingle with adrenaline and something far more powerful. The prince revelled in it. Using Fortune to play cards now seemed a trivial thing.

The whole experience lasted less than a minute, and Luke found himself at the edge of the fighting, staring back at the chaos and laughing. Despite being the one who had caused it in many ways, all attention seemed to have diverted away from him. He was about to make his escape when he spotted someone else slyly crawling from the wreckage. Though he appeared to have suffered a few more knocks than Luke, Hursty scrambled away into the darkness. Luke gave chase around corners and into deeper darkness until only the moon offered any illumination. Hursty suddenly ran to a dead end. When he turned, he saw Luke staring back at him. Hursty pulled a knife. "You!" he said.

Luke skidded to a halt. Despite the thrill of using Fortune in such a way, he wasn't foolish enough to suddenly think he could now go one-on-one in a fight against a knife and come out on top.

"That's my knife," blurted Luke, taking note of the weapon.

The two boys began to circle each other. Luke realised he'd made a mistake, and he suddenly found it was now him with his back to the wall and a dead end.

"You shouldn't have left it on the table then. Besides, it's what you get for cheating!" shouted Hursty as rain ran down his face.

"What?" replied Luke, insulted by the accusation. "I didn't cheat."

"Yes, you did. No one beats me like that. No one!"

"I didn't," argued Luke, although maybe using a Gift would be called cheating by many.

"Well, I was cheating, and you still beat me!"

"Well, I wasn't… Wait! What?"

Hursty lowered the knife, and that bellowing laugh ran out into the confined space. "Hey, if you're good enough to cheat and not get caught, then it's fair game, that's what I say. Just gotta be prepared in case you do get caught. I guess you were," he laughed, looking at the knife again.

"I need you to tell me more about the men from Varliant. I need to know about the gold."

"You know, you could've just asked, gghhhh!"

Hursty's voice cut off in a choked gurgle as an arm snaked around his neck and squeezed. The small knife fell from his grasp as he was hoisted into the air, manhandled by someone far bigger and stronger. He choked and gasped as his eyes locked with Luke's.

"Get off him," commanded Luke as he ran forward, picking up the knife and holding it as threateningly as possible. "I'm warning you! Get off… him."

His voice trailed off as Hursty was dropped to the floor, falling to his knees, putting his hands to his throat as he spluttered and gasped for air. His attacker stepped over him.

"Put the knife down, you fool and come with me. Your father is already mad enough!"

Soaking long hair stuck firmly to Hunter's still bruised face as he stared down at Luke. Aron was in the grasp of two men dressed in the colours of the City Guard. Hunter turned away and pointed a thumb back at Luke. "Someone grab him, and the other one as well. I think the king will have some questions."

Despite being so brutally attacked, Hursty suddenly knelt up straighter. "Did someone say the king?"

ANGER AND UNDERSTANDING

Branthony crossed the small row made up of his sons, his jaw locked with anger. Up and down, he walked, his body tense as the boys watched on in fear and apprehension.

"We had a deal," growled Branthony. "We had rules that were ***not*** to be broken. Did I not make myself clear enough?!" He shouted the words as he came to a stop and stared straight down into the eyes of the First-Born. Aron merely looked away, unable to match his father's glare.

Branthony stepped to the side and was face-to-face with the Second-Born. "Did I give you reason to believe you had a choice?" Luke shook his head. Branthony stepped again to the eyeline of the Third-Born. "Was I unclear in any way as to the terms of our arrangement?" Joshua shook his head. Branthony stepped once more to his side and looked down at the Fourth-Born. Jacob, though the youngest, could no longer be called a child. Even he would not escape Branthony's wrath this time. "Did you not understand my words?" Another shake of the head.

Branthony stepped back and surveyed his sons, all soaked to the bone and shivering with cold and adrenaline.

"I am not just mad, I am disappointed. Do you know why I allowed you to go out into the city? Despite all the risks! Despite the dangers! Do you know why I allowed my young, ***royal*** children to go unsupervised into the city?"

They all kept their eyes down now. None dared even look him in the eye, never mind offer a reply.

"I did for you what my father did for me and my brother and sister. I allowed it so you could learn the lessons we learned. You will rule this kingdom one day. Aron may be king, but you will ***all*** rule together! Do you think I let you out there just so you can have fun?! No. It was so you could see how life is for the people of this city. Not the pampered, rich lords and ladies. Not the lives of princes offered every opportunity, but the real people of the Cross. The people are what make a kingdom. I wanted you to see their lives, their struggles. To learn the trials that they live through every day! I hoped it would give you a sense of perspective and responsibility. A sense of gratitude for all you have! I had hoped you would take the trust I had placed in you and use it wisely. Instead, you have squandered your opportunity, and you have failed me. You endangered yourselves. You started a fight!"

He saw Aron and Luke stir slightly at that, and though they didn't voice their thoughts, he could guess that they were about to argue that they hadn't technically started it. They may be right, but he was in no mood to hear arguments now.

"I had to send my men into the storm at night to go hunting for my delinquent children, and they are found amid a brawl! You should know better. Especially you, Aron." His eldest tensed, as though he'd been hit with a physical blow. "You are a man now. If I were to die today, then you would be king." He softened his voice a little with his following words. "I hope, at the very least, that this has taught you all once and for all the real dangers that exist out there. The dangers that most people face throughout their entire lives. They are not princes who can rely on their station for protection! They do not have Gifts that help them navigate such situations."

"But we—" The faint and short-lived argument came from Jacob, and all three of his brothers looked at him with surprise and a hint of admiration that he had dared to try to make a point. The attempt was quickly thwarted.

"But nothing!" Branthony shouted. "I have heard the reasons you gave to Hunter, and they do **not** excuse your actions. We knew about the card games already. We knew the men from Varliant had been gambling with golden items. Did you think you were the only ones out there looking for a lead? Do you think you know better and can do better than me and all the men at my disposal?"

This truly made the boys feel ashamed and foolish. None of them had stopped to consider that their father could already be one step ahead. They had felt, all of them, that this was somehow their job to do. They looked to each other, and, with silence, they spoke to one another. They knew they had made perhaps the biggest mistake of their lives, and that was saying something.

"We're sorry, Father." The apology came from the most surprising source. Luke looked up at him with shame-filled eyes.

Branthony had seen the interaction between his sons, and with Luke's words, his anger faded. At the very least, he could tell they now saw their mistake. He knew it sometimes took great effort to admit to being wrong.

In his mind's eye, Branthony could hear his wife telling him not to leave whilst still angry. His anger and frustrations had often caused a rift between him and his children, and he knew they were growing up now. They had proven themselves over the last few weeks, and despite this slip-up, they had all grown closer in the process. He knew if he could train them right, he could come to rely upon them, and they would be significant assets to the kingdom. He was determined not to let that hard work go to waste.

"Do you know why I am so upset?" he asked. "It is not just because I am angry. I am not simply mad because you broke the rules. Do you remember when Aron fell off my horse, Corv?"

They all nodded. It was something none of them would ever likely forget. Aron had seen a vision of Corv, so he stole the horse and took it out. It had ended in disaster. Aron fell from the horse, breaking his arm and nearly doing much worse.

"This is the same as then. I am angry because I fear for you. You are my children. My boys. Before anything else, you are ***my boys.***" He thumped a fist against his chest with the words. "I know the dangers of allowing you into the city. If you were hurt, it would fall on me for allowing it. Whenever you're out there, it feels like a knife in my gut, but I know the difference it can make."

"Yes, it is important to me that you obey the rules I have set. It is important to me that you learn responsibility and respect for your position. But it is most important that you stay safe. I am angry because I could not bear to see anything happen to you. I cannot keep you wrapped in a bubble of safety and naivety. This world is dangerous, and you know the threats we face."

His boys looked to each other again, and it was perhaps the most surprised he'd ever seen them look. It wasn't so much his words. It was more that he had said them himself. He knew Debreace would tell them this sort of thing all the time. Such conversations were not his strong suit.

"Now," he said, drawing himself up straight. "We will discuss punishments later, and there will be punishments, but for now, let's see what this young man brought in with you has to say. This is your lead, and I'll let you follow up. But understand this. Times are changing. Your mistakes will begin to cost you dearly. Worse, they will cost others. Try not to make them."

"You're princes?"

The boys nodded. It seemed odd to admit it. In all the time they'd been going out into the city, only two people had learned their true identities: Ollie and Joe. That happened on one of the first times the boys had journeyed past the castle grounds, and they weren't exactly clever about hiding the truth.

"You're the Four-Born?" asked Hursty as he stared at them from his seat with an expression of numb surprise. That cocky yet not disagreeable smile was nowhere to be found for a brief moment, but it came back with vigour as he looked at the four of them one at a time.

"That name?" said Aron. "We've heard it before. What is it, exactly?"

"Well, it's you—the Four-Born. The four princes, born to bring about a new age. The four that will change the kingdom and will raise those who are low to new heights."

"Well, that part's new," said Joshua. They had all heard people talk of them. Some believed the birth of four children of the Fait meant a great time of peace and prosperity. The end of the war against the Sile had only strengthened the conviction of those who thought this way.

Some believed the birth of four children of the Fait meant that a great war was coming. A time of death and destruction. The fact that the Sile had managed to reach the Centre had only furthered this point of view. The boys knew they all leaned toward the latter. The title of 'the

Four-Born' they'd heard before. This whole 'raise those that are low' part was extra.

"What does that mean?" asked Jacob.

"Well," Hursty said, a little unsure of himself. "It's just what people say."

"What exactly do people say?" pushed Jacob.

"Well, you know."

"No, we don't."

"Well, just that you…erm… Did you take some kids off the streets and let them live with you in the castle?" He blurted out the question with excitement.

Ah, so that's what it was all about. They understood now, at least in part. Rumours and stories had begun to circulate. Like most of these things, they held a hint of truth, but now people were turning that into something more. Yes, they'd met Ollie and Joe on the streets of the Centre and now both had access to the castle grounds, but they had earned that right themselves. Yet now the story made out that the so-called Four-Born had done all the work. It seemed ridiculous, yet these things often had a way of catching on and growing beyond control. Besides, the boys found nothing 'low' about Joe and Ollie.

"Boys," came a stern voice from behind them. They turned to see their Uncle Michael trying hard to pull off a serious face. Even after his lecture, Father had allowed them to follow their lead, albeit under strict supervision. Michael was supposed to be part of a punishment, but it was hard for the boys to see him in such a way.

"Look," said Luke to Hursty. "We just want to ask you a few questions about the men from Varliant."

"Why didn't you say so?" came the reply, and Hursty gleefully jumped into a tale. "When they first arrived here, they only spent time with the well-to-do folks. Making business deals or whatnot. The usual thing, I guess, but nothing that would involve anyone like me."

"So, when did you meet them?" asked Joshua.

"Hold on, mate, I'm getting to it." The words seemed to come out before he'd thought about what he was saying, then he remembered who he was talking to. He offered a wide, toothy smile that displayed his embarrassment. His eyes glanced nervously at Michael, waiting for a reprimand. Michael waved him to carry on. It was hard to be mad at Hursty, who had such an agreeable persona. "Well. After a while, the word got out that someone was hosting card games on a ship at the city docks. No one knew who at the time.

"It was strictly invite only, and the only people invited were those of a certain disposition. People from a certain way of life. People not accustomed to abiding by the law."

"We get it," stated Luke. "Criminals. Get on with it."

Hursty smiled and, despite his situation, seemed quite relaxed.

"I wouldn't call them criminals," he said sympathetically. "They just got no other option. They never had anything and barely had a chance to get anything. It's the only life they've ever known. Not everyone's bad. Some people are just desperate. Not everyone can be a prince, eh?"

The boys had another of those moments when they appreciated all they had, and their father's lesson was drilled home a little further. At that moment, they also appreciated Hursty. He cared; they all liked that.

"So, these people went and started playing," the story continued. "Only."

"Only what?" The question came from Michael, who was no longer leaning casually on the wall, arms folded. Now he had stepped closer, interested.

"Well, this is where it all got a little off-putting, ya see."

"Go on," urged Jacob. It wasn't as though Hursty had any inclination to keep the story to himself, but Jacob still thought he would add a touch of his Gift just to be sure none of this was a lie.

"Well, these people who were going to play. They were losing, most of'em. Losing what little they had to begin with, and believe me, it won't have been much. Only, when they came back, having lost, well, it didn't seem like they'd lost at all."

"What do you mean?" asked Joshua. "They had money? Gold?"

"No. But they were different. None of them would say what'd happened. Tight-lipped. Tighter than a cat's a..." He remembered whose company he was in and decided to speak with a little more tact. "It was their eyes," he said, voice slightly different now. The humour that carried through many of his words had gone. "You could see it in their eyes. They'd seen something. It had taken over them. It was all they could think about."

"They'd seen the gold," said Joshua.

"Yeah, but I didn't know it at the time. Thing is, those who came back. They were angry. Real angry but not about losing their money."

"What about?"

"I'm coming to it. Trust me."

"Well then, get to it," pushed Luke.

"So, it took some time, but eventually I managed to ring myself an invite to a game. It wasn't easy. They were real careful about who got to play. You had to be recommended. It became known that I may have had a little debt hanging over me. More than a little," he admitted. "I owed a fella named Gabor for a night of cards gone wrong, and he put my name forward. I go to the docks. I get blindfolded and shuffled onto a ship. That's when I saw them. The Varliants."

"Did they have the gold?" asked Joshua.

Hursty smiled. "I'm getting to it. So, we started to play, but they seemed more interested in talking. They started jabbering on and on. Trying real hard to make a point."

"About what?" asked Aron.

"About you. All of you."

He looked at the boys, each in turn, and they could only look back in confusion.

"They were talking about the Fait," Hursty elaborated. "About how much money you've got, talked about how you want to keep it all for yourself. That you shut down the deals they were making that would have put that money back into the hands of the people. Said you even paid em off, so they'd leave. Talked about how great Varliant is because they share the wealth. Sounded like a dream if you ask me. Pretty sure it sounded like that to others. That's what they were angry about, ya see, the other players who came back. I told you they were angry. They were angry at the Fait."

"So, the Varliants were telling people the gold came from us," said Joshua. It wasn't a question.

"That's right," answered Hursty anyway. "Said it all came from right. In. Here." He tapped his finger against the table with each word.

"Those lying bas—" Luke paused mid-word as his uncle placed a hand on his shoulder.

"Finish your story, lad," said Michael.

"Well, it's like I said. They were saying the gold came from the castle, from the Fait, a payoff to piss off, so to speak." No one cared about his choice of language now. "Only thing is, Luke, erm, Prince Luke, is right. They were, well, lying ba's," he said with a smile.

"How so?"

"Eventually, they brought out the gold. So much." Hursty's eyes glazed over, as though he could see the shining metal right then and there before his eyes. "More than most men could even imagine. They had all sorts. By the God, there was a solid gold helm. Who needs a solid gold helm? Thing must have weighed, well, a lot." He shook his head as though clearing his vision. "They said the gold came from the Fait, that you were willing to pay them to leave rather than have them make deals that would make others rich. To tell the truth, I believed em. I mean, who else but the royal family would have so much?"

"It didn't come from us," argued Aron, obviously upset by the deception. "Do you know how much my father spends trying to rejuvenate the city? To patrol the trade routes and roads so people can stay safe."

"Let the boy finish," said Michael, offering a comforting hand to his nephew's shoulder. "You said they were liars?"

"Damned right they were. You see, I said earlier that most players who went to the game lost. Well, I ain't most players," he said with a grin as he leaned back and placed his hands behind his head as though he was still at the tavern.

"So, you won," said Jacob. "Why does that make them liars?"

"I didn't just win," declared Hursty, sitting forward again and practically slamming his hands on the table. "I won again and again. They kept trying to beat me, but they couldn't. I won and won and won."

"I bet you were cheating?" said Luke with a grin.

"No, I wasn't."

"He's lying," confirmed Jacob.

"Listen," he said dismissively. "You're missing the point. I won, all right, who cares how? By the time we were finished, I was a rich man by anyone's standards. There I was, standing in front of that gold, and it was all mine. I picked some up. That's where I got my golden dice. I started to tell them everything I was gonna do. I could rebuild the old mill that burned down with that much money. Get people back to work. I could fix so many wrongs for people like me, but then."

"Then what?" the four boys said in unison, eager for the story's conclusion.

"They stabbed me in the back. Literally!" He pulled up his top to reveal a nasty scar that looked like it had been crudely stitched. "Stabbed me in the back and tossed me overboard to die. Lucky to survive I'wa."

"How did you survive?" asked Jacob, amazed.

"Come on, I'm from the Centre. Not so easy to get rid of."

"What aren't you telling us?" Jacob couldn't detect a lie exactly, but he could tell something was missing from the tale. Hursty seemed reluctant to elaborate, but finally, under the glare of everyone else in the room, he relented.

"I was fished out of the water by kids looking to see if I had anything of worth on me. They stole the dice and left me for dead, but one of the kids knew me. Dragged me to a Stitcher. They did their best to stitch me up, but they weren't exactly healers. Kept trying to take me to one, but I didn't want the attention. Thought it best to lie low for a while in case anyone came to finish the job."

"That's who you thought we were at the tavern," said Luke. "Someone sent to finish the job."

Hursty nodded.

"I only started showing my face again once I heard the Varliants had skipped town. Thought it was safe. Plus, I was running low on money. Besides, I was sick of crappy players winning my games. Mergo? What a joke. He's a low-hand swindler at best. I didn't need to cheat to beat him."

"So," said Joshua. "Let's piece this all together. The Varliants begin inviting some of the poorest people in the city to card games, then, when these people lose, the Varliants show them a hoard of gold like they've never seen. Only they tell the people that the gold came from us. From the Crown. This gets the people mad. Mad enough to cause a riot and even attack our father."

"But where does the assassination fit in?" asked Jacob.

"I guess, and it's only a guess, that if some of those people voiced strong enough opinions to the Varliants, they were made an offer. Some of that gold, say. All they had to do was kill a Fait, which they were all too eager to try, considering what they now knew. Or what they thought they knew. This is where the man named Gabor came in. He could offer the names of people willing to go the extra yard and do the recruitment."

"That's a great theory," cut in Michael. "The only problem is we can't prove it. Gabor didn't know who he was dealing with. The Varliants are gone. Even if we could identify it, their ship is most likely gone as well."

"But we've got Hursty," declared Jacob. "He saw it first-hand. He can place the Varliants with the gold."

"I'm afraid to say that a cheating card player won't convince the lords to go to war."

"Hey, no need for the cheating part," said Hursty, genuinely offended.

"We need proof," continued Michael, ignoring him. "Something solid."

"Well," said Hursty, and once again looked reluctant to speak. He rocked his head from side to side as though physically forcing the words to rise from within. "When you say solid, do you mean like solid gold?"

He pulled two solid gold playing cards from somewhere on his person, a Farmer and a Peasant, which was extra surprising considering he had been searched. "I liked the look of these," he said, placing them onto the table and sliding them over. He looked like he was handing over his dreams. "Was keeping them hidden. Given what happened, they could draw unwanted attention. Even the little rats who pulled me from the river didn't find these two."

The boys inspected the cards. They were perfect, just as Mini had described. The pictures engraved on the metal looked like they'd somehow been taken from a painting and placed within the gold. None of them had ever seen anything even close to such craftsmanship.

"Their best player wagered them," said Hursty. "Tall guy. Black hair and beard. He's the one who stabbed me."

"Did you get a name?" asked Michael.

"Sal. Salvador. Something like that. They didn't use names, but I overheard them when they were tossing me overboard."

"Salvadire," said Michael. "The leader of the Varliant delegates."

"That's the one," said Hursty.

"My young friend, do you have any idea how important this tale could be?"

WEDDINGS AND WAR

"Beautiful," Branthony said as he rubbed his hand down the horse's flank. "Just beautiful."

"Boxy says he's quite the character."

Lord Richard Dawsel stood at Branthony's side. A longtime friend and ally. Someone whose opinion he valued.

"Boxy also says he can be hard to control."

They both circled the horse, examining it closely. It was a large horse, though not so big as Branthony's own, Corv, and would be a fine palfrey rather than a war or charge horse.

"The best ones always are. That's what makes them exciting," said Branthony, who couldn't keep the smile from his face. These rare moments where he could simply enjoy something were priceless to him. He and Richard had always shared a love of horses. Put Stable-Master Boxy with them and they could 'talk a glass eye to sleep' as Boxy was fond of saying.

Branthony grabbed a handful of grain and fed it to the horse, looking around to be sure Boxy wasn't there to see. The man could be fierce when it came to his horses, and even a king was not beyond reproach.

"Come on then. Out with it," said Richard.

In these more personal moments, Branthony enjoyed it when his friends talked to him like a normal person. He thought of his friend, Malf, who was always too happy to let his feelings be known. Branthony spoke as the horse snaffled food from his hand.

"A week ago, the boys found an interesting young man named Hursty."

"And what is so special about this young man?"

"Well, besides being a card player of some skill and a card cheater of even greater skill, he is the one solid link we have to Varliant. He had in possession two solid gold playing cards."

"Some of the mysterious items the Varliants have been using to pay their way."

"Yes. He won them in a game against Salvadire himself and took a knife in his back for the trouble."

"You're hoping to use this boy as proof against them?"

"Yes, though we both know it won't be enough. At the very least, it is proof for me. I know I was right, even if others don't believe me. This boy tells the truth, Jacob confirms it. I feel vindicated."

"There's something I don't understand," said Richard, taking a few steps away to lean back on a nearby fence. "If all this is by the Crone's design, then to what end? She wanted your son dead, that much, at least, is easy to understand from a tactical point of view. But the sense in some of this eludes me."

"She hopes to drive us to war with each other," said Branthony, taking another handful of feed and offering it to the horse, who gratefully accepted. "I have known war was coming to us. I just didn't know when or where the threat would come from."

"Even if it comes to civil war, that doesn't give her an edge, does it?"

"That would be a war merely meant to weaken us. Then she would come with Varliant."

"You believe they can truly wage war against the Cross?" It was obvious that Richard did not believe Varliant, which was essentially just one city-state, could have the power to match the entire kingdom.

"I've had spies there for some time now. They tell me that Varliant has made deals with some of the largest and fiercest mercenary groups in the known world. According to my source, the Clouds of Strife and the Lionheart Squalls have signed contracts. Excessive contracts that they will not break. More groups have likely already had their allegiance bought.

"Divide and conquer, then mop up what's left."

"Precisely."

"You seem certain?"

"I am. Varliant has risen to wealth that perhaps even I couldn't match. They seemingly have more gold than all the combined Points of the

Cross. They have used it to buy the loyalty of the two largest mercenary groups, and they have used it as a tool to cause friction here. The only thing I cannot figure out is the source of their wealth. It falls to reason that the Crone is somehow behind it, yet I cannot fathom exactly how. Though when it comes to her, who knows what's possible."

"So, if you are certain, what are we to do?"

"Simple. We prepare for war. The first part of that is to ensure we have a unified Cross. I must put an end to this discord."

"And how will you do that?"

"Well, for starters." Branthony gave the horse's head one more stroke before he walked away. Richard fell in step beside him. "I will bring the people together. Everyone, from peasants to lords."

"And dare I ask?" Richard said with a slight grin. "How you intend to do that?"

"That, for once, has an easy answer. We shall have a royal wedding."

The sun was setting when Morbius stepped inside the large tent currently playing home to his Cross counterpart, Sir Walter. The tall man stood at the other end of a huge table, talking with two subordinates. Morbius decided to wait patiently as they finished their conversation, but the ever-so-slight look of irritation that crossed their faces was not missed. Some may get angry at such things, but Morbius found it entertaining. Though he knew it was petty, he enjoyed irritating the men of the Cross, especially Sir Walter.

Taking a moment to look down at some of the many scrolls and parchments that littered the table, he was not surprised to see that many were lists. Walter seemed to want to count everything: food, boots, arrows. Anything within the camp had to be counted and catalogued. Well, Morbius would say this for the man: He was diligent.

Walter finished his conversation, and the two men left, offering Morbius respectful head dips. He knew such actions were forced, it only made him enjoy them more.

"What can I do for you, Lord Morbius?"

"Always so proper, Walter. Doesn't it get tiresome?"

The man raised his eyebrows, as though every second in Morbius' company was tedious. The moment dragged on before the taller man responded.

"If you only came here to insult me, I must insist you leave. I am a very busy man."

"Oh, I can see." Morbius lifted some of the parchments and scrolls and feigned reading them. "Riveting. Will you spend your evening making more lists? Perhaps I should ask my men to start counting their bowel movements."

"It may be useful. Any sudden change may provide early warning of sickness that could run through the camp."

"By the sands of the plains, man, I was joking."

"I am well aware of that, Lord Morbius, but those lists you insult may be the difference between life and death. We have no idea what enemy we may face here. Knowing the exact depth of our resources could be vital to gaining victory."

"My men will gain us victory," Morbius argued, suddenly finding his entertainment in the situation had faltered.

"Your men?" said Walter, his eyebrows raised once again. "Your men have done little more than laze the days away, contributing little to the work needed to secure this site."

"My men are warriors. I have brought some of the best fighters here to do just that. Fight!"

"My men are warriors," Walter spat back. "The difference, My ***Lord***." He made no attempt to hide the insult and contempt from the word. Walter believed Morbius to be a lord, less than he believed a pig would fly. "Is that my men are disciplined and carry out their duties. ***My*** men train. ***My*** men know that skill with a sword is not the only thing that matters in warfare. If it were, then perhaps your Sile may have done more than simply raid our southern border in all the years our people fought one another."

"Ah, so it is in the name of discipline that you have your men running training drills in the midday sun?"

"What would you have them doing? Getting drunk? Gambling? We could always have more challenges and watch our men beat each other to a pulp."

Morbius released a low growl. "Are you so arrogant that you will not admit to the good that challenge did? There has not been a challenge made since, not one that has been allowed by witnesses, at least. That's how it works, you see. It is the will of the people. If they deem a problem worthy, they allow the challenge. They decide the severity of the challenge. Allowing weapons or simple fists. The man of yours who accepted did what you could not. He gained the respect of ***my*** men."

"Is that what it takes? Well then, perhaps I should challenge you. Then, when I beat you, your men may finally listen."

Morbius clenched his hands into fists, the skin of his knuckles turning white.

"Careful, Sir Walter. Be very careful. Those are words you could come to regret. I have been challenged many times. I have made many challenges. I have won them all. How do you think I united the clans?"

Walter merely stared across at him, expression straight, with little emotion showing through. Morbius would swear the man was thinking about it. It would be a fine fight.

"You see us as nothing but savages, don't you? You talk of discipline. You say we are lazy. Do you know what many of my Sile are doing right now in the northern stretches of the plains where the rain falls more often? For the first time, they are ploughing land, planting crops, and grazing cattle. I have clans that have never done anything but fight, cultivating the resources you love so much, so we can feed ourselves and grow stronger. So that clans will not see the need to raid each other or your southern border. That is the reason I united them in the first place. ***We*** are evolving, Sir Walter, bettering ourselves. Are you?"

That finally gained the smallest of reactions from the man. Morbius couldn't tell exactly what he saw on Walter's features, but he blinked many times, and Morbius thought those words had stung. Yet the man offered no words to confirm such a thought.

"What's the matter?" pressed Morbius, knowing this could be a moment to let the tension fall away, but having no desire to be seen as backing down. "Nothing to say from the great and noble Sir Walter of the Cross. Maybe that challenge still seems a good idea, eh?"

Now Walter's face twisted into a snarl. He leaned over the table, massive hands pressing onto the wood. He glared at Morbius. Walter was a big man. Not a muscular hulk like the Crone's former champion, but tall, thick and powerful. It would be a good fight. Morbius had no doubt. Yet one that he was confident of winning.

Walter seemed intent on burning a hole through Morbius with his eyes alone. Morbius felt a familiar energy begin to build within him. He had not expected to use the Sword-of-Answers this evening, but if humbling this man was what he must do, then so be it.

"You seem eager for the fight," growled Walter, his voice low and menacing. "Do you feel confident?" Morbius offered an assured nod. "Perhaps with good reason, but I assure you that confidence is misplaced."

"Really," said Morbius, his adrenaline starting to pump. He relished the feeling. He always had. Nothing made a man feel alive like a good fight. "You forget who I am, Sir Walter. You forget that I have survived a direct battle with your cherished king. Twice! You are no Branthony Fait."

Walter leaned even closer, if the table weren't so damn large Morbius may have expected the man to come crashing over in attempt to get at his throat. Walter's stare only intensified, which would have seemed like an impossible thing, yet the old knight pulled it off. The intimidation would have been overpowering for others, but not for Morbius. For him, it only strengthened his resolve.

The following words would be decisive.

It was Walter who spoke.

"You really don't remember me, do you?"

Morbius was utterly taken aback. His chin retreated into his neck in a show of obvious shock. "What?" was all he could say. Walter straightened, turned and took a few steps away, reaching for a flask of wine and two cups. He filled them both and slid one across the table, deftly avoiding the scrolls and parchment.

The tension faded in an instant, but Morbius's confusion remained. He tentatively took the wine and sipped, shocked by the sudden change in atmosphere. Damn, it was good wine. Had the sly dog been hiding the good stuff? Morbius took another sip whilst Walter downed his and refilled. Maybe the drink helped him relax. It seemed Walter was willing to de-escalate the situation. Morbius now regretted missing his chance to do so. Now, Walter seemed like the bigger man in more than physical size, which riled Morbius more than any insult.

"When I was younger," said Walter. "It was common for men to come south and fight the Sile raiders that plundered our southern border. A way of proving ourselves. A way to get a taste of real combat." Morbius was still lost and waiting for an explanation. "You were much younger yourself. This was long before you united the clans."

Ah, now he understood a little better.

"We fought against one another?"

Walter nodded.

"Is that the reason for all your hostility? It was a different time, I a different man. Men of the Cross weren't the only ones looking to prove themselves."

Walter looked insulted again. "It has nothing to do with my hostility, and we did not exactly fight one another. But I remember you. A good warrior, a great warrior. Much potential even then. You organised your men and had them fighting together rather than individuals chasing glory. Our troops were shocked to come against an organised Sile resistance."

"Ah, so you're disappointed?"

"I most certainly am. Many of my countrymen spoke highly of you after your unexpected appearance at the Centre. I came here expecting great things. Instead, I find the Sile to be lazy and you to be a leader who seems unconcerned about the behaviour of the men under your command. I do ***not*** see you as savages, Lord Morbius, far from it. I see you as missed potential. The men who serve under King Branthony are always eager to impress. Desperate for his respect. Going above and beyond to gain it. Your men seem to have no such desire."

"There is the difference. My men already ***have*** my respect. I do not look down on them."

"That is not what I meant, and if you think for one second that His Majesty looks down on his people, then you do not know him at all."

Morbius could tell his last words had riled Sir Walter, and that was not his intention. He was starting to have some appreciation for the man and the conversation. He paused before speaking again, instead choosing to slide the cup back across the table, avoiding the parchments just as skilfully as Walter, who took the cup, refilled it, and slid it back.

"Is that why you're here, Sir Walter, to gain the respect of your king?"

Morbius chose his tone carefully to show it was a genuine question. Walter downed the contents of his cup again and refilled once more.

"I've had the respect of my king for a long time, and he mine. More than respect, he has my devotion."

"A strong word."

"The correct word. The only one I could use. I do not expect you to know how I earned my knighthood?"

Morbius shook his head as he swallowed his drink, not wanting to be seen as falling behind. The sidestep in the conversation once again had him off balance.

"When the king was a young man, not even a king, he too travelled south to the Edge. He came as all the others did to test himself. I was already there when he arrived. It was the first time we had met. Though I was older than he, we were both young, impetuous, eager for battle. He was there only a month before being called back north. There had been an… incident, and rebellion had swept across the kingdom."

"The Western Rebellions," said Morbius, now vastly enthralled by the tale that had barely begun. "The first civil war in the Cross for over a hundred years." Walter nodded back at him with a tip of the head, impressed that Morbius knew his history.

"Yes," said Walter, and there was a sudden weariness at the mere memory. "We rode back north with all haste. He barely made it back, you know. The western lords sought to take out the biggest threat against them. In the war's first major battle, the rebels attacked the loyal western region of Rodley, killing the then lord, Eric Dawsel. His son, Richard, escaped and fled east to warn King Branthony the First."

"I have met Lord Richard. Your king spoke highly of him. He seemed a good man."

Again, Walter nodded.

"Whilst the king led his forces west, the western forces sailed from Rodley to lands of The View in the Southern-Point, then moved on to Wraith Castle. Before the Crown had gathered its full strength, the west had taken much of the Southern-Point. Their leader was an excellent strategist. If he had killed Branthony there and then, the war may have turned out very different."

"But he didn't. Branthony escaped."

"Barely, and at great cost."

"Is this how you earned your knighthood? You helped him escape?"

Walter shook his head and downed another drink, signalling for Morbius' cup, which he refilled again.

"Far from it. We met the western forces slightly north of Wraith Castle. We snuck around, desperately trying to avoid them and make it to the Centre or anywhere loyal to the Crown. It was not to be. We were intercepted as we made our way to South Crave Castle. Though relatively small, it was a bloody battle. The king escaped, but that was the last I would see of him for some time."

"You were captured?"

"No, I stayed. My father was a minor lord in the Bolgar region of the Western-Point. I saw my family banners at the battle, fighting **against** the Crown. I had to choose between my family and my king. I chose my family." Morbius didn't speak. He knew how hard a choice like that must be to make. "The next time I would see Branthony was from the opposite end of the battlefield."

Morbius' eyes opened wide.

"That's right," said Walter. "You're not the only one to fight him and live."

"You fought directly against him?"

Morbius couldn't keep the excitement from his voice. This was a greater tale than he'd expected. Walter pulled at his clothes and lifted his shirt, revealing an old but gruesome scar across his chest.

"By the sands," whispered Morbius.

"You should see his."

For the first time, Morbius saw a slight smile crack Walter's lips

"You lie," he barked at a volume he had not intended. Sir Walter merely raised his eyebrows again. Morbius believed him. Walter did not seem to be the type of person who could lie even if he wanted to. A smile cracked his lips.

"A year later, the forces of the Crown came crashing down on me and my men near Kay Town. The king's forces were desperate for a quick victory so they could join with their other forces for what would prove to be the decisive battle of the war. They vastly outnumbered us, yet we kept them at bay for three days. That delay nearly cost them the war. One more day, and the king's forces would not have made the rendezvous. Without them, the Crown would have lost. You see, I know something about defending a position.

"When the war was done and the rebellion crushed, and believe me, in the end, we were crushed, I thought I would die. Branthony offered me a pardon. When I asked him why, he told me of his vision of a better world. A world where men of all kinds can be free. A world where your skill in a fight was not the most important thing in life. A better world, where men could raise their families and love their women, without looking to the next fight. A world where even the poor did not struggle for a meal. Where education was not the sole property of the rich. A better world, for all, not just for some."

Morbius thought on this. It was much the same as his own vision for his people.

"He told me," Walter continued. "That he needed good men to help him accomplish his dream. Me, who had turned against him, a good man? I thought he was mistaken."

"Your knighthood," said Morbius after a moment's contemplation. "You still haven't said how you got it."

"Hm," said Walter, and now he seemed more at ease after telling his story and moving on from the reflections of his troubled past. "Though I was offered a pardon, I would have to earn it. All was not simply forgiven. The king remembered where we first met, so I was sent south again. The Sile were attacking and becoming bolder. Taking advantage of our weakened state. A new leader was emerging."

"So, you gained your knighthood killing Sile."

It was more a statement than a question.

"Once again, Lord Morbius, you have chosen quite the opposite. I was charged with repelling the Sile but with minimum casualties. We were not to let it be known, but those in charge had been told the king was seeking peace, and that although we were not to allow the deaths of anyone from the Cross, we must gain victory with as few Sile casualties as possible."

Once again, Morbius felt an almost unwelcome sense of adulation for both Sir Walter and Branthony.

"The king's brother, Prince Christopher, should take most of the praise. He knew the land like he had lived there his entire life. He knew the Sile numbers, their tactics, their weapons. It all stuck in his head, and he recalled it as easily as we recall words."

"His Gift," said Morbius.

"One's ability to fight is not always what wins wars,' said Walter. This time, the point landed home with a dissatisfying blow.

"You're telling me that I not only lost my war but that you were not even trying your hardest to beat us."

Walter drank yet again, by the sands, the man could handle his alcohol.

"Oh no. Make no mistake. We did not hold back when the fighting was on our side of the border. Yet we never pressed our advantage onto the plains."

Damn it, the man was right. Morbius had often wondered why the men of the Cross never marched further south with their full strength.

"It was after the peace treaty that I was allowed to return home and receive my knighthood. Not long ago, if truth be told. So, you see, I was knighted because of my ability to lead. I was knighted because I kept the men under my command in check. I kept them disciplined. I kept them from doing what many of them were there to do, and believe me, it was not easy. Many doubted me. Many thought me mad for not allowing them to press the advantage when we had it. We could have followed your forces south and finished you off, but we didn't. More than once, I faced challenges to my leadership."

It was a sobering thought, so Morbius drank again. He did not say that they had been hoping to be followed many times, that they would have had an advantage on their own ground, and that they sometimes attacked with the very intention of drawing the men of the Cross to them. What difference would it make? It didn't change the fact that the Cross never followed or chased them down as they could have. Morbius had always thought they were too weary of falling into a trap, which they certainly would have. He mentally cursed and praised Branthony for never telling him this.

"So," said Morbius eventually. "Why return?"

"Because I believe in my king and his vision. I believe we can work together and become stronger together. But I also believe my king when he says there are far greater enemies out there for us than each other. What has happened to both our people in recent years should be proof enough of that?"

Morbius nodded his agreement.

"You have given me much to think about this evening. I thank you for your time, Sir Walter, and the wine."

With that, he abruptly left, leaving Walter staring after him.

The next morning, Walter woke with a heavy head, but no one else would know. He dressed in his pristine tunic and polished boots. As always, he carried himself with a stiff posture and high chin, and as always, he exited his tent before the sun was fully up.

Walter stood shocked to see the Sile warriors standing in organised ranks before him. If they were disgruntled by this, they showed no sign. They stood, heads held high with stiff backs.

Morbius approached Walter.

"You talk a good game, Sir Walter. I hope you can back it up. I expect my men to learn great things from you."

In typical fashion, Walter simply nodded in response and turned to address the Sile.

Celia was on her way to a meeting she did not want to miss; however, a rare opportunity presented itself. It was almost with a clatter that she ran into Princess Susan.

"Your Highness," Celia blurted as they both came to a sudden halt on the dissecting corners of the corridors. Celia dipped her head, an act she hated. She should bow to no one. Susan paused in her step and smoothed her dress.

"Lady Celia. How are you?"

"Very good, thank you. Oh, and congratulations. The king has recently informed the council members of your upcoming nuptials."

Of course, Celia could never say it, but she had been genuinely happy to hear that Susan had found love again. Susan's problems and what happened to her were known throughout the kingdom. Celia had heard the story when she was a young girl. She even had faint memories of the rebellion that came after the death of the young Lord of Bolgar. Celia's father took the forces of the Five Fingers to join the then-young Prince Branthony's troops against the rebels. Her father was away for over two years. They were perhaps the best years of Celia's young life.

"Yes," Susan replied. "We will announce it more publicly soon. Nothing brings people together like a wedding."

"It could be perfect timing with all the trouble lately." Susan merely nodded, and the unplanned meeting suddenly became uncomfortable. "Well then, congratulations again. I shall be on my—"

"Actually," Susan cut in. "I have been looking for an opportunity to speak with you in person. More importantly, in private. It seems a harder thing for us women of the court to do than it should."

"Oh," Celia replied with genuine surprise. "What can I do for you?"

"In truth, I wish to thank you. I have not been here at the Centre enough. Though I do not use my Gift, I never intended to leave my family weakened. Even without my Gift, I could have done more. My sister-in-law tells me your support has been invaluable to her, especially during my brother's absence. So, I thank you, Lady Celia."

Celia was taken aback for a moment. Insults and arguments she could handle, even the fake niceties of the court were well within her usual parameters. This genuine giving of thanks was different indeed.

"I was, and am, happy to help," she said with a smile. "As any loyal subject should be."

Of all the lies she had ever told in her life, of which there had been countless, that was perhaps the greatest. Only a lifetime of practised deception allowed her to say it with confidence and cover the fact that she was likely the biggest traitor the kingdom had ever known. Strange, how people spoke of the late Lord of Bolgar with such disdain after he led the rebellion. What would they say of her if her secret were ever discovered?

"Well," said Susan. "I shall keep you no longer."

"I am sure we shall get the chance to speak again, even if only briefly," Celia said with a humorous shrug.

She left the short meeting with a mixture of emotions, none of which she had time to contemplate. She was now overdue for her appointment. She approached a nearby door, knocked and waited for a command to enter. When she stepped inside, she was greeted by Prince Aron, who smiled warmly as he stood from the floor.

"No, no," she said, gesturing for him to remain as he was, knowing he'd been practising meditation and using his Gift.

He sat back down and resumed his position, but Celia knew that meditating only helped on rare occasions. Would Aron ever figure out that his premature birth was the reason for his lack of control? She felt sorry for him. For all life's troubles, one of the greatest solaces was a good night's sleep. They were rare for Prince Aron.

She sat and looked down at him, taking a moment to survey the man he'd become. A short man, no doubt, but filling out. Stocky and strong. Though he may not have his father's Gift of Strength, he was undoubtedly his father's son in terms of personality and temperament. The refusal to submit, the determination to fight on. A sometimes short temper. Those were attributes Aron got from his father, but in terms of appearance, he was most certainly his mother's. Funny, she would say Prince Joshua had the most similar appearance to the king, but more of his mother's calmer, more balanced demeanour.

"Have you had any success today?" she asked.

"It's hard even to know. I see images and write them down, but they don't make sense. I can't help but wonder if my Gift is only making things worse."

"Worse?"

"Well, the few times I've had clear visions, they've all come true, even when I don't understand them. Like when I saw the pleasure house where we found an informant. I'd never seen it before, but my vision led us there."

"You found a valuable lead," she added as encouragement.

"Yes, but I saw the tavern where Luke got into trouble. If I hadn't seen it in a vision, I wouldn't have known to go in there, so Luke wouldn't have been caught in a fight."

"But you also wouldn't have found the young card player whose story corroborates everything about our theory. He may be instrumental in proving that Varliant was behind the attempt on your brother's life."

"Maybe, but I knew Luke would get caught up in that fight. I'd seen it, and yet I let us go in anyway. Things would have been different if I'd acted differently and made us stay out. How do we know we wouldn't have found Hursty anyway? I keep walking straight into the visions when maybe I should walk away from them."

It was a complex subject to think about. Was knowing the future the very thing that made it happen that way?

"I just… I just want things to go differently for once. Different from the way I've seen it."

"Why?" she asked, and it was easy to see he was troubled. She'd never seen him this way, even on the mornings he'd woken screaming, as he often did, he never seemed as troubled as he did in that moment. What was it inside Celia that made her genuinely want to comfort him? By the God, why did she have to be such a constant conflict of interest?

"I've never told anyone this, but maybe it will help. Can I trust you, Lady Celia?"

"Of course." There was that skill at lying again.

Aron still had obvious reservations but needed to get this off his chest. "I had a vision a few years ago, just after the battle at the Centre. It's the only vision I remember properly. I fight so hard to remember my other visions, but this one, this one I wish I could forget. I see it over and over. Every few nights at least. It changes slightly. I change what I do. The decisions I make, but it always ends the same."

"What do you see?" asked Celia. Hearing Aron's story, she felt a tinge of fear, such was the dread in his eyes.

"I see." He paused, and she reached out a hand to him.

"Go on," she urged. "You can tell me?"

"I see myself and my brothers die. We fall in battle. We fall, and they cheer. I saw them pick up Joshua's body above their heads, chanting and laughing as they parade him like a trophy."

Celia had to take a moment. It was a lot to take in for many different reasons. For that moment, she decided to concentrate on the scared young man before her. What must it be like to see your own death? Not only your own but those closest to you, and not just once but over and over.

"That is…" she searched for a word. "Terrible. I am sorry you had to see that. But perhaps it can help you. Perhaps knowing that end will help you avoid it."

"It hasn't worked like that so far."

"Perhaps not. When will this vision take place? Do you know such things?"

"Not exactly, but I do know it is some time away. We were older. Men grown, all of us. We were leading the men of the Cross and," he looked up to her with fresh vigour. "There's a traitor. We discovered a traitor. It's the reason we are defeated. A traitor will bring us down."

Celia hid the shock from her face, surprising herself with how quickly she adjusted.

"That must be the reason for the dream. Why show you your death if it is not avoidable? Now you know there is a traitor, and you can find him before your downfall."

"Maybe," he said, sounding not at all confident.

"Was there any clue in your vision as to who the traitor may be?"

She swallowed her nerves. Aron only shook his head, and she had to stop herself from sighing in relief.

What am I doing? she wondered. The traitor was surely her. Was she really trying to help catch herself? Celia didn't show any sign, but she was awash with emotions. She had come to quite like Prince Aron. The thought that she would be responsible for his death, for the death of all the princes, set her stomach turning a little, but did their defeat mean her victory? After siding with the Crone, such a thing was likely unavoidable.

"My Prince," she said softly. "Is it only your future that you see? Do you ever see anyone else's?"

"There are other people in my dreams, but usually I'm there as well. I don't think I've ever had a vision that didn't involve myself."

"Have you ever seen…" she hesitated. "Have you ever seen me in your visions?"

Aron decided to try something at that moment. He took her hand and closed his eyes. Celia felt her heart begin to pound. It was a good job that the prince had closed his eyes because she could not hide her fear. It was strange; she was usually so good at controlling herself, but she had never experienced this. She knew she ran a significant risk. Perhaps she would give herself away in this very moment, all her hard work undone. Could her destiny be to hang at the end of a rope as a traitor? No, this was the best way to avoid such a thing. Get close, learn his secrets. Throw him off the scent. Implicate someone else. She could get glimpses of the future and use them to her advantage.

Aron did his routine, picturing something tranquil and allowing his Gift to take over. It did not last long on the occasions it worked, and he saw only brief visions.

"I see you." His words were a whisper. Celia drew a deep breath and held it. She was terrified but also invigorated, unable to stop it. She had to know. Who else got such an opportunity? To glimpse her future, what a thing. Her heart pounded in her chest. Was this what the soldiers felt as they lined up for battle? Knowing the next few moments could be their last.

Her worries eased a little as Aron smiled, his eyes still closed. "You look beautiful. Even more so than usual." She felt his grip on her hand tighten a little as he concentrated.

"What else?" she asked. "What do you see?" She was gripping his hand back now, squeezing tightly.

"You are older, but not much so. You are wearing a beautiful dress. You look happy. Smiling, laughing."

"Why?" she asked, desperate for more.

"You're." He paused, and Celia could barely stand the suspense. "You're holding something. Examining it."

"What is it?"

She watched as Aron moved his head a little from side to side. She could see his eyes flickering beneath closed eyelids. She recognised the signs now and knew he was losing his vision. She could see the puzzlement when he opened his eyes and looked at her.

"What?" she asked again.

"A crown," he answered. "You were holding a crown. One made especially for you. You will be queen."

So, there it was, laid out plainly, she ***would*** be queen. She had begun to doubt. She had started to think that maybe she could not do what needed to be done and that perhaps she was on the wrong path. But Aron had said himself that his visions ***always*** come true. He and his brothers would die, and she would become queen. The Crone, it seemed, would be good to her word. The thought of being queen made her skin tingle, and the Crone had promised far more. Celia smiled at Aron. It perfectly disguised the fact that she now looked forward to his death.

The prince stared up at her with an odd look in his eye. "That's,' he paused. "That's good. You would make a good queen. A good queen to any king."

Oh, does he think that I will become queen through marriage? He obviously does. Oh, the poor boy. I will become queen by walking over your cold corpse.

THE ARRIVAL OF FRIENDS AND TROUBLE

"It's clever really," said Joshua as he tied his belt with a small ceremonial dagger at his hip. He checked himself, dressed in his finest tunic, the Cross displayed on the front.

"What is?" Jacob asked, pulling on his perfectly shined boots.

They checked each other over; only the finest would do today. Finally, convinced they would pass even the strictest inspections, they made their way to the door.

"Having a royal wedding," Joshua answered. "The lords have been at the Centre for months, and nothing has been resolved. Father can use the wedding as a way of bringing everyone together. It could ease tensions. Be an end to all this."

"Do you really think any of the lords would rebel?"

"No," Joshua answered, and his younger brother turned to look at him as they walked. Jacob didn't have to speak. His expression said it all. He knew Joshua was lying, and Joshua knew he knew. "Well," he said, resigned to telling the truth. "The Western Rebellions happened because the Western lords doubted our family. The other Points stayed true to us, so we won the war, but I don't know what would happen if all the Points doubted. From a strategic point of view, this would be the perfect time to turn on us. Now more than ever, they could burn it all."

"But what could they have to gain?" Jacob asked. "They're lords of the Cross. Rich and powerful, every one of them. What more could they want?"

"Surely someone with your Gift would know. It's one of the sad things about this world." Joshua shook his head. "Power! Some people always want more. There will always be those who see opportunity. There will always be those." He looked at his brother. "That want a crown."

This time, Jacob knew that Joshua was telling the truth. "Why doesn't Father just let me walk in there and ask every one of them if they're traitors?"

"Hmm," Joshua mused. "It would be fun to watch, but most would be insulted. That's the last thing we want right now. Besides, most wouldn't see themselves as traitors. Today is the day we find out, I guess. Father is going to announce the wedding, and he's going to demand an end to this. It's decision time."

They remained silent for a moment before Jacob spoke again.

"So," he said, deciding to change the subject. "Are you excited for your name day?"

Joshua's name day was approaching fast, but it wasn't something he'd thought much about. It was hard to think about such a normal thing as a name day when there was so much else to fill his mind. He didn't want to burden his brothers, but he found his spare time often filled with conversations with the voice within his head. The voice of his Gift. It spoke to him frequently, trying to guide him. It seemed like an endless chess game with himself that he could never win. Move and countermove of battles that may never come to pass.

Guards stood at the door as the two princes approached and opened it upon their arrival. It amused Joshua sometimes to think about how comfortable and at ease he and his brothers had grown in their positions as princes. Yet, they could step beyond the castle walls and talk slang, stand slouched, spit on the floor and walk casually down any street as though they were born to that life instead of this. All the lords that his family had spent so long trying to impress would be horrified to see the princes of the realm behaving in such a way.

They were met inside the room by several smiling faces, including ones they had not seen in some time.

"Uncle Christopher," said Joshua as he opened his arms and went to hug his uncle. Joshua knew full well that Christopher found the interactions a little uncomfortable but took amusement in forcing them upon him.

"Grey!" Jacob cried out in surprise. Joshua turned from one uncle to another. Grey looked back at them from between his brothers, Michael and John. Of the three brothers of House Ken, Grey was the rarest sight at the Centre.

"Hello, boys. Well, that's the wrong word. Look how big you've gotten."

He embraced them both.

"When did you get to the Centre? I heard you'd travelled all the way to Nebrank."

"I did, and many more places. I will tell you all some stories later. I came on a cargo ship this morning. Sailed straight up The Way and into the city docks."

"That must be why you smell so bad," said John, cheekily knocking a light fist into his brother's ribs. Grey ignored him. "I hope you don't mind me wishing you an early happy name day, Luke," he said.

"Erm, that's very kind of you, Uncle, but I'm Joshua."

Grey scowled for a moment before smiling again. "Apologies, you've all changed so much. I'll wish Luke a happy name day when he arrives."

"But it's not Luke's name day for months, Uncle, and he has the same name day as yours if you remember."

"He does? Well, there's just so damned many of you I lose track," he said with embarrassment as Michael and John took him by the shoulders and led him away with smiles and laughter. John filled his ears with promises of drinking until they passed out.

"Well," came a soft voice, and the boys both turned to see their mother's smiling face. "I do so love having the family together." She hugged them both fiercely.

"A growing family," said Jacob as he looked again at Christopher, who stood beside his wife, Karin, who clutched the hand of a young boy with bright blond hair, Cousin Oliver, the baby the boys had saved from the Crone. Karin's other hand held her daughter, Harriet, while also nursing a swollen belly. This time, as the third child, they knew it would not have a Gift. It would not pass any further down the indirect bloodline.

Finally, Branthony entered the room, and it occurred to Joshua that he had perhaps never seen so many of his family together. This was a rare occasion. He felt happy for his Aunt Susan, and he'd never been to a family wedding, so why did he feel apprehensive? His Gift wasn't like Aron's. Joshua couldn't see what was coming; however, his Gift tried to plan for every eventuality. He wouldn't tell anyone, but he had a bad feeling. Nothing he could define. Just something there in the pit of his stomach. He thought it was because his Gift couldn't work. There was too much happening.

Ever since the discovery that the Crone, likely in league with the Varliants, had plotted against the Gift, Joshua felt a significant shift in his ability to harness Guidance. It was impossible to formulate a solid strategy when the full extent of the enemy's capabilities was unknown. Every decision he and his family made risked falling directly into the Crone's trap. If she was capable of devising plans against the Gift, she could be anticipating the moves dictated by Guidance. It made his head pound whenever he thought on it.

"It's nearly time," Branthony announced, but then he turned his eyes to his children. "Whatever happens in there, try to stay calm. There may be harsh words spoken. There may be insults. Maintain your composure. It's why I've kept your brothers busy. I don't think they could hold themselves back. Your Gifts may be more useful but don't speak out of turn. What happens in that room will have profound consequences for us all. Let none of us make any rash decisions."

As a united family, they moved to the double doors leading to the great hall. The doors opened, and the Fait and House Ken members entered the hall and gained the instant attention of the gathered lords and ladies.

Joshua surveyed them all with interest. Each new face he looked upon forced his Gift to deliver a fresh wave of nausea as it tried to give him information on each of them. He couldn't help but assess each as an ally or a threat. Guidance seemed to think of people as little more than pieces on a chessboard. How could they be moved? How could they be used?

He didn't like it. Such a way of thinking seemed cold. Surely people were more than that. Surely people were not supposed to be seen in such a way, but the more his Gift grew, the more it seemed to be happening.

Jacob leant gently toward him and whispered. "What's it telling you?" he asked, obviously spotting what must have been the telltale signs. "I still don't even know who most of them are. Their lands, sigils, or banners. Not a clue."

"My Gift isn't Knowledge," he whispered back. "It's Guidance, and it's telling me that some people in this room are a threat."

Branthony took the lead as he directed his family to the Dias.

"Thank you for all coming," he said loudly when everyone had taken their place. This was it. After this meeting, he would know. Either his kingdom would be united or divided. "I have asked you all here today because I have some announcements. I have both good and bad news to deliver." That caused slight stirrings around the room. "Before I make these announcements, I want to say something. I want to remind you all who ***we*** are. I don't mean my family and me. I mean ***us***." He held out his hands, encompassing the room. "All of us. Together. It is easy to think of us as separate entities: North, South, East, West and Centre, but we are all parts of a whole. We are the Cross." He clenched his fist together with the word.

"When we work together, we cannot be matched. Our combined strength has made us the most powerful nation in the known world. Remember that. With this in mind, I make my first announcement, in the hope of bringing this kingdom together again. My sister Susan is to be wed. She will be bonded by marriage to Robert of House Dooley, who resides in the Northern-Point in the fine lands of The Shield."

Roberts House was small and had no representation in the room, but Branthony saw Lord Phillip Greaves and his young son Edward stir at the mention of their land, a tip from Joshua to gain some favour. The small things can often make a big difference.

The announcement was met with applause and, as far as Branthony could see, some genuine happiness. In troubling times, a day such as a wedding could be a salve on a burn.

"I hope to use this wedding to bring us back together and forget the troubles that threaten to divide us. I hope it will remind us that together we are strong! Together we have thrown back every enemy who has ever tried to march upon these lands, and together we can do it again."

His words seemed to fall on some quicker than others. Glances passed around the room as realisation dawned. Finally, someone stood. Lady Marrice Stowland of the Gauntlet. Branthony knew her well. Her husband had died during the Western Rebellions fighting for Branthony's cause. He couldn't tell whether her being the one to stand was good or bad. It had the potential to be both.

"Your Majesty," she addressed him. "Are we to gather from your words that we may soon be called upon to repel another enemy?"

"You are correct, Lady Stowland. I believe an enemy approaches."

"And who may this enemy be?"

Branthony could see she was nervous yet determined. She held her head high, her back stiff. As well as trepidation, immense pride ran through her. She was the embodiment of a noble lady.

"Varliant," he replied. The answer was met with mixed reactions ranging from outrage that a city such as Varliant should dare to oppose the might of the Cross, to great anger that a supposed ally who had recently been seen to practically throw money at the Cross had now somehow turned to an enemy.

"May I ask His Majesty what has led him to this conclusion?"

"I believe Varliant was responsible for the attempt on my youngest son's life. I believe the representatives of Varliant have been here under false pretences. Making deals and promises they never intended to keep, all hoping to drive a wedge between the Fait and the people of the Cross. I now know that Varliant is hiring mercenary groups and drawing forces to itself. I believe an attack will come, eventually."

Another figure stood. Lord Basel of the Black Fort. The lead opponent of the Crown. Branthony would swear there was a grin on the old man's face like this was the exact moment he'd been waiting for. It did not bode well. Branthony felt something in his gut and knew the next few moments would not be good. Basel's revelation at the previous meeting regarding Valfargs had cost Branthony dearly. He still didn't know how Basel had come by such information.

"These are very severe accusations," Basel said. "Does His Majesty have any proof?"

Here came the hard part.

"I have a witness that can place the Varliants with golden items used to bribe and mislead the populace into believing that the Fait have been withholding great wealth in order to sow—"

"Your proof," Lord Basel interrupted. The act alone sending different waves of emotion rolling over the room. Some seemed disgusted that he would dare do such a thing. Others seemed intrigued by what would push him to such an act. "Is that the Varliants told people the Crown is rich?" He spoke the words with the smuggest of faces, looking at those around him as though Branthony was a jester making jokes.

Branthony swallowed down his rage, yet Basel was far from finished.

"I do not mean to be impertinent," he said, even though everyone in the room knew that was precisely what he intended. "But does His Majesty not have a member of the Varliant delegation held here at the castle? Is this man a prisoner? Could he not be questioned by Prince Jacob? Surely if the power of the Fait is as strong as you say, then the Prince's Gift would get the truth from him."

Ah, so there it was. The trap had been set, and Branthony had walked right into it. He knew, in the end, it was inevitable. Was Lord Basel on the payroll of the Varliants? Was this always a part of their plan? Or was he simply following a logical course of questions?

"We have already questioned the man named Meroth. He was the last member of the Varliant party to remain here in the Cross. The others disappeared when they knew their plot had been discovered."

"Ah, I see," replied Lord Basel, his voice now a contemptuous whisper. "So, I gather we have a signed confession?"

"We do not," answered Branthony.

"No, we do not." His tone, his eyes, told everyone he knew perfectly well that there was no confession.

The arrogance and sarcasm oozing from the man were hard to bear. Lord Basel stepped out from his table toward Branthony, staring up at his king with defiance. *Here it comes*, thought Branthony. He already knew that this was the breaking point. Here and now, the split in his kingdom would finally come.

"Would His Majesty care to tell ***us***, his loyal subjects, what he does have?"

Branthony hesitated. It was unlike him. He hesitated and it cost him. Lord Basel jumped on the initiative, and Branthony realised that this wasn't a lord defecting but a lord attacking.

"I shall tell everyone what **I** have?" The first blow came, and in a rare experience, Branthony found himself almost struck dumb. He could only stand and listen as Lord Basel sent his subsequent attacks.

"I have the transcript from the interrogation of our Varliant friend, Meroth. A man who came here to this kingdom with nothing but good and honest intentions to grow relationships and business. The Varliants came to us with the hand of friendship offered firmly out. They were repaid with insults and accusations from our king.

"The king, the queen, and all four of their sons carried out the interrogation. The so-called combined might of the Fait, even Prince Jacob with his Gift of Truth. Would anyone care to hear the transcript?"

There were obvious nods, and Branthony, rage flowing through him, knew what was about to come and could do nothing about it. If he stopped this now, it would only be worse for him. He listened with clenched fists as Lord Basel read from the transcript that Meroth had declared his innocence and Jacob had confirmed he was telling the truth. Of course, the conversation between Branthony and his family was not included. They had whispered among themselves. The damage, however, was done.

The transcript was public record, yet it still stung that Lord Basel had obtained it. Branthony thought that perhaps he should have confiscated it, but he did not want to lie to his people. He wanted to convince them. Besides, maybe it was better that this came out now rather than later. This way, there was nothing to hide. Surely someone would have demanded a more public questioning. Yes, at least this way it was out.

"What does His Majesty have to say?" asked Lord Basel loudly. "I would say this is another sign of his incompetent leadership. This is another in a long line of bad decisions that could again lead us to war! I must wonder if the king himself will remain with us this time, as an enemy comes to our borders?"

Branthony would allow anyone to argue against him, but he would not allow insults. His rage grew, and only Debreace's gentle touch on his hand held it at bay. She cupped his fist and whispered, "Remember who we are."

"Perhaps," Lord Basel continued, knowing that he had already gone too far but that this could be his only opportunity to convince others.

"This is a sign that the power of the Fait is failing. Until a few years ago, we believed ***they*** were the only magic wielders. We now know this is not true. We know," he drew his eyes over the room. "The enemy that came for us showed magnificent strength with magic. Perhaps others are stronger still. For all the supposed strength and power of the Fait and their Gifts, none of them saw the attack on Prince Jacob coming.

"The king talks of the outrageous act of open insurrection in his capital. Do I have to remind you all that the attack came ***not*** from the Varliants but from the king's own citizens? People so poorly ruled that they would dare to attack their king in the streets. Is this the leadership we want? Is this the leadership we deserve?"

That blow was the worst. The truth, Branthony knew, was a bitter pill to swallow. He allowed a moment for the commotion to die down. Lord Basel stood defiantly, staring at Branthony, who drew a long, deep breath through his nose. He released it slowly, composing himself. Rage would do nothing here. By the God, he hated politics.

"I know," said Lord Basel in a quieter tone. "That the king could choose to go back on his assurances of safe passage and put me in chains, perhaps hang me from the rafters or take my head, but if he does, then let the rest of you see the truth that he is, indeed, a liar.

"After this meeting, I am returning to the Black Fort. I suggest the rest of you consider the facts and do likewise."

"And what are the ***facts***?" asked Lady Stowland.

"The facts are these. Number one." Basel held a finger in the air. "The Fait are not the only ones in this world with magic. They lied to us. Number two!" Another finger raised to join the first. "King Branthony's leadership, or lack thereof, led to an enemy breaching the walls of the Centre. Number three, he has spurned the offer of friendship from a possible powerful ally, all at the expense of his people. Number four. His own son's Gift declares the Varliants ***innocent***. Either we can assume this is the truth, or if he would deny it, we can assume the Gift is not nearly as dependable as he would have us believe."

Branthony felt Jacob stir at his side and held out a hand to stay him.

"And number five."

Basel's voice turned to a growl as he looked Branthony in the eye. All Branthony could do was hold his glare.

"The king knew of possible Valfarg movement. He ignored it and kept the information from us, deeming his problems more important. Finally, we now seem to be on the verge of war yet again, caused by his actions. Will you deny any of these claims?"

Branthony breathed deeply. Everyone in the room was waiting for him to explode, and despite Lord Basel's harsh words, he could see the man was trembling. Partially from adrenaline, maybe, but the quivering in his eyes showed his fear.

Oddly, a wave of calmness washed over Branthony.

"I will not," he replied, and a fresh set of dismayed murmurs broke through the room. "There is some truth to all your words, Lord Basel. It shames me to admit it. Whilst you are entirely wrong, in more ways than you know, there is ***some*** truth to your words.

"This is also the truth. The Varliants are our enemy. They are working with the Crone. She is the one behind all of this and an enemy to us all. Together, the Crone and Varliant try to divide us. I understand that some of you may feel wronged, and if you wish to leave with Lord Basel, my guarantee of safe passage stands."

This time, Branthony had to stay Joshua. Was his Third-Born about to counsel against letting them go? Was Guidance telling him that this a bad tactical move?

Lord Basel signalled to his retinue, and they stood to leave. Basel himself turned to the room one last time. He still seemed uncertain if he would be allowed to leave. Foolishness, if Branthony did go back on his word, it would persuade others to turn against him. Then again, it may also deter some from doing so. Either way, the result would be the same regarding the Black Fort. Branthony had lost them.

"The time of the Fait is at an end," said Basel loudly. "Their power is not what we have been led to believe. Not anymore. He is using you to fight his battles for him. Many have already had to do this in their lifetimes. What did it cost you? He dooms you to save himself."

That was a step too far. Finally, Branthony's anger erupted.

"YOU GO TOO FAR!" The fury in his voice shocked the room, and the tension rose to new levels. Men bristled, and suddenly there seemed to be a threat of violence. Branthony calmed his voice a little, but it was now impossible to keep his frustrations down. "I am your king! As such, my battles should be ***your*** battles, as ***yours*** are ***mine***."

It was Branthony's turn to stare down the room, and it was not hard to see he had mastered the process much more than Lord Basel.

"Anyone who wishes to leave should do so now. They will not be stopped, but when this fight comes, and it will, know that those who stand with me here today will be the first under my protection. If anyone chooses to turn against me in battle, remember you had the chance to stay loyal. Remember the Western Rebellions. Remember every story or vision you have of me in battle. Remember it all when we meet on the field."

Basel had no response. He turned and left the room. It pained Branthony to see others stand despite his words. Not a majority, but enough to weaken him severely. Worse, there were people from every point of the Cross. Men and women, Branthony had hoped to count on. He held their eyes as they left, though many would not return the look. He wanted to be angry at them. In truth, he knew the Crone had once again planned to perfection. Planting Meroth had been a master stroke. At least Lord Hive had the strength to look him in the eye as he passed. Branthony had lost the Red Fort in the east and the Black Fort in the west. It did not make for a good picture.

Those leaving filed out, and another form stood just as the line was about to end. Lord Dwayne of The First Fort. Branthony hid it well, but this made him shudder. The First Fort was the Cross's westernmost stronghold, the first line of defence against an invasion on that border, where Varliant would come from. It would also mean Branthony had lost two of the largest Western lords. Even during the rebellions, they had remained neutral. They'd not sided against the Crown, though they did not fight against their neighbours.

Lord Dwayne was a large man, a renowned warrior and a great if not unconventional leader. He looked at Branthony with a single raised eyebrow.

"Your Majesty," he began. "Varliant being our enemy, I can accept," he said with a shrug. "This Crone, that you claim is the true enemy. I can certainly accept that, especially after hearing the stories of her attack. I can even look over the obvious fact that you seem to have known about her for a long time and chose to leave us in the dark. You're right. Your war is our war. We've fought your wars for years. Travelling to the Edge to fight the Sile. I lost a brother in those wars.

"You sued for peace with the Sile. Not a choice I would have made, but one I could understand, and so I could accept it. But then the Sile broke that peace and attacked. They reached the Centre, and though the day was won, it came at significant cost. I lost another brother that day. Gutted by a Sile axe.

"Our enemy for generations, and even when they broke your peace, attacked your capital, murdered your people, you chose to let them go. You had Morbius Duvec here, and you let him go. Now, we send our men, good men, to Sile lands. To protect them. This, this I cannot accept. It has stewed on me for the past years, and it rots my soul. All of this combined is too far. So now I will make my stand. Of all Lord Basel's talk, he forgot the biggest betrayal. Peace with those ***animals***!"

Branthony wanted to argue, to make his point. He didn't get the chance. Lord Dwayne stalked from the room. His words had resonated with some, as several more stood and left with him.

Branthony watched them go in silence, then waited a moment to address those who remained.

"Many of you will believe I have gone too easy on those who have chosen not to stand with us. To those of that opinion, I say this. Our real enemy is coming. Be assured of that. I will not divide us further by going back on my word. I understand many of you have doubts, but I say this. The power of the Fait has been underestimated before, and every time it has proven itself. It will do so again."

Lady Stowland decided to have one last word before retaking her seat.

"I will stand with the Fait, as my family always has. I will reach out to some of those who have left us and hope their anger fades with time. The people of The Gauntlet will be ready when our enemy comes but know this. We are weakened. Now is the perfect time for an enemy to strike. I hope the Fait are ready for what is to come. I hope they can see us through these difficult times. I hope they are everything they have always claimed to be. Perhaps, they need to be even more still."

She took her seat, and Branthony nodded his acknowledgement and gratitude.

"The Fait will be ready. I guarantee it. I thank you all for remaining, even if it was a hard decision. I hope you will join me soon in celebrating my sister's marriage."

Let there be one small day of happiness before the real war comes.

WORDS OF THE FAITHFUL
ACTIONS OF THE SUSPICIOUS

"Well, well. Look at you?" said Michael as he entered the room to look upon his nephews and brother-in-law, all dressed for the occasion yet again. "Not often I see you with these things on your heads." He gestured toward the crowns they all wore. Though Branthony had worn his many times, he never seemed to have grown comfortable with it.

"Is everything ready?" asked Branthony

"As it can be. How did everything go this morning?"

"As well as could be expected," Branthony answered.

"The last few days passed quickly, as Lady Stowland promised, she talked to some of those who decided to leave. I, too, tried to sway some. The efforts succeeded in some cases, but unfortunately, the argument goes both ways. Some lords who stood by me have now decided against it. Mainly those whose neighbours stand against me. It is all painfully understandable. We regained six of those that left and lost four the other way, so I supposed I should be grateful.

"Anything else I should know?" Michael asked.

"All those who have chosen to depart have now left the city and are making their way home. I have tripled patrols on the main routes and sent word to all four Point-Wardens to do the same. All lords are expected to secure their lands. I can't have people taking this as an opportunity. Some may see this as an invitation to banditry. Our patrols at sea are to double in case of any moves against us.

"All lords will make a full listing of food, grain and armaments and prepare their people for what is to come. The Western-Point is to be set on a battle-ready status. Lord Richard Dawsel will depart the Centre soon and return to Rodley. From there, he will take his men further west as close to the First Fort as possible. When Varliant comes, it will most likely come at the Western-Point, though the south and north shall also be ready in case they attempt to bypass our defence."

"You're preparing to fight the Varliants, but how can we fight an external enemy when the biggest threat is within? Is sending an army west simply about preparing for Varliant?"

"If Lord Dwayne or Basel decides to make a move, I want to be ready. The last rebellion relied on surprise and quick movement. I won't make the same mistake again.

"I gave my word that all would be allowed to return home, but that is where my patience ends. By tomorrow, a decree will be sent across the kingdom that all must swear fealty. Any who do not will be at war with the Crown. I won't force anyone to fight for me, but I will have guarantees they wont fight against me."

"Has it truly come to this, old friend? Civil war, maybe on all four Points?"

"I hope for the best but plan for the worst. When the decree is received, many may have second thoughts. I will give each lord their own choice. I will not hold any accountable for another's decision."

"But if we do this, if we fight them all, on each Point, we are doing the Crone's work for her. We weaken ourselves whilst giving her the time to grow stronger."

"I know, my friend. I know. It is hard to accept, but once again, the Crone has outmanoeuvred us entirely, but I also know she needed this. She needs us weakened. Even with the mercenaries and Varliant together, they do not have enough to defeat us. She needs time to grow her forces. They need time to prepare. We have the ground, the defences, the numbers, and the experience."

"So, we will give her the time?"

"Unfortunately, though she is not the only one who needs it. We desire it as much as she."

"For what?"

Branthony looked to his sons.

"My children are growing strong in their Gifts. Though it is the might of the Cross that will fight off any enemy, it is my sons who will defeat the Crone. It is what they were born for. I know it. She thinks she is giving herself time, but she also gives us it. My sons will grow stronger, and they will be ready when she comes. We all will."

"Wow," said Michael. "There he is."

Branthony raised a questioning eyebrow.

"Boys," said Michael, gesturing for them to come closer. "Your father has dedicated his life to peace. He has fought and strived for it. Peace with the Sile. Peace for the Cross. It is a noble and admirable goal." Though he stayed close to the boys and talked to them, he now locked his eyes with Branthony. "But your father is a man built for war. His Gift is meant for battle. This is where your father thrives. This is what he does best. Learn from him now. You are learning from a master."

"Together we will win," said Branthony in a firm, powerful voice. "Together! However, today is not a day for war." He ushered his sons to the door. "You all head out. It's almost time." He patted Michael's shoulder. The little speech, though unexpected, was welcome. They exited the room, leaving Branthony alone. He checked over himself once more and had to admit he was nervous.

"You look fine," came a voice. He turned to the other end of the room and smiled warmly at the sight that met him, his sister standing before him in a splendid white dress with a long white fur cloak at her back. "Well," said Susan. "What about me? How do I look?"

He felt foolish for his pause but took an extra second to search for the right word. "Beautiful," was all he could think of. Simple, yet perfectly fitting.

"I take it you met with Robert?" she asked.

"Of course. You didn't think I'd let my sister marry someone without inspecting him first."

"I hope you weren't too hard on him," she said with a smile. "So, what did you think?"

"He's a fine man, Susan. If he makes you happy, then he is a fine choice. Are you ready?"

"As I'll ever be."

"Then I shall see you out there."

"What?" she exclaimed loudly. "Branthony, you are my eldest brother and the king. Our father has long passed. I expect you to walk me down the aisle."

Branthony was taken aback. It took a moment to compose himself.

"All the preparations, the rehearsals. I did not attend."

"You have had a lot going on and many distractions. I didn't want to burden you further, but if you think you're getting out of this, you're sadly mistaken."

"I…I didn't think you'd want me."

"Who else would I have?"

He smiled as he offered his arm.

"It shall be my honour."

She took it, and together they walked to the door.

The four princes stood just before the large wooden altar and looked over the huge hall filled with long benches occupied by some of the most powerful people in the kingdom. Their eyes glanced at the top balcony stretching around the upper circumference, the people up there looking down on those below. Worth as much note as the people in attendance were those who were not. The missing faces of those who had decided to stand against the Fait were very noticeable.

Everyone had dressed in their absolute finest. A royal wedding was a rare thing indeed. On the first bench closest to the boys sat their mother, who smiled at them all, pride swelling. Next to her was Uncle Christopher, who tried to show his usual calm persona, though Jacob had already confirmed that Christopher had lied when he said he wasn't nervous. Other immediate family members sat close, and it seemed they were all intent on focusing on the four princes who stood in waiting. Uncle John pulled faces, determined to try to make one of them break their stiff facade. He also seemed intent on looking at Lady Margaret, a blond-haired woman who blushed and smiled at every gesture offered to her by John.

The only two people besides the boys who stood were the priest, who was wearing a long grey gown as was customary, and Robert, the man who would soon become their uncle. The boys felt a pang of sympathy for the man. He barely knew anyone here. There had been talk that Susan, as a princess of the Cross, was marrying beneath her station. The boys cared little for such things. They had learned young that anyone can play a significant part in the world. Did Joe and Ollie not sit at the back of the room, a testament to how someone could rise, how anyone could make an incredible difference?

Robert stood with his back to the room, hands on the holy book, and eyes down, as was customary. He was a devout man and would not turn until his bride was standing ready at his side.

"What's taking so long?" whispered Luke.

"Not sure. I thought Father was going to be here with us," replied Aron.

As though they had heard him, the doors at the room's far end opened and everyone stood. The boys straightened at the sight of their father standing beside Aunt Susan. Together they made their way down the centre aisle.

Each of the boys dipped their head as their father and aunt moved past. Susan smiled, her face beaming with happiness. Finally, she looked at Robert as he turned to see her.

The boys stepped back as their father handed Susan over and sat beside Debreace. Much to their annoyance, the boys had to remain standing. They had been given a place of great honour. They were happy to do it but hopeful the ceremony wouldn't take too long.

The priest began his reading as the room sat quiet, listening. The words seemed to drone on as the priest's monotonous voice rang through the hall. Perhaps it was the sound of his voice or just standing in concentration that led Aron to begin feeling an odd yet familiar sensation. Luke noticed the change first.

"What are you doing?" he whispered, his mouth barely moving as his eyes flicked to Mother to be sure he hadn't been seen.

"My Gift," he confirmed. "I've seen this before."

"Does that mean there's trouble?"

"No, it's just strange for me."

Aron tried to still himself and ignore that odd feeling of déjà vu. He pondered how many dreams he'd had and moments of the future he'd seen. Why show him these particular moments in time?

The ceremony proceeded, and soon all four of the boys were beginning to shuffle on restless feet. Finally, the priest announced the couple as married in the eyes of the King and the God, which was met by rapturous applause and cheers.

"Finally," said Luke into Aron's ear. The four of them stepped to the centre aisle. It was their job to safely escort the bride and groom from the room, not that there was any danger; it was ceremonial role. They lined up and began to walk back down the centre aisle. Susan and Robert took in the congratulations and best wishes of those who passed, so it was a long walk despite the short distance.

His aunt's back dominated Aron's eyeline. He stared absentmindedly into the fur of the long white cloak she wore. Joshua's voice almost woke him from a daydream as he spoke.

"I don't know that man."

'Huh?" said Aron, blinking.

"That man," Joshua nodded, but didn't point. "I don't know him."

Aron glanced in the direction of the gesture and saw a man about halfway down the hall, sitting to the far end of one of the pews, standing and smiling like all the others awaiting his moment to offer his congratulations. Not that he'd have much of a chance at that distance. As Aron stared, there was certainly something off about the man. He looked uncomfortable. Unsure of himself. Out of place.

"So what? I couldn't tell you who most of them are."

"Neither could I, but I don't know his face. My Gift assesses people, factors them in."

"Factors them into what?"

"A plan."

"A plan for what?"

"Everything," he said with weariness.

"So, what does it say about him?"

"It tells me I don't know him."

"So?"

"So that means he could be a threat."

"You're paranoid. That could be true of anyone."

"Exactly, yours isn't the only Gift that's becoming annoying."

"Always having a plan. Sounds terrible." The bitterness and sarcasm weren't hidden from Aron's voice. Not that he meant to be that way. Sometimes it was simply hard to hold back his frustrations.

Slowly but surely, they made their way down. None of the boys could help their attention from falling on the man that Joshua's Gift had singled out. Especially as he stood and began pushing forward towards the aisle, his hands held out as though grasping for Susan and Robert. He pushed hard, bumping those around him in desperation to get closer. Joshua began to edge toward his aunt, and the others grew tenser with him. The man was close. He was so close that he practically jumped over those before him to overcome the final gap. The boys began to move, reaching for the daggers they wore at their sides.

At that moment, Robert turned to the man and beamed in delight as he took the outstretched hand in his own. Even Susan embraced him warmly. He was one of the few people there specifically for Robert, so it was no wonder he looked out of place, and the boys had thought him a threat. They relaxed and fell back to a normal distance, ashamed of their earlier suspicion.

"I knew it," said Luke, bullishly. "Your Gift is stupid. You gonna get scared whenever you see someone you don't know?"

"It's not like that," retorted Joshua angrily. Jacob was about to speak up after hearing the lie but decided otherwise after a quick nudge from Joshua. Luke seemed almost shocked by the sharp response, as though insulted that his brother would dare even stick up for himself. In truth, it was a rare occurrence, at least with such an elevated level of exasperation.

They reached the end of the hall and began to file out. Joshua looked back again at all those happy faces. If they were all so happy, why couldn't he be.

BLOOD AND WATER

Cutter-of-Men watched as the Crone stood uncharacteristically still in quiet consideration. Her lips and eyes moved slightly as though she were speaking with someone who was not there. Finally, the Crone opened her eyes and looked straight at Cutter. Those cold, black orbs that made the soul quiver.

"The time has come."

She extended her arm before her, gazing intently at a hand of immaculate white bone. It was a relic of death, an object that defied the very essence of life. There were no muscles, no tendons, nor any sinew to bind it together; it was a hollow appendage, devoid of warmth and vitality. Yet, astonishingly, this lifeless hand responded to the Crone's thoughts like any living limb, obeying her commands as if it were as natural as any other.

Odd, that of all the things people found so strange and disgusting about her, this hand was to many the worst, yet it was not ***her*** hand.

She grabbed the ulna and radius, the two bones that made up the forearm, wrapped a hand of rotted flesh around them, then pulled. With an effort and a squelch of blood, the bones came free without so much as a whimper of pain.

A cloud of black mist formed from the Crone's elbow and swirled before dissipating. A perfect arm remained in its place. Not the arm of the Crone, a youthful arm with soft, smooth skin.

She turned it over. Delicate fingers curled at the end of a soft palm. She rubbed a thumb over her fingertips, and her lips twisted into a snarl at the sensation. She pushed her power into the arm and watched as the skin blackened, cracked, and shrivelled until it looked the same as the rest of her.

"Better," she growled.

From the room's shadows, Cutter-of-Men stepped closer, her head tilted as she watched the Crone's transformation.

"Why?" she asked, her dark skin and jade green eyes shining in the torchlight.

"Why what?" the Crone growled.

"Your skin. You choose to look this way."

"Not exactly, but tell me. What is the alternative? Look normal? Beautiful? What are these things? No. I detest such an appearance. Why should I conform to this world when I am beyond it? This world should conform to me. Is man made in the image of the God? Then I will ravage that image. Besides, is it not amusing to see the horror in the eyes of those who look upon me? I find their discomfort delightful."

The Crone looked down at the bones that had served as her hand for so long that she could not remember the number of years. She had strange emotions as she looked upon it, but such things were not to be discussed. She plucked one small bone from the end of a finger, keeping it for herself.

"Lady Celia has sent word from the Blood River. They are building defences, fortifying their position. We need to move now. The Cross is divided. Weakened. Now is the time to strike. Take this." She offered the rest of the bone hand.

"Why?"

"The village at the Blood River is protected. I cannot enter, but you can with this. It greatly weakens me to lose it, but sacrifices must be made. Now that we know the camp's defences, it is the perfect time to strike."

"What is it?" asked Cutter as she took the skeletal hand. "Much more than simple bones."

"So much more," the Crone's gravelly voice replied. "That hand once belonged to an angel." Cutter's shock was obvious. She stared at the bones with fear and reverence.

"How did they come into your possession?"

"It matters not. All that matters is what they can do. They can get you inside the village. Past the defences that are in place there. Not the things of man. More powerful things. The rest will be up to you."

"There are many men there. I cannot kill them all."

"You will not be alone," crackled the Crone. She reached within her black, ragged cloak and withdrew a vile of blood which she drank with a glorious shudder.

"Will they heal like last time?" asked Cutter, remembering the glorious days when she and Forty-Of-Hands had cut through the men of the Cross and could not be stopped. No, that was wrong. Even with the Gift supplied by the Crone, Forty had eventually been killed. The king of the Cross crushed his body, and Morbius Duvec took his head.

"No," answered the Crone. "This time they will be different. Pushing Gifts into others takes them from me. I have only enough of the Gift of Healing left to maintain myself. This time, I will give the Gift of Concealment. A Gift from the first days. A Gift from the other side. The creatures I send with you will be one with the night, and they have a touch of another Gift. Something to mock the men of the Cross and ensure victory."

Cutter was once again amazed by all the Crone could do, yet as always, she had questions.

"Can the Fait do this? Pass on their Gifts?"

"No," the Crone chuckled. "The passing of power has nought to do with the Gift. This is something only I can do. A power that comes from far more than the blood or the river. This is a power left to me from a time beyond this realm. It is my reason for being here."

Cutter stared back at her, once again feeling little understanding of the Crone's words.

"Magic," said the Crone, addressing Cutter's bafflement. "It is a thing not of this world. The blood of the Fait is not of this world. That is how they use the Gift. You have been given the Gift of Healing, which offers some resistance, but I warn you again, too much use will kill you. Your predecessor had more of it than you, yet he was dead that night, even if he had won that battle." Cutter was momentarily taken aback by the revelation. "He was careless, reckless. You must be smarter. The creatures I send with you will not live past the dawn. Be sure to accomplish your objectives before the sun rises.

"Trust me, my champion. As I have always said, I am far more than the Fait even dare to dread. Do this, and from there we shape the world anew. Now go!"

With that, the torches flickered out. Darkness filled the room, and Cutter-of-Men was now far away.

Merleal entered the tent to the exhausting sound of arguments. It had seemed the Sile and the Men of the Cross had worked out many of their differences, but something had reignited their passions.

She pushed through the crowd to find the two men she sought at its centre. Morbius and Walter glared at each other over the large wooden table in a stalemate of anger and frustration.

Merleal stumbled a little. She felt dizzy. Unsettled. Something was wrong, but she could not figure out what. It felt like when a headache was coming on, but so much worse, like there was an approaching tide that threatened to wash her away.

"Daughter," said Graf, noticing her presence and sickly appearance. "What's wrong?"

"I don't know. I think something is coming. I can feel its approach, but this is new to me. It may be nothing."

He looked at her momentarily before turning to the arguing men surrounding him.

"Enough," he barked to no avail. "ENOUGH!" The room grew quiet as those around took notice of both Graf and Merleal.

"By the God, My Lady," said Walter. "You appear unwell. Forgive us for disturbing you at this late hour. Let some of my men escort you to your bed."

"Something is wrong," said Graf for his daughter. "Danger may be approaching."

"Danger," said Morbius. "What danger? How can you be sure?"

"I'm not," answered Merleal. "Not entirely, but I can feel something strange. Something is getting closer."

"There is nothing to fear," assured Walter. "We have scouts out beyond the perimeter. If something approaches, they will see it and give a warning."

She wasn't so sure. Whatever she was feeling, it was getting stronger.

"Perhaps Sir Walter is correct, Merleal," said Morbius. "Let us get you comfortable, somewhere you can rest."

The feeling only intensified. "I don't need rest," she argued. "Something is—"

She never finished her sentence. A horn blew out somewhere in the distance. The men inside the cabin looked at each other. The horn blew again. Morbius and Walter locked eyes one more, the argument between them was gone this time.

"Swords," said Morbius with a grin.

"Swords," agreed Walter, oddly for once matching his counterpart's eager expression. With that word, all the men in the room quickly and efficiently prepared themselves. They could all argue relentlessly but let it not be said they were not warriors.

Merleal watched them leave and was surprised by their compliance. She was sure the pressure within her head started to fade somewhat. "What were they even arguing about?" she asked her father.

"Who can drink the most," he said with a shake of his head.

Sir Walter headed straight for his tent and emerged clad in plate and mail. That was when the first cries came, a sound that sent a shiver running through a man even as steeled as Walter. He arrived at the edge of the camp. The only recently erected wooden wall marked the line of their defence. The Sile warriors were already waiting, their bare skin glistening in firelight despite the chill of the night.

Walter stood on a raised platform beside Morbius, and together, they looked out into the night. Silence fell again as they waited for sight of their enemy. There was the normal tension that came before every battle, yet there was also something more, a sense of something supernatural. None of the scouts and guards placed beyond the perimeter had returned. An eerie silence greeted the watching eyes from within the camp.

"This reminds me of a night not too long ago," whispered Morbius.

"What night would that be?"

"The night I lost everything," he whispered, looking the taller man in the eye. "The night I was usurped. The night the Crone sent her champion to kill me."

The men startled in their lines as the darkness beyond the wall was suddenly broken by yellow piercing eyes. They stood out like words on parchment, seeming to hover in the air, yellow and terrifying.

"What are they?" asked Walter.

"Our enemy," answered Morbius. "We shall meet them in the field."

"We need to stay behind the wall where we can defend," argued Walter.

"No, Sile do not fight well this way. You stay here. We will meet them."

"Defending a fortified position against an unknown enemy is not cowardice."

"I do not think you a coward, Sir Walter. I think you are stubborn and self-righteous, but I also believe you can defend this wall. My men can not. I should have listened to you earlier. Perhaps we would have been better off having trained more, but we are wasted here. We will go and meet the enemy and fight like Sile. It is what we do best."

Morbius held Walter's eye briefly, then looked over his shoulder at Merleal. "If we fall, it is on you to save her. She is why they are here."

Reluctantly, Walter nodded and watched as the Sile warriors made their way through the open gate. They flooded out, and the gate was barred behind them. Walter had to admit the bravery of those men. The yellow eyes that peered back at them through the night held a terrifying effect. He stared at them a moment longer through the smoke of the perimeter fires, then turned and began barking orders at his men.

Looking from the darkness toward the village, Cutter-of-Men stepped forward. The creatures were all around her. She didn't know what they were. Men, not so long ago, many of them Sile. Many of them sent from the dungeons and prisons of Varliant. They were not men anymore. Now they were creatures of the Crones' making. She had changed them, much like she had changed Cutter herself once. Cutter was glad she had not received this Gift. She could feel the presence of these creatures; they seemed otherworldly, like they did not belong here. What did the Crone mean when she said a Gift from the other side? Their warm and rancid breath filled the air, yet all Cutter could see were yellow eyes shining as bright as small flames in the night. Something they'd done on purpose to intimidate.

She could feel something else, a pressure pushing her back. An invisible force told her to leave. She stepped forward again, struggling as though wading through thick mud. Holding out a hand, she would swear it was almost swatted away by the invisible force. She was not welcome here and would not be allowed to pass, not without a key.

She raised the hand of bones before her, pointing it like a weapon. It throbbed within her hand with a strange energy. She took a step, then another, and another, feeling the pressure growing, trying to push her back. She refused, holding the bones higher. She took another step and screamed. A black mist formed around her, healing her from whatever strange wounds were inflicted. It felt like she was being flayed, the skin pulled from her bones. Still, she pressed forward. A step, then another, and suddenly the resistance was gone, melted away like snow on a warm morning. Whatever spell was holding them back now ceased to be. Whatever protection surrounded the village of the Blood River, it was now gone. Or she had passed through it at least. Cutter-of-Men growled.

She did not need to give an order. The creatures felt it as well. They surged forward like a sudden wind blowing hard at her back. The battle began.

Beyond the camp's perimeter with the newly built wall at their back, the Sile formed a line with Morbius at the centre, the Sword-of-Answers in his hand. Shimmer-of-the-Night stood at his side; double-sided axe hefted at the ready. Morbius was now glad for the pits and spikes that filled the land between his men and their new enemy. The Blood River was on the other side of the camp, so as planned, it had left the enemy with only one real avenue of attack. Morbius would meet these things head-on.

He tried to calm his men, sensing their desire to charge. He watched as the yellow eyes moved closer and he waited for them to fall upon the traps. His heart sank as the eyes leapt into the sky, passing over the pits, then dodged perfectly between the spikes and obstacles left to hinder them.

"They know of the traps," he said, more to himself than anyone else. How else could they avoid them so perfectly? How could they know? Well then, so be it. Hand-to-hand it would be.

"Hold!" he cried, waiting for the enemy to get within range and be sure his men did not fall victim to the traps set to protect them. "Hold!"

Almost. Almost.

"Charge!" he cried, and the Sile warriors exploded forward. The enemy was one with the night. The only thing giving them away was the yellow eyes that seemed to hover in the darkness. He slashed his blade down but found nothing. The creatures, whatever they were, looked human enough when up close. They carried dark blades that seemed extensions of their arms. They appeared naked but blended so well with their surroundings that it was hard to be sure. Their very skin seemed translucent. He could see the trees and bushes through them, though the image was marred slightly.

Morbius smashed his blade against an enemy and found himself knocked back. When he defended a blow, his bones rattled with the impact. He was sent sprawling back as though kicked by a horse. He gasped. He had fought a battle like this before, when he fought against the King of the Cross. He knew then these creatures had more than one Gift. They also had Strength. No, a blow like that from Branthony would have crushed his ribs. They had a touch of a Gift, like some of the Sile that had gone with the Crone's former champion had a touch of Healing—nothing so potent as Forty-of-Hands and his chosen few.

Morbius had survived that fight with Branthony, and he would survive this.

"THEIR LEGS!" he cried. "TAKE THEIR LEGS!"

He threw himself into the battle.

Sir Walter heard the fighting raging just beyond the wooden wall. He heard the expected cries and grunts of men, but the sound was at the very edge of the wall. As though the enemy had already passed the killing field and reached deep into the Sile ranks. Surely not.

"They're getting slaughtered," said a voice to his side. "We've got to help."

"No," commanded Walter. "Defend the wall. That is what we must do. That is what we've trained to do. Positions!" he called. His men climbed onto the small parapet on their side of the wall with spears ready to be thrust down at any enemy attempting to climb. Arrows were ready to fire, but the battle was already too congested.

Walter stepped up beside his men and looked out at the fighting. The dark of the night hindered his vision. It was broken sporadically by torches and fires, but he could make little sense of the sight before him. The enemy could barely be seen. Invisible almost. There were short glimpses as they engaged, but when they moved away, they disappeared into the surroundings.

A cry from somewhere to his side grabbed Walter's attention, and he turned just in time to see one of his men being pulled over the wall like a rag doll. Walter swallowed his panic. He had expected this. Well, not exactly, but he had expected the unexpected. King Branthony had told him that when the Crone came, she would come with something not of this world.

"Fire," bellowed Walter. "We need more fire!" His men responded, lighting torches and throwing them over the wall. "More," he commanded. "More!"

The men of the Cross threw torch after torch, lighting arrows and sending them into the night. Eventually, some began lighting branches and cloth, anything that would take a flame. All were thrown far enough that the fire would not threaten the wall but deep enough to illuminate the battle beyond.

In the darkness beyond the wall, Morbius felt warm blood running down his chest. He slashed at his enemy but missed. Again and again, he missed. How could he fight what he could barely see?

He felt another hard blow knock him backwards again. His feet were swept from beneath him, and he was on his back.

He rolled but felt a weight bear down on him. Instead of trying to escape, he pushed into the weight, wrapping his arms around the shape before him and gripping it tightly. At last, he had hold of something. He swung his head forward and felt it connect with something that felt entirely human.

There was a problem. Though Morbius could tell he had hurt the thing, it still had a strength beyond that of normal men. It pushed back. Morbius felt hands on his face, shoving him into the dirt. Blows rained down; the wind rushed from his lungs. He felt hands around his neck, squeezing.

Suddenly, the weight lifted. Air filled his lungs, and Morbius felt hands lifting him to his feet.

"Rise, My Lord," said a young man who seemed familiar. "These creatures will not be the end of us."

He watched the young man leap forward with a spear in hand. He was as fast as anyone Morbius had ever seen. He disappeared into the carnage of the battle.

"Who was that?" asked Shimmer as he retook his place at Morbius' side. He was wounded but still able to fight.

"No idea," said Morbius. That was when the fire began to rain down. Torches were thrown from the wall, landing on the floor and illuminating the night. The more fire that fell, the more the enemy became visible. The skin that could barely be seen shimmered in the firelight, reflecting it oddly. "Walter, you old dog, you're not the fool I took you for." Morbius took his opportunity and attacked. Finally, he felt his blade cut deep into an enemy.

Fearing the light, the creatures moved away from it, but they did not retreat; they drove past the Sile defenders and began to charge the wall in numbers. Morbius could only look on as they leapt over in a single bound.

From inside the camp Sir Walter saw the creatures jump over his defensive perimeter and straight into the midst of his men. The slaughter began. Suddenly, the fight was inside the camp as well as outside. The creatures, whatever they were, could now be seen more clearly as the camp was more illuminated. It took mere moments for Walter to gauge the extent of their deadliness. He watched his men get batted aside as though they weighed nothing. He recognised the effect. He had fought alongside it before, and he had fought against it.

The enemy began tearing through his men, cutting, slashing, kicking, and punching. The surprise of having the enemy so suddenly amongst them caused panic. Discipline was lost, and order abandoned.

Walter felt momentarily frozen at the sight of so many of his men falling so quickly. His heart sank. All his preparations, traps and strategies, the building of the perimeter wall, the felling of trees, hours and hours of drills, practice and hard work, all for nothing. Morbius had been right. Walter had wasted his time.

He shook himself from his daze. This fight was not over yet; he had at least done one thing by illuminating the ground beyond the camp.

He had forced the enemy to split their numbers. With the added light, they lost some of their advantage and sought to achieve a quick victory by simply tearing through the camp and the village beyond. Walter would not allow it. He would not allow discipline to fail. "To me!" he bellowed. "To me!" He would force order upon his men and then force victory from this battle.

Merleal and the people of the village retreated to the water, feeling safer within its depths. She looked across the shimmering surface to her son. The children had been carried out as far as possible without being forced to swim. She turned back to face the camps, and already the fighting was spreading. Men were dying. Blood was being spilt on a level this place had never seen. She had done this. She had brought this blight upon her people. No, this was not her. This was the Crone's doing. She must remember that.

She began to pray.

"What are you doing?" a hysterical voice asked. Res was at her side, his panic obvious. "Praying will do nothing here," he argued. "We must flee." He looked back at the fighting. "They're working together." He turned back to her, hands gripping her shoulders tightly. "She told them about the defences. They must have known. It's the only explanation. She is a part of this. Don't you see?"

"Calm," Merleal ushered gently. "You're right, Res. She has sent them. These creatures are of the Crone's making."

"Yes," he said, voice weak but suddenly calmer. "Yes, the Crone. The Crone." Again, he turned back to the fighting. "They ***all*** work for the Crone."

There was an odd inflection to his voice. Was it the terror that had shaken his senses? Merleal wondered if he was, in fact, talking about the Crone. If not, then who? That was when Merleal saw her—the Crone's champion. Cutter-of-Men stalked forward. The creatures hung back. They would not enter the water. The power there was strong. It held them back, though Cutter was different. With a determined stare aimed directly at Merleal, she entered the river.

Morbius swung the Sword-of-Answers and felt it dig deep into the creature's side. When he pulled his weapon back, the creature fell, squirming. Morbius turned the sword and rammed it down through skin and bone into the earth. The squirms and movement came to an abrupt end. These things ***could*** be killed. It was getting to them that was the hard part.

As he surveyed the battle, he realised his men were being driven apart, separated from one another, making them all the easier to pick off. It was evident that the battle inside the camp was just as fierce. Some of the enemy had managed to leap over the wall, but others, it seemed, were being repelled. The defenders were having some success.

Morbius looked to the ground, which was littered with the dead or dying, and far too many of them were his men. He needed a plan, or this battle would be over, but chaos had gripped the situation with a firm hold. His cries and commands were lost to it.

The gates to the camp suddenly flung open. Morbius's first thought was that the creatures had opened them to allow their fellows inside, but he saw men of the Cross standing in a tight group, shields held high, spears and blades protruding from the gaps between them. Men in full suits of armour stood at the forefront.

He saw Sir Walter within the group, screaming commands. The men of the Cross ushered Morbius and his men to join them. Regroup, form a unit. It was not how Sile usually fought their battles, but it was obvious the men of the Cross were having more success. He thought back to their drills in the midday sun. He knew how well they could fight like this.

"On me!" he called. Though unsure, those who could hear him obeyed, rallying to their lord, forming a circle. They didn't carry shields and wear armour as the men of the Cross did, but even so, the new strategy had an immediate effect.

Sile and the men of the Cross came together. The young man with the spear was at Morbius's side, though he was bleeding from several wounds. Shimmer hobbled along, his leg displaying a deep cut.

The Sile took position alongside the men of the Cross.

Sir Walter saw the enemy make their adjustments and quickly devise their strategy for defeating the tightly knitted group now facing them. A creature ran at them and slammed into the line with the force of a boulder in a rockslide, sending men sprawling. It was quickly killed but had done its job. The formation was momentarily broken. Other creatures leapt into the gap. One of them went straight for Morbius.

Walter raised his sword and charged. He thrust his weapon forward and felt it clash with an enemy's blade preventing it from slipping between Morbius's ribs. Walter screamed as the enemy found a gap in his armour at the thigh. He fought on, relentlessly throwing his sword at the enemy who tried to put distance between them, to take refuge in the shadows again. Walter would not give it a chance. He pressed the attack, grunted as he finally found an opening, and thrust his sword through the creature's chest.

Gritting his teeth against the pain in his leg, he turned back to the battle. Suddenly, his leg seemed a trivial thing as another of the creatures leapt from beyond the firelight and plunged a blade into Walter's back at the shoulder. He stood frozen as the pain threatened to overwhelm him. That was when the Sile warriors swarmed past him like crazed bees protecting their nest. The creature was quickly put down.

Walter stumbled as he reached up and yanked a small knife from his shoulder. With heavy breaths, he fell to a knee, only his sword prevented him from falling face-first into the dirt. Damn, his armour felt heavy. He tried to swing an elbow as he felt something grip him from behind, but his arm would no longer obey his command.

"Relax, my friend." Morbius hoisted Walter from the ground and took Walter's weight upon his shoulders. "You have fought well. Damn well. And your quick thinking has given us the key to victory. Look."

Walter looked out at the battle, the night still illuminated by the torches that burned on the ground and the growing fires that had started within the camp. Though the fight was not over, the enemy's numbers had begun to dwindle. The men of the Cross and Sile had formed together. Those with shields and armour formed a front defensive line, and the faster, more agile Sile leapt out from between them to pounce on any of the creatures that came within range.

"Well," said Walter, grateful for the aid as they hobbled back toward the camp. "It seems your Sile reprobates finally learned to fight as a unit." He spoke the words with a grin that offered the most minor reprieve from the pain.

"Well, it seems your cowardly men can't quite move quick enough to kill the enemy in their foolish suits of metal. Do not worry, my Sile will finish them off."

Walter tried to laugh, but it was a step too far. They hobbled through the open gate, and Morbius helped Walter sit, his back against the wooden wall.

"You were right," said Walter, his head falling back a little as he removed his helm. The effort of pulling his head up again was substantial. "All our traps. All our effort. For nothing!"

"Don't be a fool," said Morbius. "Your wall held many back, and your men fought with valour. Your formations were the difference. You were right to be cautious. These things would have torn us apart if we had not been so well prepared. I was the fool." Walter offered a weak, appreciative nod. They had both made mistakes. "I must leave you now, my friend. This battle is not yet over. The villagers are still at risk."

Walter's eyes suddenly opened wide with fresh energy. The villagers were not the target.

"Merleal. Where is Merleal?"

Cutter-of-Men stalked into the river, her path taking her straight to Merleal. Some villagers tried to stand in her path, but a quick crack of her whip turned the water red with blood.

Determined that if this were her end, she would meet it with dignity, Merleal stood firm, watching the woman, who seemed more a goddess of death, get closer. She only held regret at coming this far, at finally regaining a connection with the Fait, only to have the Crone stand in their way yet again.

She closed her eyes and silently prayed, waiting for her end. Her eyes opened again at the feel of hands upon her shoulders.

"What are you doing?" called Res as he pushed at her. "You're just gonna stand there and wait to die? Run!"

He tried to push her away, further into the water's depths.

Merleal flinched as she heard the crack of the whip. Res's shoulders suddenly hunched backwards, his face contorting in pain. He fell into the water. Merleal pulled him up, coughing and choking after swallowing down mouthfuls. Her fingers felt the gaping wounds that now covered his back. When she looked back toward her would-be killer, she saw a new figure standing between them—her father.

"NO!" Merleal cried as Graf stood defiantly before the Crone's new champion. Cutter-of-Men grinned as she drew back her arm. When it leapt forward, it brought the whip, cracking, eager to land its bite.

Graf raised his staff from the water, and the whip coiled around it. He yanked hard on the staff, and Cutter-of-Men stumbled before catching her balance. She was close to him now. A forked tongue stretched from her lips to lick at him as though he were freshly cooked meat.

Oddly, Graf looked past her, his attention over her shoulder. When he looked back at her, they locked eyes, and Graf spoke faintly.

"If you manage to scramble back to your master, tell her that she will never win this war. This world is not for her."

Cutter-of-Men growled as she drove a knife down through his neck. His body went limp, and she pushed him off into the water.

Merleal cried out in despair at the sight of her father's death. She still tried to scramble away while carrying Res's weight. All these sacrifices, for her. She felt their weight. Cutter now returned her attention to the fleeing prey, stalking once again.

Morbius ran to the water's edge just in time to see the old man look at him. Then the woman cut him down. Morbius' heart sank at the sight, but he leapt forward as he saw Merleal still alive and well, though in peril. He wouldn't make it. He needed to do something.

"Did you see? " he shouted at the top of his lungs. "Did you see when I cut his head from his body!" Cutter-of-Men turned to face him. "Your pale-skinned friend with the red hair. Were you there at the Centre? When the witch's ***first*** choice for a champion fell. Did you see when I took his head? I've kept it, you know, as a trophy!"

Cutter growled in anger and contempt. However, she did not move toward Morbius as he had hoped. She was much brighter than her predecessor, who had been unable to control himself and complete his mission. The former champion, Hands-of-Forty, had been unable to resist Morbius' challenge. The new champion was determined not to make the same mistake. However, Morbius was not in the mood to give her much of a choice. He'd closed the distance during his short distraction. He had hoped to fight on dry land, but instead he'd waded further into the water, his weapon ready.

Cutter-of-Men looked to Merleal. She could not reach her target before Morbius reached her. With no other choice left, she turned to meet his challenge head-on.

She sent the reclaimed whip lashing forward, but the water diminished its speed. Morbius dodged to the side, though he still felt a sting on his arm as one or more of the blades glanced him.

Water splashed around them as they came together in a clash of steel. Cutter used a small dagger like an extension of her arm, and Morbius had to be careful not to let her close. Neither of them could fight properly in water, their movement slow and awkward, but Morbius held the advantage with the Sword-of-Answers in his hand.

He knocked her dagger aside and slashed down, his sword cut deep, but the water around Cutter-of-Men did not turn red as it had when she had killed Graf. Instead, a black cloud flowed over the wound and in an instant, she healed.

Not this again, thought Morbius as she came at him. The Lord of the Sile found himself on the back foot as he was forced into a retreat. The water grew shallower as they got closer to the river's edge. Soon, they were on a slight embankment of grass and sand and getting closer to the camp. Good, the further away from Merleal, the better, and at least now, Morbius could fight properly.

Unfortunately, the benefits of leaving the deeper water went both ways, and Cutter-of-Men started to use the whip again. Morbius dodged as best he could and deflected with his sword, but Cutter used the opportunity to get closer.

She was a dancer in the night. Her movements precise and practised. The Crone's first champion had been a brute, all muscles and strength but no finesse or skill. Cutter was the opposite. A true warrior. A far superior choice. Add that to her ability to heal and the battle was not going Morbius' way.

As magnificent as Cutter was, Morbius still had his skills. He allowed her to get close, then grabbed her arm, twisted at her wrist, breaking it, which sent the blade falling from her hand. The wound healed, and Morbius felt bone knit itself back together beneath his grip, but he did not let go.

Cutter threw her head forward, and Morbius felt his nose crunch. An all too familiar pain, but still his grip held. He threw his own head forward, and though she would heal, it was still satisfying to hear her grunt of pain. It was more concerning, however, when her forked tongue licked out over a smile. She was enjoying this.

Somehow, in the midst of battle, Morbius found a brief moment to consider that this woman was a Sile who had chosen to side with the enemy. A great shame. Such a woman was a treasure amongst his people.

She tried to twist away from him. His grip held firm, but she reached for the fallen knife. It slashed toward him, and he was finally forced to relinquish his hold. Their weapons clashed again. Morbius tried to think. He needed a way to end this. How do you put down an enemy that can heal from every wound? He couldn't pick up a giant boulder as Branthony had.

Morbius remembered Branthony's words. Magic is poison to those who use it. If he could cause enough damage, then healing would be the very thing that stopped her. But he remembered how much the former champion had taken before he finally succumbed. This could be a long fight.

That was when a spear came flying past Morbius' head, so close he felt the wind rush by. The spear took Cutter through the abdomen and dug deep into the sand. Immediately, the black mist came, but the spear accomplished more than just injury. It had pinned her to the ground.

Cutter writhed and screamed in pain and anger. Morbius was astonished as he watched her begin pulling herself up along the spear's length despite the obvious pain it caused. What a woman. What a warrior.

The young man who had thrown the spear, the same man who had used it so deftly earlier when fighting outside the camp, now stood at Morbius' side with a drawn sword. Together, they approached their enemy just as she freed herself from her impalement. Not only that, but she pulled the spear from the ground and wielded it against them. The two Sile men fought against the Crone's champion.

The battle should have been one-sided, but the champion's healing ability meant otherwise. Again and again, they cut and stabbed at her, but the black cloud swarmed over her body, healing wounds as fast as they were made, though it seemed the champion understood her predicament. She could not win. Skilled as she was, she could not beat them both.

Suddenly, the champion turned and ran back into the water towards Merleal. If she could not win the fight, she was determined to complete her objective at least. She dived into the water and out of sight.

Merleal watched the water, trying to see where her would-be killer would emerge. She was startled as a splash came from behind her and dived away as Cutter-of-Men raised her knife. Merleal knew it wouldn't be enough. She gasped as an arrow zipped past her head and thunked into Cutter's chest. The Crones champion stumbled backwards, then another arrow took her, then a third. Cutter growled and began pulling arrows from herself. Men of the Cross were aiming, lined up on the shore. Others gestured for Merleal to move, get away, create distance. Cutter thrashed in the water, sending frothing splashes mixed with foaming black mist. That was when Merleal saw a hand of bones, somehow still holding itself together, strapped at Cutter's waist. The moment she laid eyes on it she could feel its power. It thrummed in the air with a pulse. The same feeling she had felt before the attack, but also different. It had been warning her, she realised. Now, it called ***to*** her. It wanted to be taken. Merleal leapt forward, much to the dismay of the archers who cried for her to get back out of the way. She didn't listen. Instead, she barged into the Cutter. Merleal grabbed at the bones and pulled them free of their bindings.

"No!" cried Cutter as she realised what had happened. She made to give chase but paused, then convulsed and vomited violently into the water. Her skin now carried a sickly green colouring. She'd used too much magic, and her body was failing. With one last hate-filled glare, she fell backwards into the water and disappeared beyond sight. Merleal moved away, watching the calming surface, expecting another sudden emergence. None came. She cautiously moved back to the shoreline and the protection of those fighting men who were left.

Morbius took her and dragged her behind him. The others surrounded her in a protective circle, but suddenly, it seemed the battle was over. Everyone looked around, panting with heavy breaths, waiting for an enemy to spring from the darkness. They didn't come.

Where the translucent skinned creatures had fallen only the corpses of normal men remained. Their skin was the usual different shades found on men, yet their bodies were shrivelled and ravaged.

By both firelight and that of the rising sun, the survivors surveyed the ruined camp. It was destroyed. The village itself, however, though not untouched, had survived.

The people slowly began to wade from the river and gather together. People of the Blood River, men of the Cross and Sile, all mingled together as the cold realities of the battle began to set in. Many had been lost.

Morbius placed a comforting arm across Merleal's shoulders as others pulled Graf's body from the water.

"I'm sorry," was all he said. Merleal hugged him, her sobs muffled by his shoulder.

"My son," she said, lifting her head.

"Safe," he assured her. "All the children are safe."

Merleal turned and looked over the carnage. This place had known nothing but peace for so long, but they had been isolated, closed off from the outside world. Now, they had ventured back out into it and reconnected with the Fait. That decision had come with a heavy price.

"Res!" she said, turning back to the water's edge as a young man lay back, eyes to the sky. "Are you alright? Your wounds, you were choking."

"I'll be fine. I'm not so easy to get rid of," he said with a grin, followed by a wince.

"I am glad. Thank you for what you did. For trying to save me."

She hugged him as he stood, and to Morbius's eye, the boy seemed sheepish, reluctant to repay the kindness. Eventually, he returned the hug. Whoever he was, he'd brought a brief smile to Merleal's face, for that, at least, Morbius was happy.

Right, Walter, where are you? Morbius thought, casting his eyes around. He couldn't see the old knight anywhere. That wasn't like him, injured or not.

Morbius strode across the camp, embracing his men as he passed them, and he even embraced the men of the Cross. *By the sands, how quickly things can change.* He was back in the camp, near the wall, which bore unmistakable signs of battle damage, before he noticed the crowd. Morbius pushed through. No one resisted. No one even spoke. An unsettling quiet hung over the group. Finally, Morbius made his way through. He had prepared himself to find a corpse. He saw no one. Walter was gone. In his place were words written in blood upon the wall. 'I take this one as a prize.' It felt like a blow from a hammer. A fate worse than death. Morbius could only stare at the words, his jaw clenched tight. Walter was now in the hands of the Crone.

WHITE AND RED

The four princes sat at a table toward the back of the hall. The festivities were in full flow. Music played, wine was drunk, and people danced and laughed. The king and queen did all they could to keep the mood high and instil confidence in any of the lords who had doubts—and there were many.

The tension in the air could not be missed. Everyone relaxed and tried to have a good time, yet the knowledge of what had happened and what was likely to follow hung in the back of everyone's mind. A dark shadow that should not have marred such a happy occasion.

The boys had played their part for a while, standing alongside their parents, trying to seem strong and confident. Aron, especially, was called upon as heir. Even Luke was asked many questions and treated like a man by most. Joshua and Jacob, though still young in many eyes, had also been included. Everyone knew they would play a big part if war were truly coming. Everyone wanted to know if the so-called Four-Born were ready. As the night had drawn on, the questions seemed to die down, and they finally found a moment of peace.

"They look happy," said Jacob, nodding towards their Aunt Susan and her new husband, Robert. With the formal dancing finished, the two simply swayed in the centre of the room, wrapped in each other's arms. The sound of a gently picked harp fluttered through the air, and the boys thought of Mini as the music played.

"They do," said Joshua with a smile.

"More than I can say for you," said Luke with a hard nudge in Aron's side. The eldest looked sullen. He sat slumped in his chair, chin tucked firmly into his chest, watching the room through the tops of his eyes.

"Do that again and I'll beat you down in front of all these people."

The response was far more aggressive than any of them had expected. Luke felt his temper rising. "Give it your best shot," he said in defiance as he stood ready for an attack, as always completely unwilling to bend an inch to his brother's authority.

"Whoa," calmed Joshua. "You'll both be knocking on Death's Door if you ruin Aunt Susan's wedding night."

Aron merely turned sunken eyes back to the room.

"What's gotten into him?" asked Luke, retaking his seat.

"What's wrong, Aron?" asked Jacob.

"Nothing," the eldest replied.

"Lie," Jacob declared.

"I think I may have the Gift of truth as well," said Joshua with a grin. "Something, I'm not sure what, just told me he wasn't being honest."

"Ha, ha," mocked Jacob. "I'm serious, Aron. What's wrong?"

"What's wrong?" Aron replied, indignant. "Don't you know what's happening. Some of the lords turned against us. We're going to be at war against our own people. That's before the Varliants come. The Crone has beaten us again. We failed."

"We haven't failed. Not yet." Joshua's tone was now serious. He wasn't even looking at his brothers. His eyes stared into the crowd. "The game has started before we were ready, but at least soon we will know the pieces on the board."

"What are you talking about?" retorted Aron angrily. "This isn't a damned game, Joshua. This is real. We have a divided kingdom, exactly how she planned it."

"I know it's not a game." Joshua retorted with anger. He knew the stakes. He knew exactly what was coming, perhaps even more than his brother.

"There's more, though, Aron, isn't there?"

"Don't do that, Jacob. Don't use your Gift on me. Not now."

"I'm not trying to trick you. I can just tell. If you don't want to say anything, then don't. If you want to lie, then lie. I won't give you away. Sometimes we need to lie. For our own sake and others."

Aron's head finally rose, and he turned to his youngest brother.

"By the God, Jacob, when did you become the old wise one?"

Jacob offered him a weak smile. "I'm not old, but maybe a little wiser. I think we all grew up some time ago. The things we've seen. The ways our Gifts change us. We've got to grow up quick with these things."

Aron stared at him momentarily, and something in Jacob's words made him think. Eventually, he sighed and resigned himself to answering.

"I keep looking at Susan, at her cloak." They all glanced at their aunt, who still wore the thick white fur cloak. "I made a list of my visions. One of them was 'white.' I think it has something to do with her cloak. The next thing on the list was 'red.' I think it was blood. I think something is going to happen to her."

"What," said Luke, making to stand.

"No!" declared Aron, thrusting a hand over his brother to hold him in place.

"What are you doing? If you think something will happen to her, then we need to help."

"That's just it, though. All my visions, everything that's ever happened has happened ***because*** we've acted. I saw you in a fight at the tavern. So, we found the tavern and guess what, you ended up in a fight."

"Yes, but we needed to find the tavern, just like we need to do something now."

"But what if ***us*** doing something is what gets her hurt?"

"So, what's your plan? Just sit there and stare menacingly at the room, hope that your glare puts people off."

"Listen to me. When we act on my visions, that's what makes them happen. If we do nothing, then maybe nothing will happen. It's like Corv, remember? I had a vision of riding him, so I did, and what happened? I fell off and broke my arm, and we got in more trouble than ever before. If I'd done nothing, none of it would ever have happened! We gained nothing. The vision didn't do a thing."

They all fell silent for a moment, thinking it over. It made sense, they all had to admit. Aron sat back again, convinced of his decision and that he'd finally gotten through to his brothers.

"But wait a minute," said Joshua, breaking their uneasy silence. "If you'd never taken Corv, we'd never have gotten in trouble."

"That's what I'm trying to tell you."

"But then," Joshua pressed. "We'd never have been separated. Jacob wouldn't have been in the right place at the right time to hear the guards talking about the body sent from the Brayfort. Even if he had, would he have cared as much as he did? He thought it was a good way to bring us all together."

"It was," Jacob cut in.

"Exactly, and because of that, we went to the crypts, that's how we found the tunnel, remember? If you'd never taken Corv, we'd never have found it. Which means we'd never have gone out into the city. Which means we'd never have met Ollie and Joe."

"Which means Ollie wouldn't have been there to save the baby and stop the Crone," Aron finished for him, sitting forward again, freshly invigorated.

"Exactly," said Joshua, looking his brother in the eye. "Taking Corv, getting us in trouble, saved us in the long run. The fight at the tavern led to Hursty. We know the Varliants were responsible for the attack, even if we can't prove it. Your visions work, Aron. They help. We can't always see how and sometimes it takes a while before we can make it out, but they ***do*** help."

Aron contemplated whilst the others waited patiently. Luke's eyes were open wide as though waiting for some grand epiphany, his agitation growing by the second. He began to shake with anticipation.

"How can I know?" Aron pleaded. "How can I know if acting will be the thing that gets her hurt? How can I know if my visions are what will happen if I do or don't act?"

"You can't," answered Jacob. "The future is the future, whether you've seen it or not. That may not make sense, but it's the truth."

Another moment of hesitation. Finally, Aron stood, slamming his hands down on the table. "Something is going to happen. I saw Aunt Susan's white cloak covered in blood. We need to stop it."

"Alright," Luke said, eager for action. "So, what's the plan?"

"I don't know," Aron replied. "Ask the smart arse, he's the one who's supposed to be good at this sort of thing."

The three of them turned to Joshua who was looking out at the room. It took him a moment before he realised they were waiting for him.

"Oh," he said, surprised that they would want to listen. "Smart arse?"

"I'm just playing, you big baby. Tell us, what does your Gift say?"

"Well, erm, first we need to find out what doesn't fit. Is there someone here who may want to hurt Aunt Susan?"

"Maybe someone who has allegiances to the defectors," Jacob offered.

"Maybe, but that doesn't seem like the right move. We're not officially at war yet. Besides, they can't expect to escape. Or maybe taking Susan out could be worth the cost. Her Gift is powerful."

"Then who?" asked Aron, frustration growing.

"I don't know. Everyone here should be allies."

"Supposed allies," said Luke.

"No lord or lady would sacrifice themselves."

"What about the servants?" pondered Jacob.

They looked around the room and saw a multitude of people they could not identify. Any one of them could be anyone. They had full access to the room, moving freely among the guests"

"There's so many," said Luke, looking around. "What are we supposed to do?"

"It won't be a direct attack," said Joshua. There are too many guards." Again, the boys looked around and saw that Joshua was right. There were guards at every door, stationed all around the room, and more waited just outside. Any obvious threat would be met with stiff resistance. "The food? The wine?"

"Poison?" asked Luke.

"Maybe."

"We keep trying to do things ourselves," said Aron, causing the others to look back at him. "We learn from our mistakes. This time, we do it right, like we should have done with the hunt for the gold. We go to Father."

They all looked across the room to where their parents stood mingling. Guards stood close by, though they seemed relaxed, unsuspecting of any danger. The boys approached their parents hesitantly. Branthony glanced at his children and immediately halted his conversation, staying the lord that had his attention with a simple hand gesture. He looked his sons in the eyes, instantly turning serious.

"What's wrong?" he asked, his voice calm yet reassuring. The boys had felt almost foolish in their approach. No longer.

"We think Aunt Susan is in danger," Aron answered.

Branthony's eyes quickly darted to her. She stood with her husband, as happy as he'd ever seen her.

"Aron thinks he's seen it in a vision," offered Luke as an explanation.

"We think it could be one of the servants," added Joshua. "They're the most likely."

Branthony took a moment of consideration. Over the last weeks, trust had been built between them all despite their slip-up in the city. All of a sudden, his mind was made up. He stood straight and strode across the room to his sister, his arms wrapped around the shoulders of his children, ushering them along with him. Debreace followed as they approached Susan and Robert. Branthony leaned into his sister and whispered one simple word.

"Danger."

Susan looked over the room, suddenly suspicious. She looked hesitant for a moment, then drew a deep breath. Branthony put a gentle hand on her arm.

"No, Susan. You don't have to. Come, let's get you somewhere safe."

Susan smiled at him and looked relieved. She did not wish to use her Gift on her wedding day, especially on her guests.

They all began to move to the closest door. The guards walked with them, staying close. They may not have known what exactly was happening, but it was obvious something wasn't right. Two more guards opened the door as the family approached. Guests around the room noticed the family leaving. Believing the royals were retiring for the night, the guests moved in to say their goodbyes. The path in front of Fait was suddenly congested. It only worsened as the guards stepped forward, trying to clear the way.

Luke was near the back of the group. He could see others approaching with smiles and hands held out, searching for some kind of embrace. Luke saw their opportunity for a quick escape fading. He pushed forward. "Let us through," he called. "Let us through!"

He wasn't sure who it was, but someone pushed him backwards. He stumbled into Jacob, who fell to the floor. They heard a strange "cling" sound, and then Jacob's crown fell from his head. Luke offered a hand and pulled his brother up.

"Are you alright?" he asked.

'Yes," replied Jacob. "But I think something hit me." He picked up his crown and saw a small scuff on the metal. Then they heard a scream. Susan stumbled, her hand clutching at her chest. She pulled it away, and a single drop of blood marred the cloth of her dress. She held up her hand and opened it. A small dart lay within her palm.

There was sudden panic. People began scrambling in all directions. Swords were drawn, the sound of steel ringing out as the guards looked to protect their charges. The commotion only made it harder.

"EVERYONE WHO IS NOT FAMILY, KNEEL!"

Almost everyone in the room immediately fell to the floor. Some moved with odd, jerking motions, fighting the sudden desire that had come over them. The commotion and panic quelled in an instant. Eyes darted around, confused. Even the guards dressed in armour now knelt.

Susan stood panting, her breath heavy and laboured. Then she fell to the floor.

The family turned to her. Robert knelt at her side, gently taking her head within his hands. Branthony leaned over her, panic in his eyes.

"Boys, get Healing-Master Fredrick."

Jacob was the first to move, turning around, ready to run and fetch Fredrick. Only he didn't. "Erm," he said, voice soft, a hint of confusion in the delicate word. "Father."

Branthony turned to see what was wrong. Jacob looked back on the strange scene of a room filled with people forced to kneel, but not ***everyone*** was kneeling. Three men now stood staring back at them with cold, menacing eyes. Branthony stood, stepping forward, putting himself between the men and his family. The men looked to each other, though no words were spoken they seemed to communicate and come to an agreement. It appeared that whoever these men were, this was not exactly part of their plan, but they were now moving forward despite the unexpected change.

"How?" mouthed Branthony. How had they disobeyed Susan? No answer was forthcoming. Instead, the three men drew blades.

As one, they attacked.

Branthony threw up an arm as the man at the centre came at him. He felt the cold touch of steel on his forearm, quickly followed by the warmth of flowing blood. The other attackers moved past him. He was not the target. Jacob was.

One of the attackers leapt at the Fourth-Born only to find himself plucked from the air like a feather floating on the wind. Branthony grabbed his leg and threw him across the room. This time, he was not chained. This time, he would defend his family. A grown man hurtled like an arrow from a bow, smashing against the hard stone of the hall with a disgusting splat. A sound and sight the boys had never imagined. This wasn't like when the Crone's champion was thrown against the stone; this was like throwing a rotten apple against a wall. The man disappeared, leaving a strange pulpy mulch of blood, bone and skin. The other two attackers did not hesitate or falter.

Another blade swung toward Jacob. This time, it was Luke who prevented it. Though not a man grown, he was well on his way. He pushed all his weight against the attacker. It was an awkward, unpractised motion, yet somehow his head rammed perfectly into the attacker's gut and forced a squeal. Still, the knife lashed out and Jacob's head whipped backwards, blood spraying. He fell to the floor; his top lip completely split with a ghastly wound.

Debreace cried out, throwing herself on top of her youngest son as a human shield.

"Aron," called Joshua. "The guards, their weapons."

Aron moved to a still kneeling guard who sweated and groaned as he fought against Susan's command but to no avail. Aron took the sword from him and leapt at the downed assailant who wrestled with Luke.

The attacker raised his blade to stab down at Luke but stumbled. He kept trying to stand, to gain some footing but seemed to trip and fall over the youngster scrambling at his feet. Aron stood before him, all his training and practising almost completely forgotten. Seeing the sword, the attacker turned his attention to the First-Born. A man grown and with training, was the bigger threat. A knife lashed out once, and on reflex, Aron deflected the blow. A second slash came at him. Aron tried to lean away as he'd been taught but wasn't quick enough. This time, the attacker found his target. Aron cried out in pain as the knife slashed down his shoulder, cutting cloth and skin. If that had been a sword, he'd be dead.

Joshua leapt onto the attacker's back, wrapping his arms around a neck. The man reached back, grabbing Joshua and flinging him over his shoulders. Joshua landed with a crunch, his head bouncing off the stone floor.

Aron took his chance. He planted his feet, stepped forward and plunged the sword into the man, who gargled as blood began to run down the blade. Aron withdrew the sword and dropped it, staring at his own hands, shocked that they were capable of such a thing. The man fell to the floor and Aron stared at him in disbelief.

Whilst the boys fought against one of the men, the third moved towards the crouched figure of Debreace as she protected Jacob. She held out an arm to ward him off. The man grabbed her and yanked her aside, revealing Jacob beneath, blood streaming from the wound on his lip. The man reached back, weapon raised. A hand wrapped about that arm and squeezed. Bone crunched as though nothing more than a rolled parchment. The man screamed in agony as Branthony lifted him from the ground. The man lashed out with a fist, but it had no effect when it struck. Branthony grabbed the other arm and twisted with rage in his heart, snapping it like a twig. The man screamed again. When that scream died away. An odd quiet fell across the room.

"Who are you?" Branthony demanded. The man's eyes stared coldly back at him.

"Who are you?" said Jacob, spitting blood with muffled words.

The man resisted before blurting one word. "Nerium."

He seemed confused that the word had spilt from him. He knew he had failed. His two companions were dead, and his bones were broken. He threw his head back in an odd gesture, when it came forward again his eyes were wide and growing red. A froth formed around his mouth as he coughed. Just a moment later the man hung limp in Branthony's grip. Dead. Choosing to take his own life rather than be captured.

Branthony inspected the body. Something was wrong. Something was hanging from the man's ear. It had become dislodged in the fighting. A sticky, waxlike substance. So that's how they'd done it. He thought back to how Ollie had withstood the Crone's attack. These men had taken that knowledge and used it. Branthony discarded the body to the floor with disgust and turned to survey the aftereffects of the short battle. It had lasted mere seconds, yet he and all four of his children were wounded.

"Susan." Aron's voice broke the silence.

They all ran to her.

"You may rise," said Susan, her voice weak. Though soft, without the commotion of fighting, her words carried through the room, and the kneeling forms began to stand. No one spoke, not a solitary word. They simply stared on in shocked silence, shocked at the power of Susan's Gift and at what they had just witnessed: the remains of one assailant dripping from the wall like spilt paint.

"Susan, Susan, are you alright?" Robert asked. He held his wife's hand in his, his face streaked with tears. She looked into his eyes and seemed to find comfort in the mere sight of him. She smiled gently as he kissed her hand.

The bleeding from Susan's wound was minimal, the wound small. The offending object was little more than a needle, yet Susan's breath drew shorter.

Branthony leaned over his sister and delicately lifted her from the floor. He would not wait for the healer to come to him. He carried her from the room, and his family followed, leaving behind a crowd of bewildered people in the company of three corpses.

ANSWERS AND TRUTH

Aron stared in a trance-like state at his aunt's life drained away. She lay on the table in the healer's chamber. Her long cloak hung to the side; the once-perfect white surface was now stained with blood. Aron's vision had been right again, only he had misunderstood it. It was not Susan's blood that stained the cloak. It was his father's, and his, and that of his brothers. The result, however, was precisely as predicted. Susan was dying.

Fredrick, the Healing-Master, worked with frantic speed. He had always seemed a dithering old man to the boys, but right then, in that moment, his years seemed to roll back. He moved about the room, grabbing at jars and bottles filled with herbs and who knew what else. He mixed them, his hands as steady and sure as those of a man half his age. He had to find an antidote, but first, he had to identify the poison. He used the dart that had struck Susan, seeing how it reacted to different substances. All the while, Fredrick's face told a story. He knew he would not be fast enough.

Susan looked at her family and, strangely, seemed the least concerned. Everyone was there except for Christopher, whom Branthony had begged to tend to his wife, children, and all those who had witnessed the attack and suffered the power of Susan's Gift. Susan herself offered words of comfort to Robert as he held her close, words only for him.

Aron looked up from his trance. Was it suddenly cold? He shivered against a chill.

"*Look at you all,*" came a harsh voice. "*Look at all that wasted blood.*"

"Bran," said Susan, her eyes wide as her brother leaned closer to her side, taking her other hand. "I can hear her. She laughs at me. The blood has drawn her to me."

"I hear her too, Sister,"

"We all do," said Jacob, from behind the cloth he held to his lip.

"Branthony?" questioned Debreace.

"The Crone," he told his wife. "We can hear her." He looked at Susan. "If we can hear her, she can hear us. Tell her, my sister."

Susan closed her eyes and drew her strength. "Kill yourself." She directed the words to the voice in her head that laughed and taunted her. It only laughed harder.

"*Oh, that won't work,*" said the voice. *"Even your Gift cannot force someone to take their own life. Self-preservation will always overcome. Poor little thing. Did you think you could command someone to kill themselves? Whatever gave you that idea?"* The crackling voice of the Crone laughed louder than ever.

Susan closed her eyes again and felt a fresh tear roll down her cheek. She understood in that moment that she had not taken the life of the man she had once loved. She understood that the Crone had tricked her somehow. She didn't say anything. There was no point. If the Crone had meant her words to cause more pain, she had made a mistake. Susan felt a great weight finally lift.

The boys looked at each other. They had heard the Crone's words. They understood. They looked to their father, and his pain was visible. All this time, all the fallout with his sister because of what happened. All the lives lost in the subsequent war. All because of a lie. Another trick. Another manipulation by the Crone. How many more were there? His sister, his father, who else?

"She comes to torture us," said Aron.

"No," replied Joshua. "She comes to gloat. She's conceited. She wishes to revel in her victories, but she reveals weakness."

The Crone's voice faded. She had pulled away, and her presence was no longer felt. The temperature rose again. Joshua looked around the room, almost excited. "I know how to play against her."

"How many times?" shouted Aron. His anger suddenly boiled. "This isn't a game!"

"But it is," argued Joshua with more intensity than ever before. "At least to her, it is. It's like playing the war game against Hunter. My Gift didn't just tell me about the game; it told me about my opponent. That's how I beat him. That's how we can beat her. She's made a mistake. My Gift has seen it."

"What mistake?" asked Branthony.

"Don't you see? She came to us to gloat. She's overconfident. Coming to us like this gives us something we can use. She can come to us when we bleed. She did it years ago when Aron was wounded. She did it with Jacob when he was attacked. She does it now. We're all bleeding, so we all heard. I should have seen it before."

"How does it help us?" asked Luke.

"The blood is the connection between us. She can come to us, or maybe, we can call her to us."

They looked at each other, thinking about what this could mean. The implications. They had known of this link and this ability, but none had thought to use it against the Crone.

Branthony shook his head. "It is too dangerous. We don't know the strength of the link. What she could do when summoned here."

"Branthony," came the unexpected, pleading voice of Debreace. "An enemy has reached us here in our own home twice. If we are not safe here, we are not safe anywhere. You were right before. Our boys are the key to defeating her. It's time to start fighting back."

She looked at her sons. Fearful for them as any mother would be, but resolute that the time had come to act.

Branthony nodded.

Joshua reached a hand to the back of his head and prodded at the wound there, wincing as he drew fresh blood. The others did the same. Branthony grabbed his arm and squeezed until the blood ran freely, dripping to the floor.

They first felt the chill, then an ephemeral presence, like a ghost hovering fleetingly above them. Finally, as more of the blood fell, she was there. They stood in silence, staring at her as she stared back. Her anger was so deep that the dark orbs that were her eyes twitched.

The moment seemed like it had been coming for years. It was a destiny that had been building their entire lives, even longer than that. For generations, the Crone and the Fait had intertwined. Now, they finally faced off as enemies, a cold stare-down between them. The boys tried to push down their fear. Even Branthony had always had a phobia of her. An apprehensive trepidation. It was a part of her aura.

"You ***fools*** think to summon me!" Her anger had faded, replaced by a snarling, sickening confidence. "Have the little children finally found their testicles? I'll cut them off one day, well, three of you at least. The other shall be forced to use his on the lowest form of female I can find. The result will be the same for me," she chuckled to herself. "What do you hope to achieve by this?"

"The very thing you fear the most. We will get some answers." Joshua stood firm before the Crone despite the way she made him feel. It was more than simple fear. Fear was what you felt when another person was across from you. The Crone's presence had a power that made the worst, darkest thoughts and feelings bubble to the surface. "You have tried to kill my brother again. Susan was not the target today. The poison was meant for Jacob. What poison was used?" Fredrick paused as he listened to one side of the conversation, hoping for a clue.

The Crone smiled with those black lips. Those toothless gums dripping with drool.

"I cannot take credit for today's events. It was not my doing, so I cannot tell you the poison. The attack on the streets was by my design. This was someone else. Though I shall laugh when her strength finally fails."

Fredrick still worked on his antidote regardless. Susan's eyes were barely open. Her breaths shallow with long pauses between.

"Be that as it may, you want my brother dead above the rest of us. That is because you fear his Gift the most. You fear the questions he may ask."

Joshua put his hand on Jacob's shoulder. Once again, the youngest knew it was his turn to be the weapon they could wield. The sword that could stab at her. They instinctually knew that they could not physically hurt her when they communicated like this. Though they could see her clearly, it was still obvious she was not there in a physical form. It didn't matter. Jacob could make this moment count. He stepped closer. Tongue licking at the wound on his lip. Sharp pain came in response. He used it as motivation.

"Who was responsible for the attack?"

"An underling," she answered with a ghastly smile. "They are so desperate to gain favour. They know who truly holds the power. Fear can motivate, but I do not fear you."

"If you do not fear ***us***, what do you fear?" The Crones' eyes opened a little wider at that.

"Oblivion. Judgement. Being forced to return." An answer they were not expecting, one that gave them little, but Jacob could tell it was the truth. He wanted to ask more, but knew time was precious.

"How do we kill you?"

The features on her shrivelled, grey-skinned face contorted. Her breath seemed held as she fought against the urge that compelled her.

"How do we kill you?" Jacob repeated, pushing every ounce of his will into the words.

"Arrrggghh!" The scream that came from Crones' black lips was a terrifying sound. The boys fought against their urges to run far, far away. "There are ways," she answered, her voice calm now. "This is a mortal realm. All things must die. When my power grows weak, mortal wounds can be inflicted. My Gifts are not infinite."

"Ask her what she has planned," Joshua said. "Ask her how she plans to defeat us."

Jacob repeated his brother's words, and this time, the Crone seemed more willing to answer. The black-lipped, toothless mouth smiled again.

"I will crush you," she answered, her croaky voice groaning with each word. "I shall bring death and fire upon you from all sides of the Cross. I will swarm you with forces you do not even know exist and starve you. I shall suffocate you and pull the very breath from your lungs, and when the time is right, I shall drain the blood from your veins. The last of you will come to me and ***beg*** for my forgiveness and give himself willingly to me, all in the desperate hope that I will make his pain stop! All I need is one. It matters not which. From there I breed more. It is so easy."

Jacob could tell she was speaking the truth, and he knew she chose her words carefully. She answered, but without giving away any details.

"Specifics," said Joshua. "We need specifics."

"I know," replied Jacob, but the Crone continued before he could ask another question.

"I will win. It is already written. You will die! Ask your brother." Her eyes drifted to Aron, who felt colder still beneath her glare. "He has seen it. He knows what will come!" Her voice held taunting tones. Every flicker of emotion was like nectar, and she salivated for them.

The others looked to Aron in expectation.

"I had a vision," he said, words a whisper, eyes lost to the memory of what he had seen. "I saw us fall in a great battle. I'm sorry, I should have told you all. But how does she know about that?"

"I have seen it myself," she replied with another groaning laugh.

"You lie," said Jacob, assuredly.

Joshua stepped closer, doing as he said he would and listening to his Gift. It spoke to him, desperate for information it could use. "What are your powers?" he asked. "You claim to be so powerful. What exactly can you do?"

They could tell by her grimace, making every horrible feature all the worse, that Joshua had asked a question she did not wish to answer. Jacob was about to repeat the question and force the reply when she offered it anyway, knowing it was pointless to resist.

"I can do all that you can do and more. A part of every Gift I have ever tasted resides within me. I can gain the Truth like you. I have Fortune, Guidance and Foresight. So, you see it is hopeless to fight against me. Everything you can do, I can do, and so much more. Every Gift that ever was resides within me, yet even that is not the limit to my power."

It was terrifying. How could they beat such a thing?

"She's holding something back," proclaimed Jacob.

"Why?" asked Joshua. The question seemed more spoken to himself. The words came on a whim. "Why do you do all this?"

The Crone flinched; it was a minute action, but Joshua saw it, nonetheless.

"Why?" he asked again. This time, her response was visible to all, not only to the eyes, but they could also sense it. She tried to pull away from them, to end the connection.

"You're going nowhere," said Branthony, squeezing at his wound again, forcing more blood to the surface. The Crone could not help herself. She was pulled back to them.

"Why?" Jacob asked the question this time, and the Crone visibly fought against the compulsion to answer, but the truth could not be withheld. "WHY?" he shouted and could feel the power of his Gift in the word. It tingled as it left his broken lips.

"To live!" she answered.

"There's more. Tell me why? Why do you want to live? Why do you hate us? Why do you come to gloat?"

She growled and groaned, dark eyes bulging. Black lips twisting. Her fingers bent as she tried to resist.

"You cannot compel me!" the Crone screamed, but she did not look or speak to Jacob. Instead, her words and gaze were directed upward. She talked to someone, or something else. She writhed in pain, then finally she sagged. Wheezing breaths drawn as she crumpled into a heap. For all the grotesqueness of her body, it was the first time she had truly looked frail.

From her crumpled form, she spoke.

"I told you this is a mortal realm. Everything must die, yet I do not. Every day of my existence is a victory. Every second spent in this realm is spit in the face of the powers of creation. Powers that think themselves so mighty, and yet I defeat them with my very existence here.

"Why do I hate you? Because you are the closest thing to those powers. You carry their touch. You carry the God's very essence within you. Why do I gloat? Because it is my right. Why should I not gloat and revel in my victories against such power?"

"What do you mean? Explain yourself."

She looked up at them again, such deep hatred and revulsion in her every shrivelled feature.

"The God created this world, He and the Other. They fight over it. Both think themselves so mighty, so powerful. Yet I defeat them both by being here. I am not a part of either of their plans, not anymore. Both have spurned and rejected me, neither can step upon this plane of existence, yet here I stand. I will do what they cannot. I will take this world for my own. Those so powerful, those that create worlds, create existence, and they cannot do what ***I*** do."

Silence again. She was telling the truth, though it was cryptic. No one truly understood what she meant. Yet they knew her words here would define so much in what would come.

Luke stepped closer, a question on his lips. It was his Gift again, helping him stumble fortuitously onto the right path. Normally, Fortune left no impression on him. He did not feel it like the others did. It simply was. It came to him like Breathing. This was different. He could feel Fortune pushing at his mind to find the right question. He knelt next to her crumpled form of the Crone. It was with a delicate voice that he asked his question.

"Who are you?"

Her eyes widened again at the question. It surprised her. Perhaps a question she had not heard in a long, long time. Then her face contorted to a snarl once more. "Isilbisk," she answered. The single word held more menace than all she had uttered before. "My name is Isilbisk."

Luke looked back over his shoulder at the others. No one seemed to know the name, yet they undoubtedly knew that they had just uncovered something important. Perhaps the most important thing possible.

"Branthony," said Debreace. He looked to his wife, who looked to his sister. She was fading.

"We must end this, my sons. We know a name now. We will call her to us again another time."

"Oh no, you won't," the Crone snapped. "You think yourselves so clever summoning me, but you have ***wasted*** your chance. You have gained little. You have not asked the right questions. This will not work again. I will not allow it. My ego gave you your opportunity, and your rashness wasted it. Now I will stay with you as she dies and laugh in your faces."

Aron felt the world falling away. Had they really wasted their one opportunity? Jacob hadn't said she was lying, so it must be true. He had finally felt like they had gained some small victory, that they had managed to take one solitary step off the Crone's chosen path. He could not let it end like this. He thought desperately for a question that would help them. Something she couldn't twist. It was hard to think. The Crone's laugh blared, invading his thoughts. He thought of his Gift. Surely, there was something he could do. He had to believe that his Gift was meant to help, so surely something he'd seen must be important. Something must help them. He thought of his list, of the memory of things that had not yet happened. Something on the list stood out. He replayed the vision over in his mind. A vision he had seen more than once. An older Joshua stood over a map, pointing. Aron stepped closer to the Crone as she laughed and danced maniacally. Bouncing and hopping on her thin, frail legs like a giddy child. Joyful at the pain of others.

"What is in the White Mountains?"

The Crone froze, her back to them. She drew a deep gasp, and her laughing stopped as sharply as if she'd been stabbed with a knife to the heart. Her neck twisted unnaturally, her head coming all the way around to stare back at them, eyes massive and bulging. They continued to grow until they began to bleed. Then they popped from their sockets. Black blood oozing down her face. They hung from her skull, dangling on black optic nerves.

"Jacob," prompted Joshua. "Ask her."

"AAARRRGGGGHHHH!!!!!" the Crone screamed. It was a sound they'd heard before, piercing their minds and exploding their thoughts.

"JACOB!" shouted Joshua over the Crone's scream and their anguished cries.

Jacob tried to step towards her but felt like a great wind was pushing him back. Fighting against a storm, he shouted. "WHAT IS IN THE WHITE MOUNTAINS!?"

The scream ended.

Silence.

Tantalising silence.

The Crone's face looked back at them, her eyes suddenly back in their sockets, the damage erased in an instant. Her other features returned to their usual gruesome appearance, yet it seemed much less terrifying than moments ago.

"Life," she croaked. "Death. Victory. Defeat. All lay in the White Mountains."

"Crone," came Susan's voice, breaking the strange moment. Susan snarled at their enemy and spoke with a burst of power. "Be gone!"

The boys and Branthony all spun towards where she had stood. Nothing, no sign that she had ever been there.

"Susan."

Branthony fell to his sister's side. She retook his hand, but he could feel she was weak. Fredrick knelt to her side, ready to attempt his antidote.

"Do not worry," Susan said. "I pass from this world a happy woman. I have my family. I have my husband." She squeezed Robert's hand with the last of her strength. "I have one last command that you will all obey. Don't let her win."

With those words, Susan's beautiful light flickered from the world.

WORDS TO THE DEAD

Walter felt the grip of cold iron at his wrists. He slumped against tort chains, his head lolling downward. To watching eyes, he would look unconscious. He was not. He'd listened the Crone talking. He'd watched in the darkness of a cave with barely a touch of light. There was no one else there, but he'd heard her words. He knew she had somehow been talking to the Fait. Even with only one side of the conversation, he'd discerned that much, at least.

He'd also heard her name. He ***knew*** that name. It made him tremble.

When she'd finished talking, she stood motionless for a long time. Walter watched as she held something in the air and peered at it with what he could only describe as reverence. A small, white bone. A fingertip. Then, with apparent reluctance, she threw it to the floor and stamped upon it until it was dust. Then her eyes snapped to him.

"You cannot fool me, man of the Cross. I know you are awake."

With great effort, he pulled his head up and looked her in the eye. "Why have you brought me here?" he demanded, his throat dry, voice raspy.

"My champion will soon return, but she has failed me and grown weak, sickly. The very Gift that has kept her alive is now killing her. I need another."

"I will never fight for you."

"Oh, but you will," she chuckled as she approached. With a black tongue, she licked him and laughed at his disgust. "You heard the words I spoke to the mongrels. I did not lie. I hold the Gifts that I taste. Susan is dead, now there is no one to override my commands. I have saved Obedience for so very long. All for this."

She whispered in his ear. Walter felt a great darkness fall over his mind. He wailed as her words took hold of him.

Bolevard struggled to contain himself. He'd spent so much of his recent life in constant anger and tension, always fighting to hold down the emotions that threatened to boil over. His carefully crafted persona as the Scroll-Master was forever on the edge of shattering. Very few days indeed offered any reprieve. Yet now, he felt as though the floodgates had opened.

A strange sound escaped his lips, and he quickly clasped his hands to his mouth. He cast eyes about the darkened room, though he knew no one else was there. It would have been hard to identify the sound even if there was someone. It could have been heard as a sob, a short yet powerful breaking through of sadness. The truth was quite the opposite. Bolevard had laughed.

It took every ounce of self-control to stop that short yet sweet burst. He wanted to let it go and gain momentum into the bellowing, full-bellied sound he knew it would become. He wanted to laugh, to let it out. He dared not. He felt like a child trying not to laugh at an adult who'd fallen, fearful of the repercussions once the adult climbed back to their feet.

He took a step forward and bent down, then whispered into the ear of a corpse.

"I am glad you're dead, you ***foul*** thing. I am glad you are gone. You deserve it for what you did to me. For what your family have done to this world."

Of course, the dead could not reply.

Bolevard knew he had taken a risk coming here, yet some things had to be done. He had to come and see for himself. Years ago, he'd had the Gift of Obedience used on him and raged against its control with no success. Now the one that had defiled him was gone. Bolevard felt a thrill. The first Fait had finally fallen in this war.

"You are merely the first. All the Fait will join you. One by one, I will see you all die. So, rot. I will soon see your wretched family join you. Your brothers, your nephews. All of them. Until the Fait are no more."

Merleal remained where she was as the others began to move away. They had buried the dead, and there were many of them. Men of the Cross lay next to Sile and with people of the Blood River. All their differences in life mattered little in death.

She had spoken at the funeral, hoping to comfort those who remained. It would typically be her father's job. Graf had a great affinity for things like that. Yet this time, he lay amongst the dead, the last funeral he would ever attend. Now that she was alone, she approached her father's grave. She had kept some words solely for him.

She kneeled as she spoke, thanking him for all he had done for her and for always keeping her faith strong.

"I promise, Father. I will not fail. I will not let the Crone break the bond we have reforged with the Fait. I will not let it be for nothing."

Her heart ached as she stood. Thoughts of the Fait only made it worse. She could feel them, even now. Despite the distance, she could feel them. They were in pain, much as she was.

Word had already been sent north to the Cross. The Fait would soon know what had happened here. She suspected they may already. Though she could not commune with the Fait, she could feel them. Did the sensation work both ways? This was part of the connection between the Fait and those who delivered the Gift. She'd felt similar when Christopher's second child was born. The connection was strong.

A figure was waiting as she walked away from the graves towards the village. Morbius Duvec stood patiently. She smiled weakly as she approached, grateful that the Lord of the Sile had given her the moment she needed with her father.

"Lady Merleal," he said with a deep dip of his head.

"Lord Morbius," she replied. They both smiled at the titles, knowing they didn't fit, but neither could escape them.

"You did well today. These things are never easy. You should be proud."

"I am proud of us all," she said. "We have stood firm in the face of great evil. Yet that evil remains."

"Then we shall stand firm when it returns."

They fell in step alongside each other as they strolled back towards the village.

"It will return, won't it?" Morbius asked.

"Most certainly," Merleal answered. "Though I am unsure where or when. I have a feeling the village is safe for now. I believe the Crone has used her chance to get us here. She failed, thanks to you and your men."

"And thanks to you. You realised the key to banishing those things. And, thanks to the men of the Cross," he added. "Thanks to Walter. My men were being slaughtered before he intervened."

She looked at him with a fresh wave of dismay.

"Why take him?" she asked.

"Who can fathom such a mind as hers. I promise this, though. I will find him. Have you discovered more about what you obtained from the Crone's champion?"

"No. Though I have not put my mind to it." Even now, she could feel a strange power pulsing through her mind. The bones had allowed the champion access to the village. Whatever they were, they felt not of this world. She had her suspicions, though she would keep them to herself for now.

They reached the camp's edge where they found a figure waiting for Morbius, much like he had waited for Merleal.

"I take it you wish to speak to me?" asked Morbius.

"I do, My Lord." The young man spoke Sile now, the most common dialect.

"I keep telling people," Morbius replied, matching the man's dialect. "Though it seems to do little good, I am no lord."

"If it's all the same to you, My Lord, I'll keep using the title. My father taught me it means more than land ownership. It is a sign of respect."

"Your father sounds like a good man. Perhaps we could all do with learning more respect for others. Sometimes these lessons are taught the hard way."

"My father was a great man, My Lord. You knew him well."

Morbius looked surprised to hear this and stared at the young man until it finally dawned.

"You're Farlik's boy."

The young man smiled, not just out of joy but out of pride.

"His father was my guard," Morbius told Merleal, excitedly. "And a dear friend," he added, facing the youth again. "I owe him my life, and much, much more. He saved me from the Crone's first champion. Without your father, I dare say the Crone would have won this war already. Well, it's no wonder you're so good with that spear. You've grown since last we met."

"My name is Wind and Sun. My father called me Win, and he taught me well. I have come to ask if I may stand as he stood, by your side."

Morbius looked to the sky as Merleal looked at him. The Lord of the Sile was fighting back tears.

"Damn you, Farlik," Morbius said to the sky. "Even after death, you're still protecting me."

He put his arm around the young man's shoulders and ushered him into the village. "Let me tell you some stories about your father."

"Well," said Merleal as she found an unexpected smile upon her face. "These sound like stories I would love to hear."

Celia sat in quiet contemplation, thinking over all that had happened yesterday. An odd mixture of feelings and emotions raged inside her like a tempest. She'd heard from Aron about the confrontation with the Crone and the revelations revealed before Susan's death.

On the one hand, Celia felt great sympathy for Susan. To spend so long believing herself responsible for the death of the man she loved, to finally move on, only to find the truth mere moments before death.

On the other hand, she felt relieved that Susan was gone. Celia had been in the hall after the wedding. Like everyone else, she had been completely powerless against Susan's Gift and had obeyed without question. She had knelt and watched in stunned silence as the assassins revealed themselves. She had witnessed the king's Gift up close and personal, and though it was terrifying in its own way, it seemed nothing compared to Susan's.

Celia hated being so powerless. She hated being controlled in such a way. A part of her was certainly glad to see such power gone from the world. The Crone was right to dissuade Susan from using her Gift. Such a power would have been difficult to combat.

Celia also had to admit to a sense of sympathy for Bolevard. The Scroll-Master had once opened up about Susan using her Gift on him. Celia thought he had exaggerated. She now knew better.

All the inner turmoil was suddenly buried deep down with the force of an avalanche. If Celia had a gift, it was suppressing her doubts. The door creaked open, and Prince Aron stepped inside.

Celia stood to meet him and dipped her head. "Your Highness."

"Lady Celia."

'How are you feeling today? Did you manage to get any sleep?"

"A little," he offered with a polite yet forced smile.

"Have you spoken more with your brothers or father regarding the vision you told me about?"

"A little," he repeated, looking to the floor. "I think they're mad at me for not telling them. They don't understand. How do I tell the people I care about that they're going to die because I can't control the one thing that could save them?"

A tough question. One she did not have an answer for.

"You're still of the opinion that it will come to pass?"

"Everything else I've seen has come true, even with Aunt Susan. It wasn't exactly what I thought it was, but it still happened, and the result was the same. She's gone."

"Could you try the meditation again? Instead of inviting any vision this time, concentrate on that particular one. See if you can recall it." She could see by his expression that he didn't want to. Who could blame him? Who would want to watch that again? He was already forced to do so without voluntarily trying to. "Perhaps not that vision then," she said, seeing his distaste at the thought. "Another. The one you had of me, perhaps."

She made her voice gentle and enticing. It was easy to see that Aron found the idea more desirable. He nodded his acceptance and moved closer, offering out a hand, which she took.

Aron closed his eyes and began to breathe deeply. She watched him closely. It was odd, watching him in such a vulnerable moment. Aron was a man now. A young man, yes, but a man, nonetheless. A man with the weight of a kingdom on his shoulders. A man born for greatness. He had even taken a life, and he was using a power far beyond her comprehension. She saw him in a new light in that moment. As he held her hand, she would admit she was slightly in awe of him.

"I see you," he said. "You're smiling. You look beautiful. Radiant." It was good that the prince had his eyes closed; otherwise, he might have seen her blush. "You have a crown, like last time, and you're putting it on your head. I think you're checking it fits," he said with a smile.

"Is there anything else? Anyone else? Where am I?"

"It's hard to tell where you are. There's nothing I can see that would help, but someone, a handmaid, I think, is helping you dress. Brushing your hair. She's talking to you."

"What does she say?"

"She…"

He hesitated as though trying to listen in on a conversation that was taking place right there and then. How odd that it was a conversation Celia would actually have one day. Would she know what to say because she'd already heard it today? Is that the reason she would say it? Did seeing the future create the future? It was all too much. No wonder Aron suffered headaches. No wonder he struggled.

"She's saying that she looks forward to the ceremony. She can't believe you're going to be queen. She…" he strained harder, trying to listen, as though the conversation were growing quieter.

Celia knew the visions never lasted long. The Crone had said that Aron's premature birth could mean he never gained complete control of his Gift.

"She's saying it's hard to believe how far you've both risen. You, a queen, and she, a noble lady, where once she had been a—"

Celia jerked her hand away as though burned, and Aron jolted at her reaction. "I'm sorry," he said, confused. "I didn't mean to offend."

"No, no. Don't apologise. You did nothing wrong. It's just that I feel like I'm prying, spoiling the surprise, maybe. I have also just remembered that I have an urgent meeting with your father. He seemed annoyed in his summons for me."

Like all good lies, it held a hint of truth. Good, her heart pounded in her chest, and she needed to get out of there. If they'd continued, what would he have discovered? What word would have been uttered? Something that could ruin everything? Who was the girl? Too many possibilities that could lead down dangerous paths.

"Yes," said Aron. "He's angry that your father hasn't replied to the decree. As Point-Warden it sends a bad message."

It most certainly did. What was her father playing at? She'd always hated Carter Trone, and he her. He hated that she'd done such an excellent job as his representative. He hated that she hadn't failed, as expected. He hated her for what was between her legs, or rather, wasn't. He'd hated her since the day of her birth. Could he be delaying simply to jeopardise her position? She would not put it past him.

"We shall continue later, I promise." By then, she should have thought of a distraction. That line of vision could be dangerous. Almost as dangerous as Aron seeking the traitor's identity, whose betrayal would lead to the fall of the Fait.

Celia bowed and left, leaving Aron alone.

"Celia will be queen," he said to himself. "But she could only become queen through marriage."

He stared after her, and the door closed.

END OF THE GAMES

"Do we really have to do this?" Joshua asked as he gestured at the war games board. Luke stared at him from across the table, and though he seemed equally uninterested, he appeared to have a different approach to trying to get out of playing. He thought to get it over quickly.

"I apologise, My Prince," said Hunter. "Though it may not seem so, this is perhaps the most important lesson. Now you have suffered a real loss. You now know the genuine cost of war. Does it feel the same as you dispense the lives of your men? Will that sense of loss affect your judgement and decisions? Every leader must face this scenario, eventually."

"Let's get it over with," Joshua said morosely.

Hunter turned the timer and revealed the newest conditions of play. As usual, they favoured Luke. It was windy, and the wind was blowing toward Joshua's attacking forces, reducing his attack points.

"Make your move?" demanded Luke, impatiently.

Joshua eyed his brother, who was aligning his defensive pieces, knowing he had a good chance to inflict heavy casualties.

The younger brother didn't move. He didn't do anything. He just stared across at his older sibling.

"Well, you just gonna stand and stare dumbly all day?" said Luke, his mood darker than usual since the wedding. Joshua gave no reply. "By the God, do something."

Hunter didn't interject. He watched on expectantly.

"My Gift helps me against the player, not just the game," said Joshua.

"Yeah," said Luke with a huff. "You've told us already."

"It's telling me about you."

"Really." Luke looked up, folding his arms. "And what does it tell you?" he asked with a grin.

"It's telling me that you want to win this game."

"Well, I'll be damned. The Crone stands no chance at all against you. I thought your Gift was Guidance, not stating the bloody obvious."

"It's not that you want to win the game, you do, but that's not what's important. You want to win because winning means beating me. Beating me is what's important to you. Proving you're the best."

"I am the best," spat Luke.

"Then I know how to beat you. Because to my Gift, the game doesn't matter. It's just a game. Hunter, I surrender."

"What?" asked Hunter, baffled.

"I surrender my forces." Joshua reached onto the board and toppled his pieces over. "There, the game is done."

Luke stared at him in utter bewilderment. "Then I win?"

"Sure," said Joshua. "You just didn't beat me. I've just had enough."

"Your Highness," said Hunter, about to interject and tell him that's not how it worked. He didn't get the chance as Luke broke into a furious tirade.

"You can't do that! Pick them back up! I'll beat you. You think you're being clever?"

He continued, using more and more explicit words and insults. He didn't even notice as Hunter smiled at Joshua.

"Not exactly what I had planned, but you've made an interesting point. Your surrender is accepted."

With that, Joshua gave one last glance to his brother. "I'll see you in the morning. Father wants us ready bright and early." Then he turned and strode from the room, leaving the game and the others behind. He only flinched slightly as some wooden horses flew past his head to clatter on the wall.

It was a full minutes later, after Luke had flipped the game board over in rage and fury, that he finally stopped. He surveyed the mess and carnage he'd caused as his deep breaths finally calmed him. He looked to Hunter with sudden apprehension. Remembering how dangerous the man was and how much power the tutors had whilst the boys were in their lessons. Hunter merely looked back at him with raised eyebrows. An expression that asked the question, are you quite finished?

"He did beat me, didn't he?"

"Was that the reaction of someone who has just won?"

Luke looked back at the carnage and mess, feeling foolish. "I haven't been beaten at anything in a while. Damn," he said with a smile, then a chuckle, then a full, deep, belly laugh. When it died down, he slapped a hand on what remained of the table. "We might just have a chance after all."

"Yes," said Hunter. "Yes, we might. And if you can start acting your age, we may have more of a chance."

Luke smiled ruefully.

Salvadire stepped out of the carriage and breathed deeply through his nose. Ah, the smell of home. To be truthful, the city stank, as most cities do. The stench of too many people, all that sweat and waste. Still, this was his home, and he was glad to be back. How long would he be here? That was the real question. There was much work to be done. He would find no respite, even here in Varliant.

Salvadire arrived at the Prelim's palace and entered through one of the back entrances. He sent most of the others off to rest. The journey had been long, and they had each performed admirably whilst away. They deserved their brief time of relaxation. Salvadire knew the real work would begin very soon. Before the sun would rise again, everything would be different.

Though Salvadire sent the others away, he kept Karim close. He trusted Karim, not that he didn't trust the others; he did, but Karim had a cautious mentality about him. Salvadire thought this might come in handy over the next few hours. He spared a thought for poor Meroth. The man was loyal to the core but deceiving him was necessary.

There was a reason Salvadire had entered the palace through the rear entrances. He didn't want to be seen. Not yet. He had to make sure everything was in place. He traversed the palace in secret, meeting and speaking with certain people, his people. He wanted to know precisely what had been going on. He needed to make sure everything was in place. Salvadire had set Varliant on a perilous path. He needed to make sure it was one that they were all ready to walk. There could be no turning back, especially after tonight.

Finally, he approached the chair of the Prelim in the great hall. From the shadows, he watched as Vol vomited into the bucket of pure gold at his side. When the bout was over, Vol leaned back in his chair and made a feeble attempt at wiping the leftovers from his chin, leaving slimy residue on the sleeve of his once delicate garments. He breathed deep; exhaustion evident as he dropped the bucket to the side. Odd, how such a thing once held such value. Now it seemed as common as a clay cup.

The door creaked as Salvadire pushed it open and entered the room.

"My Lord," he said as he approached. Only when he got close did the light let him see his so-called master properly. He startled at the sight, cupping a hand to his mouth, lest his vomit join Vol's.

"Salvadire?" asked Vol in a strange mumble, the voice sounding nothing like the one he remembered. Vol then erupted into a bout of coughing that nearly led to another round of vomiting.

Salvadire merely looked on in shock. This was far worse than he'd expected, and he expected it to be bad.

"I am sorry, old friend, that it has come to this."

Vol's eyes suddenly looked outwards as though they saw nothing at all. The fleeting moment of coherence was over, and now his mind was lost. He struggled to speak. He struggled to breathe. When Salvadire had last seen him, Vol had been a grossly overweight, glutinous fool who had nearly led his people and city to utter destruction. Now, fortunes had been completely reversed. The city and the people were thriving, but Vol was a shadow of his former self. Less than a shadow.

He was skeletal, the skin around his eyes was sunken and dark, and the eyes seemed to bulge and protrude grossly from his skull. His gums had receded, making it seem like his teeth had grown, threatening to drop to the floor at any moment. Some had decided to forego a drawn-out departure and had taken an early exit. Even now, one hung on by some thread, threatening to fall at any moment. He was completely unrecognisable. If not for the assurances of others, Salvadire may not have believed this was the Prelim.

He reminded Salvadire of the Crone in many ways. The difference was in the eyes. Despite her frail body, the Crone's eyes held an enormity of emotion and knowledge. One glance told anyone that behind that frail façade was a creature of great malice and power. Vol, well, Vol looked broken. Little, if any, mind was left behind the crumbling shell that held what was left of his consciousness. He seemed a simpleton, the smallest of tasks beyond his body and mind.

"Oh, you fool," said Salvadire. "I am sorry, but you left me no choice. You would have ground us all to dust if left unchecked. We were failing, Vol. On the edge, just when the world is changing. When such opportunity was arriving, you knew that this was our chance, but you didn't have the mind to see how we could capitalise. I had to send word to her. To ask for aid in return for our service. She was clear, there had to be a sacrifice."

Vol stared at him, emitting an odd moaning sound. There was a hint, ever so slight, of clarity in those eyes. Perhaps he understood. Maybe he had suspected as much for some time.

"I had hoped to keep you alive. What you can do is amazing. We could have prolonged your life if we had been smarter and more measured in using your abilities. It was not to be. You hired assassins! You went against orders. Though your efforts gained unexpected fruit, they were not authorised. You pushed the Fait to make a move. This act cost her dearly. She is enraged. So, I must bring you to an end sooner than planned.

"I want you to know I will lead Varliant to glory, old friend. Your name will be sung from all corners. You shall be the hero who drives our people forward. Your sacrifice will not be forgotten. You are the man who brought power and wealth back to Varliant. You shall have a golden statue in the centre of the city for the people to pay their respects."

"G…" Vol tried to speak. A thick, bloated tongue flopped from crusted lips. "Gold," he said, the word muffled. "I…hate… gold."

Salvadire smiled sympathetically.

"I know, old friend, but gold has been our salvation. Look."

Although it sickened him to touch his old friend, he grabbed Vol by the shoulders, feeling the bones beneath his hands. He turned Vol, and they both watched as Karim pulled a cover from something huge in the corner of the room. A gigantic clay statue of Vol. Not like he looked now, how he used to look. Despite being a horrendously fat man who did next to no good for anyone, even Salvadire would say the statue implied some grace and nobility.

"You see," said Salvadire, head next to Vol's, whispering in his ear. "We will say that the Cross killed you in retaliation for the attack on their royals. They blame us for the attack. Claims they cannot prove despite your failure in hiring the Nerium. How different that could have been. All our work to hide a link between us and the attack, all to stop Prince Jacob gaining the truth, and you hire the Nerium directly. Foolish! However, the Scroll-Master did precisely as I asked. He took a record of Meroth declaring us innocent. You see, you will be the catalyst to spur our people on. They will want revenge on those who took their great leader the one who enriched them.

"What do you say, old friend. One last time. Do it one last time and know this is the image of you that shall be remembered. This is what people will see when they think of you. Let this be your legacy."

He wasn't sure if Vol truly understood. Did Vol know he would die anyway and think to leave a better image of himself? Or perhaps he had grown too stupid, too empty of mind to know any different. Either way, he reached a hand towards the statue, a fingertip pressed against it.

"Do it," urged Salvadire. "Use the Gift. Use ***Alchemy***."

Vol pushed his hand against the statue, and before their eyes, it turned gold, solid, gleaming gold that shone even in the weak light. Now, Vol's image really did look magnificent.

Salvadire looked down as Vol slumped in the chair. He remembered the Crone's words to Vol at that first meeting. 'You shall soon be dead at the hands of your own people.' Well, Salvadire thought his old friend may already be dead, but he drew a blade across his throat just to be sure.

He felt the briefest moment of something bordering on sorrow at the sight of Vol. This meek, disgusting thing was all that remained. The stories were true; using magic was fatal. Oh well, that was why he'd given the power to Vol instead of taking it himself. Now, he had to let the people of Varliant know that the Cross had assassinated their brave leader. Then, in time, he would take them to war.

Merleal and Morbius rode side by side as they crossed the border between the Angosh plains and the Southern-Point of the Cross. Neither of them had expected to return to this border so soon, but after the attack on the Blood River and news of the fractures that had formed in the Cross, both thought it wise to speak in person to someone with authority.

As they pulled up with what they had thought to be an extensive array of wagons and men, they looked out and saw how wrong they had been.

The sight of a massive camp stretching out into the distance met them —the camp of an army, thousands of tents and horses, tens of thousands of men. The fires filled the horizon. The smells created by such reached their nostrils. The clamber of men was everywhere. Banners blew in the wind to mark the different forces that had come together to make one.

"By the sands," said Morbius. "All those years we fought against the Cross, thinking ourselves mighty. All the small victories we gained, all the times we fought them back. We thought ourselves great. Now I see he could have sent this against us. Walter was right. All that time, Branthony held back. He toyed with me."

Merleal heard the growl of anger in his voice. She knew Morbius was proud and would feel embarrassed at his realisation.

"That is not technically correct," she said, looking at him. "It takes a significant effort to mobilise like this. It comes at great cost. The lords of the Cross are not so quick to dispense with their coin. They would not mobilise like this unless absolutely necessary. They often bicker. They come together now because they are threatened."

"So, you're telling me they did not even see us as a threat?" he asked defensively.

"In a battle, a fight, yes. Most certainly. They knew you were a threat as much as any opponent, but in terms of conquest, no. They knew their homes and land were never truly at risk. Things are different now. Whichever side the lords have chosen, they know if they lose, the cost will not only be their lands but likely their lives."

He had to admit that made some sense.

"Maybe Branthony should have been harder on those who rebelled last time. Many of them kept their lands and their heads. If he had taken them, I suspect many new rebels would have thought differently."

"Perhaps," said Merleal. "But I suspect the king had had enough of killing. He sought to make peace. To unite. Many of the lords are good men at heart, but sometimes even good men find themselves disagreeing. If Branthony had been harsher on those who betrayed him, Sir Walter would have been one of the first to feel that wrath."

Morbius winced at the mention of Walter "True, but it is often not the lords who do their own fighting or dying. If they were Sile, this could all be finished with a challenge."

"If you made a challenge and lost, would all the Sile simply accept it, or would many fight on regardless?"

Morbius looked back out at the camp. He didn't reply. He knew the answer as well as Merleal.

"So, this is the strength of the Cross," he said instead. "He is certainly ready for war."

"Oh no," said Merleal with a knowing smile. "This is just a good portion of the Southern-Point." She saw Morbius' eyes open wide. "Although I notice some banners are missing. The Crossed Hills would be the largest area I don't see represented. That is north of here. I don't see the Dawn either. Another powerful region. Troubling."

"You seem very familiar with the lands of the Cross. Not to mention the politics."

"I am. I was taught much of this in my short time at the Centre, and Sir Walter carried on my tutelage." There was that name again. "I don't seem to forget anything anymore. It all comes easily to me since I delivered the Gift. I believe I have a touch of Knowledge. Look, here is someone I think would completely understand."

Morbius followed her gaze to see Prince Christopher riding towards them. The queen's brothers were at his side. All three of them. Michael, Grey and John. The presence of such high-value individuals showed how seriously the king was taking this. The poor men had travelled up and down the Southern-Point these last few months.

The two groups came together amid awkward greetings. Merleal hugged them all, even Grey, whom she had never met. Morbius offered a hand, which they each grasped at the wrist in a short embrace. Any former misgivings about their alliance were now forgotten. Too much blood had been spilt to doubt each other now.

"That's some force you've got there," said Morbius.

"Yes," said Christopher, "but will it be enough? I've seen the reports from the Blood River. Those creatures you fought against. They sound terrifying."

Morbius nodded bleakly. "What are your plans?" he asked.

"Well," said Michael. "We've had an official response from Basel and the Black Fort. They've declared war on the Fait and the Crown. Lord Dwayne and the First Fort have joined them. That alone makes this a bigger rebellion than last time. Some of us are heading back north to converge with our forces at Wraith Castle. From there, we will see how far those who have not sworn fealty wish to take this. As for a portion of this host." He glanced at Merleal, and she understood.

"This force isn't for the Cross," she said. "It is for the village."

Michael nodded. "Some of it, yes. Branthony wishes he had sent more in the first place. He regrets his miscalculation and promises not to repeat the mistake."

"In time, I will join you at your village," said Christopher. "It is hoped that with our minds we may discover something new and come to understand our enemy better."

"We need to know what she can do," said John. "The little witch keeps pulling new tricks from her sleeve. We need to know how to kill her. I don't care what name she goes by. She'll die all the same."

"Name?" asked Merleal.

"My brother and nephews had a confrontation with Crone. They learnt her true name. Isilbisk," said Christopher, and Merleal paled at the word.

"That cannot be," she whispered, breathlessly.

"You know it?" asked Michael. "You know the name?"

"She lies. She lies to spread fear."

"No," said Christopher. "Jacob confirmed it. She spoke the truth."

Merleal's eyes glazed over in horror. All they had seen recently did not have half the effect of hearing that name.

"It is the name of the fallen. The one who..." She swallowed, closed her eyes, and said a silent prayer.

"Who what?" urged John.

"It is the name of the one who fought the angel. Two beings of such power that their battle tore the fabric of reality. They ripped the heavens open. She and the mightiest angel crashed from a higher plain of existence to this mortal realm."

"The story you told Branthony," said Christopher. "Of an angel falling into the river. The beginning of the Fait."

"The story is true," she said. "The Crone confirms it with that name. We thought the other had perished after the battle. All this time, she has been here among us. Don't you see? The Crone is far more than a deliverer gone mad. She is a demon." Her eyes refocused. Sharp and alert. "Get a message to the king. We are in far more danger than we realised."

Celia walked the thin corridors of the library, surrounded by scrolls and tomes stretching upwards on shelves twenty feet high. She found Bolevard, precisely as expected, at his desk. It was the same enormous and incredibly ostentatious desk, yet the man behind it seemed very different. Could it be? Was that a smile on the face of Bolevard Bront? A sight Celia never thought to see. It only made the man all the more menacing. She didn't like it one bit.

"Lady Celia. What brings you here this time?"

"Our friends," she said quietly. "They must be home by now."

"Yes, though I suspect we will see them again in time."

"Certainly," she agreed. "You seem awfully chirpy."

"I am. I really am. A Fait is dead. The kingdom is divided. The Varliant plan came together quite nicely."

"We are at war," she said, unsure if Bolevard desired this.

"Yes," he said with a smile. "It seems we are."

"What do you hope to get out of all this?"

"Simple. The end of the Fait. The king confirmed with his own words that the witch they have suckled from will also die once they are gone. They have fed each other for far too long. Now they shall all starve and die." The joy with which he spoke was off-putting. "But what, Lady Celia, do you want to get out of all this?"

Celia would not say she liked Bolevard, not by any stretch, yet she had found over the last years that he was perhaps the one person besides the Crone she could be even half honest with. What did that say about her? She didn't want to think about it. Of course, if Bolevard ever discovered she was working ***with*** the Crone, that could be the end of her. His hatred was all that was left to him. Well, that and his library. All other aspects of his life had been consumed, burnt and shrivelled beneath his hatred.

"I have come to see a bright future for the Cross. A future with a queen of great intellect and glorious beauty," she said, not so humbly.

"Ah, so you finally admit it out loud."

"I do," she said. Perhaps she would even find a place for Bolevard in her new queendom, though she doubted it. Something about the man scared her. Greed and desire were one thing, determination another, but Bolevard hated the world. He seemed to hate himself. No, such insanity was too dangerous, but he had his uses for now.

"If Varliant comes, what makes you think they will want a queen?"

Varliant and I beat to the same drum. We all do, except you, who has no idea whose side he is on.

"It is all in the plan," she said. "Did you think I was helping them for no reward?"

"You place great trust in them."

"I trust only myself. The Varliant part in this is over, for now. Lord Basel and his co-conspirators will play the greater part in the coming years. There are already rumours of gathering forces at every Point."

"War can offer many opportunities," Bolevard mused.

"All that is for later. For now, let us take a moment to revel in our victories."

"Now that," he said with a grin more menacing than anything Celia could hope to muster. "Is certainly something I can do."

RISE AS MEN

The four princes rode out together. Not just out of the stables, but out into the training yard. Then out past the castle walls into the city beyond. They rode through streets they knew so well, but they rarely travelled those streets as the people they were today. Today, they were themselves. Today, they were each a Prince of the Cross.

Guards rode fore and aft, but the princes took the middle. People noticed and called out as they passed. More than once, they heard the name the Four-Born. They had such an odd feeling. It was like they were hiding in their own skin. Like they were impostors yet pretending to be themselves. Eventually, they came to the city walls, passing beyond them and out of the Centre.

The city's noise died away as they reached more open ground beyond. Luke was the first to put heels into his horse. All four were accomplished riders now. They'd never imagined it, once upon a time, especially after Aron had stolen Corv. Times change.

They laughed as they followed Luke's initiative, kicking their horses into gallops. They felt the rush of adrenaline that comes with a charging horse beneath you. They powered across the grassy hills, putting distance between them and the city. The different roads stretched away in all directions like the legs of a spider, but the princes chose to stay on the natural terrain. On and on they went, the guards following frantically but laughing themselves in a moment of pure enjoyment, enthralled in the sudden jubilation of their charges. Nothing could be heard but the sounds of laughter and the thunder of horses in gallop.

All too soon, it came to an end. Luke slowed his horse first and brought it to a stop, while the others were just seconds behind. They were at the bottom of a sharply rising hill that they knew led to a dramatic cliff drop.

They took a moment to look back at the city, now in the distance. It seemed odd to see it in such a way, as a single thing rather than all the small parts that made it up the whole. How could it be so big, yet seen from this viewpoint, it also seemed small?

The castle sat towards the centre. Even at this distance, they could still make out the training grounds. An odd break in the mass of structures. Beyond that, thousands of rooftops packed tightly together. Small billows of smoke rising from thousands of fires. They could see the streets and roads as they cut their way through the city. The docks and ships within the Way River. The market streets with their tents and canvases. The wealthier districts that housed the merchants and traders gradually gave way to the poorer areas, where the buildings became smaller and more compact. Finally, these reached the city walls with their huge portcullis gates. Odd that they had just travelled through one of those gates. They seemed so much more intimidating up close.

It was beautiful. The Centre. Their home. They each knew that their time there was ending. They knew the Cross needed them.

The princes turned their attention from the city and stared up at the figures at the top of the hill: four, all on horseback.

"What do you think they're talking about?" asked Jacob.

"We'll find out soon enough," said Aron. "They're coming down."

Three figures turned their horses away from the fourth and began to trot them down the hill. The fourth figure remained at the top.

Ollie and Joe rode well, considering they'd only been training for the last few years. They reached the princes and stopped their horses. The six of them stared at each other. The other figure descending the hill did not ride so well.

"Hursty?" said Luke, surprised. "What in the name of the God are you doing here?"

"Well," replied Hursty with his broad smile as he slid a hand through his hair. "Your father wanted to thank me for my help. The gold cards and my story have convinced some of the lords of Varliants guilt. Though not many, which ticks me off to be honest. I'm a very reputable man. Besides, I owed quite a lot of money, you see, and your father, well, he paid off my debts. Debts that even two solid gold playing cards wouldn't have wiped out, and thanks to you lot, I don't have to sneak around the city anymore. So, as repayment, he demanded I pledge myself to you." Ollie clapped a hand on Hursty's shoulder in a 'he's one of us now' motion. "I'm still not exactly sure what help he thinks I'll be, but who can refuse the King of the Cross. Especially when you owe him money," he said with a laugh.

"Can someone remind me how, in the name of the God, any of us have ended up here?" said Joe, his large smile spreading across his face. "How have we all reached this point? It seems like it's all been one big dream."

"Not all a dream," added Aron. "Parts of this journey have been a nightmare." They all solemnly agreed.

"What did he say?" asked Joshua.

Joe glanced at Ollie, up the hill, and back to the princes.

"Most of it was just for us," he said. "Right, Ollie?" He looked to his brother as he spoke the words, and Ollie nodded agreement. "But I'll tell you this, he's put a lot of trust in us."

"Trusting you to do what?" asked Luke.

"That's obvious, ain't it. Look after you four fools."

"You do remember we're princes, right?" said Joshua.

"Yeah, and when there are others around, we'll be careful how we talk to you, but your dad says it's good for you to have friends that aren't afraid to speak up and speak honestly."

There was a coughing sound, and they all looked to Ollie, who gestured back up the hill. Of course, he was right. They didn't want to keep their father waiting.

The princes set their horses to a trot and made their way up the hill, approaching their father with apprehension. He'd been quiet the last few weeks since Susan's death. Once, they would have taken that as a sign that he was unhappy with them. Now they knew it was simply his way of dealing with things.

They stopped alongside him. Together, the five of them stared out over the land beyond. They could see the northern branch of the Way River as it stretched off into the horizon to reach the Autumn Sea eventually. No one spoke for a time. They all looked out and took a moment of thought and consideration. Finally, a father turned to his sons.

"I'm very proud of you." He turned to look at them. "All of you. So very proud." The princes shuffled on their horses, unused to such words and sincerity from their father. "Things are about to change," Branthony said. "Things will move quickly now. We are at war. First, we must fight our own people. I know this is hard. I have done this before. I know what it did to me, and I am so sorry that you must suffer the same fate, but it ***must*** be done. Then, when that battle is won, we move on to the next. The Crone and Varliant."

"What makes you think she won't make her move sooner?" asked Aron. "Attack us whilst we're still fighting amongst ourselves."

"Because she needs this time as much as we do. Even with Varliant and her mercenaries, she knows she cannot defeat us. She wants us to fight amongst each other, then, when we are weakened, she will make her move."

"Attacking could risk uniting the lords against her," said Joshua. "Father is right. She'll let us tear each other apart, then swoop in."

"So, we do exactly what she wants?" asked Luke.

"Unfortunately, yes," said Branthony.

"She's beaten us at every turn," said Aron. "All her plans have worked perfectly. Do you think we can win? Do you really think we can beat her?"

"Yes," answered Branthony with confidence. "Jacob, do you hear the truth in my answer?" Jacob nodded. "Then have faith. You say all her plans have worked. They have not. She failed to capture your cousin, Oliver. You have seen the letters from Merleal. You know the Crone failed to kill the new deliverer. She failed to kill Jacob. You four have helped bring about some of these failures. We can win, my sons. We ***will*** win."

Branthony directed his gaze back outward. "Climb down from your horses."

The princes obeyed, climbing down and then standing in a line. Their father looked back at them.

"I want you to kneel, but when you do, know this. You will ***always*** be my boys. Always! But once you rise again, you rise as men. Men of the Cross." The brothers glanced at each other with thoughts of previous conversations between them.

"Much will be asked of you. Not just of your Gifts but of you as leaders and princes. You will need to fight." They all nodded their acceptance of these things. "You will be separated."

That caused them to take their eyes off their father and look to one another again. It was something they'd never really considered. It made sense, it even seemed inevitable. Yet, they had all become accustomed to always having each other. They looked back at their father with stiff jaws, resigned to the fact that they must all step out on their own.

"We are ready, Father," said Luke.

"Then kneel, my sons."

They did. All four of them, side by side, with heads dipped. Branthony rode his horse just in front of them. Then, one by one, they heard a soft thunk. When they looked up, a sword was dug into the ground before each of them.

The princes looked on in wonder. Each was a sword fit for a prince. At the base of each blade was an inscription.

Aron stared at his. It had the shape of an eye with a hawk behind it. Luke saw three shooting stars. Joshua's had a compass etched onto the symbol of the Cross. North pointed to the tip of the blade. Jacobs had the shape of a sun, but within it was the shape of tipped weighing scales. Each blade held a symbol of each Gift. Yet the swords themselves were symbols of more. They symbolised that now the four princes of the Cross were men, and they would be joining the fight.

"These swords come from the Raven Forge, the greatest swordsmiths in the kingdom. Dare I say the world? They will not fail you, as I know you will not fail me. Now rise," said Branthony, "and take your swords." They did, and Branthony drew his own. He held it to the sky. "For the Cross," he said, his voice alone a wall of strength. The princes raised their swords to join their father's.

They spoke as one.

"For the Cross!"

EPILOGUE

Aron would admit to making many mistakes, but he now believed he knew the greatest mistake of all. He had tried to hide from his Gift, to ignore it. He had tried to keep parts of it secret from his family. No more. He thought of Susan again, her words to him. He would embrace his Gift. He would master it. Or at the very least, he would keep trying. When he lay in bed that evening, he did so with fresh resolve and determination. More than ever before. It was time to confront the vision he feared the most. He would go through it and learn from it, even if he had to live it over and over again. Even if he had to see his death a thousand times, he would do it, so that when the day finally came, he would know how to avoid it. He would know how to win.

Four swords stood together, their points pushed into the dirt at the top of a cliff edge. The army that approached would look up and see the four gleaming weapons. They stood like a monument, a sign, a message that said, 'We are here! If you want anything beyond this point, you will fight for it.'

The four princes of the Cross stood in gleaming armour, staring down at the enemies below. Aron rubbed at a bearded chin. "It's time," he announced. As one, they took their swords from the ground and lifted them into the air. Then, with a sense of finality, they lowered the tips and pointed them towards the approaching enemy. Those below then heard the cries and the crashing of hooves as the army at the princes' backs began its charge.

Aron was in the thick of the fighting. He would not be denied. He had seen this too many times. Ollie was at his side, ready to protect him.

He was not needed. Aron watched the battle play out exactly as he knew it would. He knew every step he had to take, every swing of the sword he had to make. He knew when to stop, when to duck, when to step to the side. He traversed the battlefield as though the whole thing were one giant, orchestrated dance. As though everyone was simply playing a part, their steps and movements all planned and rehearsed to perfection.

Luke watched Aron and laughed. Aron was doing what Luke had been doing for years. Walking through the fighting as though untouchable. The Second-Born's steps were fumbled. His avoidance of death always came at the last second through some seemingly random act of his or someone else.

"You've never done this before," Luke called as he raised his sword to defend against an incoming attack. "By the God, you look like you've got Fortune."

Usually, Aron was a torrent of anger and emotion in battle, fighting furiously and often recklessly. Not today. Not for this fight. He was calm. Assured. Completely at ease.

"I've seen this day too many times," he shouted back to Luke over the noise of battle. "Of all my visions, this is the one that has come the most."

"This is the one you told us of?"

"Yes."

"Then we need to fight harder!"

Luke redoubled his efforts, while Aron looked to his right where he knew Joshua would be approaching. Joshua fought through the battle with Joseph at his side. Ollie looked at his brother as Aron looked at his.

"Brother," cried Joshua as he fought off the enemies that were beginning to become more numerous. There was panic on Joshua's face. Aron saw it. He'd expected it, yet still he winced. He had hoped this time would be different. He'd hoped that after so many visions, adjustments, and alterations to their actions, they had finally managed to stave off what Aron feared was about to happen.

"Something is wrong. We are defeated. We must retreat."

"Retreat," called Aron, offended by the word. "No, brother. This is where we need to be. Look."

He pointed with his sword. Joshua followed its direction and saw why Aron was insistent on pushing forward. Lord Basel was before them.

Old as he was, Basel had still joined the fight. Aron would admit to some small amount of respect for the man for this.

"This is part of it?" asked Joshua. "In your visions."

"Yes," replied Aron. "We need to get to Basel. He's the only one who knows what's happening here. We need him to question him. No one else will do. Basel and Basel alone can tell us who the traitor is."

Joshua did not look convinced. He never did, not once in all the versions of this day that Aron had lived. Despite his reservations and complaints, Joshua trusted in Aron. Aron just needed to make sure he was worthy of that trust.

Joshua turned and signalled. A moment later, Jacob appeared, and he and his guards were fighting forward.

"Come," said Aron. "We get to Basel. Jacob can find who the traitor is."

"Well, what are we waiting for?" called Luke.

They fought their way forward, cutting through the enemy ranks. Their Gifts seemed almost as adaptable to battle as their fathers. They were all men grown. Veterans of many battles, and they had mastered their Gifts. This was the true power of the Fait.

Time seemed to shift and blur, and in moments, they had their man. Basel was on his knees, staring at them with anger and hatred. That expression suddenly turned to fear. He knew it was over. He would die. Perhaps right there and then.

Jacob knelt in front of him. He looked the old lord in the eye and placed a gauntleted hand on Basel's pauldron in an almost friendly manner.

"It's over, Lord Basel. Now is your chance to show remorse. Make amends for all this death. Tell us, who is the traitor?"

They all leaned in, waiting to hear the answer.

Basel whispered in Jacob's ear.

"Who?" demanded Aron. "Who is it? Jacob, who is it?"

Jacob turned back to look at his brothers, then his gaze switched to stare off behind them.

"We're too late," he announced.

"Jacob," Aron demanded. He felt a familiar sensation taking over him. "No, no, this can't be. I could swear this was it, that this was real. Jacob. Who is the traitor? Tell me, Jacob. Give me a name?"

"Brother," said Jacob. He stood and put both hands upon Aron's shoulders. "This isn't right. Truth, brother. Can't you see the truth?"

"Just tell me a name," he raged as he felt the world slipping away from him. He fought against the feeling, trying desperately to keep himself there and then. He saw the enemy suddenly rush their position. He knew how this ended. They were overrun. His brothers died. He died.

Aron startled awake.

He looked about himself, the scream that had escaped him cut off with a hand to his mouth. He looked up to see Joshua staring down at him. His face looked much the same as it had in the vision. A man grown, a man who knew the hardship of war.

"Relax, Aron. Relax. You're safe. We're on the ship, remember? We should be at the rendezvous soon. Luke and Jacob should be waiting. Years of civil war, Aron, it could all be over soon."

Aron looked around at his surroundings. He drew deep breaths, noticing the motion as the ship bobbed in the water.

He swung his legs off the end of the bed and sat on its edge, scratching at his beard.

"I had the vision again."

"And?"

"And we failed, again."

"Anything new?"

"We got to Basel. We finally got to him. Jacob asked him the question, but I still didn't get a name." He shook his head. "FAll the times I've had the same vision, hundreds, maybe thousands, I've never seen us win the battle. For years I've been trying, yet I've never managed to get the name of the traitor." He sighed. Why couldn't he get a name? They'd got to Basel. Jacob had asked the question, and yet he still had no answer. He was getting closer, though. He would not give up. He knew the time for visions was almost over. One day soon, that vision would become reality. If he failed, then all was lost. He had to know.

"Who is the traitor?"

ABOUT THE AUTHOR

Joshua M Fitton is the third of four brothers. He was born to his parents in Bradford, West Yorkshire, and raised in the small country town of Silsden. He is a bricklayer by trade and works with his father and eldest brother in the family business. An avid fan of all things fantasy and science fiction, he was raised in a household that revered such things as Star Trek, Star Wars, The Lord of the Rings and more. He now lives with his wife, two children and dog, all combining to make for a busy life.

www.ingramcontent.com/pod-product-compliance
Ingram Content Group UK Ltd.
Pitfield, Milton Keynes, MK11 3LW, UK
UKHW022013281125
9243UKWH00003B/45

9 781919 348803